W9-AQR-270

CONTENTS

INTRODUCTION

Mary Ann Rasmussen

HOW DID RADICAL WOMEN WRITERS in midcentury express what we now understand to be feminist concerns within the context of a left-wing movement that tended to subordinate women's issues to its class struggle, anti-fascist, and anti-racist priorities? What are the historical roots of their feminism and how did they articulate the relationship of gender to class and race? Josephine Herbst's *Pity Is Not Enough* (1933), the first volume of her Trexler trilogy, published in the heart of the Great Depression when the author's attraction to the Communist movement was at its height, demonstrates how a materialist-feminist sensibility and implicit political analysis transformed an apparently conventional realist historical novel into a rich and complex work of art. *Pity Is Not Enough* speaks powerfully to the importance of reclaiming the compelling literary works and contradictory lives of radical women writers, women who struggled in the absence of any systematic understanding of the intersections of multiple oppressions to integrate their gender consciousness with their knowledge of racism and classism.

Josephine Herbst was a prolific and critically successful writer in the 1930s. With three novels, numerous short stories, and journalistic essays published over the course of the decade, she became a major figure of the proletarian movement that inspired and mobilized left-wing artists and writers. Herbst shared the political and aesthetic commitments of her male Marxist contemporaries to expose the cruelty and hypocrisy of an exploitative and dehumanizing capitalist economic system and to create class-conscious depictions of the individual in society. Yet as a feminist writer, she was also critical of the male-dominated literary world and of the suppression of gender as a category of difference in its theoretical discussions and representational practices. In *Pity Is Not Enough* Herbst spoke back to her politically committed peers about the limits of their assumptions and interests, prefiguring terms of the debate on the relationship between Marxism and feminism waged since the late 1970s.[1] Herbst's novel discloses the effects the sexual division of labor in the family and in society had on women and historicizes the rules governing the production of gendered subjects. Even more radically, it suggests that a collective sense of the inherent instability of the subject is critical to dismantling the power and authority of the ruling class and that the uneven and unfinished business of subject formation is a key battleground of revolutionary struggle.

In this introduction I ask today's readers to view the literary accomplishments of this often misunderstood leftist woman writer in terms of the political discourses, ideological tensions, and artistic milieus from which they emerged. *Pity Is Not Enough* invites us to contemplate women's distinct experience of American radicalism in the first three decades of this century. The materialist-feminism of Herbst's novel is rooted in the personal circumstances and cultural context of her artistic development as well as in the history of the American political Left, particularly the long, often troubled, but indispensable relationship between feminism and socialism—the very alliance, with its manifold possibilities, that first drew Herbst to American radicalism as a young woman in Iowa.

The Legacy of Prewar Radicalism

To understand the American writer's leftward turn in the late twenties, Daniel Aaron has argued, one must look back to the period before the outbreak of World War I, to the young radicals of prewar bohemia who rejected bourgeois morality and rampant materialism for the liberation of the self. Although lacking in feminist analysis, Aaron's *Writers on the American Left* provides a key to tracing the origins of Josephine Herbst's materialist-feminism in *Pity Is Not Enough* back to the crosscurrents of the feminist, socialist, and bohemian movements that nurtured political and literary radicalism in the first decades of the twentieth century.[2] From 1917 to 1921, Herbst participated in the cultural life of what the historian Mari Jo Buhle calls the "new intellectuals" of the American Left: young college-educated men and women living in the avant-garde enclaves of American cities who made sexual egalitarianism and the liberation of women central to socialist revolution. In their journals and newspapers, new intellectuals advocated a "new morality" that swept past the class reductionism of their more orthodox elders in the Socialist party and represented their flights from their small towns and rural communities as both personally liberating and politically necessary.[3]

In 1917 at the age of twenty-five Herbst fled Sioux City, Iowa, her small hometown, for a final year of college at the University of California. Herbst brought to Berkeley hard-won lessons about the injustices of capitalism and the destructive nature of gender stereotypes. After graduating from high school in 1910, she was forced by her parents' failing economic circumstances to live at home and attend a local church-run college for two years before enrolling at the University of Iowa. After her father's farm implement business went bankrupt in 1913, Herbst reluctantly moved back to Sioux City and worked at a series of intellectually uninteresting "women's jobs" to support herself and to help her financially strapped family. In 1915 she enrolled at the University of Washington but illness forced her to withdraw before she completed her studies. Back again in Sioux City, she felt all the more intensely the limits of small-town American life for an ambitious and talented young woman. As early as 1914, the year she taught eighth grade in Stratford, Iowa, Herbst knew she wanted to leave home to become a writer; yet in 1917, while literary and artistic revolutions were flourishing in New York and Paris, she was still stuck in Sioux City, reading the public library's copies of the socialist journal *The Masses* and the experimental literary magazine the *Little Review*. Living at her parents' house and working as a secretary in a local law office, Herbst at last saved enough money for a final year of college. This time she was determined not to return.

Herbst experienced the Bay Area socialist-feminist group she joined soon after her arrival in Berkeley as a "milky way of daisies"—an apt metaphor for the romantic expectations and political idealism of the "radical new women" of her groundbreaking generation.[4] Telling her new companions—the feminist poet Genevieve Taggard and journalists Max Stern and Carl Hoffman, both editors of Bay Area socialist newspapers, among them—that she was twenty, Herbst subtracted five years from her real age (the time elapsed between enrolling at the University of Iowa and entering the University of California) and reinvented herself in the prevailing terms of her new community. After years of social isolation and economic frustration, Herbst expressed in a letter to her mother the relief and joy she felt in finally finding like-minded peers: "I always knew that somewhere in the world there were people who could talk about the things I wanted to talk about and do things I wanted to do and in some measure I have found them."[5]

Evidence of the impact of prewar radicalism on Herbst's work is present in her earliest writings. As a student at the University of California, Herbst published five poems in the campus literary journal the *Berkeley Occident* that foregrounded conflicts and issues the Socialist literary and political establishment tended to exclude or deny. In one poem a rebellious working-class daughter pursues self-emancipation over the brooding objections of her unemployed father. In another Herbst critiques the mind-numbing boredom of a well-coifed and carefully dressed middle-class housewife treated as a beautiful and expensive pet by her shadowy and distant husband. In the poem "Pagan" a free-wheeling bohemian insists on her right to self-determination and sexual freedom against the social constraints of traditional femininity. The feminist theme of the poem "Silences" is found on the listless faces of the poem's working-class wives trapped in loveless marriages of prevailing male dominance.[6]

Herbst's early poems suggest the influence of the new moralist Edward Carpenter's vision of "companion love" between a "new man" and a "free woman" expressed in his revolutionary guidebook to the new intellectuals, *Love's Coming of Age*. Carpenter called for a "natural harmony" between the sexes to replace the artificialities and conventions of love in the Victorian Age and disputed notions of women's passionlessness, claiming that women possessed sexual instincts and erotic desires repressed and contained by Victorian culture.[7] Emma Goldman's anarchist-feminist critique of women's economic and emotional dependence on men in her infamous essay "Marriage and Love" may well have inspired Herbst's representations of the psychological consequences of domestic confinement and submission to patriarchal authority: "The institution of marriage," Goldman wrote in 1914, "makes a parasite of a woman, an absolute dependent. It incapacitates her for life's struggle, annihilates her social consciousness, paralyzes her imagination and then imposes its gracious protection."[8] Goldman praised women who withstood the onslaughts of public opinion and the tyranny of the state to risk everything for a romantic love defying all laws and conventions. To the prewar radical new woman, the "perfect romantic love" would not split desire from intellect nor intimacy from equality but would be "the cornerstone of egalitarian relationships with men."[9] To Herbst, an aspiring young female artist with socialist sensibilities, prewar radicalism's promise of passion and freedom with a new man struck a particularly responsive chord.

After graduating from Berkeley in 1918, and after a brief stint in Seattle, Herbst moved to New York to establish herself as a writer, quickly becoming a member of a circle of radical artists and intellectuals for whom, as Herbst's biographer Elinor Langer says, "love-and-revolution" were "sacred watchwords." Through her friend Geneveive Taggard, who had moved East a few months earlier and was publishing in leftwing journals and magazines, Herbst met Helen Black, a writer for *The Nation*, and some of the most important male literary radicals of the day: Mike Gold, Joseph Freeman, Max Eastman, and Floyd Dell.[10] In 1920 Herbst became sexually involved with the playwright Maxwell Anderson. In many ways Anderson seemed the epitome of the new man of prewar radical vision, sharing Herbst's socialist values—his pacifism got him fired from two teaching jobs in the Midwest during the war—and her literary ambitions. Though not her first romantic interest, Anderson was Herbst's first attempt at "free love" with a married man with children, and the affair soon became more complicated and painful than she imagined at its bohemian beginning. Not the heroine of a new morality play, Herbst instead found herself the traditional romantic victim, obsessively jealous of Anderson's wife, possessive, insecure, and, worst of all, passive and self-denying, agreeing to an abortion she did not want to save Anderson's reputation.

Not surprisingly, Herbst's writings of this period evince an uncomfortable familiarity with the debilitating contradictions of women's place in bohemian communities.[11] In Herbst's unpublished novel "Following the Circle," written from Berlin in the early 1920s, the circular motion of escape and enclosure pursued by the novel's female protagonist suggests the experience of a generation of women who, having fled their Victorian homes for bohemian communities, discovered they had not escaped fundamental gender roles and rules that constricted their personal lives.[12] "Following the Circle" was based on the social paradoxes and tragic consequences of Herbst's own life in Greenwich Village. For reasons she spent a decade trying to understand, Herbst hid her abortion from her closest confi-

dant, her younger sister Helen, who was married and living
with their parents in Sioux City. Helen found herself unexpectedly pregnant and sought Herbst's advice about having an
abortion. In letters to her sister, Herbst concealed the unhappy circumstances of her affair with Anderson behind a veneer
of the bold and daring free woman, encouraging Helen to seek
a life beyond Sioux City even as her own life in New York was
confusing and hurtful.[13] Helen had an abortion and died a few
days later. Rightly or wrongly, Herbst held herself responsible
for her sister's death and suffered an emotional and physical
breakdown. In May 1921, after a brief stay in a New York sani-
tarium to recover her strength, Herbst followed the expatriate
path of many of her generation and set sail for Europe. There,
Herbst transcribed the bitter memory of her unwanted abortion and her sister's abortion-induced death onto an emotionally charged first novel whose sexually explosive subject was not
likely to appeal to publishers. Nor would its feminist perspective be read sympathetically by her leftist contemporaries when
she returned to the United States in late 1924.

In the conservative and consumerist twenties, the burgeoning advertising industry transformed the sexual freedom of the
new woman into a marketable commodity. Popular psychology
linked sexual satisfaction to political apathy, and popular culture represented single women as romantically retarded, sexually unsatisfied, or worse—lesbian.[14] By middecade, as Elaine
Showalter has shown, dozens of confessions of former feminists
filled the pages of American magazines as pressure to conform
to traditional gender roles led many to abandon their prewar
feminist ideals. Ruth Pickering, who had joined the prewar radical feminist group Heterodoxy, for example, described herself
in *The Nation* as a "deflated rebel" who had learned a more
"adult attitude" than the socialist-feminism she had espoused
in her youth—that "my deficiencies and my capacities are my
own—not those of my sex." Stripped of its leftist politics Pickering's feminism became a personal matter disconnected from

larger social and political issues, "part of my ego and perhaps nothing more."[15]

Pickering's response was symptomatic of a general loss of feminist consciousness and radical vision in the twenties. Prewar materialist-feminism had flourished in an anticommercial and self-consciously ideological context that challenged authority, linked gender transformation to socialist reconstruction, and endowed personal life with multilevel political significance. In the twenties, however, the Left abandoned its earlier integrative politics, eschewing feminism as "bourgeois" when feminist organizations appealed to economically privileged women in support of—except in the area of equal political rights for women—the status quo.[16]

In her published work from the twenties, Herbst explored the consequences to herself and her contemporaries of the postwar sexual and social conservatism of American culture and the loss of radical consciousness among young bohemians in flight from the "Philistines." Herbst's writings are highly autobiographical in this period, revealing both her inscription within the regime of "modern womanhood" established by popular psychology and the new advertising industry and her resistance to its antifeminist and corporatist message. Writing in a culture increasingly fearful of gender incompatibility and wary of the "lesbian threat" posed by the new womanhood, Herbst courageously drew from the painful memories of the deaths of her mother and sister to critique the social pressures on women to disavow their friendships with one another and the distrust and jealousy between women placed in ruthless competition for the admiration of men. Herbst's novels affirmed key elements of prewar radical ideology even as they represented their cultural marginality and social displacement, suggesting the "bohemian futility" of a world without a redeeming vision of social change.[17]

The transformation from the prewar romantic quest for a "new man" to a postwar compulsive search for the "right" man was played out in Herbst's difficult marriage to John Herrmann. Herbst met Herrmann in the spring of 1924 in Paris, where he was a twenty-three-year-old refugee from the family shoe business in Lansing, Michigan, studying art and literature with ambitions to be a writer. After returning to the United States and under pressure from Herrmann's parents, Herbst and Herrmann married in 1926, and in the following years each pursued a writing career—Herbst methodically and with ever-increasing success, Herrmann erratically but with occasional brilliance—while living in rural Connecticut, New York City, and Key West, Florida.[18] In their postwar radical and modernist circles—their friends included Katherine Anne Porter, Nathanael West, Ernest Hemingway, Alan Tate, John Dos Passos, and Mike Gold—more women fulfilled traditional gender roles in conventional heterosexual relationships than in the previous decade. Herbst was often described by her twenties contemporaries as a "masculine" woman with an argumentative and aggressive style, a portrait she accepted with both pride and discomfort as she struggled to hold together a troubled marriage she had once hoped to be "an even race between us or nothing."[19]

In 1928 Herbst and Herrmann moved to an old farmhouse in Erwinna, Pennsylvania, not far from where Herbst's mother had grown up. Determined to keep her marriage intact yet frustrated by the emotional and intellectual costs of Herrmann's drinking and affairs with other women, Herbst sought to put her personal life on more solid political ground. In Erwinna Herbst and Herrmann began a serious study of Marxism and their growing interest in radical causes led to their attendance at the International Congress of Revolutionary Writers in Kharkov in 1931. Not long after the trip to the Soviet Union, Herrmann joined the Communist party and Herbst began work on *Pity Is Not Enough*.

Marxism clearly provided Herbst with more than a theory of the dialectically inevitable economic demise of bourgeois society critics have found inscribed within her novel. It was after the trip to the Soviet Union, she wrote in an autobiographical essay written in the 1960s entitled "Magicians and Their Apprentices," that she first began to connect the house in Erwinna with "the bigger stonehouse twenty miles away" that had belonged to her mother's family.[20] When Herbst's mother, Mary Frey, died in 1925, she left behind the sacks of family letters and documents that had hung from the rafters in the attic of the old Sioux City house, and Herbst claimed them soon after moving to Erwinna. The origins of Herbst's fictional reconstruction of her family's past are suggested in the association between these bounded domestic spaces and Marxism's liberatory project. In *Pity Is Not Enough* Herbst employed to feminist purposes the same dialectical process as her male Marxist contemporaries who made art a political weapon of class struggle. Overturning yet another set of hegemonic categories and metaphysical concepts, Herbst revealed the material conditions of women's oppression within class society and the difference of women's historical experience of wars, economic depressions, political revolutions, and cultural transformations.

In the thirties, Daniel Aaron claimed, the young bohemians became "more serious" about art and politics, putting aside issues of personal life for the more pressing work of initiating class struggle, righting racial injustice, and combating international fascism.[21] But prewar radicalism's socialist-feminist legacy was not so easily forgotten by at least some leftist women. Nor did they leave uncontested the pattern Aaron describes. Just as Herbst had protested when men and women abandoned sexual egalitarianism and the companion love ideal in the 1920s, she voiced her concern when her Marxist contemporaries dismissed the personal implications of their dialectical materialism in the thirties. In *Pity Is Not Enough*, Herbst tried to make gender once again as central as class to her generation's revolutionary conversation, but it was not an easy task.

The Materialist-Feminism of *Pity Is Not Enough*

Positive critical response to the novel established Herbst as an important American woman writer but the novel did not escape criticism in the left-wing press for its unorthodox subjects and formal complexities. A year after its publication, Granville Hicks, a major critical voice of the proletarian movement, declared his disappointment in an article in the Communist-led journal *New Masses* imposingly entitled "Revolution and the Novel: Part 1: The Past and Future as Themes." Tellingly, Hicks's criticism centered on the very issues of emphasis and proportion that signal to contemporary readers their transgressive relationship to the norms of proletarian fiction.[22] Reproving Herbst for failing to integrate the novel's multivocal narrative form with its class-conscious political function, Hicks found "uncertainties of attitude, conflicting emotions, and inconsistent interpretations" in the novel, flaws that stemmed, he surmised, from the author's only recent conversion to Marxism.[23]

Contemporary readers need only look to Herbst's letter to the *New Masses* in response to Hicks's review to see the stifling effect of the male-dominated proletarian movement on the voices of women literary radicals.[24] Herbst begins her letter by denying Hicks's claim that the material of her novel "was not relevant to class struggle," but then fails to explain the relationship between the parts of the novel Hicks objects to and the tale of "the defeat of rugged individualism" he valorizes. The closest Herbst gets to communicating her materialist-feminist perspective in this forum is through speaking metaphorically of her characters as "border people . . . falling by the wayside" who "must throw their forces with the proletariat or perish."[25] Troping her own position within literary radicalism, Herbst's language implies both fragmentation and connection, suggesting the historic split between feminism and the Left that came in the aftermath of World War I and the "border identities" of those who continued to believe that socialism and feminism were inseparable.[26] Herbst's reticence to more directly challenge Hicks's views should not be construed as the absence of feminist consciousness but rather as the difficulty of expressing it. Herbst's materialist-feminist perspective, historically rooted in the radical new womanhood and its disappointing aftermath, honed by Marxist critiques of universality, objectivity, and ruling-class ideas, found form and meaning in *Pity Is Not Enough*.

The novel begins in 1905 in Oxtail, Iowa, with Anne Wendel and her four daughters running to the storm cellar to escape a cyclone, an annual event, the narrator explains, that always resulted in the mother's telling of the same sentimentalized family stories. There, under the earth, after lighting a lamp and passing out apples, Anne invariably recited tales about "the dead and gone Trexlers and Joe, the most generous brother, poor Joe," who briefly lifted his working-class family out of economic hardship and social deprivation into the privileged world of the leisured middle-class. During one particularly violent storm that nearly destroyed the family house, Anne reveals for the first time the events following the collapse of Joe's good fortune: a life on the run after a railroad scandal in post–Civil War Georgia and the failure of prospecting ventures in the Black Hills to return him to his glory days of wealth and power. Yet though the "tragic" outline of Joe's life is revealed here, Anne provides her daughters with no greater insight into her brother's life on this occasion than on any other. Shut out from "learning why Joe ran and why he was poor Joe," the Wendel girls must construct their own versions of the Trexler family history from a maternal narrative of revelation and repression.

"Oxtail, 1905" is the first of seven transgressive interchapters written about or from the point of view of Anne's daughters. Interchapters, as Barbara Foley has shown, often function in radical novels from this period as "political mentors," "foreground[ing] interpretation as an ideological enterprise" and positioning readers to think about relationships and interconnections.[27] Shifting the narrative voice from "we" to "I" to "they," speaking both of what connects the sisters to their mother and of what divides them from each other, Herbst presents the writing of history as a collective yet deeply personal interpretive act shaped by the historical moment in which the writer positions herself and is positioned. The past the Wendel girls must sort through involves not only Joe's life but the lives of his two brothers, Aaron and David, and two other sisters, Hortense and Catherine, his favorite, who dies mysteriously of a "brain fever." Speaking in the "I" voice of the fourth interchapter, Victoria Wendel discerns familial relationships her mother cannot and will not see—that the death of Catherine was connected to the reasons "why Joe ran" and that Catherine's death from "brain fever" foretold, and in some sense engendered, Joe's insane end. In the daughter-narrator's tale of the "good brother," Joe's economic demise reveals the interlocking tale of his sister's sexual oppression.

Through the trope of the daughter-narrator, Herbst figures her own family's history and the materialist-feminism that infuses the novel's form.[28] In "Magicians and Their Apprentices," Herbst described her mother's tales of her "roving brothers" as "our first oral library" and recounted how they shaped her awareness of the injuries of class and the inequities of gender long before she entered the radical scene.[29] In the fictional Trexlers Herbst recreated people and events from her mother's stories that illuminated a complex web of economic and gender relationships. Like Anne Wendel, Mary Frey grew up in rural Pennsylvania, one of six children raised by an impoverished widow who supported her family through piecework and small farming. Joseph Frey, the uncle for whom Herbst was named, died in 1892—two months after Herbst was born—destitute, nearly blind, and insane, and the major events of his life are the central focus of the novel. Mary's older sister Priscilla, like her fictional counterpart Catherine, died of a "brain fever" of uncertain origins after Joseph fled the family home to avoid arrest by local authorities. In 1883 Mary Frey married a local farm implement salesman, William Herbst, five years later following him to Sioux City, Iowa, where he started a farm machinery business that never prospered. David, the spoiled and close-fisted younger brother in the novel who lords his success as a wealthy Oregon businessman over his siblings, mirrors Herbst's uncle Daniel Frey, whose real-life stinginess forced her to postpone college for several years after her father's business went bankrupt.

There are also strong autobiographical elements in Herbst's representation of the "Wendel girls." Like Herbst's siblings, the four Wendel sisters were divided by generational outlook into companionate pairs. The two older sisters, born before the move West and nearly ten years senior, were religious and conventionally domestic. The two younger girls, restless and rebellious, learned to read the "things unsaid" by their mother as an underground tale of resistance to unequal power relations in the home and the moral platitudes of the middle-class. Like their fictional counterparts in the interchapter "Seattle, 1918," Herbst and her sister Helen lived in a boardinghouse in Seattle during the time of the flu epidemic at the local naval encampment near the end of World War I. Herbst's clearest memory of that period, she later wrote, was of working as a typist in a law office and hearing the sound of Chopin's funeral march rising from the street below. In the novel Herbst uses this same motif to focus the reader's attention on the censoring of disquieting images by those in authority. Because they reminded the public of the lethal consequences of the war, the military banned parades of coffins through the streets of Seattle. If no one saw the funerals, the logic went, the war would remain invisible and the violence and havoc it wrought would be buried with the coffins quietly sent home. In *Pity Is Not Enough* Herbst will not allow her reader to ignore either the sexual power structure that dictates women's economic choices or the history of gender violence buried beneath the mother's stories of the "good brother." Constructing her historical narrative from the "material of her mother's telling"—both things said and unsaid—and the crucible of her own gendered class history, Herbst makes visible capitalism's illusory separation of private life and public world.

The family is a crucial site of political struggle in *Pity Is Not Enough*. As readers witness the production of asymmetrical heterosexual relationships within the Trexler family—the boys learn to differentiate themselves from their mother and sisters while the girls acquire the passivity and pietism necessary to the maintenance of separate spheres—they learn to connect sexual politics with the needs of capital. The Trexler sisters repeatedly sacrifice their own desires and interests to increase their brothers' chances of economic success. Anne helps pay for David's schooling at a pharmaceutical college while her own educational aspirations are put aside. After Joe flees Atlanta under cover of darkness, the sisters move out of their expensive Philadelphia home into a small farmhouse in rural Pennsylvania to give Joe a second chance out West. Mother Trexler "cheat[s] her girls and favor[s] her boys" despite her own girlhood desires for education and independence, encouraging her daughters to seek satisfaction in their difference from men while exhorting her sons to "make a lot of money and to take care of them all."

Herbst's representation of the ideology of sexual difference that shapes her characters' emotions and actions anticipates Nancy Cott's study of the "canon of domesticity," a hegemonic but paradoxical set of discourses that empowered and imprisoned nineteenth-century middle-class women. Asked both to rein in men's worst instincts and to accept male control, Catherine is granted moral authority to critique the values of the marketplace yet is admonished to provide "disinterested love" to those who uphold them.[30] Herbst's exploration of "the culture of sentiment" at the heart of nineteenth-century American society is accomplished in many moments in the novel: in Joe's obsessive desire to alter his family's economic status so that he might claim a proper domestic lineage; in the role of guide books, inspirational essays, and sentimental poetry in the formation of middle-class identity; in sections on Joe's fascination with the Blondell sisters, Georgia women warped by a conservative Southern code of loyalty and self-sacrifice; and in Catherine's systematic efforts to justify and forgive Joe's moral transgressions if not to prove his innocence.[31]

Pity Is Not Enough manifests a Foucaultian sense both of how discourses have been deployed in the service of hierarchical relationships and of how subjects resist normalization.[32] In the chapter "Catherine Dispossessed," Catherine's overwhelming desire to comprehend the events culminating in the family's financial decline compels her to read the newspapers and court documents stored in Joe's trunk in the attic. Although previously she had been content to let Joe act as her "window to the world," after learning the true story of his role in the Georgia state railroad scandal she realizes that she knows no more of life than "a child" or a "nun, closed in and shut tight." For Catherine, "it was as if the scales had fallen from her eyes," yet insight into her brother's sordid economic ventures does not produce lucent vision. Dispossessed of belief in her own moral separateness, Catherine struggles to resist the dictates of the "code of domesticity." In the chapter's final scene she obsessively rereads the record of her brother's crimes while being attacked by wasps. Engulfing Catherine in a "sudden darkness," Herbst evokes a multitude of metaphorical configurations: the "dark" side of capitalism, men and women "in the dark," and the darkness of the other victims of Joe's crimes—the Georgia ex-slaves for whom the failure of Reconstruction banished any hope of building a new South based on racial equality and economic justice.

Joe Trexler is also subjected to the contradictions of "separate spheres" at great emotional and physical cost. Unlike the

successful capitalists he tries to emulate, Joe cannot completely separate his ruthless public conduct from the gentility and
generosity he expresses at home. Herbst's text reveals Joe to be
often troubled by what he sees around him. Like Catherine
swatting off the garret wasps, Joe tries to avoid the disturbing
elements within his situation and, like his sister, his confusion
results in a critical mistake. Because he treats the public world
and his private life as interrelated, he becomes the scapegoat of
the Georgia Reconstruction scandal. After his arrest, Joe refuses to testify against Blake Fawcett, the superintendent of the
state railroad, because of a promise he made to Fawcett's mother and he flees Atlanta rather than break his oath. The dupe of
his rivals who claim he master-minded the fraud, Joe is defeated by his allegiance to a private code of conduct that proves
fatal in the economic sphere. In sharp contrast to Joe, David,
the successful capitalist of the Trexler family, never blurs the
distinction between home and workplace. While Joe is swayed
by the domestic pieties mouthed by the Southern gentleman
with whom he lives and works, David is unencumbered by the
moral niceties of women, possessing "the good sense never to
be too generous with the women folk . . . or encourage them to
dictate to him." Unambiguous in his assignation of power to
men, David creates a unified and centered masculine self in
contrast to Joe's divided and contradictory subjectivity.

The "materials" of Herbst's "telling" of the Trexler family history are the artifacts and tools of contemporary materialist-
feminist historians: lost documents, forgotten events, buried
lives, and the contradictory subjects and ideological tensions
that emerge in their reconstructions of the past. A materialist-
feminist history presents gender "as an organizing category,"
Judith Newton argues, and portrays "hegemonic ideology . . . as
internally divided, unstable and in constant need of construction and revision."[33] Herbst represents Catherine and Joe Trexler as conflicted subjects whose contradictions illuminate the
social construction of a class and gendered self in a racialized

American landscape. Anticipating postmodern critiques of the unified self as the ground of revolutionary politics, Herbst's characters are essentialized by discourse but inwardly in motion, at odds with the divisions of class, race, and gender at the heart of capitalist relations of production.[34] Their "nervous breakdowns" become sites of a political struggle devalued by the thirties' Left, one waged in opposition to capitalism against the binary organization of sexual difference and the psychic divisions of sexual organization.

Yet if *Pity Is Not Enough* manages to foreground gender equally with class, it also suggests through a key character the author's anxiety about her own materialist-feminism. Tellingly it is the text's most "bourgeois" female character—the term of opprobrium frequently deployed by the Left against feminists—who drives Joe Trexler insane. After several years of prospecting in the Black Hills, Joe marries the beautiful daughter of a wealthy Eastern stockbroker. Agnes Mason reminds Joe of his glory days in the South and he likes the "shine and spectacle" of her. Yet in private Agnes does not act like any other woman Joe has ever known, defying his traditional notions of female nature and the role of men in preserving women's proper place. At home, Agnes talks and acts like a man, swears like a whore, berates Joe for not acting more like a man himself, and relentlessly criticizes him for the kindly way he treats the workers at the silver mine he manages. In her bitter refusal of the pietism, sentimentality, and moral virtue expected of nineteenth-century middle-class women, Agnes ironically personifies the "gender trouble" of the woman Joe most wishes his wife to emulate.[35] The trauma of Catherine's psychic defeat by the very code of domesticity Agnes flaunts is reenacted in Joe's imprisonment by this most unlikely angel of retribution. Although Joe expects Agnes to act as a mirror in which to recover an idealized and static image of himself, she instead reflects back to him both what he lacks—ruthless individualism—and what he most wishes to be—a "feminine" man in nurturant affiliations with others, an anarchist like his friend John Huber, freeing himself from his unremitting capitalist aspirations. The "masculine" woman who tears Joe's psychic world apart and the "bitch goddess" of his phallic gaze, Agnes is both a "grotesque figure" and a "signature of protest," marking the author's estrangement from her male-dominated literary world and her refusal of the essentialist notions of gender difference that confounded radical men and women of her generation.[36]

Historical Forces in *Pity Is Not Enough*

Herbst's research into the life of her nineteenth-century carpetbagger uncle produced a tale of the defeat of post–Civil War Reconstruction remarkably similar to the one told by the contemporary leftist historian Eric Foner.[37] In Foner's account, Republican men throughout the South viewed Reconstruction as a field for personal advancement. Captured by the "gospel of prosperity," they appointed themselves spokesmen for blacks and poor whites, but their real interests were in attracting Northern capital and in inducing economic development primarily through the building of railroads. Throughout the South Reconstruction efforts were undermined by widespread greed and corruption. Bribes, risky loans, and lavish entertainment drained state resources and increased state debt. Government indifference to the concerns of freed slaves encouraged Klan violence and gave heart to all those who desired the restoration of white supremacy.

Herbst's story of the demise of Reconstruction in Georgia, where the Democrats won control of the state legislature in 1870 and took the governor's office a year later, depicts the historical forces at work in the reinstatement of traditional class and racial hierarchies. Throughout his tenure in office, Georgia's first Republican governor, Rufus Bullock, a transplanted Northern businessman, gave special deals to his friends that undermined his reform agenda. High on the list of recipients of Bullock's largess were Foster Blodgett, the former mayor of Augusta whom Bullock appointed the first superintendent of the state railroad in 1868 and later supported for U.S. senator, and H. I. Kimball, a Northern entrepreneur known as the brains behind the Bullock administration who made a fortune in postwar Atlanta as president of a railroad car company. Both men were involved in scandals that reflected badly on the Republican administration. Blodgett, twice under investigation for plundering state funds, was indicted in 1871 for cheating the state out of $40,000 for railroad cars purchased from Kimball's company but never delivered. Kimball fled the state in 1871 with a debt of $5 million under a cloud of accusations regarding the illegal use of state bonds and the shady circumstances surrounding the purchase of his Atlanta Opera House by the legislature for use as the state capitol. Neither man was ever punished for his alleged crimes. Blodgett was pardoned by Governor Conley in 1871; Kimball returned to Georgia in 1874 at the invitation of a group of Atlanta businessmen and made a fortune in the new cotton mill industry.[38]

The Atlanta that Joseph Frey migrated to in 1869 was wracked by legislative chaos and racial violence. Black officials had just been expelled from the Democrat-controlled state legislature and white men in Camilla, Georgia, had ambushed three hundred blacks on their way to a political rally, killing and wounding at least forty. Governor Bullock used the Camilla massacre to persuade Grant to return the state to military rule, and from January to July 1870, General Terry and his forces took control of the state and reconvened the original 1868 legislature. Terry required lawmakers to reorganize under the test oath prohibiting supporters of the Confederacy from holding public office and to ratify the Fifteenth Amendment, which guaranteed the right to vote regardless of "race, color, or previous condition of servitude." Bullock celebrated Grant's promise to return Georgia to military supervision with a lavish party for his supporters in Washington at the Cafe Francaise, an event that reinforced his reputation among Georgia Democrats as a radical usurper and a swindling politician. Bullock was ousted by the so-called Redeemer legislature of 1871 that quickly moved to disenfranchise black voters. Like his friend H. I. Kimball, Bullock avoided arrest by fleeing the state, returning five years later to be acquitted of criminal charges by an Atlanta jury. After his exoneration, Bullock was offered the job of treasurer of Kimball's Atlanta cotton factory, and the former governor, eager to return to his previous life as a successful Southern industrialist, readily accepted.

In *Pity Is Not Enough* Herbst's antiracist perspective is conveyed through character, narrative voice, and ironic juxtaposition. Republican allegiance to a discourse of black rights is countermanded by the words of the drunken businessman Joe Trexler meets his first day in Atlanta, who claims the governor's efforts to help "the poor downtrodden nigger" are the logical consequence of his enlightened policy of "free enterprise." White characters express traditional myths of blacks' passivity and docility while Herbst pointedly reminds her readers of the Camilla massacre and the rantings of Democratic newspapers about "uppity blacks clamoring for their rights." K. I. Trimble, Herbst's fictionalized version of H. I. Kimball, lies to himself and his abolitionist aunt in letters home about his work of spiritual uplift for blacks while plotting to defraud the state government. Blake Fawcett, the Foster Blodgett character, fondly recalls the material extravagances and social stability of the Old South as he praises Joe's efforts to get in on the graft at the state railroad office. In the section sardonically entitled "Bones of the Saints," the Falstaffian Ton Ferris, Fawcett's legislative aide, exposes the real motives of the "do-gooder" governor to the naive newcomer, Joe Trexler: exploiting violence against blacks to consolidate his power, Bullock turns the votes of "ole Sambo" into a flood of Yankee cash. Republicans and Democrats alike express fears of the dangers of unbridled democracy and the political inadequacies of the poor and the colored;

discourses of social Darwinism are deployed in the service of traditional racial and class hierarchies; and the rhetoric of "free enterprise" and "universal prosperity" make poverty a sign of moral weakness and mental inferiority.

In her representation of the death of Reconstruction in Georgia, Herbst presents a reading of Southern history in which the ascendancy of Hooverism is forcefully linked to the rise and preservation of Jim Crowism. The advancement of free market capitalism, Herbst suggests, was integrally linked to the abandonment of the North's commitment to racial justice. Racial violence was surely on Herbst's mind when she wrote this first volume of her Trexler family history. Herbst supported the work of the Communist party in the South against race terror in a 1931 article in the *New Masses* entitled "Lynching in the Quiet Manner" on the Scottsboro trial of nine young black men in Alabama falsely accused of raping two white women. The article outlined the conditions of black servitude in the aftermath of the demise of Reconstruction—tenant farming, vagrancy laws, chain gangs, and a corrupt legal system run by "white men still dominated by a slave owner's code"—and took to task all those who decried the ignorance and poverty of blacks without situating their social circumstances within the material conditions of their oppression. To counter racist stereotypes of black women, Herbst provided a brief sketch of the mother of two of the Scottsboro boys in her article, an account in which female agency and maternal desire for a better life for herself and her children bravely functioned within a cruel environment of economic exploitation and race hatred.[39]

Herbst's reference in "Lynching in the Quiet Manner" to the "gentlemanly way" the South perpetuates racism suggests the very relationship between codes of gender conduct and racial politics she depicted in *Pity Is Not Enough*. Joe's swaggering masculinity, his devotion to his "whitest little angel," his fine clothes, and his expensive gifts to his family, Blake Fawcett tells him privately, perpetuate traditions of the Old South threatened by a Republican ideology of social mobility he publicly advances. These same manhood issues are manipulated in the trial of Fawcett when Joe's working-class background is used by the former superintendent's lawyers to undermine Joe's claims to bourgeois integrity and racial purity, key elements in the return to power of elite members of the Bullock administration in the post-Reconstruction period. In a last-ditch effort to raise himself and his family, Joe heads West following the siren song of "free labor" to the mining towns of Wyoming and Colorado only to find himself engulfed in the contradictions of an exploitative and impersonal marketplace. In the end, Joe's ambivalence about joining the managerial class and succeeding in a man's world that separates home and workplace, joined with his former doubts about Fawcett's moral guidance and his revulsion at racial violence, reinforce the reader's sense of the socially transforming potential of the resisting subject seemingly reified by class, race, and gender ideologies.

Enduring Values

Josephine Herbst's resistance to the notion that revolutionary movements need coherent, stable subjects was a product of her own history and experience as a woman of the American Left. So, too, was her commitment to class, race, and gender justice. As we recover the work of radical writers, it is worth noting that Herbst never repudiated her past and that her literary reputation has suffered as a result. Hilton Kramer, Herbst's literary executor and the editor of the conservative journal the *New Criterion*, has publicly called Herbst a Stalinist, a failed writer, and a neurotic woman for refusing to disavow the "whole political outlook" of her life as an American radical: not just her relationship to the Communist party and its policies in the thirties but her feminism, her bohemian lifestyle, and even her prickly, "masculine," personality.[40] Similarly, arch anticommunist Stephen Koch, without a single shred of archival evidence to support the charge, claimed Herbst was a secret agent for the Soviet Comintern in the midthirties. Like Kramer, Koch tellingly uses Herbst's feminism and bohemianism to bolster his argument for her moral degeneracy and her status as a second-rate literary talent.[41] Kramer's and Koch's virulent admixture of misogyny and anticommunism, in fact, points to the critical task of today's readers of *Pity Is Not Enough* to lay claim to Herbst's feminist past and the socialist roots of her commitment to gender justice and to revalue the cultural work of her materialist-feminist novels.

In the early forties, as former Communists and fellow travelers expressed guilt and remorse for their involvement with leftist causes, Herbst lived alone on the edge of poverty in her farmhouse in Erwinna, largely cut off from literary and intellectual circles. Holding to her belief in the significance of her generation's achievements, Herbst fought back at the height of the cold war. In a remarkable essay published in *The Nation* in 1956 entitled "The Ruins of Memory," Herbst's defense of her radical past and the artistic achievements of her contemporaries speaks powerfully to today's readers of the value of the radical novel:

> If you can bear to lift the black cloth placed over the thirties by the revisionists, some of whom seem more infatuated with the revelation of their own private sense of guilt than in the situation as it *then existed,* you may be surprised to discover work not entirely marred by "innocence" nor requiring the afterthought of "shame." The reaction in the forties, the Second World War, the new cynicism, the new prosperity and the new smugness put the thirties, its work and the sources of its potential, into a time capsule where it has been effectively isolated. But the fact remains that work marked by vitality and venturing did emerge in the arts, the theater and in the writing of that decade and found a new dynamic.[42]

Warning readers of "the stern father image of an arbitrary authority" looming above both the Left and the Right, Herbst rightly perceived the seductions of power and privilege both sides had succumbed to and the logic of domination inherent within masculinist thinking. To think dialectically about subjects in history is the founding principle of Herbst's trilogy of novels from the thirties. *Pity Is Not Enough,* too long buried within the ruins of America's radical past and under the wreckage of Herbst's once considerable literary reputation, is richly deserving of our fullest attention. The issues raised by Herbst's novel—the relationship between feminism and Marxism, the contradictions of leftist political discourses and cultures for women and "others," the value of postmodernist critiques of subjectivity to revolutionary politics, the dynamics of racism and capitalism, and the occlusion of left-wing fiction from the American literary canon—remain for us to address today.

Notes

1. Key readings in the debate over the relationship between feminism and Marxism include Combahee River Collective, "A Black Feminist Statement," in *Capitalist Patriarchy and the Case for Socialist Feminism,* ed. Zillah Eisenstein (New York: Monthly Review Press, 1979), 362–72; Michelle Barrett, *Women's Oppression Today* (London: Verso, 1980); Lydia Sargent, ed., *Women and Revolution: A Discussion of the Unhappy Marriage of Marxism and Feminism* (Boston: South End Press, 1981); Nancy Hartsock, *Sex and Power: Toward a Feminist Historical Materialism* (New York: Longman, 1983); Leslie Rabine, "Searching for the Connections: Marxist-Feminists and Women's Studies," *Humanities in Society* 6 (Spring–Summer 1983): 195–221; Christine Delphy, *Close to Home: A Materialist Analysis of Women's Oppression,* translated and edited by Diana Leonard (Amherst: University of Massachusetts Press, 1984); Gayatri Chakravorty Spivak, "Can the Subaltern Speak?" in *Marxism and the Interpretation of Culture,* ed. Cary Nelson and Lawrence Grossberg (Urbana: University of Illinois Press, 1988), 271–313; Rosemary Hennessy, *Materialist Feminism and the Politics of Discourse* (New York: Routledge, 1993); and Teresa L. Ebert, *Ludic Feminism and Af-*

ter: Postmodernism, Desire, and Labor in Late Capitalism (Ann Arbor: University of Michigan Press, 1996).

2. Daniel Aaron, *Writers on the American Left* (New York: Columbia University Press, 1992).

3. Mari Jo Buhle, *Women and American Socialism, 1870–1920* (Urbana: University of Illinois Press, 1981), 258–59. See also Nancy Cott, *The Grounding of Modern Feminism* (New Haven: Yale University Press, 1987), particularly "The Birth of Feminism," 13–50, for the socialist roots of modern feminism.

4. Josephine Herbst, "Pagan," *Berkeley Occident* 72 (Nov. 1917): 125. The "radical new woman" is Lois Banner's term for those women who called for "a fundamental redistribution of the wealth and social power of the nation" and the sexual and social liberation of women. "The New Woman," in *1915: The Cultural Moment,* ed. Adele Heller and Lois Rudnick (New Brunswick: Rutgers University Press), 75.

5. Quoted in Elinor Langer, *Josephine Herbst* (Boston: Little, Brown, 1983), 44. For a fuller account of these years see "Unmarried," 53–79. Langer's biography is essential reading for Herbst scholars.

6. Herbst published the following poems in the *Berkeley Occident:* "Kept Cat" 72 (Oct. 1917): 16; "Will o' the Wisp" 72 (Oct. 1917): 32; "Pagan" 72 (Nov. 1917): 125; "Silences" 72 (Mar. 1918): 317–19; and "Stardust" 72 (Apr. 1918): 368–69.

7. Edward Carpenter, *Love's Coming of Age* (New York: Mitchell Kennerly, 1911). The best critical study of the impact of Carpenter's work on the prewar American Left is in Sheila Rowbotham and Jeffrey Weeks, *Socialism and the New Life: The Personal and Sexual Politics of Edward Carpenter and Havelock Ellis* (London: Pluto Press, 1977).

8. Emma Goldman, "Marriage and Love," in *Red Emma Speaks: An Emma Goldman Reader,* ed. Alix Kates Shulman (New York: Schocken Books, 1983), 209.

9. Leslie Fishbein, *Rebels in Bohemia* (Chapel Hill: University of North Carolina Press, 1982), 146.

10. Langer, *Josephine Herbst,* 54.

11. For the contradictions of women's place in prewar bohemian communities, see June Sochen, *The New Woman: Feminism and Greenwich Village* (New York: Quadrangle Books, 1972); Leslie Fishbein, *Rebels in Bohemia* (Chapel Hill: University of North Carolina Press, 1982); Ellen Kay Trimberger, "Feminism, Men, and Modern Love," in *Powers of Desire,* ed. Ann Snitow, Christine Stansell, and Sharon Thompson (New York: Monthly Review Press, 1983), 169–89; and Cott, *The Grounding of Modern Feminism,* 43–50.

12. Josephine Herbst, "Following the Circle," ms., Collection of American Literature, Beinicke Rare Book Room and Manuscript Library, Yale University.

13. Excerpts of the letters between Herbst and her sister Helen appear in Langer, *Josephine Herbst*, 61–66.

14. On the "modern womanhood" as formulated by psychologists, popular magazines, and the advertising industry in the twenties, see Christina Simmons, "Companionate Marriage and the Lesbian Threat," *Frontiers* 4 (Fall 1979): 54–59; Mary Ryan, *Womanhood in America* (New York: F. Watts, 1983); and Carroll Smith-Rosenberg, "Discourses of Sexuality and Subjectivity: The New Woman, 1870–1936," in *Hidden from History: Reclaiming the Gay and Lesbian Past*, ed. Martin Duberman, Martha Vicinus, and George Chauncey Jr. (New York: Meridian Books, 1989), 264–80.

15. Elaine Showalter, *These Modern Woman: Autobiographical Essays from the Twenties* (Old Westbury, N.Y.: Feminist Press, 1978), 61.

16. See Cott, *The Grounding of Modern Feminism*, 59–66, for a compelling account of how hostility to radicalism in the wake of World War I and the Bolshevik Revolution in Russia turned many feminists against socialism.

17. Herbst's twenties novels are *Nothing Is Sacred* (New York: Coward-McCann, 1928) and *Money for Love* (New York: Coward-McCann, 1929). In her review of *Nothing Is Sacred* for the *New Masses*, Katherine Anne Porter criticized Herbst's novel for implying that a woman whose "true ambition is to be successful with men" ought to be "despised" for her "perfectly womanly" vocation. See "Bohemian Futility," *New Masses* 4 (Nov. 17, 1929): 17.

18. In 1932 Herrmann shared with Thomas Wolfe the *Scribner Magazine* literary prize for the best short story for "The Big Short Trip."

19. Herbst expressed to Herrmann her desire for an egalitarian marriage in a letter dated January 17, 1925, John Herrmann letters, Humanities Research Center, University of Texas at Austin. Careful readers of Herbst's short story "A Bad Blow," published in *Scribner's Magazine* in 1930, will hear what Elaine Showalter calls the quintessential voice of the "modern woman" in a "wry, self-deprecating" (17) tale of a wife's repressed anger and disappointment with the inegalitarian terms of her "romantic" marriage. The story is based on a sea voyage that Herbst reluctantly agreed to take with her husband down the coast of Maine in 1927. Piloted by Herrmann, their small sailboat nearly capsized in a storm en route to Portland harbor. The story's title refers both to a sea storm and to its effect on the wife who cowers below deck, like Herbst, terrified of the water, in fear of drowning while her husband rejoices in his exhilarating "masculine" adventure.

20. Josephine Herbst, "Magicians and Their Apprentices," *The Starched Blue Sky of Spain and Other Memoirs* (New York: HarperCollins, 1991), 41.

21. Aaron, *Writers on the Left*, 12.

22. Two ground-breaking feminist studies of the relation between gender and genre are Mary Jacobus, "Is There a Woman in This Text," *New Literary History* 12 (Summer 1982): 117–41; and Nancy K. Miller, "Emphasis Added: Plots and Plausibilities in Women's Fiction," in *The New Feminist Criticism*, ed. Elaine Showalter (New York: Pantheon Press, 1985), 339–60. See also Paula Rabinowitz's "The Contradictions of Gender and Genre," *Labor and Desire: Women's Revolutionary Fiction in Depression America* (Chapel Hill: University of North Carolina Press, 1991), 63–96.

23. Granville Hicks, "Revolution and the Novel: Part 1: The Past and Future as Themes," *New Masses* 12 (Apr. 3, 1934): 30.

24. For discussions of the damaging effects of the masculinism of the male-dominated literary Left on the voices of leftist women, see Deborah Rosenfelt, "From the Thirties: Tillie Olsen and the Radical Tradition," in *Feminist Criticism and Social Change*, ed. Judith Newton and Deborah Rosenfelt (New York: Methuen Press, 1985), 216–48; Constance Coiner, "Literature of Resistance: The Intersection of Feminism and the Communist Left in Meridel Le Sueur and Tillie Olsen," in *Left Politics and the Literary Profession*, ed. Lennard J. Davis and M. Bella Mirabella (New York: Columbia University Press, 1990), 176–83; Rabinowitz, *Labor and Desire;* and Barbara Foley, *Radical Representations: Politics and Form in U.S Proletarian Fiction, 1929–1941* (Durham: Duke University Press, 1993).

25. Josephine Herbst, letter, *New Masses* 12 (July 3, 1934): 30.

26. See Sherna Gluck, "Socialist Feminism between the Two Wars," in *Decades of Discontent: The Women's Movement, 1920–40*, ed. Lois Scharf and Joan M. Jensen (Westport, Conn.: Greenwood Press, 1983), 279–97. Gluck's analysis of the effects of the split between feminism and socialism after World War I is based on oral history interviews published in *From Parlor to Prison: Five American Suffragists Talk about Their Lives*, ed. Sherna Gluck (New York: Random House, 1976) in which several prewar radical new women discuss the personal and political consequences to themselves and their contemporaries of the absence of any guiding theory or supportive political context in the twenties and thirties for their socialist-feminism.

27. Foley, *Radical Representations*, 431, 441. See Foley's discussions of Dos Passos's use of interchapters in the U.S.A. trilogy, 425–36, and of the relation between proletarianism and modernism, 54–63.

28. *Pity Is Not Enough*'s multivocal narrative form confirms Alan Wald's sense that many leftist writers in the thirties brought a modernist sensibility to their writing and that the boundary between literary culture in the twenties and thirties—much policed in the aftermath of the cold war—was

more permeable than literary critics have previously considered. Alan Wald, "In Retrospect: On Native Grounds," *Reviews in American History* 20 (June 1992): 276–88. See also Cary Nelson, *Repression and Recovery: Modern American Poetry and the Politics of Cultural Memory, 1910–1945* (Madison: University of Wisconsin Press, 1989). Nelson demonstrates how modernism was constituted differently in the writings of leftist poets and argues that leftist writing has been occluded from the canon of modern American poetry for ideological reasons formulated during the cold war.

29. Herbst, "Magicians and Their Apprentices," 10.

30. Nancy Cott, *The Bonds of Womanhood* (New Haven: Yale University Press, 1977), 67, 70.

31. See *The Culture of Sentiment: Race, Gender, and Sentimentalism in Nineteenth-Century America*, ed. Shirley Samuels (New York: Oxford University Press, 1992).

32. See Michel Foucault, *The Archeology of Knowledge and the Discourse of Language,* trans. A. Sheridan Smith (New York: Pantheon, 1972).

33. Judith Newton, "History as Usual? Feminism and the 'New Historicism,'" *Cultural Critique* 5 (Spring 1988): 106, 102. See also Judith Newton and Deborah Rosenfelt, "Introduction: Toward a Materialist-Feminist Criticism," in *Feminist Criticism and Social Change*, xv–xxxix.

34. The postmodern feminist reconfigurations of subjectivity that have been most useful to me in the writing of this essay are Chris Weedon, *Feminist Practice and Poststructuralist Theory* (New York: Basil Blackwell, 1987); Leslie Wahl Rabine, "A Feminist Politics of Non-Identity," *Feminist Studies* 14 (Spring 1988): 11–31; Biddy Martin, "Feminism, Criticism, and Foucault," in *Feminism and Foucault: Reflections on Resistance,* ed. Irene Diamond and Lee Quinby (Boston: Northeastern University Press, 1988), 3–19; Judith Butler, "Contingent Foundations: Feminism and the Question of 'Postmodernism,'" in *Feminists Theorize the Political,* ed. Judith Butler and Joan W. Scott (New York: Routledge, 1992), 3–21; Kaja Silverman, *Male Subjectivity at the Margins* (New York: Routledge, 1992); and Lisa Lowe, "Unfaithful to the Original: The Subject of *Dictee*" in *Writing Self Writing Nation: Essays on Teresa Hak Kyuun Cha's* Dictee, ed. Elaine Kim and Norma Alarcon (Berkeley: Third Woman Press, 1994), 35–69. For a very different view of the relationship between feminism, postmodernism, and revolutionary politics, see Barbara Foley, "Marxism in the Poststructuralist Moment: Some Notes on the Problem of Revising Marx," *Cultural Critique* 15 (Spring 1990): 5–37, and *Radical Representations,* 240–46; and Ebert, *Ludic Feminism and After.*

35. The allusion is to the title of Judith Butler's postmodern critique of essentialist notions of gender identity, *Gender Trouble: Feminism and the Subversion of Identity* (New York: Routledge, 1990).

36. Here I am drawing from Rabinowitz's analysis in *Labor and Desire* of the presence of "grotesque creatures" in the writings of women radicals who feared their feminism made them "bourgeois" (30) and Nancy K. Miller's claim that "desire for the revision of story" is often embodied in women's texts in "phallic" female figures. Nancy K. Miller, "Arachnologies: The Woman, the Text, and the Critic," in *The Poetics of Gender*, ed. Nancy K. Miller (New York: Columbia University Press, 1986), 270–95.

37. Eric Foner, *A Short History of Reconstruction, 1863–1877* (New York: Harper and Row, 1990).

38. See Russell Duncan, *Entrepreneur for Equality: Governor Rufus Bullock, Commerce, and Race in Post–Civil War Georgia* (Athens: University of Georgia Press, 1994). Although Duncan's view that Bullock was a defender of black rights and a friend of the poor contrasts sharply with Herbst's depiction of him in *Pity Is Not Enough,* his book reveals just how carefully Herbst researched the history of Reconstruction in Georgia for her novel, particularly the events preceding the ouster of Bullock in 1871.

39. Josephine Herbst, "Lynching in the Quiet Manner," *New Masses* 7 (July 1931): 9–11. For the story of the Scottsboro trial, see Dan T. Carter, *Scottsboro: A Tragedy of the American South* (Baton Rouge: Louisiana State University Press, 1984). In "Lynching in the Quiet Manner" Herbst was also responding to the efforts of the Communist party during its Third Period (1928–35) to define the specificity of black oppression and to create interracial coalitions. See Robin D. G. Kelley, *Hammer and Hoe: Alabama Communists during the Depression* (Chapel Hill: University of North Carolina Press, 1991) and Foley, *Radical Representations,* 174–80, 183–87.

40. Hilton Kramer, "Who was Josephine Herbst?" *New Criterion* 3 (Sept. 1984): 1–14. Kramer wrote the article in response to what he saw as Elinor Langer's political illusions about Herbst's alleged "Stalinism" in *Josephine Herbst.* Disconcerted by revelations after Herbst's death in 1969 of her bohemian past, particularly her affairs with women, Kramer has constructed a grim narrative of Herbst's life and work that disparages both, incredibly claiming that Herbst choose him for her literary executor to "allow the truth to be told about her life" (4) in the way he now sees it.

41. Stephen Koch, *Double Lives: Spies and Writers in the Secret Soviet War of Ideas against the West* (New York: Free Press, 1994). Elinor Langer writes a spirited rebuttal to Koch's book in "The Secret Drawer," *The Nation,* May 30, 1994, 19–20. Given what her biography reveals about Herbst's life, however, I found it difficult to understand how Langer could succumb to Kramer's pressure to term Herbst a "Stalinist."

42. Josephine Herbst, "The Ruins of Memory," *The Nation,* Apr. 14, 1956, 302.

Bibliography

SELECTED WORKS BY JOSEPHINE HERBST

"As a Fair Young Girl." *Scribner's Magazine,* Nov. 1930, 513–19.

"A Bad Blow." *Scribner's Magazine,* July 1930, 25–32.

"Dry Sunday in Connecticut. *American Mercury* 8 (July 1926): 339–44.

"The Elegant Mr. Gason." *Smart Set* 71 (July 1923): 35–39. Published under the pseudonym Carlotta Greet.

The Executioner Awaits. New York: Harcourt, Brace, 1934. Reprinted, New York: Warner Books, 1985.

"Following the Circle." Ms. Collection of American Literature, Beinicke Rare Book Room and Manuscript Library, Yale University.

"The Golden Egg." *Scribner's Magazine,* Mar. 1930, 492–99.

"Happy Birthday." *Smart Set* 71 (Nov. 1923): 97–102. Published under the pseudonym Carlotta Greet.

"Kept Cat." *Berkeley Occident* 72 (Oct. 1917): 68.

"Literature in the U.S.S.R." *New Republic* 66 (Apr. 29, 1931): 305–6.

"Lynching in the Quiet Manner." *New Masses* 7 (July 1931): 11.

Money for Love. New York: Coward-McCann, 1929.

Nothing Is Sacred. (New York: Coward-McCann, 1929.

"Pagan." *Berkeley Occident* 72 (Nov. 1917): 125.

Pity Is Not Enough. New York: Harcourt, Brace, 1933.

Rope of Gold. New York: Harcourt, Brace, 1939. Reprinted, Old Westbury, N.Y.: Feminist Press, 1984.

"The Ruins of Memory." *The Nation,* Apr. 14, 1956, 302–4.

Satan's Sergeants. New York: Charles Scribner's Sons, 1941.

"Silences." *Berkeley Occident* 72 (Mar. 1918): 317–19.

Somewhere the Tempest Fell. New York: Charles Scribner's Sons, 1947.

"Stardust." *Berkeley Occident* 72 (Apr. 1918): 368–69.

The Starched Blue Sky of Spain and Other Memoirs. New York: HarperCollins, 1991.

"A Very Successful Man." *American Mercury* 29 (June 1933): 211–20.

REVIEWS OF *Pity Is Not Enough*

Davenport, Basil. "Pity 'Tis, 'Tis True." *Saturday Review of Literature,* June 3, 1933, 629.

Forum, July 1933, vi.

G. B. *Boston Transcript,* June 10, 1933, 1.

Gregory, Horace. "Wealth in Shining Dollars." *New York Herald Tribune Books,* May 28, 1933, 4.

New Republic, July 5, 1933, 216.

Springfield Republican, June 11, 1933, 7E.

Troy, William. "Pathos Is Not Enough." *The Nation,* July 12, 1933, 52.

"An Unquenchable Family." *Christian Science Monitor,* June 17, 1933, 10.

Walton, Edith H. "Miss Herbst Turns to the Past." *New York Times Book Review,* May 28, 1933, 6.

OTHER SOURCES

Bevilacqua, Winifred Farrant. *Josephine Herbst.* Boston: Twayne, 1985.

Foley, Barbara. *Radical Representations: Politics and Form in U.S. Proletarian Fiction, 1929–1941.* Durham: Duke University Press, 1993.

Kazin, Alfred. "Josephine Herbst (1897–1969)." *New York Review of Books,* Mar. 27, 1969, 19–20.

Langer, Elinor. *Josephine Herbst.* Boston: Little Brown, 1983.

Madden, David, ed. *Proletarian Writers of the Thirties.* Carbondale: Southern Illinois University Press, 1968.

Pittenger, Mark. "'Woman's Nature' and American Feminist Socialism, 1900–1915." *Radical History Review* 36 (Spring 1986): 47–61.

Rabinowitz, Paula. *Labor and Desire: Women's Revolutionary Fiction in Depression America.* Chapel Hill: University of North Carolina Press, 1991.

Rideout, Walter. "Forgotten Images of the Thirties: Josephine Herbst." *Literary Review* 27 (Fall 1983): 28–36.

———. *The Radical Novel in the United States, 1900–1954: Some Interrelations of Literature and Society.* Cambridge, Mass.: Harvard University Press, 1956.

Roberts, Nora Ruth. *Three Radical Women Writers: Class and Gender in Meridel Le Sueur, Tillie Olsen, and Josephine Herbst.* New York: Garland Publishing, 1996.

Rosenfelt, Deborah. "From the Thirties: Tillie Olsen and the Radical Tradition." In *Feminist Criticism and Social Change.* Ed. Judith Newton and Deborah Rosenfelt. New York: Methuen Press, 1985. 216–48.

Sussman, Warren I. "The Thirties." In *The Development of an American Culture,* ed. Stanley Coben and Lorman Ratner. Englewood Cliffs, N.J.: Prentice-Hall, 1970. 179–218.

GUIDE FOR RESEARCHERS

Josephine Herbst's papers, which include manuscripts, journals, photographs, and personal correspondence, are in the Collection of American Literature, Beinecke Rare Book and Manuscript Library, Yale University.

PITY IS NOT ENOUGH

TO THE MEMORY OF MY SISTER

HELEN HERBST

—

PITY IS NOT ENOUGH

Oxtail, 1905

A<small>T LEAST</small> once during the cyclone season, Anne Wendel and her four girls raced through the pouring yellow rain to the cellar. The littlest held to the bigger girls. Anne at the head shielded a lamp with her shawl and held a basket of apples under her arm. In the cool damp cellar they lit the lamp and shut out that dreadful yellow sky and the red barn a monstrous red looking as if it lived and breathed in grass that was too green and living. Down there, they huddled around and Anne brought out to still their terror old Blank and his fits, the dead and gone Trexlers and Joe, the most generous brother, poor Joe.

The day the cottonwood snapped off short and fell heavy as a horse upon the roof, cracking the plaster off the upstairs room and sending the mirror off the wall to break for seven years bad luck, that day, she let it out for the first time that Joe had run away. He had run off from the South to Canada and from Canada he had come back to the old Grapeville home and from Grapeville he had run away again to the West. She had seen with her own eyes a hat he had worn in the Black Hills where an Indian arrow had punctured it neatly with a rusty hole like blood.

We sat there. The cottonwoods outside were crackling and the tiny incessant tinny shivering of their leaves went on between the claps of thunder and the groans of trees. The cellar smelled of earth and mould and in the corner white sprouts of potatoes shot out in rays and through the leaky cellar door drafts came to smoke up the chimney of the lamp and we ate our apples, core and all.

"Poor Joe," she sighed and we waited on that sigh but no more came. "He was the finest man, always wore the best clothes. He had the most charming manners, was generous to a fault," and so she shut us out once more from learning why Joe ran and why he was poor Joe.

The cyclone never touched us. The slimy caterpillar crawled around us to the south and north, writhing from tree to house, biting corners from barns and nipping tops from silos. It was a freak that might touch us still, in spite of the superstition that between two rivers we were safe. Our town lay wedged between the Missouri and the Big Sioux that saved us from the storms for their own eating. In the spring, the Floyd overflowed its banks and wiped out the stockyards poor on the bottoms, and from our attic windows we could see the yellow bubbling Missouri toss about little islands nibbled from farm lands, sometimes with young corn still standing that was to have paid for the machinery bought from Amos Wendel. A bad year for crops. It was always a bad year. Too hot, too wet, too dry, too much Republicanism, the Democrats were ruining things. Flowers were hard to raise in that baked soil.

A wild bird in the house means death and we heard wings beating in the attic. "Don't believe such silly stories," says Anne Wendel, running up the attic stairs. "It's only a poor bird looking for a place to rest. Poor bird."

Lightning split the willow tree but we were spared. Storms played around us and never touched us. We counted days until the next lodge picnic with free rides up the Big Sioux in the *Minnehaha* and in the drugged summer heat waited for a shower to cool us and took turns writing tags for Papa's binders in his store on Pearl Street while across the way women in red and yellow kimonos dyed their hair and stuck their dyed heads from second story windows.

And when the corn was grown and those had paid that could pay, we settled down to winter with crocks of apple butter in the cellar. In the evening on the same piano Joe had given her and Catherine as young girls she played her girlhood music, "Listen to the Mocking Bird" and "Floyd's Retreat," and through all the stricken notes of Floyd running, we heard Joe. Her fingers tinkled over bass and soprano, now he runs and she hammers triumphant, but doubt creeps in, he grows tired, lags, is lost. "Poor Floyd," we say, leaning on the piano, and she turns toward us, her hands still on the keys, the crystals of the hanging lamp making little shivery shadows on her face. Poor Floyd.

We saved our pennies in a china pig and there's no state like Iowa for pigs and corn and in the spring she tried her hand at papering and did a fine job in the bedroom with a flower sprig pattern. Before the corn was in, the rains began, and the storms broke and we made a dash for the cellar, skating through the mud. Down there the clay walls shut us in and as we grew older we tried to worm it out of her why he was poor Joe.

She made a little island of her past and climbed aboard with all her dead and gone and took us children too, clinging and listening, fascinated and scared of the rushing water around us and she had to sit there on that island and see us overboard and sink or swim according to our nature and the chance. The year Amos Wendel lost his business and all the other years of ups and downs, she had her island and we had it too and kept the silver teapot shined and thought of Joe as the most generous brother, not like David who rolled around in Cadillacs the year she tried to pull us out of debt with her invention, *The Gem Scraper*, made of wood to clean the pots and pans, and sat up all night composing ads to tell the world of its superiority. And when she pretended she had paid a bill and acted innocent and shoved a man off the front porch with her "Why I'm sure that's paid, I'll have to look up the receipt right away," she always turned back toward us with a white and beaten look and once she said, "Poverty changes your whole nature, makes you lie and steal and do things you'd never do otherwise," and then again she'd praise the poor and try to reconcile us to it and paste up Emerson on her pantry door that whosoever owned the land, the horizon belonged to that one with the soul to see it and we grew up wondering why he was poor Joe. Why had he been a fugitive and what was the railroad scandal that had made him run and when we learned his other name had been Victor Dorne, we were ashamed a little, silly it sounded and not quite there, like a play with too much shooting in it, but one day we found a clipping in an old pocketbook hanging to a rafter in the attic and then we didn't feel that way any more.

Victor Dorne, an old resident of Deadwood, is insane. He has been in failing health for a number of years. Mr. Dorne's dementia has taken a peculiar form. He imagines he is in Pierre and welcomes old friends as if he had not seen them for years.

I. BONES OF THE SAINTS

O N THE day that her boy left home to go South, Mary Trexler cried and carried on in a way the other children never forgot. There was foreboding in the way their mother cried, a woman not given to scenes. She had six children. On that day her crying cast a gloom on them, all but Joe and he was in the air for joy at leaving the old "Fish Town" to make his fortune.

On the last day he had his picture taken with the pants pressed round like stovepipes and one hand resting on the back of a flimsy chair. His eyes look straight ahead very determined and conquering and his jaw is set in his youthful and at that time round face, but not so set as it was a few years later when he was in the thick of it and struggling to keep his head out of water. To see that picture anyone would say, there's a boy to make his way in the world. His new suit was nothing to what he wore a few years later when the best was none too good and he was running up to New York ordering the finest broadcloths. In the beginning his clothes were countrified looking clothes, cut out by an unfashionable tailor and sewed by his mother late at night after her own sewing girls had left for the day, but he had a bold challenging look as if he meant to compensate himself for some wrong he didn't deserve.

He was nineteen at the time, going South along with many another Northern man. Northern armies still had the whip hand, Northern politicians were running states to please their pocketbooks, land was up at forced sale for a song. Joe went with the tide, a mere chip of a boy. He would have gone anywhere to get away from Philadelphia and his long apprenticeship in a bakeshop. Let Aaron stay at home if he liked selling spools of thread and packages of bluing so well. He would become rich and famous and good and the kind of man their father had intended him to be.

Mary Trexler kept her feelings to herself when she saw Joe was bent to go. If she had learned any lesson it was that a sure thing and steady wages are best. Little good did it do her with the air thick with coming and going and big fortunes on the make. She had no chance from the beginning for anything but to let Joe, the first to go, leave with her foreboding on him.

Good and clear his handwriting came back from Wilmington, North Carolina, in 1868 a first rate town to go to, as full of opportunity as the next. Round and strong with not many sentences to the page, his hand remained on letters home all that year, holding out even in Atlanta, Georgia, for the first few months, gradually shrinking, getting smaller and narrower as to letter formation, the page more cramped. Even the Christmas of 1870, the very year he bought the solid silver tea set for his mother from Tiffany and sent a hundred dollars to his sister Catherine for a fine watch and then another hundred for fear she would not buy the best and nothing but the best would do, that Christmas even, the writing still had traces of his open frankness but it was gradually closing in and shriveling up and in seventy-one, only a year later, running to Canada, he wrote from Niagara Falls, face to face with the Governor of Georgia, also on the run, and his writing then was a cautious swift thing with the letters rushing together but the strokes hard and firm and quite confident.

It took twenty-five years to beat that hand down and to

lick it to what it was toward the end, just a dribble of letters toiling in two lines uphill at the top of a big empty page, optimistic to the last.

Joseph Trexler, going South, was his father Joshua and his uncle Jacob, he was the good Trexlers and the bad as they had lived and died in that part of the world around Locust Valley south of Allentown for generations. Solid landowning men married to long-lived Quaker women, the family came to its chief importance and its power in Joshua, who dying left debts and the memory of importance lost to all his six children.

Joseph, second eldest son, was at the in-between age. Aaron had had his schooling at Nazareth Hall and lorded it around because he knew some Latin and trigonometry and David's schooling was yet to come but Joseph to get anything at all was farmed out to his Aunty Blank at Bethlehem, to be a poor relation while his mother took her brood to Philadelphia to start her career as provider.

Aunty Blank, married to the sterile Uncle Blank, one of seven sterile brothers whose women wept in old age thinking of their childless lot, gave some comfort to Joseph and when old Injun Blank was not there to see slipped hard rock candy in his pockets. For all that she liked a good cigar better than a bottle of perfume any day, she knew how to feed a boy and he ate his fill even with Uncle's hard beady eye grudging every bite. He had his room to go to and he had his *Life of Daniel Boone* and wrote his brother that such a life would be the sort for him, hunting and fishing alone in the woods for years surrounded by none but the savage Indians, escaping from them like Daniel Boone, fighting and never being hurt. He would never need to take a mouthful from old Uncle then and he kept his pride up thinking of the future in that house where Injun Blank never for a minute let him forget he was a poor relation, hating little boys, not having any.

The day he broke Fenstermacher's window, leader of a gang all shouting, "You're name's Windowmaker, isn't it? All right, make one," he cooked his goose and Big Injun hustled him to Philadelphia to be poor with his brothers and sisters, to be happier too, even in the constant whirr of sewing machines that went on late at night because the Civil War was on, just in the nick of time to help the widow make a living sewing coats and pants for the soldiers. Sewing girls came and went. Little Anne, aged eleven, stayed home from school to help out. Her feet barely touched the pedal but she could work faster than the big girls who liked to stop and talk and stretch their arms. Aaron "kept store" below and at night they all gathered together and talked for comfort of the days when they were children, although they were children still, the eldest only seventeen. But growing up had to be quick and Joe, disgraced at Big Injun's, must go to work.

His mother did the best she knew, picked a pious master rather than the job and if her son worked in a cellar kneading dough in troughs with damp dripping all around and the heat of ovens wringing him of strength, she worked in an attic. The little that he earned was not enough to clothe him and he slept like the dead in the few remaining hours of his long day. It made her heart sick to see him lie there, too tired to eat, and she tried to cheer him with bright talk of the future and how his employer now a rich man had the same beginnings. Joe saw this Mr. Ajax getting rich and swinging into politics and rising higher and he took a tip.

Joe went South carrying the same old carpetbag that his father had taken to the state legislature in fifty-six.

Under the stack of six new shirts, finished the night before and the last buttonholes rounded off that morning, were six Bartlett pears and four Bellflower apples. Wrapped in a silk handkerchief was his mother's picture, taken full length, sitting bolt upright on a velvet chair with a handsome chenille fringe, supporting the half lolling figure of her youngest, David, aged seven. So far as the eye could see, Joe traveled light.

At the last minute as he started up the train steps, Catherine pressed her own handkerchief into his hand. He could feel the few hard coins of her savings tied in a knot and had only time to shout, "I'll buy you something nice." The train moved slowly and all the children moved slowly with it, walking along the platform in a little group, big Aaron, whether stupid or deep, walking in a mild daze, Catherine with her eyes on Joe's, Anne tagging along and Hortense, alone and apart, with long straight dank hair, and David, pampered youngest, his pantspockets bulging with forbidden marbles, all moving in a tiny crowd, a band of children moving with the train for one last look at Joe.

They stood waving handkerchiefs and Joe leaned far out waving. The train moved with a grind wrenching Joe away from them and as it was still early morning of a September day, they all turned homeward, Catherine to school to learn to be a teacher, Aaron to the store to sell thread, a bar of soap and Dr. Ruff's Vegetable Compound and perhaps toward night to negotiate a quarter from the till and make an excuse to "walk out" after supper to Concross & Dixie's Minstrel Show.

Because of their mother's crying the children steered clear of her that day. Her slow even determined tears made their stomachs feel hollow. By supper time, the tears had stopped but she sat there, a wooden figure with a wooden

face. Aaron ate with a good appetite and read his paper,
then cleared his throat and said he'd walk out, so was
gone, the quarter from the till heavy as a lead dollar in
his pocket until it was safely slid under the window and
he was stowed away in nigger heaven. There he let out a
long sigh and hunched to see the stage below.

The younger children did the dishes, got out their
school work and pinched and tormented one another.
But sleep was not so deep or sound in that house that
night, Catherine was a long time wakeful. Late at night
Mary Trexler sat for hours ripping bastings and felling
seams, found stockings to darn and darned them and after
that, just sat, trying to read her Bible.

TWO BROTHERS AND OLD MULE

Jacob's day was not Joshua's day. Jacob must wait for
another day. Before his brother was yet cold Joshua
sat down before his Journal with the picture of Holt's
Hotel on the cover and feverishly began to write his vin-
dication. That done he drafted a letter to Jacob's wife,
separated from him years before when their child was but
a baby. His clear firm hand cleansed himself and her and
all their connection of any guilt toward such a brother.

He wasted away, became weaker and weaker. There was
nothing on him but skin and bones, the latter part of
his time he lived on wine, water and sugar alone, in the
former part of his disease he lived on thin gruel, milk
and chocolate but that became too thick for him to swallow so miserable was his condition, his tongue all hollow,
there was little more left of it than the upper skin. On
the beginning of March everybody believed that the move
that had to be made with him would be to the grave but

everybody was mistaken, on the 3rd of April we moved him by loading him on a sled and brought him away without much pain.

At the word pain, Joshua's hand cramped and he stopped and for a second saw his brother's eyes gaze at him bitter and long as they took him from his exile in the little spring house and placed him on the sled. If he had talked, there wouldn't be this burden to answer and to justify. Lord knows he did his best.

Talking was painful and difficult for him during the whole of his illness but towards the end it was still more so, he could hardly be understood and it caused him severe pain. He frequently lamented during the last month that he could not speak better, what he wished to say if he had been able to do so, Heaven only knows. He never expressed any regret or repentance at his former evil course, he never spoke of his wife or child while he was able to speak, yet what came to pass within his heart I will not undertake to say. Let no man judge. He is in the hands of the omnipotent. He died at the age of 48 years, 7 months and 5 days. Never regret that you separated, he was an unreformed and unrepentant drunkard to the last pouring the liquor down his throat as long as he could swallow. I hereby send a lock of hair cut off a good while before his death.

He folded the black and silky hair into a neat package and marked it carefully *Jacob's Hair,* sealed it and turned toward the accounts, the pennies spent for wine and grave clothes; he could not rest until it was down in black and white. But he could only hint in writing at the sort of burden it was to have had a brother like this Jacob. A stallion, wild and untamed, could be no worse, better, for he would bear a rein and have a stable.

Not a maid in his father's house had been safe from Jacob. Little trundle beds that by day were pushed out of sight under the big patriarchal bed of Jacob's father and mother, held the maids at night from Jacob's prowling. Many a night the maids lay in their little beds, in the majestic presence of the great dark curtained bed of the master and mistress, moonlight falling on their faces until they gripped each other's fingers, leaning out of bed to whisper to each other, hearing creakings on the stairs, then a hinge groan, a log in the fireplace fall. Is that Jacob? Would Jacob dare? And they lived with Jacob on the brain, night and day, and then at last, first one and then the other, would fall to Jacob. Night was not the only time for Jacob.

Jacob was open as the day in all his looseness. His mother forgave him all but not the eggs. That he should fall upon six dozen eggs, laid carefully out upon the storeroom floor, and lie there, mocking, making a desecration of all their careful work and accounts strictly adhered to, their whole lives narrowed down to keeping track of things, the fields, the crops, the apples and the good things to eat, dishonored her, his mother. They turned him out and he went out to live alone down in the spring house but in the evenings the sound of his flute wailing away kept the maids twitching and was unholy as the naked flesh strutting through the godly home. All that he did was open and brazen. Bastards he had, no one knows how many. He knocked them up without regard to season while Joshua raised a proper family and Aaron played the good old bachelor uncle, sly Aaron, who had his fun and sowed his seed and no one in his day the wiser.

Jacob left a few old clothes, some chests and tools put up at sale by Joshua and Aaron Trexler, Executors, a few debts for laying out, for medicine and wine, for ice to keep the corpse sound for burial, all covered by his father's niggardly bequest to him. What was left the wife in Illinois got and treasured more than the hank of hair.

Jacob died without weak repentance and that he had scorned all that men thought good tormented Joshua even after the reckonings. The handsome mocking face of Jacob, dead, came between him and his little sons and he took it as a warning and tried to teach them beneath each outer act, the deeper moral. Exhorting, warning, talking, teaching, scrivener in his community, justice of the peace, surveyor of the roads in all his county, he pushed himself to be an example to his boys. He never missed a chance and from the legislature at Harrisburg lectured them. "We are still busy in the legislature for the good of the people," he wrote and boasted that a bill opposed by him in the house had been turned down in the senate thereby vindicating his position.

I wish you to learn from this, always to consider well before you make up your mind on a subject of any importance and after you have maturely made up your mind, be firm as a rock. I wish you to form a straightforward and upright character, to love God and his laws, to love the Bible and its truths, and to fear no man. The greatest evil in this world is if a man acts from the fear of man or with the desire to court favor of men without due regard to right and justice. Do what is right and fear no man.

And then his anxiety for his boys was greater than his pride and on the following day he got out pen and ink again and bent his thin eager face above the paper confessing.

In my last I bragged that the Senate had not passed the two bills I mentioned but they went to work and reconsidered their action and passed. So much for the stability and firmness of men! Do not place too much confidence in others, and watch and observe the doings and actions of mankind closely, by close observation a man eventually becomes so practised that he can almost read the designs

of others on their faces and by their gestures and movements.

That done he wiped his pen with greatest care and
paced up and down and planned out big futures for his
children, but he must do more than warn and guide them.
The property built up by four generations was weakened
with parceling and much use. Machinery had come in and
he saw clearly a new day to cheat him of the profits of his
inn on the post road with the new railroad cutting him
clean off from traffic as if he'd been in the wilderness.
He tried to foresee needs but he put his foot into new
ventures too soon and died too soon. The foundry was
mortgaged to the hilt, the farm was mortgaged to pay for
the inn, the inn was in arrears for taxes. Pressed on all
sides, he made another trip to Wisconsin for Miller &
Duerst to look over land for more immigrants from Ger-
many. It was a hard winter, he rode at all hours, came
home exhausted to see his new, last son. He had to lie on
his sick bed, down with a heavy cold turned to pneumonia,
and know he'd not get up again and that his children and
his wife were as stripped of all they needed as if he'd been
improvident and drunk. Jacob's pale face in its coffin
taunted and jibed at him and all the grand words he had
said to his sons were so much folly. The last few years
had twirled and twisted him and all he'd built as if he'd
been of straw, and he must go as shiftless as if he had spent
his life in vain. Great tears rolled down his cheeks and he
tried to speak but even his breath had left him and he was
as bereft as Jacob and Jacob haunted him and stuck by
him and in his dying hours he had to feel that Jacob's
corpse was the nearest thing to him. He tried to call to
Mary, his dear wife, and she could only look at him,
wringing her hands and piling on the blankets and rubbing at his feet, but there was no way to warn her, the

earth was sliding fast and he and Jacob were pitching down to where they came from.

He died during the hard times of fifty-nine, along with John Brown's body, but he was not really dead for a long time.

DEATH OF JOSHUA TREXLER

About the time the last number of the *Democrat* was going to press, we were painfully surprised to hear of the death of Joshua Trexler, Esq., a prominent citizen of Upper Saucon. We were surprised because but a few days previous he was in our office, apparently in as good health as anyone around us. His disease was pneumonia which in three days carried him into the spirit land. Verily in the "midst of life are we in death." Mr. Trexler was a man who united those traits of stern integrity and unbending honesty which constitute a high moral character in an eminent degree. He was a descendant of one of the early settlers and the father appreciating the value of an education gave the son advantages, which for those days were regarded as superior. Hence Joshua Trexler became a useful man in his neighborhood. He was a good surveyor and scrivener, for several years Justice of the Peace and during the session of 1856, represented this county in the State Legislature. In all the various public trusts which he was called upon to discharge, he acquitted himself with honor; while in his private relations he was universally regarded as God's noblest handiwork, an honest man.

His widow carefully cut the account out of the paper and kept it in an old pocketbook for an inheritance for her children. She thanked her stars she knew how to sew and was not helpless. When Joshua Trexler had taken her from the sewing room in Bethlehem and raised her up, she had thought never to be plunged down again. Now that it was to do all over, that steady climb, at least she had her own strong hands to help her. Even when rich Uncle Blank turned her down and offered to adopt a child while refusing to buy a sewing machine to help her earn her living, she knew she'd find a way without him.

"I'll leave you to your honor and your glory," she said that last day, standing in the parlor at Bethlehem with the children ranged up beside her, little David not yet two months in her arms, the last to wear the baby bonnet made from the heavy green satin of her wedding gown and lined at the rim with soft lace made in the days when she had begged her guardian to go to school and he had stormed, "What, a girl to learn to read and write, there's no sense to it!"

"We'll not trouble you," she said, braving Injun Blank's fits of rage, sure to follow, while poor Aunty hovered in the next room wringing her hands and waiting for her lord and master to begin his rollings on the floor that must end with the household turned topsy turvy, the maids routed out to heat a great tub of water for Uncle to be immersed in, mustard brought and shaken in with shaking hands and then the great heavy carcass of a man, groaning and foaming, lowered into the water to lose his dignity and his rage like any baby so that Aunty had no standing with her maids or with herself. She was wife to a great foaming baby with hairless body and clean shaved heavy pouting jowls that quivered when the fish came in too brown or the cheese cake crumbled to the knife.

Poor Aunty, then, stood in the doorway, waiting for the outburst, her fingers rolled into a wad of her dress. The maids, frightened half out of their wits, oozed in from the kitchen and banked around as Uncle rose to exert his maleness in a baby's tantrum. As he rose, one hand shaking, his finger forming to point, Mary Trexler spoke up coolly. She had nothing more to lose and nothing to gain. "Don't bother to throw a fit for me, it's not worth your trouble," and turned away, wheeling neatly on a dime and the children with her, not a lost motion and they were gone. The front door slammed, the stiff curtains in the parlor blew out with the gust and then were rigid as before. Uncle opened his mouth to yell, fell heavily on the floor and knocked his head against the old chest, bellowing with real pain and rolling, holding to his belly with locked arms. "Ungrateful, common, brats, out of my house! Out. Out. Out of my house," and screamed, while the maids rushed around and pulled out the big zinc tub and the water was poured in, splashing in torrents of steam.

Poor Aunty, her pride gone, appealed with streaming eyes to the maids who two by two hoisted the great rhinoceros in his underwear, pushing him into the too hot water. Another roar and grinning to each other, they rushed for cold and splashed him with too cold and stood back, while he roared again and then sank down sobbing into the huge tub, his hide turned scarlet with the water and his rage, while Aunty hovered over him murmuring, "There, there," sobbing for shame that this must be her only child, her great false baby.

The widow marched firmly down the street with her children two by two behind her. They caused a little stir in town and word went around that old Blank had turned them out without a nickel. "He'd take a child to raise and not help me to help myself," she said and her anger fed her. They were alike, relative or stranger, grasping and greedy as the law allowed. They had stripped her of all her means to earn a living, taken away the inn, the forge, the very furniture for debts she had never heard of and turned her out. She went out, leaving her husband's body in the graveyard of the Blue Church. Many rigs turned out that day and wound up around the hills and over the toll road but coming back, the wind was cold, snow in flurries blinded horses' eyes and some beasts stumbled.

Mary Trexler had nothing but her name and her hus-

band's honesty and the luck that war brought her. The
war brought work and she called that luck and knuckled
to it. Aunty Blank left alone with Uncle moped for Joseph
and hinted that a boy around the place would come handy.
No use trying to adopt one but they might take one of
Mary's for a time and make him useful.

Big Injun, stubborn as a mule and like a mule no good
for breeding, grunted and let her waste her breath. She
had it over him in one way. She could look him down
when children were being talked of and could make him
feel not half a man. Even his fits of rage she took advantage of, in her quiet woman's way, hanging her head
for mortification afterwards, refusing to give orders to the
maids, shrinking back and trembling behind her knitting
held up as a screen to her face. She could shame the old
mule and bring him to time by her shame and for days
afterwards he paid in little ways for his self indulgence.
She'd run and fetch for him and refuse to call the maids.
"I can't, I'm that ashamed," she'd say, hanging her head,
making him writhe at the remembrance of his fit and the
heavy underwear clammy gray against his blubber.

No way out but to yield something to her. She knew it
too and held to her course, hinting and standing around
and feeding him his favorite dishes, making him feel in
turn a fool and her lord and master. Finally he roared,
"Be still about it! Send for him if you can make him earn
his keep. But I've no money for charity brats."

"I don't know as she'll let him," said Aunty, bold for
once.

"She? She'll let him. She'll be glad for one mouth less to
feed but see he keeps out of my sight. He's not *my* nephew.
If I brought home all my relatives to roost, we'd be in the
poorhouse." He could say that, spouting out the words
like a whale, his cheeks quivering and his stomach swell-
ing, and her mother not dead a year, a woman that had

paid her way if any mortal ever did, yes, and more than paid it. How could he say that and remind her? An old woman, neat as a pin and ninety-two when she went, going as obliging as anyone ever could, without fuss or muss.

If only that dreadful thing had not happened to haunt her always. But no one could be rightly blamed, that road was bad enough at any time of year but with the ruts frozen stiff it would jolt any corpse. When they had raised the lid, her mouth had fallen open. It had looked as if she had come back to life and was gasping for fresh air. No one but Mrs. Kemmerer had had the gumption to touch her. They had stood there, stiff with fear. But Mrs. Kemmerer had fixed her mouth and then they had all cried in a natural way and after she was in the ground, they went back over the roads and got busy.

No one ever saw such food. It was a consolation to know that no one had ever put on such a good spread. Everyone stuffed and the Trexler children were sick afterwards. Little Joe had three cups of coffee at his grandmother's funeral and Aaron went around tattling. Some of the old ladies pretended to be shocked at such a boy but Aunty had told him not to mind. Better three cups of coffee out in public than to stuff down cellar the night before the way Aaron had and have no proper appetite when the time came. "Never you mind," said Aunty.

And he could say that and remind her and never a chick or child of her own. "Never you mind," and she sobbed out loud, suddenly and uncontrollably in one of her terrible gusts of crying. Alone on the attic stairs she gave way, with the bunches of herbs hanging dead and sweet on the attic beams and the rag carpet stiff and tidy under her. "Never you mind," she kept saying over and over, and she didn't know why, it wasn't only to Joe she had said it, it was to herself she must always say it. "Never you mind."

Injun Blank thrashed out of the house and came back

in time for his big meal. He was licked. He stiffened his great neck in his low open collar, settling his jaws down with authority but Aunty never so much as looked at him. She had put on her black dress, and with downcast eyes and small button red nose, sat meekly opposite him, wilting down in her chair when Lizzie brought in the food and even then she took advantage of him and did not deign to more than peck at their favorite dish of tripe.

Uncle was licked and stayed subdued waiting for his chance at another fit to even up with Aunty. Joe came, carrying all his clothes in one small bundle and Uncle held out one thick finger for the boy to shake and grunted like the Big Injun the children called him. In letters to his brother Aaron he made fun of Uncle, revenged himself as best he could for eating Uncle's food.

When Joe broke Fenstermacher's window, Big Injun Blank nearly brought the house down. The women ran out of the house, all but Aunty and she rushed up the stairs and sat on the attic steps, her hands rolled tight in a fold of her dress. She sat crouched down, aching all over, waiting for the roar that meant Uncle's fit was on him. For a wonder, it didn't come. Uncle was practical for once. He stuck by it until Joe had his few traps bundled together, smuggling the *Life of Daniel Boone* in his nightshirt. The bundle secured, he went downstairs and sat in the parlor waiting for Lizzie's beau to come for him and take him to the depot.

Aunty heard the front door slam. It went through and through her like a knife. She knew he was gone. She ran her finger over the attic floor, it was neat as wax, there was not a grain of dust. There was nothing to clean, she hung her head and waited for the tears but none came. Down below she heard Blank roar and holler but the boy was gone. Her mother's grave was too far away, there was no place to go. She sat on the attic steps and let the maids go screeching next door to Aunty Bachman's looking for her. Evening came and she stole down to supper, her face grayish, but her hair neat as a pin and she wore her brooch under her chin. At table Blank was very chipper and when Lizzie served his supper, pinched her plump arm out of playfulness.

THE EARLY WORM

WILMINGTON, thirty miles from the sea, was a good river port town and as good as any to start with. With country bristling on all sides and towns calling their names and roads branching off to other bigger cities, Joe thought of it only as a beginning. He'd be a fool to stick in one place and molder there. With Wilmington, especially, he had reservations on account of old James Ajax, brother to Confectioner Ajax whose mealy religious mouth palavering about all beginnings being hard and look at me, your boy can do the same with hard work and a will and it's something to have a good religious atmosphere, we don't put up with ungodliness, had fooled Mem. As if he didn't know about the words chalked up in that place and the men talking under their breaths. Mem swallowed it because she was a woman and good and didn't know and even a boy can realize that women are to be protected and guarded from all the wickedness they couldn't understand. If it was easier for her to let him go where someone knew of him, why he would go, and there'd be time enough to tell her his conclusions when he left the new town for a newer.

With his clear hand he got a job in a tobacco warehouse owned by a Northerner, friend of James Ajax, and stood all day before a slanting desk making out invoices and adding figures. On Sundays, Mr. Ajax invited him for dinner and talked largely about Joe's future and his own importance. He pointed out that the Northerners must regard themselves as missionaries in a benighted country where they had to educate the Southern white to his high responsibilities and to the God given charge of lifting the poor downtrodden nigger. Joe nodded in agreement, anxious to be up and coming, and with everyone so cranky about the Yankees, he had to feel he had a purpose, and wasn't just a foreigner. But even as he nodded to all Ajax said, he really was admiring the cut and quality of the man's clothes and wondering how long it would be before he wore the same. Sometimes Ajax drifted to the duties of a gentleman, and the word was often in his mouth. Gentleman. Quality was another favorite word and gentlemen must smoke only the best cigars and Mr. Ajax drank only the best wines and brandy, aged at least six years in the wood. Joe was a good listener and Mr. Ajax took it gratefully. His audience in that Southern town was too small to please him and he rewarded Joe with, "A bright boy. He'll get ahead."

After dinner, Mrs. Ajax and their little girl of twelve in dainty ruffled clothes and with large staring blue eyes sat before the grand piano and pounded out duets together, their arms moving mechanically as if on cords, their cheeks growing pinker as the part became more difficult, and Joe watching them wished Mr. Ajax would keep his mouth shut and not prattle on about how good the piano was, what a solid rosewood case and works to last forever. The music was the first outside of hymns he had ever heard and in his room that night he wrote a long letter to his sister Catherine and asked her if she did not think music was the highest art.

Catherine wrote back that music was the highest art and had the power to stir in human breasts the noblest thoughts and aspirations. What it meant to her to have a brother who could discuss the finer things of life, no one would ever know. It seemed to lift the two of them out of the dull everyday into some brighter world and even David sulking and playing marbles with those vulgar boys could not spoil it. What if Aaron was foolish and went around in a daze without a proper sense of responsibility, the day would come when she and Joe would lift the family up and Mem would not have to take in clothes to sew any more and Anne could quit pedaling that machine and take music lessons. Sometimes Joe read his sister's letters to Mrs. Ajax, taking pride that she knew Latin and could write so well. The kind woman drew him out with her nods and questions and in her loneliness in that Southern town had long talks with him and dared to voice her doubts about the life down there where everyone was shiftless and so far as she could see the poor blacks worse off than ever. He'd hunt for little jobs to do to repay her, mend the broken wire on the bird cage, put a patch on the rabbit hutch, and when Ajax roared and laughed, "Take it easy, my boy, let the niggers do that, that's what they are good for," he felt hot and sore and hated Ajax for trying to put him in the wrong.

As soon as he had money saved, he sent some home to dazzle them and bought new clothes and had a picture taken of himself in the new suit. "Well, so we're going to have a dandy in the family," Aaron said, squinting and holding the picture at arm's length. "Oh why must you always sneer and belittle like that?" Catherine said, snatching the picture from him and giving him a cold look. "I sneer? Why you exaggerate. You do me wrong, I tell you, you'll all regret it," and he'd shake his head in mock despair and snicker and go off, burning up with envy at that Joe with his good looks and his luck. He was the eldest and it was meant for him to lead the family and here was Joe walking off with the prize and getting all the praise.

He'd said it was a wild goose chase going South and he'd not eat his words yet, all's well that ends well, and the end's not yet in sight.

The family praise spurred Joe on and he began to be uneasy in that town, thought it was slow and heard stories of greater activity further South. Friends of Mr. Ajax swaggered around and told stories of what they'd seen and what they'd do until his little bit of money every week seemed foolish and he a dunce to be satisfied with it. With everybody talking easy money, money that came hard and slow made him feel behind the times. Along toward Christmas he tried his luck and won fifteen dollars in a lottery and sent the whole amount home as a present. "Business is picking up," he wrote and longed for the time when he could fit them out with musical instruments, get Catherine and Anne at the piano, Hortense at the violin and David at the flute. Mary Trexler looked at the picture of her son and his new clothes with a magnifying glass and shook her head and told the girls to write him not to be extravagant. Her letter almost made him want to cry. Why he'd show her what money meant and make it up to her for the hard years when it used to hurt to see food on the table because you knew it wouldn't go around. With some of the money he had been laying by to pay his way to Georgia, he bought a pair of earrings for Catherine of heavy gold chased with fine inlays of blue enamel.

"Don't let Mem call me extravagant," he wrote, "there's more where this comes from," at that moment not knowing where, but just as sure of it as he was of breathing. That so many Southerners were poor he laid to natural laziness and lack of gumption. The words were in the mouth of Ajax all the time and he and his friends said no one could blame the Northerners for taking advantage of natural opportunities just going to waste around them. It sounded true enough. How this crowd made money, Joe couldn't say, but Ajax had it and everyone said this was an age of opportunity with new inventions doubling every minute and wonders happening that no one could have foreseen fifty years ago.

The earrings went to Lawrence Street and lay in their white case. Mary Trexler shook her head at the sight, touching the white velvet cushion with her finger much punctured with the needle. "What ails the boy? He'll run his head into a wall, spending like water." But when she sat up late that night scolding him in a long letter written in her funny, upcountry German, he was ready for her, and answered with high promises of plenty in the future.

With young Gaskill from the warehouse he took in the races and made some easy money and one night toward spring rolling along in young Gaskill's buggy they talked of wealth and how Ajax made his money. It made Joe's blood run cold to hear young Gaskill crack the whip and get the horses in a sweat when they talked of Ajax.

"Bloody Yankee, scuse me Joey, but he's the kind, well ask my father, he knows. He can tell you. First he skinned the North and now he's here to skin us. Why he was a big pork and flour man in '64, you can ask my father any day, he sold moldy rot to the army, your own army, yes sir, and doctored up crow bait, he sure did, bought sick horses and shot them full of dope so they could walk and let them die on the Government. That's Ajax, ask my father. You ought to keep clear of him, he's no good. Oh we've got that stripe down here, they made hay while there was sun and sat at home getting their 30 per cent. But Ajax, why I'm surprised, you didn't know about him."

"I like him less the more I see him, and his brother, why he pulled the wool over my mother's eyes with his talk and his pious ways. This Ajax here, I only see the way he treats his family, he spends money pretty free but I like him less the more I see of him, I can't say why but he's always talking and pretending he's such a gentleman, well if it's clothes does it, he's a gentleman all right, he gets the best there is."

"Why that fellow is no more gentleman than—say, he stinks, I tell you the stink reached us down here before he did, that's a fact. My uncle's in the North, he's crazy, wouldn't stick by the cause and said the states had no right to secede, but he gets a hankering for home and writes my father and he said that this Ajax was a shark and to beware."

The road ran through a thicket of young trees and honeysuckle and Joe squirmed at the thought of Mr. Ajax.

"If you're right, Tom."

"Right? I know I'm right. Ask my father."

The buggy spun around a corner humming in the dust and Joe knew that now he would go away and he was glad for the excuse of Mr. Ajax and cut things short and left, following the stream of Northern money South.

In Atlanta he found his way around, stopped at the Trimble House, hung around the lobby, watched big well dressed men go by in pairs, talking each other down, passed a few cigars, got in on a few confidential conversations.

"Listen to me," and one night late, leaning against a polished bar, Joe listened. A long sleek man speaking, his quick eyes watching doors, his left leg, shorter than his right, resting on the rail. "Listen to me. You're from the North. So am I. Take my advice. I won't charge you a cent. Your one chance down here is to cotton to the right crowd. The Rads have got business in their pockets and they know what is what. A lot of old fools down here don't know the war is over and they were licked. But I ask you, who won the war? Did the Union or didn't it?"

Joe taken back by the sudden thrust of the man's thin hot face near his own, leaned backward and said, lamely, "Why they won, of course," and to himself, I hope he isn't crazy.

"That's the whole thing in a nutshell. The Union won. The law's behind the North and the majesty of the law is mighty. Now I happen to know," he leaned nearer, sinking his voice to a whisper, "I happen to be possessed of certain information and I know for a certainty that the railroad here is looking, is looking I say," and he pointed hard with his finger at Joe's middle, "for young bright adaptable Northern men. They brag down here about this road being owned by the state, outright, like you own your hat, but pshaw, that's silly, a road's owned by the money back of it and let me tell you, sir, there's Northern money in that road, why the damned car wheels are sunk up to the hubs in it."

"Mighty interesting," said Joe, nodding his head as he had seen it done only that afternoon by two men reputed to be important citizens. "Mighty interesting." He hoped no one would think he was green. His clothes fitted well and made him feel easy and happy. If he only had a good watch and chain, he would not be afraid to tackle anything.

"I could tell you things, young man, that *would* be interesting. But watch out for narrow minded little Southern fleas. Oh I don't mean the big important fellows that were clean wiped out, they're done for, but the little buggers, the fellows who are opposing our cause, who are refusing to give the black man his *rights,* for which we fought and died. And by the way," his voice dropped still lower, "I don't know why I'm giving this away, I ought to be paid for advice this good, but buy land. You'll never get it cheaper. Five dollars an acre sir. That's my advice." He snapped his fingers, wiped his mustaches carefully, and fingering his fobs that swung conspicuously on his vest, limped from the room. Joe looked around uneasily. He hoped he hadn't been made a target for talk. But no one was paying any attention. He moved up to the bar and by twelve o'clock that night had scraped up three acquaintances and one lifelong friend, by one he was back in his hotel room, excited and happy, writing home to Catherine with a short stubby pencil moistened with his tongue:

"Tell Mem this is the only place in the world. I've heard of a position and expect to make great strides."

Then he hung up his coat and vest with care, folded the trousers over the back of a chair. In bed he was too wide awake for sleep. The room seemed luxurious to him and the fascination of the rich, of lights and the hair of women in the bright dining room, their satins and their jewels and their intimate eyes made him feel a million miles from home. He felt guilty in the soft wide sheets and eased his conscience with the thought of presents for them all. Through the open window strains of music from the rooms below came softly and he could hear the flat clack of horses' feet as a carriage halted at the door. Fawcett. The Western & Atlanta Railroad. He mustn't lose that address in his vest pocket. Fawcett. He couldn't get the name out of his head and went to sleep at last to dream uneasily that Uncle Blank had given him a large copper penny that kept bouncing away when he touched it as if it were live rubber. He sweated in his sleep chasing and hunting and woke, all in a sweat, muttering "Aunty," trying to remember something, he didn't know what.

Blake Fawcett, slim, curling red hair, fine hands, shook hands with him and led him to his own capacious office with the solemn heavy desk. Joe had never met a more sympathetic man than this Fawcett and before he knew it Fawcett had drawn out all his history, his father's death, the number of his brothers and his sisters and he almost told about his apprenticeship at the confectioner's but that might have cooked his goose. Fawcett smiled and nodded and said, "Well a little Yankee gumption won't hurt us," and after a little more palaver, the place was his. He had slipped into it so easily, he felt a whole inch taller and shook hands with Roger Wallace, the other clerk, as if he'd known him all his life. What people, none of your stiff Northern manners and trying to impress. He was in clover.

He spent two days fiddling around the office listening to Roger Wallace and laying out pens and ink and hearing what a crowd it was he'd fallen into. He wrote home that he was clerk in the office of the right hand man to Governor Bullock and all the biggest politicians of the day came and went not three feet from his desk.

Ton Ferris came every few days, his four hundred pounds shuddering through the hall, his tiny eyes, sharp and fixed in fat, gimleting the place. "Who's that?" Joe asked and made it a point to remember names and faces. He wished he could get on to their way of doing business as easily as he could keep tab of visitors. It looked to him slipshod to write orders on slips of paper and be content to lose them. But he would rather get along as best he could and try to learn their ways than have them call him a damned Yankee. There was a hot enough crowd in town ready to remind him of that fact as if it were a crime. Sometimes when he had had a taste of what the rebels felt, he was almost grateful to Fawcett and his crowd for putting up with him. Why they made him feel at home and were so jovial and so open handed with their free and easy come, easy go ways, and their talk of good eating and good wine, racing and women. A fellow like Ton Ferris was coarse but he wasn't Southern, he was an Ohio man and hard and funny and a kind of Falstaff, Fawcett said.

That was the best of working for a man like Fawcett who
wasn't a sniveler like Ajax in Philadelphia but a hearty
cultured man who read and had seen Fanny Kemble and
could describe her "proud animal ways," he called it,
without an atom of disrespect, just as if she might have
been a statue or a horse. He'd seen Macready and Forrest
too and Macready had a kind of finish but Forrest had
fire. "If you could see that man act, why he's a live coal,
and then one moment so calm and the next a regular hur-
ricane. That's genius."

"His pronunciation ain't so fine as Macready's," said
Ton Ferris, rolling his huge cigar in his round rubbery
mouth. "It ain't so refined nor correct."

"Since when was acting pronunciation? Why man, acting's soul, and Macready was a lisping upstart and deserved
a licking. What do you take to the theater, a book of etiquette or a human heart?"

"I take four hundred pounds of solid meat," said Ferris,
grinning, "and I'd like to see the man that can do better."

"And have a special seat set up for you. They ought to
charge you double, Ton, I should if I were in the box
office."

"You'd skin me of my hide if you could use it," said
Ferris, winking boldly, and Fawcett flushed and said,
"That's an ungrateful speech, Ferris, to say to a man who's
given you a lift every step of the way."

"I don't mince words, I'm an ordinary man Blake, but
I can see the flaw and still admire the diamond. I'm no
saint, I let my left hand know what my right hand's doing.
You fellows are too high and mighty. You forget you
haven't got a bunch of niggers to boss any more. I don't
like this pose of Bullock's either, he's a New York man
and ought to know better, why you'd think the fellow
never got a wink of sleep for worrying about the pore
black devils and their sorrows and how bad they'll feel if

they ain't made free and equal with the vote. Now you and I, Blake, know that Bullock don't give a little finger for the black man, but he wants his vote and he's cute enough to see if he can get business going with Yankee money, he'll keep his power. And Yankee money won't invest unless it sees the South humbled, humbled low, with nigger votes choked down its throat. There's not a handful of men in this country that care what happens to the Negro, if he starves or votes or what he does, and the funny thing is that some of that handful is made up of the old masters. Yes sir, it ain't only the abolitionist but the same old masters right here in Geawgie that cares what becomes of ole Sambo."

"You're a crude man, Ferris, but it's the fault of your fat. You're too fat. You can't see anything but yellow grease. Do you mean to say you don't believe in the vision of our party, its reaching out to the future, shaking off the shackles of states' rights, growing, developing—"

"Listen Blake," said Ton, interrupting and holding up his hand. "Save your speech. I tell you there's no use talking to you boys. You're too full of organ notes for me. I like good food, a shapely woman, a fine cigar. If it's all the same to you, you can keep the music." He stopped and elaborately hiccuped, covering his mouth with a singularly delicate hand.

Fawcett flushed, then smiled diplomatically and in a sad actor's voice said slowly, "Yes, I'll keep the music."

It was like a play. The way he stood, those words, made Ton look like the coarse brute that he was and yet there was something about the man, his sharp eyes and his walk more like a lolling roll as if he were on little wheels that made him always seem a lively fellow. Besides Roger told Joe in an aside that he was an awful roué and kept a yaller girl on the other side of town. Roger thought only a coarse brute like Ton would do a thing like that, the better class of Southerner was sobered by the war and say what you like it wasn't like the old days when some of the best men were reputed to have carried on in "the quarter." Times had changed and Roger was so in love with Blake Fawcett's young widowed sister that he saw even Blake with a halo.

"Don't believe all you hear about him, just mean lies and jealousy. Besides any man who leads is crucified today, yes sir, crucified. No matter what he does, there's a hundred hands against him. Why look at Joe Brown, you'd think he'd be a bitter man, but he's stronger than most. When he was governor, there wasn't a man better liked or more thought of, but now, mention his name in a crowd and you'll get a riot. There's enough hate going around to last a million years."

"It's all new to me. I don't know who to hate and who not to, it's all the same so far as I'm concerned. Why I think it's a great place. Why don't they just settle down and quit squabbling? You'd think they'd had enough war."

"They have, but it's just going on of its own weight. Looks like. Say let's get out of here and take a couple of guns and go out and see if we can't get some ducks. It's nearly three." And they shut up the office without a qualm from Roger. Joe tried to take it easy too but it was all new to him, this shutting up in business hours, and talking for the bigger part of the day about anything but business, and now he took the gun and felt along its smooth barrel and in the bright sunlight of that Friday afternoon could hardly hold himself in for relief and happiness. This was living.

But even when they were nicest to him he had the feeling of a "foreigner" or of being on a ship and of having to part company with the crew when the ship docked. It wasn't a comfortable feeling and he hated it and smoked a lot of the best cigars walking around the streets and feeling excited about the night air and the occasional figure of a woman behind a drawn curtain. In the office the next day he'd be absent minded and Fawcett had a nice fatherly way about him and it was almost uncanny, his intuition, when Joe felt like that. He'd stand there, smiling in a quizzical way, and the day he said, "Well, young man, how'd you like to come to my house to live. Keep you out of mischief and besides I'm looking ahead, it would be convenient in more ways than one. What do you say?" Joe was flabbergasted, and wrote home that it was the greatest honor and the boss had only charged him the most nominal board, and he was truly grateful.

The girls swelled up with pride at such a brother, living with the *best* people, why Mr. Fawcett was being talked of for the United States Senate and Joe had hardly moved to their house before he was made superintendent of the road and Joe assistant to the purchasing agent who was no less a person than Fawcett's son George.

He couldn't help but feel a little important and took the best care of his clothes, read *Harper's Weekly* and the daily papers, especially the *Constitution* because its language was more elegant than the rest. He certainly enjoyed the way they referred to Cato and the classics and he thought that education had just been thrown away on Aaron who was too indifferent to appreciate it. References to Fawcett and the Governor were anything but complimentary but he did what all that Fawcett crowd did, laughed at the slander and laid it all to politics. Things looked pretty black that fall and no one could laugh at the murders going on by the dozen. But even when men were killed or chased from their beds, Fawcett saw the bright side.

"They're playing into our hands, the damned fools. If they think this terrorizing business is going to get them anything but military rule again, they're mistaken. The army'll back us up, Bullock can organize his own house and senate and compel the black vote. The test oath will keep them from getting in, not a damned one will dare take it. Why it's a good thing, actually a good thing. It can't go too far along this line, no sir, I say the further they go the tighter the rope will be around their necks."

Looked at from that angle the descriptions of Bullock in the rebel papers looked like sheer vindictiveness. "Sour grapes," Ton Ferris said, squinting up his eyes and making a wry face. "Just sour grapes." So Joe laughed when he read about the big vulgarian lolling around the senate chamber going it with a high hand in the most shameless lobbying, spending somebody's money like water and making a holy show of himself, gorging between the acts in the lunch room. He'd seen Bullock a couple of times and he didn't look so vicious, not a Nero. Fact is, he had the looks of a big portly gorgeous sort of person, free with cigars and drinks, they said, a little vain of a fine red beard and wearing flowing black tie ends over a spotless expanse of shirt. He wasn't *tight,* didn't have mean Yankee ways they all thought so low, spent his money like water, treated his friends, was a man with some daring, but nothing risked, nothing gained. Why look at Napoleon.

"These fellows surely like to exaggerate," Joe said. "Just listen to this":

The celebrated Café Française was the scene Wednesday night of a Bacchanalian feast, given by Governor Bullock in honor of his triumph over the people of Georgia, to the aiders and abettors of the scheme. Wine flowed like water, and rich viands were greedily devoured in the midst of which the company gloated in fiendish triumph over the vengeance they had wreaked upon an unhappy and defenseless people. What mattered the expense? The people of Georgia would be made to foot this and many other bills of like nature. With his hands to the elbow in the State Treasury Mr. Carpet Bagger Bullock can well afford to be sumptuous and to dine and wine, and feast and flatter the men who have done his bidding on the floor of Congress. Whether or not he has inaugurated a gift enterprise, in which these servile and traitorous congressmen are to participate, we cannot say.

Roger wouldn't vouch more of an answer than to cluck his tongue and shake his head, staring out the window, getting his mouth black with ink from the pen, and now and then he'd yawn and wish to Gawd that the damned war was over and let a man have peace. The way he looked at it, there might as well be an actual war with guns popping. He'd like to join a few good lodges and then once or twice a week leave the little wife for a smoker and men's talk and going home along the dark streets it would be fine to think of her snuggled down in bed, sweet and warm, waiting for him. "Take it easy, Joey," he said and sometimes when he'd look at Joe he'd have a worried look. It puzzled Joe to see a good fellow like Roger so indifferent and so unlikely to get ahead. When Joe was telling him about the tips Fawcett had given him to buy some property up for sale for taxes as cheap as you'd ever get land that good, he just stood there, his eyes so sleepy it reminded Joe of Aaron. "What's the matter Roger, you ought to be more interested for your own good."

But Roger looked up, laid his pen down, scratched his ear and holding his inked lip between his thumb and finger said, "Well I haven't the daring, at least they call it daring, I can't find my way around in all this maze, and so I just go along in my little way, not taking any risks and I suppose not getting anywhere." He looked doleful for a minute, then brightened and suggested they close up and take a ride, the two of them needed a little shaking up, and they hired a buggy and rode out to a country place and had some wine and lobster. It was almost midnight when they came out together leaning toward one another like weak reeds and Roger moaning that she'd never forgive him, his whitest little angel, if she knew.

Joe felt like his Uncle Jacob and wondered what his mother'd think and he told himself he must keep a tight rein on those impulses and not be ridden by them. He had an ugly feeling thinking of Uncle Jacob, half pride, half shame, mixed up with the talk of the men around the barns about how Jake was hung like a stud horse and their admiration and their shame and dirty looks and yet, even now, he couldn't help but think Jacob must have been quite a fellow.

It wasn't hard to like the South with everyone so nice to him. Fawcett couldn't have been nicer to his own son and he'd insisted on advancing Joe money to make an investment that no young man could afford to miss. Everyone in the Fawcett family from Grandma to the house boy was ready to fall on his neck with kindness. He laid it all to the Southern hospitality he'd heard so much about and the North seemed cold and stiff necked in comparison. When he and Roger Wallace made calls among the circle of Fawcett's friends he could feel his ears turn red at Roger's nudging and whispering, "Did you see the eyes she made at you? That's Nancy Collender." He bought a book of etiquette and read it through. There was a lot of nonsense in it but it had some good points and he liked the passage about good clothes because he was spending quite a little on his suits and was glad to know clothes had real importance. He read it over several times:

A proud well dressed man generally does everything well. It takes a man of wit and pride to wear a well fitting suit of clothes. Wellington said his dandy officers were his best officers. There was a dash of dandyism about all the great heroes of

Greece and Rome. There were swells in those days as well as now. Alcibiades, was the nobbiest boy in Greece. Aristotle was the swellest fellow on the Fifth Avenue of Athens. Pride makes politeness, makes a man treat his wife well, dress her in rich pongee and camel's hair and makes him hate paper collars and deception generally.

That was one thing about the Fawcett crowd, they all dressed well, were careful of details and picked the best cloth for their suits. It was something to be sure about in a place where he often felt at sea. He'd had ladies carry on to him about poor Miss Angela or Miss Pruella who had never had to lift a finger all their lives and now their pretty nails were broken with the hard degrading work they had to do. He'd stand there, commiserating, feeling kind of sick thinking of his mother and her hard work and when a letter from her came in her plain upcountry German that was so hard to read and so like a photograph of herself, it was almost a reproach to him. He couldn't rest until he had bought her something nice to take the sting out of the way he felt. She was as good and better than any lady you could name and when he sent her a camel's hair shawl on her birthday, he picked out one fit for a queen. No one could blame him if in his talks with Grandma Fawcett he emphasized his father as an important legislator and gradually wiped out of his mind the simple ways he'd had, and the early days that his mother used to tell of, how he'd been a "finder" and could locate water with a hazel twig and all the jobs he liked to do even when he could well afford the hire, the wood-cutting and the long walks and the talks with every farmer up and down the valley. He'd write their letters for them and their wills, say prayers and swap tools and harness, why no one could blame Joe for not telling that kind of thing when in the South everything was different and they could never understand, with darkies waiting on them hand and foot all their lives.

Roger Wallace's mother was one who never could get out of her system that her father had owned a thousand slaves and the night that Joe went home with Roger to dinner the old lady with her sharp cold stare made him feel that he was personally responsible for all her losses and her grief. She had a cast in her right eye that gave her the look of an old mare and her strong curved nose with the mouth drawn back on strong old yellow teeth twitched slightly as she talked about the vulgar Fawcetts and all that tribe. She couldn't understand what Joe's mother could be about to let her boy so far away from home among such rascals but then Yankee women were a different breed.

Roger said scarcely a word and acted glum and when the two were alone he told Joe that his mother was doing all she could to break off his engagement with Fawcett's sister Estelle. "I'm so tired of her high and mighty notions, even if she is my mother. She as good as killed my father, was so ashamed she'd married beneath her that she made him get into the war and he was the kind, you know, mild and gentle, didn't want to fight. I can remember him as well as if he had just walked through that door and the look he had the day he went away. He was shot down before he'd had a chance to fire, just like that," he raised his hand and snapped his fingers. "Now she wants me to go on redeeming the family name with some poky marriage."

"I don't know much about the war," Joe said, "but she surely makes me feel guilty."

"Course it's hard on her, she doesn't know what it's all about. I don't either. But I've thought a good deal about it and when people talk about the older people having the hardest part to bear, it seems to me they're wrong. We are the ones, only we don't know it yet. I feel it in my bones." He heard the door creak and in a raised cheerful tone of voice pointed to a portrait on the wall. "That's my grandfather," and out of an uneasy corner of his eye, Joe saw Roger's mother look pleased and lay her hand upon her son's arm.

Joe was glad when the ordeal was over and Roger told him he had come through with flying colors. "Why I even think she likes you," he said the next day in the office and if it hadn't been for the press of work, he would have spent the whole day talking it over and wondering if he should buy or rent when he married. With Bullock given power to convene the legislature the office buzzed and no one knew whether any railroad business was transacted or not. Ton Ferris was there early and late, beginning the day in muffled conversations behind closed doors but by noon the air was stifling with smoke, the door to the outer rooms opened and Ferris's voice, fat and smoothly oiled, like himself, trickled out in tantalizing whiffs. "Can't fail," he said. "It's foolproof. Who thought up the blamed thing? Why it's a stroke of genius. Not a man jack of the Democrats is going to be able to take the test oath. Doesn't Barrow himself give it as his opinion that it wipes the slate clean by its very nature? Barrow's in a position to know, he's attorney general, above politics, for he's a man of law, even if a Republican. When you come to think of it, it's a mighty funny thing, the law. Now I heard that on this very point of the test oath Joe Brown was quibbling. He's a man of law too and he differs from Barrow but then he's one of your on the fence men, got sense though, doesn't like the medicine any more than Toombs but knows he has to take it. Great spirit. By the way Fawcett, have you anything in that line? A little Bourbon?"

"Here you are Ton," said Fawcett and a drawer squeaked.

"No? Well, I'll drink alone, here's to *Senator* Fawcett."

Cawkins, the little auditor, sitting modestly near the door clapped ostentatiously. He had not been offered a drink by that big tub of a Yankee and he was angry but there was no use showing it. He'd get even some other way. If they thought they could blind him to their doings, and not let him in, they were fooled. As if he didn't know that money was pouring out for supplies that never showed up. Supplies. That was pretty good. Reckon he knew as well as the next where cash came from to buy Thornton's paper. Where did they think they were getting money for Bullock's hundred dollar a day stay in Washington when he pushed the test oath through? It didn't grow on cotton patches, why demn it nothing grew there. He edged nearer the great ones and coughed.

"Well Senator," he said ingratiatingly, "I see your friends won't regret putting you where you'll be, you know, the Senate." He winked and nodded to take the cold look from Fawcett's face and something in the man's eyes wiped the coldness off and replaced it with a cordial smile. "I always stick by my friends, Cawkins, no one can say I haven't."

"That's right," Cawkins murmured. Ton Ferris chewed his cigar and tried to lift one leg across the other. He said he'd never seen anything so funny as the time they'd put the niggers out of the legislature. "Why, let's see, no that was the time they were trying to get them back in, I remember Tumlin, you recall him? Why he roared and bellowed more about the Constitution and all its damnable amendments and called on God oftener than any preacher. His collar button burst, or no, come to think of it, that was someone else. Then the Democrats who replaced the ousted niggers gave him a gold watch. Wonder if they'll take the watch back now because they sure will lose their seats. Lucky if they don't lose the seat of their trousers, yes sir, damned lucky."

They all had more time to talk than Joe and Roger did. The pay roll had to be checked before tomorrow if Joe was to take the roll to the end of the line. It was almost double the size since Fawcett took over the road and some of the names were down twice. He'd have to speak about that. And let's see, George had drawn money, several hundred, from the safe the day before and had forgotten to put a slip in to say where the money went. The money certainly ran out like water but that was the way to get things done Fawcett said. The road had been run down and the thing to do was to build it up. He made a few notes and had an uneasy feeling for a second wondering if he should poke his nose into all the business that didn't concern him. He'd like to hear Ton Ferris tell that story again about how the Israelites became carpetbaggers with Moses down in Egypt.

Laughter was rumbling into the outer room and in the silence that followed Ton Ferris cleared his throat and wondered if any gentleman present had heard that Lady Thorn had dislocated her hip.

"Why Harbeck told me. She was a good little mar, too," someone said. "A good little mar."

"None of you boys know racing if you were never at Saratoga," said Ton Ferris. "If I never do another thing, I'm going up there, if it's the last thing I do, and I'm going to see Longfellow run. He'll beat the Belmont string any day, got a lot of power in him yet. And then give me one of Moon's dinners. Mrs. Moon was in her prime when I was there last. What a cook. We had woodcock, soft shell crabs, trout, champagne impregnated with just a suggestion of orange flavor and Moon could make the best Roman punch you ever swallowed. I can taste that punch now, slipping down from the tip of the tongue to the pit of the stomach. You don't know what food is if you've never eaten with Moon. No sir."

"How about Willard's?"

"What, that depot? I'm surprised at you. That's good for nothing but General Grant's bummers. No, for a fine liver, there's nothing to beat Moon's." Roger came around to Joe's desk and whispered that he didn't half believe Ton Ferris's stories because according to him he'd been everywhere and done everything and it wasn't human.

When the batch of dispatches came from the governor's office, Joe took them to Fawcett's desk and Ton Ferris leaned over Fawcett's shoulder reading. Another proclamation was in the batch.

"I don't know, looks to me—" Fawcett was muttering. "Look that one over Ton, didn't he put out identically the same thing a few months ago?"

"Hm, hm, why it's enlarged. Let's see, the Colby outrage, Eli Barnes, yes they're old, but here's a new one. *Ten or twelve gunshots fired into a camp of colored laborers on the line of the Macon and Brunswick, three killed,* why this stuff isn't good enough. I tell you, people are too inclined to say what's a few niggers more or less. This proclamation is to get votes, you have to remember that little fact and figure the way people's minds work, not the sound of the thing."

"You're wrong Ton, this is aimed at the North, more than down here. Why look how they stirred themselves up after that shooting at Camilla. I tell you we owe our victory to this kind of thing. So long as this goes on we'll have Terry backing us up—with guns, if need be."

"I still think it ain't the best policy. Half the time I think Bullock is a nigger-lover like the Honorable from Pennsylvania, he acts so blamed consistent and *sincere.*"

"Oh Rufus is a good politician," said Fawcett.

They talked politics all day long and in the afternoon

Joe and Roger eased up with their scribbling and read the papers. The language of the *Constitution* was certainly a contrast to Ton Ferris and Joe didn't understand why Mr. Fawcett tolerated such an ignorant man who was always taking the conversation away from everybody else. George Fawcett was almost never in the office except for a half hour in the morning and another half hour in the evening and Roger said he had a bar and gaming place that brought him in all the money needed. The Fawcetts were perfect gentlemen in their home and Blake Fawcett was very tender and considerate with his widowed sister Estelle. He treated her as if she had never married and if she stayed up too late would ask, "Miss Estelle isn't it your bedtime?" Joe thought the courteous way they treated one another wonderful and knew that if his sisters had the chance they could be as fine as anyone.

The best part of the day was the moment he could wash his hands, scrubbing the ink from his finger, and with his hat tilted at the right angle swagger out with Roger and know that he was looked at enviously by other young men in town as standing in well with the Fawcett crowd. He priced horses and planned to own a span of grays as soon as he could turn some of his investments to ready money. As soon as the state was firmly Republican, property would surely rise. "Joe you're born to be lucky," Roger said. "Look at the way the ladies bridle when they see you." But even as he laughed Joe knew he was really scared of the young ladies and liked best to chat with Nannie Ellis, Blake Fawcett's little niece, because she was just a child, like one of his own sisters, and when he began to collect photos for his album he and Nannie exchanged pictures. He bought two pictures of actresses too and stuck them in his album planning how he'd make old Aaron envious and let him think they were good friends of his and had given him their photos with their own hands.

He bragged in letters home about his "investments" and

in the morning when he stepped across the carpet of the Fawcett's dining room with the roses in the purple background thick and soft under his feet and the window full of birds in their cages whistling and singing, he thought he'd made quite a stride since bakery days and took it as a good omen for the future. Fawcett was always telling him how sharp he was and George certainly reposed confidence in him. He ought to feel proud and content but Sunday was the best day in the week when he and Roger hired a rig and drove like mad with guns and lunch for hours. He'd get so tired of the word Yankee, they might as well spit in the eye as say it with that intonation and for every person looking on him as a favored son of the Fawcett crowd, there were a dozen ready to tar and feather.

But the very notion that he lived in a kind of danger was exciting and if he had gone West, it would have been Indians shooting at him. He made up his mind that the first chance he got, he'd make a quick trip North and take the family a fine array of presents. No use thinking of it now until the row in the legislature was over. George Fawcett was so seldom there, everything was on his shoulders and he had even begun to sign the papers, writing *George Fawcett per Joseph Trexler* with flourishes and a big extra loop in the *J*. Two days before the legislature opened F. V. Langford of the firm of Langford Brothers gave him the first chance to do a little private business.

"George has been putting through the bills for me, using his influence with the board so I don't have to discount at the bank. He said you'd take care of it. That right?"

"That's right," said Joe, picking up the slip of paper.

"You'll get the usual split, of course. What do you think is going to happen at the State House?"

"Oh, Bullock has the thing well in hand," Joe said. He had heard Ton Ferris say that a dozen times.

"Think so? Well, perhaps. He's got some opposition. I hope you're right for the sake of business. Conditions are terrible. Terrible."

"Yes, there's a lot of suffering," Joe said.

"We've got to get Yankee capital down here, there's no money in the South. We're ruined." He looked at Joe warily and in not too friendly a way then pulled himself together remembering that after all he wanted the road's patronage and perhaps this young upstart really had the say around here. "Much obliged to you."

"That's all right," said Joe.

When the door had closed he added up the items. They totaled a puny $365.75 but even that would net him somewhere around twenty dollars. Not much in comparison to the big sums he handled but all his own.

The papers were howling because the road had paid nothing to the state for the last three months but if the former superintendent hadn't been so anxious to keep his seat by making payments the road couldn't afford, it wouldn't be in the shape it now was, just a skeleton with some of the bones missing. "Let them howl for their meat," Ton advised. "They'll howl even louder if you let the beef die that makes the steaks. No matter what you do today there's bound to be a howl go up. My advice is, watch out for number one, keep your seat and let the old mare ride."

Cawkins cackled appreciatively at this sally. "What good's the road if we all lose our jobs?" he said but Mr. Fawcett hearing them gabble from his inner room came out and fixed the little auditor firmly with his eye. "I'm surprised to hear you talk like that. Tragic as our personal destinies may be, there is the greater destiny of the state. This is the critical year. If the breach isn't healed with the Union, we'll sink."

Ton Ferris let out a snort and said, "Blakie you're good.

I like you better all the time. How about an oration on the noble Negro?" But at a look from Mr. Fawcett, even he closed his mouth. It took something to make that big hippo quiet. Joe looked at Roger and Roger slyly winked.

They talked it over afterwards when the office emptied. "The big fool, blabbing like a fish. He's no dignity but he has a great deal of influence, so Mr. Fawcett says. Knows a lot of monied men up North." Joe surely got tired of all the little gossip and detail and in the evenings he enjoyed going to the Ellis home and talking foolishness with little Nannie. But even there, the talk would veer around and Ellis thought as a Union man Joe ran risks.

"You wait, you'll see, there'll be a riot and God knows how many bodies strewing the streets," said Ellis stroking his walrus mustaches. All the Fawcett crowd took pride in recounting how the Democrats inspired riots and bloodshed and violence and yelled "tyrants" at the Republicans to hide their own dark doings. When rebel papers screamed figures that blackened Bullock, Ton Ferris shrugged his shoulders and said, "It's a subterfuge."

It was a joke around the office and "It's a subterfuge" said with a shrug was an answer good enough for anyone. Sometimes a scream in the night made people shiver in their beds but no one stirred. The clock ticked loudly in the hall. The little dog barked nervously and subsided to a snarl. Smiling K. I. Trimble, the brains of the Fawcett crowd, put the gas out in his hotel room and went to bed to lie there thinking of his deals, the opera house, the hotel, the Tennessee Car Company, and how hand and glove with Bullock he could split the state wide open like a melon. Money was nothing, he'd had money all his life, made it in wagon bodies in New York State but to see buildings spring up, have papers write about him as the Jim Fisk of the South, that was good. Southern men were lackadaisacal, mixed up in old ideas, thought too much of horse and female flesh, spouted Cato while Grant was sitting in the White House with bummers swarming over him. Then this fear they had, was it that the pure female stream would be polluted by Negro blood? He'd heard there had never been a nigger rape before the war, well the whites did plenty of it judging from the yaller skins. A funny people, pride enough to sink a ship and God knows they needed it to cover up the dark pits. Chivalry like leaves to cover blood. But some fine men, as fine as any in the land, Gordon and Joe Brown. Toombs was more the Southern hero but not so bright. The die-hards couldn't recognize history when they saw it. But you had to admire the man for his convictions. Blake Fawcett now, he smiled contemptuously in the dark and reached for the stand by the bed, felt around in the box and fished out gingerly a long cigar, struck a light firmly with a sure stroke and lit it, puffing gently, pleased with the glow it made and pinching the burned match slowly into little pieces.

The day the legislature opened K. I. Trimble stuck close to his hotel, shut in his room, playing solitaire. He had his dinner up there, and growled because the knife was too dull to cut the bloody steak. By evening the air was thick with cigar smoke and cigar butts choked the cuspidor. The cards were cool and crisp as ever and he laid them down with precision. He'd made a good thing on that deal about the opera house and Bullock was a man to stick by his friends even when he'd made a bad bargain. At eleven o'clock George Fawcett tapped and was admitted. Fawcett's hair was sweated to his forehead and he had a streaked look around the eyes but he grinned and said, "You should have seen Ton. He was immense. Bullock was a genius to put him in the chair."

"Bullock? *I* told Bullock Ton was the man for that job."

"You had judgment. But were they crazy? It went to their heads that an Ohio man should take the chair. Why, where's their logic? Bullock is in his rights. Terry is military overlord down here and this is still a military business, Bullock can appoint anyone he sees fit."

"Get on with it, what happened?"

"There stood Ton, cool as a cucumber, with catcalls, yells and cursing buzzing around him and he paid no attention to it. Just kept rapping the gavel and recognizing whom he pleased. Course when Bryant got up and objected to Barrow's construction of the test oath, Ferris called him to order. You could hear yells all over and someone got up and hollered out that even that traitor Joe Brown disagreed with Barrow's construction. Peabody was crying, yes sir, big tears dropping into his beard."

"Oh get on with it, what do I care about Peabody, what happened?"

"Well it isn't over yet, but Bryant gets up on a chair and starts to say that Ferris has no authority as speaker. Ferris just orders him arrested. Bryant jumps to another chair with all his crowd shouting and cheering and says he refuses to be arrested. Then Ferris turns to me and Hinton and says, 'Arrest that man.' We start toward him and when I got where I was able to grab him, Ellsworth from Rome stuck out his foot and tripped me. See, hurt my forehead, this bruise, why I could have broken my head."

"What next?" said Trimble. "What next?"

"Why next, Tooley's man, a black, I can't think of his name but he was Tooley's man all right, a foreman, good man, pulled a gun and started toward Bryant. Bryant shoved out his arm and says, "Ain't you ashamed, put up that thing.' Trouble with the blacks is that they are cowed so easy and of course Tooley's man put the gun up. I was on my feet again and coming toward him and Hinton was trying to get away where someone had pinned him down in a chair but Bryant was cute all right, he was up again shouting and he made a move that Caldwell be chairman. Some of the damned conservatives, the white livers, they'd been too scared before but now they spoke up and seconded but Caldwell didn't budge, he shook his head and stuck to his seat. It was funny, why he would have died if they had got him in the chair, he was so scared. Then Bryant kicked out with his foot at Hinton who was trying to pull him down and yelled with his hands to his mouth like a trumpet, 'Move we adjourn!' Ferris stood smiling and making jokes and keeping all those around him in an uproar and now and then he waved his hand toward Bryant and said, 'You're under arrest.' When Bryant put his motion, a few of his crowd seconded it and then the bunch starts toward the door but Ferris just kept calm and seeing they were leaving, he began again to call the roll just as if nothing had happened. When the conservatives saw that, they began slipping back one by one. We got O'Neal to read a protest against a number of Democrats today."

"Keep our men out of that, they can be prosecuted, don't forget, the line's fine as a hair—it says anyone caught scaring another from taking the oath."

"O'Neal's a nigger."

"That's good. Keep our crowd out of that. How did the roll show up?"

Young Fawcett moved uneasily. He lighted a new cigar and bit the end off and said slowly, "Can't tell yet. Not as good as we expected. But if it goes against us, why we've still got Terry. Bullock can get an order from him to suspend the legislature and put a military committee on to inquire into the eligibility of members. We think we can kick out some Democrats under that little regulation. So in any event, we aren't lost."

"Bungling somewhere. You've had enough money. It's

been pouring out. Lack of organization. I've said it all along. Fawcett is too openly what he is. Don't care if he is your father. Why that deal in Augusta where he was up for perjury is still held against him."

"No, he's got a big popular following. You'd be surprised. A lot of Democrats are behind him. No, I think he'll get the race for the Senate. And I think we'll hold the legislature, have to, there's no if about it."

"That's the talk," said Trimble. He pulled the bell rope and to the darky, "Whisky." When he brought the drinks the two men swallowed solemnly and K. I. Trimble began fumbling with his cards and finally he shuffled the deck and commenced laying out the kings and jacks. George Fawcett saw he wasn't wanted and left. It was nearly one o'clock but Mr. Trimble never went to bed until three. He finished his game and wrote a long letter to an aunt in Brooklyn. The aunt was a member of Dr. Beecher's congregation and she always sent K. I. Trimble long excerpts from his sermons. She had the feeling that her nephew had the instincts of a great preacher like Henry Ward Beecher and had missed his calling. K. I. liked to encourage her in her illusions and he liked to write long letters about the rôle a Northerner could play in the South where passions raged and the still small voice was completely drowned in the shuffle. Writing the letter soothed his nerves and made him sleepy and it also took away the irritation left in the room after the departure of young Fawcett. He rinsed his mouth with a new patent preparation and bared his strong teeth to see the effect upon them, that done he turned out his lights and undressed in the dark.

He couldn't get to sleep. Once he heard a gun go off but no scream followed. A man went by under his window whistling. He yawned and stretched and finally lit the gas again, dug around for an old New York paper and read the rest of that story about the horrid abortionist trials in New York City.

When George Fawcett left Trimble at his hotel he made straight for the Turf Exchange. On a night like this he didn't care to be roaming the streets. Gangs of toughs had like as not been hired by those Democratic assassins to fire on any Rad. He was cold although it was a mild night and he felt the damp between his collar and his skin. A crowd of friends at the bar moved as he came in and nodded and he had a quick feeling of relief to be safe with them. Joe Trexler came forward to hear if Trimble had made any comments and he took pains to answer Joe with all the cordiality he could muster. He had the feeling lately he couldn't look Joe in the eye and he told the old man he thought they'd made a mistake to take him on. There was no use worrying about anything but the row at the legislature now and he spoke to Charles behind the bar and started toward the little green room at the head of the stairs. One of the Dace boys followed. When the door was closed Ed Dace said, "How's it look?"

"Bad," said George.

"It does? I heard Ferris had wielded things with a strong hand."

"Looks as if the Democrats had squeezed in more than their share but that will iron out, they can't take the oath, but they'll make trouble, start fights and then lay it to us. If they could just get a few Democrats murdered, they'd lay it to us."

"Why not call out Terry's troops? What's he here for if not that?"

"Later. Later. Have you seen Father?"

"He was in here an hour ago. What's that?" Both men

put their glasses down and listened. A dull crash sounded downstairs and loud voices cackled, and outside yells and people running. George didn't know whether to hide or go downstairs. He did neither and the door opened and Jim Dace put his head in. "Stone went through the plate glass, George."

"Who threw it?"

"Gang of toughs. It crashed through and broke a coupla glasses and scared Ginger Will into fits. That's all."

"Get them to board it up. I'll be glad when this is over."

"Here too," said Ed Dace.

"They are an excited bunch of men downstairs, George. They got strong superstitions. Old Withersmoon is drunk again and he's raving about the ship sinking in the storm and we'd have to find the Jonah to heave him out."

"Well he's harmless. Crazy, but don't pay any attention."

"All right, it's your bar, not mine, but everybody's nervous. It's a nervous evening."

"Perhaps I'd better go down, what'd you think Ed?"

"I would, on a night like this."

"I'll go," said George, getting up and trying to stiffen his puny shoulders. "I'll put a stop to all the foolishness." He stepped out and started down the stairs. Two barmen were dragging in planks and were fitting them across the broken glass. There was a buzz of talk, remonstrating and commands, but the high insistent voice of Withersmoon shrieked above the rest. "I told you boys. Look what's happened already, jib boom's been carried away, next thing you all know fo'castle's liable to go, her side will be stove in. Boys, remember the good book, get down on your knees. There's a Jonah on board and we must pray for a sign to cast him over. Lord thee knows there is a Jonah." He stared around with his small bloodshot eyes needling the crowd. Each man turned and shifted uncom-

fortably from that bloody stare. People stopped talking
and somebody tittered. Someone said, "Take the old man
home." George advanced but as he came toward Withersmoon the old man backed and bumped into Joseph Trexler. Trexler moved aside but the old man caught at his
coat collar and glared at him and then turned slowly and
kept on backing from him. "Jonah," he said. "Take your
hands off me."

"You've got your hands on me," said Joe pleasantly.
"I'm not touching you."

"Come now," George said, "can't I help you home, Mr.
Withersmoon? I'm going your way."

"Jonah," repeated Mr. Withersmoon. "Watch out for
Jonah. The cold sea is bashing in our ship, boys, all hands
to the boats, lower away there on the sta'board, lower
away, we are lost." As he said lost, his raised white face
poured tears.

"He's raving," Ed Dace said. "The poor old idiot is out
of his head."

"What's the matter with him?" a newcomer said, trying
to edge nearer.

"Give him a drink."

"He's had too many already."

"Stand aside please," said George. The old man let
George take hold of his arm but he turned his head to look
at Joe once more and again he said "Jonah." Joe turned
pale and the way he had said "Jonah" would freeze anybody's blood. George told him not to pay any attention,
the old fellow was absolutely dotty. And drunk.

"Yes," Joe said, "I knew he was drunk."

"That's it," George said. "He's drunk."

"Yes, he's been drinking," Joe said. He made his way to
the bar and had a drink. Was it only his imagination or
did the others really stand off a little from him? He was
crazy to get nervous about a poor old man. He went home

and the streets were quiet and there was no sign of the
crowd that had flung the stone.

He was glad to be safe in his own room. He drew the
curtains of heavy stuff and again admired them. They
must have cost a pile of money. He swung out of his coat
and vest and to cheer himself commenced humming but
remembering that Grandma Fawcett slept in the next
room he stopped abruptly, his necktie in his hands, his
head cocked on one side listening. Was that a noise on the
street? Must be his imagination. He was getting nervous
and no wonder with everyone strung tight as a wire. When
the row at the State House was over, everything would be
easy again.

He wished he had gone to see little Nannie Ellis tonight
instead of to the bar. Today he had heard that she was
very sick with inflammation of the lungs. All the time
Roger had been telling him about her, Ton Ferris had
been holding forth and keeping the office in an uproar.

He would go up to Philadelphia the first thing after the
elections were over. Before long he would have enough to
buy the girls a piano. Those lots had resold to a man from
Cincinnati for a pretty penny. They were going to put up
an ice factory. Old Mamie, the Fawcett's cook, said it was
agin nature to make ice, they should let the Lawd do that.
He was going to be in on the company that would start the
ice house. There were no end of enterprises. It wouldn't
be long before he would be independent. Cawkins and
Ferris were building houses as fast as they would go up
and he couldn't see any reason why he shouldn't do the
same. He wasn't going to be laughed at for a fool and if
the others took chances he could also. They no doubt kept
an account with the road the way the Fawcetts did. At
least that was what Fawcett had told him. When Fawcett
came to make a down payment on the Walton Street house
he had taken it from the big safe in his office. He had

peeled off three thousand from a roll that had come in that morning from the post office, government money allotted the road for carrying the mail.

"Well," he had said, "I don't know if this will put me or the road in the hole. I'll have to get that account between us straightened out before long. If the road owes me I shall expect to be paid. And vice versa. Mrs. Fawcett," he says, "Mrs. Fawcett put some of her money in this road and she'll be expecting that back too. Said she thought if she couldn't have faith enough in an enterprise that her husband headed, she wasn't a good wife. It was her own money too." Joe had been impressed with Mrs. Fawcett's public spirit. But Grandma Fawcett was the nicest one in that family. He felt sorry for her because she was so bewildered and didn't have an idea what was going on. She hated to see her son getting so involved in politics. "He'd do better to stay quiet and not go seeking ructions," said Grandma Fawcett. And how kind she was to Joe and to his birds. He had bought a cardinal and a mocking bird and had a great cage for them. When he went to the end of the road with the payroll, Grandma always fed his birds for him. She said they just seemed to know he was gone.

He walked over to the bureau and started taking off his shirt. His own image reassured him. He looked like a swell all right in those nobby clothes. No one would ever know he'd been a candy maker. Of course he had told Roger Wallace but then Wallace had confided pretty nearly everything to him. The family would be pretty surprised to see him so changed and when they heard he was going to buy a piano, they wouldn't know whether they were asleep or awake. He'd like to know the Blondell girls better. The youngest one reminded him a little of Anne. Lucy Blondell was a beauty and how polite she had been to him. He fingered his part and wondered if he could start growing a mustache soon. He heard the front door slam and knew that George had returned, so quickly turned out the light and got into bed himself. He would certainly be glad when the row was over.

The row at the State House went on for four days and it might have kept on until kingdom come if Bullock hadn't taken matters into his own hands and ordered a recess to inquire into the eligibility of certain members. General Terry backed the Governor and created a board to inquire into the six Democratic senators regarded as doubtful. When the legislature met, five senators and representatives were kicked out and they were squeezing Republicans from the next highest candidates into the ousted members' places. The *Constitution* jeered that the Rads didn't dare risk an election but Fawcett's crowd laughed it off. Why what did they care what was said so long as they got results? Success made anything right. With Bryant defeated for the chair and driven from the room with a bloody nose, enough order was restored to pass the Fourteenth and Fifteenth amendments. Several die-hards wept publicly on the street.

On the fifteenth of February, Fawcett was elected to the Senate. A bunch of Negroes came down from Chattanooga in the state elections and Joe went around to the polls with them to show them where to put their marks for Boss Fawcett's men. Afterwards he herded them on the train to Tunnel Hill and they made their marks again. There must have been seven carloads made the trip down that day. He wrote a letter home the same night and said that he was coming to see them soon. Late at night bonfires were lighted along the tracks of the W. & A. and the company wood surely made a nice bright blaze.

But the election was no sooner over than a new set of troubles came along. Now Bullock was really in hot water. The Democrats had raised such a howl and even compromisers like Joe Brown had complained so much that Congress was ordering an investigation. Money was needed more than ever for Bullock in Washington. Some of those Senators wanted as much as a thousand dollars for a vote. Why they were too greedy for this life, Ton Ferris said, and he was very bitter about them. He said somebody ought to write a letter to Senator Morton. People were beginning to boom Morton for the next President and he was making a tour and getting off some pretty popular speeches. "Listen to this," said Ton. "That fellow knows how to put it:"

I think I may say with perfect truth, there never was before, since our government was formed, a condition of such universal prosperity as prevails this day. Every condition of society is prosperous. There never was a time when labor was better rewarded or wages would purchase more. Labor was never so honorable as now; every man is free and equal with every other man and each has within himself the power to do what he will. But notwithstanding, they are croakers and grumblers. There always are.

"He doesn't want to come too far South with that speech or he'd run up against the biggest delegation of grumblers ever was," said Cawkins.

Ton Ferris frowned on the little man. "Why do you always want to see the dark side of life? Well, it's like Morton says, there always will be grumblers."

THE BITCH GODDESS, SUCCESS

JOE WAS sending money home now. He talked of coming home for a visit but not until the trouble blew over. Bullock was putting up a stiff fight in Washington. The House had gone against him. The Atlanta *Constitution* blared that Bullock was spending eighteen hundred dollars a week at the Hotel Willard, living like a lord while thousands were starving in Georgia. These sums certainly made Joe's savings look pretty small. He couldn't help but admire the way Fawcett took all the criticism. One morning someone sent him a New York paper marked with a blue pencil. He ripped it open, read,

"The people of the U. S. are just about sick of the name of Bullock. A senator last week remarked that Congress had Bullock on the brain."

Fawcett laughed, shrugged his shoulders, turning to Joe. "I suppose some *friend* sent this," he said. "Never let scandal or rumor disturb you, my boy."

It was good experience to work for a man as worldly as that. Joe was bothered by a good many things going on that he didn't exactly understand but George Fawcett said that was the way all businesses were run. "You don't make a fortune on cheeseparing," George said. George took things coolly, that was certain. He simply added two plate glass to an order and when the glass came he sent it down to the Turf Exchange. The bill went before the board and was paid without comment. Joe also made no comment. When Mem wrote that she hoped the day would come when they had enough dishes, Joe went white around the mouth and got in touch with Hector Cornbolt, one of the road's big customers. Hector put in an order for some of the finest French china, chaste, with a lovely eggshell finish and a little band of rosy pink. Joe got encouragement from Mr. Fawcett for making gifts like that.

"I like to see that you are generous, Joe," he said, pushing back his cuffs and exposing the fine wrist and the heavy gold cuff links on the white linen. "There's nothing so contemptible as meanness about money. One of the great heritages of the old South is a lack of meanness about money. They knew quality, sir, and were willing to pay for it. Nothing but the best would do for our fine old fam-

ilies. We imported rarities from Europe for their consumption. It's the duty of the new families to take up that
tradition and not to let it die in the kind of commonness
running rife." He certainly enjoyed hearing himself talk.
Joe never knew just how to take the old man. When he
got oracular, Joe just sat back and listened. He couldn't
help being impressed but he was beginning to have another feeling. He didn't want to examine this new attitude
too closely. It made him very uncomfortable and he hoped
that Fawcett did not suspect him of it.

Bullock actually lost out and trailed back to Georgia
feeling dejected. Fawcett talked of the Governor as if he
were a great martyr. But the game was by no means lost.
The legislature meeting in April demanded an investigation into the railroad. No one in the railroad office took
that very seriously. The committee would be picked and
they would order a lot of fine Northern cigars, six year
old whisky, sherry, plenty of lemons, get an orchestra and
have some dance music. Women had an influence on affairs of this kind. If members of Congress hadn't been so
greedy, Bullock wouldn't have to feel humiliated. They
were born pigs, Ton Ferris said, and nothing would satisfy
them.

Joe's commissions had grown considerably in the last
couple of months and he wrote to his mother to expect
him soon. His letter puzzled her. It didn't look like his
hand. It was written in a hurry, she thought, but she was
troubled. It wasn't a good sign to see a boy's hand change.

It didn't set her mind at rest to see him either. He was
taller and broader and his clothes were of the best. Anyone
could see that he was somebody. When she turned the coat
back to see the lining and how they sewed the pockets in,

he laughed at her and said that if she had wanted to see
his coat, he could have shipped it to her and saved him
the trouble of coming himself. The girls couldn't take
their eyes off him. He had presents for everybody and
bought theater tickets and ribbons and new gloves for
them all.

Aaron came up from Grapeville, New Jersey, to see his
brother. He had gotten into a town promotion scheme and
was busy surveying and laying out lots and town sites.
Mr. Flemmer was a wealthy man who had ideas he had
picked up in Italy. He planned to get Italians into his
town and start the grape industry. Joe talked of Mr. Fawcett's schemes and ideas and the two compared Fawcett
and Flemmer. Aaron had his own private idea of Mr. Fawcett and told Joe he had been reading the papers and he
had better watch out. Joe laughed and said Aaron was full
of small town notions and would never make a fortune.
His clothes were sloppy for one thing and Joe lectured
him on the importance of his personal appearance. Aaron
grinned as if he were concealing something and Joe felt
suddenly immature and foolish. What kind of fellow was
Aaron with his wrinkled clothes and stringy blue tie that
just emphasized a sort of naked blueness in his eyes? He
stood there, absent minded, scratching his head and rummaging in his vest pocket for something that he never
found. He got on Joe's nerves and Aaron told his mother
that Joe was flying high but it would be nice to have a rich
brother. Too bad there weren't more railroads. From all
he had heard, it was as good as a gold mine to be connected with a railroad.

Joe realized that he had broadened and did not think
the same as Aaron on many subjects. The pleasure that the
girls took in all his presents and in showing him off to
their friends made the time go fast. He brought out his
album and displayed little Nannie Ellis, the Fawcetts, pic-

tures of Grant and a few Southern generals with flowing beards, and let them be completely mystified by the picture of the actress in the black lace veil that he had bought in Atlanta. His sisters hung around him with shining eyes and he thought that they were as lovely as any girls he had seen in Atlanta. He wanted them to have the best and his mother to relax just once and not sit as if she were made of steel. He couldn't help but compare her to Mrs. Fawcett with her pretty soft ways and wavy hair. His mother's hair worn so uncompromisingly hurt him more than her hands. She could not seem to stop her ripping and pressing and steaming. He leaned toward her across the table and sketched a picture on the back of an envelope. "Look here," he said, "how do you like your new parlor?"

She worked her hands into her pocket, got out her steel rimmed glasses, put them on, looked at the paper, her plain combed hair ruffling up at the back of her neck. "What's this?"

"See, it's like Fawcett's parlor, here a fireplace and in this corner a cupboard, kind of, to put things on."

"What things?"

"We'll get things. Curios, things like that. Then carpets. How'd you like carpets so thick you couldn't hear a step on them?" She held the sketch steady in her hands with all the children swarming near and Catherine was just a little put out at Mem's composure.

"Can't you get just a little bit excited, Mem?" she said and was sorry as soon as she had said it because she saw the paper trembling and Mem's lips twitching the way they always did when she was moved and didn't want to show it.

Even David was impressed but he didn't think much of all the talk about a piano and a flute. If he got a flute he would have to practice. The girls went with Joe to the piano dealer's and were more impressed with his manners than with the big shiny instruments. The way the clerks stepped around delighted them and they came home and told Mem she should have seen Joe. He made Catherine and Anne take off their hard white collars and took them to buy wide soft collars to button over their plain wool dresses and wide soft ribbons with roman stripes and the two of them had their pictures taken, their hair strained a bit too tight, but their eyes shy and withdrawn.

He carried the pictures back to Atlanta with him and showed them around with pride at the compliments they drew. He took them with him on the night he went to see little Nannie but she was too ill to look at them, saw Joe only for a moment, smiling at him above a mass of white coverlets. What had been a bad cold had turned into consumption and she would die. He tried to think of something to say to Mr. Ellis, who went to the door with him as he left the house, standing in a half hearted incompetent manner in loose slippers, with his long straggling mustaches seeming to trickle down his neck beneath his stiff collar. He'd lost all in the war, he said, and now he was to lose a daughter. He said it grudgingly as if she were a possession of value only to him, her father, as if he not Nannie were the loser, so that Joe wanted to knock the old fool down; he was a liar too, because everyone knew he had risked nothing in the war, not even his own skin. Asthma had saved him to see his daughter die. People died in spite of the best of care but she was so young and he could see her too bright, wide and frightened eyes staring at him and imploring. It was raining and he took consolation in feeling himself get wet and soggy. He tried to get relief by blaming Mr. Ellis and when he could not, he thought what must be, must be. But his throat ached all the same, and he wished he could write a poem like that one in the *Constitution* a few days before. It had the melancholy of rain in it and as he thought of it in that way he was pleased at his own idea. Perhaps he could write poems too. Grave where is thy victory. Death where is thy sting. Mr. Fawcett would be pleased if he wrote a poem about little Nannie. It was awful to keep thinking of her as dead when she was still above the ground and might get well. He hoped no one would ever find out his thoughts.

All the next day he kept thinking of rhymes for Death where is thy sting, Grave where is thy victory. He pasted invoices in the book and between times found himself drawing birds and spirals. He couldn't keep his mind on the business and almost sent the safe that Fawcett had added to the Lenghorn bill to the board as a safe. He changed the item for $175 to bolts as Mr. Fawcett had suggested and looked up the catalogue to get a reasonable number for the order. That patched up, he took it over to the board room but no one was there but Culberson and he was not there for business, he said. Joe left the invoice and went out again.

He didn't know what to do with himself because when he was alone he thought of little Nannie dying and death. He went back to the office feeling aimless and foolish and Roger had just come in. He told Joe that Nannie had died that afternoon. The two young men were upset and went out to dinner together and tried to talk about the pain those missed who died young but they both knew it was not true and so suddenly shut up. Walking home alone Joe thought something was wrong or he would not be able to think of anything else but Nannie but bits of business kept poking up. He wondered if he had really made out that invoice correctly. The safe was going to Fawcett's house and there was no use explaining all that to the road. It was easier to mark it as bolts intended for the road only. Had he torn up the original invoice? He thought so. His head ached and when verses learned from the pages of the newspaper came to him he felt ashamed. There was something wrong about remembering verses when that little girl was dead.

Someone did write a poem for little Nannie Ellis and it was printed in the *Constitution*. Joe flushed as he read it and when he came to his own identical lines, Death where is thy sting, Grave where is thy victory, he felt as if someone had stolen something from him. He cut it out carefully and during the day looked at it several times. Roger got the idea Joe had written it. He had talked to Roger about things like that and it was in Roger's head that the poem signed *Anonymous* must be his. He complimented him on it and said, "Why you're a genius." Joe denied it was his but with a half guilty air and Roger just poohpoohed and thought he was entirely too modest. When Joe wrote to Catherine that night he inclosed the poem and asked, "What do you think of this? Give me your honest opinion."

The Blondell girls were at little Nannie's funeral and at the grave he found himself standing beside Lucy and feeling very close to her. He wished he had been the one to think of the poem for Nannie. When he looked at Lucy crying he almost felt that he had really been the author.

He kept thinking of Lucy and a few days later dressed in his best and hiring a rig, he drove out of town past the big Blondell place, his hat a little to one side, his cuffs set right and himself straight and at ease in the freshly washed buggy. He passed the house and coming back, stopped and hitched, got out and leisurely walked up the path between the stumps of once fine trees. The door opened and Lenore, the younger sister, came out to meet him. He found himself shaking hands with Blondell surrounded by little Blondells and Lucy bringing up the rear, and in an aside she said to him, "I saw your poem. Roger told me," and squeezed his hand, her eyes filling with tears.

Joe flushed and knew that was the time to tell the truth,

but he let it pass with nothing but a shake of the head that Lucy took only for false modesty. Blondell, inept, small and frightened looking but with a firm mouth that gave to his shy appearance the courage of a bird battling a hawk, brushed his wife's sewing out of a chair and Joe sat down. The family surrounded him, the wife with her interested face and the two older girls, reserved in the presence of their parents. Lucy was a real Southern belle but when he talked Lenore was the one who listened. She stood there with her greenish rather small eyes shining in her pointed freckled face, her straw colored hair pulled tight back giving her high white forehead a precocious plucked and rather forlorn look that made Joe look twice and then turn to Lucy who stood easy and graceful with nothing to feel sorry for.

He couldn't help noticing the chipped china at supper and compared it to the Fawcetts'. The fine old house was almost bare and a high scolding Negro voice singsonged from the kitchen when the door opened. He wished he could fix this place up for them. It must have been a mansion in its day. Mrs. Blondell kept apologizing for her poor table in a timid way and once he had it on his tongue to tell about his mother and her struggles but he was afraid they might look down on him and kept his mouth shut. Going home the streets were dark and as he came to Fawcett's house the front door opened and Fawcett let out a guest. Joe brushed past him in the dark, a tall handsome man whose straight profile he had seen from the fanlight over the door. K. I. Trimble. Fawcett was standing in the hall absently handling his watch. He smiled at Joe cordially, opened his mouth and then shut it, turned away and said abruptly, "Good night, my boy."

On the table in his room was a letter from Catherine. She had read the poem. "Don't try to deceive me with your false modesty. I can tell your style of thought and turn of phrase. How proud I am of you and how I cried for that poor girl." He ought to sit right down and write her that the poem wasn't his but it was hardly important enough to make a fuss about and perhaps it would be better to wait until he saw her. Besides he was certain he might have written that very poem, why two of the lines were out of his own head, almost. He sat down at his table and with a pen began drawing birds and plumage and singsonging noises and sights came to his mind and made writing poems seem so easy that his pen hung there, just waiting for the word. But dollar signs got tangled up with the birds on his paper and he must be sure to remember to see if George Fawcett had put a slip in to account for the batch of bills he had extracted from the safe the day before. Now his thoughts were thrown off the track and he put the pen down, felt dejected and got into bed.

Talk about the way the legislature had been organized didn't die down very fast. The Democrats kept the story moving adding something to it all the time to keep the people worked up. Ton Ferris said they had regular spies who spent their days and nights digging up rubbish to infuriate the people. "Why they'll take some little innocent thing like Miller's frogs and make a mountain out of it. Can you imagine anything more innocent than those poor goggle eyed frogs of Miller's? No, you couldn't. It just shows the paucity of their imaginations that they must pick on a poor defenseless frog." He couldn't get over it. Miller was the head mechanic in the railroad yard and he had had iron frogs made at the works, weighing about five pounds each and painted a nice green. If it was railroad paint and iron, it wasn't *much,* only a mean person would kick at such a little item. He sold them around for fifty cents apiece and there wasn't an official of the road that didn't have one squatting on his desk. Miller was a pretty popular fellow and they were all glad to buy a frog to help out Miller.

With many of the railroad men building houses no one could blame Miller for wanting to sell a few frogs. With times so hard it was every man for himself. If it kept on like this Miller said he would have to quit using butter.

"Butter," says Ton. "Why man you could butter every chair in your house if you wanted to, you sly old fox."

Miller grinned in a foolish way but he went right on saying that if things didn't get better he would have to eat dry bread. He had the reputation of being about the most mercenary fellow in Atlanta and Ton Ferris told Joe he hoped he'd take a warning from that scamp and never tie up his purse strings in such a miserable fashion.

Joe sent money home every week and he planned to buy the girls the finest piano in Philadelphia on his next trip North. Mem could not bear to hear of such extravagance. She could not bring herself to believe in the piano and in spite of the money Joe sent home continued to take in suits from a tailoring establishment. She was an expert on buttonholes and had taught Anne the trick of rounding them off. While Catherine and the others were at school, Anne rounded off buttonholes, went to market and stared in the windows of music shops. The piano came in June on an order from Joe, crowding the front parlor and making everything look shabby and kind of sordid. Every day Anne dusted its beautiful surface with a rag lightly soaked in linseed oil and every evening she practiced hard at scales and runs. By July she could pick out "Listen to the Mocking Bird" and wrote Joe that she had beat Catherine and should have the soprano part in all the duets.

Joe liked to watch Lucy Blondell at her piano and think what a picture she made and fancy how Anne and Catherine could not be looked down on now for not having the accomplishments young ladies should have. Lenore was almost certain to poke her nose in the door, her eyes scared and her straw colored hair braided like the ears of a little rabbit. She had more to say than Lucy, prattling and caressing the wood of the piano as if it were a pet animal. Once he accused Lucy of not hearing what he said and she answered, giving him such a look, "No, I didn't hear but I was thinking of you and that's more important," so that he really thought he was very lucky.

Blake Fawcett took an almost paternal interest in Joe's visits to the Blondell home. "That's an old family but Seth is the weakest link in the chain. He won't corrupt you even if he is a Democrat. I hear his line has run to seed on girls." Joe said he'd seen a boy of four. "Let's hope the boy lives. I thought that family had gone to seed," Fawcett said. He was like that one day and the next snappy and irritable.

"Why a bedbug couldn't put up with him," Ton Ferris said. "I guess that's what you call the mercurial temperament. Geniuses and fools. Take your pick."

Ton sat every morning in the office snorting and blowing over the papers. He took them all and read them moving his heavy cabbage head with the thick mussed hair slowly up and down as he followed the columns. He liked to read aloud the perorations of the *Constitution,* throwing his head back and orating like a Roman senator:

How long, O Cataline! As old as time and stamped with the imprimatur of Holy Book, is the utterance, that when the wicked are in power their people groan in tribulation. Georgia is no exception. Her rulers are against her, not for her, they seek personal aggrandizement not public weal.

And then he'd stop and snort and cackle and call out, "Hey Blakie, we are all out of public weal. Order a little of that from New York. They've got a heavy shipment there, I'm told." And he'd double up until he looked as if he might die of apoplexy. Blake Fawcett didn't appreciate Ton's spasms and told him on the side not to indulge himself like that in the office. Ton could sober in a minute and sit solemn as a judge, emitting heavy sighs and mournful looks like an undertaker.

When it came to any tricky business, Ton was the best one to manage it. But even his oratory and the seven thousand cigars, fifty-seven dozen lemons, fifty gallons of whisky, fifteen gallons of sherry, cases of champagne, sugar and bitters, all of the very best from R. M. Rose and Company could not save the day at Lookout Mountain. The committee turned in a report that Fawcett might have dictated and the dance at Dalton lasted all night with high jinks and music by Polk's string band. Hacks were hired from Lookout Mountain and no expense had been spared. The committee was in the best humor and the railroad crowd did not worry much about the bills that came rolling in. The grand total came to around sixteen hundred and fifty dollars but by boosting a few board bill accounts and holding back a little government money for carrying mail that item was taken care of. Everything was taken care of but public opinion. Nobody was satisfied with the committee report and even Republican papers were disloyal enough to say that what was needed was an investigation by experts, not by politicians.

"The dirty yellow bellies," Ton said after reading a long fulmination in a Republican paper from Savannah. "Poking their noses into something that isn't their business. What do they know about railroads? Here we are sweating in this beastly weather trying to pull an old wreck through that a bunch of Democrats got into such bad shape that nothing but the Holy Ghost could resurrect it, and what do we get? Thanks? Oh no, that would be polite. It might be beneath a Southern gentleman to notice a few poor sweating toilers who work like niggers." His face actually turned purple and his eyes were blood-shot with his efforts to work off steam. He sat fanning himself and sending out for mint juleps, wiping his huge head with pocket handkerchiefs taken one by one from his vest and coat. The heat crackled in the office and in the midst of the talk and bubbling foolishness of Ton and his cronies Joe felt homesick for the Blondells and for Lucy. He could hardly wait for evening and the chance to drive out to the big old house and stand around and talk with Blondell and sit with Lucy on the veranda or out by the arbor. In letters home he talked of the Blondells and made light of the rumors in the newspapers.

Aaron read the news even in Philadelphia of the railroad frauds and the money leaking out and he didn't know what advice to give to Joseph. Joe's explanation that it was all politics sounded plausible. Everyone knew the Democrats were moving heaven and earth to get the Northern influence out of the South. Let them show that they understood the lesson of the war if that was what they wanted. It was all against the grain of the time to be lenient with old Southern notions. With so much bloodshed and wreckage there should be something to show for it. He wrote a long preachy letter to Joe about his own business in Jersey and that he was making money on crates for the grapes that season. He didn't think it worth while to tell Joe that Mem was helping him with money Joe sent her but he thought it would be a shame if Joe left the South just when the family was beginning to feel prosperous for the first time in its life. He made Mem feel that Joe had a good many extravagant ideas and she was very careful of the money he sent and saved most of it for David's schooling. She forgot how she had cried for education when she was a girl and made plans to cheat her girls and favor her boys. The girls could be frugal, love birds and plants and sniff the fresh morning air as if it were a treat. It was wrong to get high notions and she even doubted the piano, until the girls came to look upon it as an instrument liable to vanish.

Coming North in August, Joe tried to shake the family out of their caution. He scattered money around and had the girls playing the piano all day long. Mem went around complaining that she couldn't get anyone to do a thing. When letters from Lucy Blondell came, he read snatches of them to Catherine. Mem always came into the room and sighed and complained of headaches for hours afterwards. Joe could see that she wouldn't make it easy for him to get married and the only way would be for him to make a lot of money to take care of them all.

The Philadelphia house seemed very cramped after the Fawcett house in Atlanta and all the furniture so shabby that in the mornings when he woke up the first feeling was a kind of sinking at the heart. But the sun came in early in his room and he got to like it, waking and thinking about the grand things bound to happen. Even when Mem pulled a long face, he still felt happy and started to learn a duet on the piano with Catherine. He thought a little contemptuously of Aaron plugging away in Grapeville and wouldn't even go down to look over the proposition. It was more fun poking around Philadelphia with Anne and Catherine telling them how different everything was in the South. He talked about the high society and spoke so chummily of Governor Bullock that the girls had a kind of awe of him and thought he was pretty extraordinary to find himself in such company.

When he got back to Atlanta everything seemed a little flat after the stories he had told the girls, but Fawcett went out of his way to be nice to him and put a number of small private matters to his advantage. There was a constant barrage of criticism of Fawcett and his management of the road in all the papers but they were all used to the gunfire by this time and paid little attention to it. The test would come with the elections and it was pretty doubtful if the Republicans could carry the legislature. Fawcett was being warned by letters and editorials that his seat in Congress was in danger and only K. I. Trimble went his way smiling and unconcerned.

A tension in the office made even Roger Wallace uneasy but he was all wrapped up in plans for his marriage and much as Joe liked him he thought of him privately as something of a stick-in-the-mud. He couldn't understand a young fellow being so content in times like these and he was on fire himself about the country opening up, the inventions multiplying and the chances Northern capital had for investment in the South. Under all the talk of profits to be made he could feel the hurry and the excitement and he and Mr. Blondell worked themselves up wondering what the West was like.

Joe got the old feeling he had when reading the *Life of Daniel Boone* and when he walked into the office in the morning he wondered if he weren't wasting the best years of his life when there was so much adventure to be had for the taking. He and Blondell talked of fortunes to be made and how small the world was and that travel wasn't anything any more until the world seemed to spin around like a top and all he had to do was to twist a string to make it hum for him.

One night he hit on the idea that fortunes were like continents in Columbus's day, just waiting to be discovered, and he and Blondell sat discussing it until Lucy got impatient and began playing and singing all by herself in the big almost empty parlor. He could hear her lovely voice, plaintive in its sadness, and it was a pleasure to sit there and prolong her singing and know that the song was meant for him. The talk about the continents got all mixed up in his mind with Lucy and when they at last walked out to move around the ragged lawn and stand in the shadow of the grape arbor he began to talk crazy and before he knew, he'd blurted out that she must marry him. She was as cool as a little cucumber, looking at him with her great mocking eyes as if she were surprised he had had any doubts at all about their future and yet suddenly by her very gaze putting a wall between herself and him.

"What is it Lucy?"

"What is what?" said Lucy, holding her head far back and looking him straight in the eyes from under such heavy lids that he could hardly bear it and squeezed her hand until it hurt and she said, "Don't," with a kind of furious admiration that made him feel it wouldn't be so easy to be married to her and he was glad of it. Walking home that night from the livery stable where he'd left the horses, he wished again he could write poetry and little Nannie lying in her grave hurt him to think of more than the day she had died. He couldn't understand why he thought of death on such a happy night when he was almost wild for joy of living in a world like this, but tiptoeing up the stairs in the Fawcett house the cuckoo clock sounded in the hall and one of the birds in its cage rustled.

He put off writing home for days, uneasy, thinking of his plans for himself and Lucy. He'd better wait to spring the news until after he had bought a house for Mem and furnished it from top to bottom. The Fawcetts moved out of their old house into the new and Joe moved with them, taking his music box, shotgun and rifle, the two birds in their big cage and his clothing neatly packed. In spite of fires the house was damp and Joe came down with chills and fever. Grandma came to see him every day peering down at him shaking her head and moaning that it was a bad sign to have sickness in a new house. Lucy wrote him little notes and in the daze of his fever he worried about the office and suddenly felt alarm for his books and that they might be tampered with. Alone in his room, some of the doings at the office bothered him and he tried not to think and took a double dose of medicine to keep himself half sleeping.

Still weak, he got up after two weeks in time to make the trip with the pay roll and coming back, found that Grandma Fawcett had fallen from a chair as she was feeding his birds and had broken her hip. Now it seemed as if the house had real ill luck in it and Joe was frightened, the more so because George kept assuring him he was in no way to blame. The entire family were more cordial to him than ever, Mr. Fawcett even coming into his room the first night with a hot drink to brace him.

"Don't trouble yourself," he said heartily. "It's not at all your fault. None of us feel that way. A mere accident that the birds were yours." Something about Fawcett's cheerful manner disturbed Joe and sent a shiver up his spine. He was only weak, he told himself, and imagining things, but a few days later when George urged him to get in on one of the good games at the Turf Exchange he had the same feeling. No one without a wad to lose sat in on the green room games at the Turf Exchange. They were staged for Northern financiers looking the South over for cheap land and factory sites. Many an Ohio or New York man steadied his nerves at midnight play at George's. What had he to do with that kind of thing? He consulted Roger Wallace and Roger urged him to try it. "You can't more than lose and perhaps you'll get in with some of these big fellows and get a chance to make an investment that will set you up for life." That won Joe, and he went to the Turf Exchange that night. George met him and whispered he was not to worry.

"I'll take a chance on you," George said. "We've got some people from your own town, Philadelphia, here tonight." Joe laughed and moved uneasily toward the group. He hoped George wouldn't say anything about his being from Philadelphia. He didn't want to tell the neighborhood he lived in. The next time he went North he'd see to it the family moved and he'd see they had the house furnished with fine stuff so no one would ever need be ashamed again. His head up, he looked the Philadelphia customers in the eye and felt a kind of contempt for them.

They looked him over too and suddenly as he began to play he felt cool and calm. The coughs and the shuffling of the cards, the smoke and now and then someone crowding behind his chair, his feet sweating, marked the progress of the game and before he knew it he had won and lost and won again. He made up his mind he'd quit before he had a chance to lose again and went to the bar. George came after him and said he couldn't leave the game so early, not when the others wanted their revenge. It was now past three and Joe shook his head. A man from Boston had quit and was putting on his tie. He said, "It's late enough, if we all get revenge, the thing will never end. Not tonight George," and walked out disturbed again at a sudden look on George's face, baffled and half angry. Hadn't George wanted him to win? He should have thought he would, and he had paid him back, dollar for dollar. What was wrong then? He couldn't fathom all the ins and outs and lately he had imagined something stealthy in people's looks. It must be because he was still weak from his sickness and nothing more.

But one night coming home late, he was not surprised when Fawcett stepped quietly from behind the portières of the parlor and in a hesitating way suggested that he

might do better for himself further north. Somehow it
seemed as if he had always known this would happen and
he looked back at Fawcett now, steadily, thought a minute
and then said, "I don't see that. I've got investments here.
I like it here."

"Perhaps," said Fawcett looking at his long hand and
the starched cuff and the heavy gold link that in the reflection of the purple glassed hall lamp looked very ghost-
like and unreal. "But Bullock is hard pressed. The road
will be turned over to private management. You might
find it uncomfortable if an investigation took place."

Joe opened his mouth to ask why he, more than another,
then shut it without a word. He saw it clear enough. He
was a Yankee and in the rush he would be the bone thrown
to the dogs. It was like that, the pack had yowled and
howled for blood for a long time now. He felt trapped
and at the same time stubborn. After all, what had he
done that Fawcett had not fully approved? He lifted his
head, looked Fawcett in the eye, and said, "Thanks. I think
I'll stay." Fawcett shrugged his shoulders and said he
hoped he'd not regret it, then turned and went up the
stairs, his shoulders sagging a trifle heavier like those of
an older man. Joe was happy at what seemed his own bold-
ness and went upstairs to dash off a letter to Philadelphia,
full of confidence in the powers of Joshua Trexler's son.
He had looked Fawcett in the eye and he had won.

But now the talk about the road that had been bottled
up in rebel newspapers and certain circles spread over the
town and no one thought of sitting down at table without a few remarks about those Fawcetts and that bunch of
scalawags and whatever will become of us. Even at the
Blondell's Joe had to face comment and Blondell with a

half laugh asked what about that Tennessee Car Company.

"That's Trimble's company," Joe said. "It's all right. Look at Trimble. There's no one else so enterprising."

"Easy enough to be enterprising on somebody else's money," said Blondell. "What do you think of the talk that that company exists only in the minds of a few people?"

"I think that's a lie," Joe said. He did think so. He couldn't believe that cars would not be delivered yet. True enough a check had gone to pay for cars in advance and no cars were to show for it, but anyone on the inside knew how closely linked politics and the road were. Some enterprise on which the whole thing hung doubtless called for money. You couldn't explain these things and only being on the inside made them seem real. He was uneasy thinking of them as he stood there facing Blondell trying to make up his mind what was the truth. There wasn't any truth. That was what he had learned. There were a dozen sides to every question. He had to believe that in order to get ahead. Or go back in the basement and knead dough. Blondell seeing his troubled look laughed and said, "Take it easy, Joseph, only look out."

Mrs. Blondell looked at her husband and shook her head. "Why should you worry him? He's not to blame. I can't see how you can blame anyone for the dust in a dust storm. It's over everything, the dust, on all alike. Why Millie Gaskill was here this morning, worried into a fit almost, because she was afraid her husband had been polluted by Western & Atlanta gold. He's a loyal Democrat, an honest lawyer, and he'd got some lordly sum for drawing up a few miserable papers."

Lucy was tired of the talk and had moved toward the door, standing there, indifferently, with only her eyes steady and insistent on Joe's face. Lenore was sitting with her schoolbooks and kept looking uneasily from Joe to

Lucy. She couldn't bear it if they left the room together. She made a desperate effort to talk and forced out of her dry throat, "How do you like the new house?"

"Fine," said Joe, smiling and moving toward Lenore. He felt easy and happy talking to her as if she were one of his sisters. He liked her small sharp wrists and the little pathetic nape of her neck. He wished he could think of something to say to her now. He smiled again instead and Lucy made a movement by the door. He turned and followed her, looking back at Lenore, smiling. The child slammed her book shut and stared across the table. "Why whatever?" said her mother.

"Excuse me," said Lenore. "I'm tired." Her lips trembled. She didn't know why she should feel so alone in the world when she had wonderful parents and a brother and sisters and was doing well at school. In a few more years she would teach and be able to help the younger ones to a good education. Oh that was it, she would always be helping others all her life. She felt it in her very bones. Not like Lucy, who would be tended and loved. She could feel the tears itch as they began trickling, and went quickly to the window. From there she could see the back of the grape arbor where they were. They would be sitting there talking. And what would Lucy have to talk about when she didn't have an idea in her head except her face? She was a cat, just content to stretch and bask and feel her own fur patted and lap her milk and purr. She'd never read a book. Lenore wiped her eyes and crouched in front of the big dictionary pretending to look up a word. The tears came faster and she left the room. Why should she cry? Nothing, nothing at all. And she cried the harder, feeling her way up the stairs in the dark.

When Joe went home from the Blondells' garden the Fawcett house was dark but for a light from Fawcett's study. He entered quietly into the dark hall. Tiptoeing past Grandma Fawcett's room he strained his ears to hear if she were stirring in her bed and was relieved when all was quiet. She'd live and even walk again, he knew that now, and something of the fear he'd had lifted. He knew that nothing he could ever do for her would be too much to compensate her for her pain. It frightened him to think of this obligation. He took off his coat and laid his watch open on the table. It wasn't a good enough watch, cheap, and cheap things were degrading. He'd get the very best watch made and see that Catherine had a good watch too. By Christmas he would have enough to buy a house and furnish it. This year would be a Christmas to remember. When had the family ever had such a day? He couldn't remember one, while people like the Fawcetts had them so often it meant nothing to them. That very afternoon when Langford had given him the knives and forks, George Fawcett had hardly looked at them. A dozen solid silver pearl handled knives and forks and spoons were worth considerable and yet George had acted careless and indifferent and had told Joe to think nothing of it, it was customary to give presents like that.

"You did him a favor," George said. "Why shouldn't he do you one? We don't need to buy from Langford Brothers, in fact I'm not so sure Cuppy & Treader wouldn't give us a better price."

"They bid lower," Joe said.

Then George said that price wasn't everything. Quality ought to be considered and he'd added that it might be practical to buy up that Cuppy lot and hold it to resell to the road later. He had rubbed his chin and left the office and Joe still felt disturbed and uncomfortable remembering that remark. Did George do that kind of thing himself? He couldn't go to sleep wondering and forgot all about Christmas and the presents.

He lay in his bed and longed to feel at ease. A kind of shame that George might think him just a fool not to be making the most of his chances kept him wide awake. He could see that the old railroad crowd were not so optimistic lately as they had been. Some pretty greedy goings-on took place in front of him every day. He didn't want to be laughed at by older and more experienced men. Probably what he felt was just old fashioned or Yankee. They did everything differently in the South. He told himself that a dozen times a day and he said it to himself now, in bed, and it made him feel easier. His father with his ideas wouldn't have understood business in the South. But everything was changed since his father's day. The war did that. People had different ideas now. He thought with a kind of pity of some of his father's old fashioned precepts. His mother was like that now, old fashioned. There was no use trying to explain things to her. The best he could do was to make life easy for her. He wasn't a boy any more. He felt very old at that moment and considered that he had been growing up fast.

He didn't like to be alone any more and began going a good deal to the theater in the evenings. Sometimes Roger Wallace went with him but Roger was tiresome with his complete belief in Fawcett and that crowd. "Do you really think Bullock will hold out?" Joe asked coming home from a gloomy but spectacular *Macbeth*. "Who? Bullock? Why, of course, and why shouldn't he? The man has zeal, give him time and he'll really pull the South out of the mire."

"Suppose he doesn't?"

"Don't cross bridges. If he doesn't—he won't be much of a hero and they'll get fun out of blackening him. It's

too soon to judge what's going to happen. Aren't thinking
of leaving are you?"

"No, what made you think I was?"

"Fawcett said something. Maybe it wasn't Fawcett. I
wondered."

"No, I'm not leaving. Nobody else is, why should I?"

"Don't fire up at me," Roger said. "I was only quoting
what I'd heard. And perhaps I didn't hear it." He began
to whistle in an irritatingly cheerful way but still Joe
couldn't help liking the fellow he was so good natured and
innocent. Joe thought of himself as anything but innocent
any more.

By December 1, it was certain the road would be leased
to former Governor Brown and his outfit. The elections
were over and it looked as if Governor Bullock would find
the next legislature a tough nut to crack. Fawcett was
agitating about his seat in the Senate that was up for
investigation and going back and forth to Washington,
left the road clear for the minor road officials who were
transacting all the business they could before it was too
late.

Orders for twine, bolts, nuts, lard, oil, poured through
Joe's hands. He stayed at the office late at night reading
the New York papers and keeping notes in a small black
book about accounts and transactions he alone knew.
The little office seemed remote and obscure and safe at
night but reading the papers he felt small and out of
things. Prices were high, businesses failing and yet Northern papers talked about good times and all the Fawcett
crowd were building houses, fences, and making improve-
ments.

News like the hanging of Reuben Wright, a Negro,
upset him and reading it at ten o'clock at night with
street noises muffled by the window shades, he felt kind of
ill and wondered what he'd had to eat to upset him.

Reuben Wright had shot Ezra Pease, also colored, over some black wench or maybe she was Reuben's wife. He was hanged, out in public, with a big crowd looking on "for a lesson." They'd worked it so he made a speech and told how he deserved it and hoped they'd take warning from him, a sinner, and then the noose had tightened and he swung. The crowd went crazy and a white man stuck a knife between his teeth and rolled in the dust yelling, "Kill him, kill him, kill forty more like him!" and no one thought it was out of the way to hear him yell like that. Joe could tell by the calm way the papers wrote it up that it was just what they might have expected, or were they so used to shocks and yells and murders that one man howling after forty more meant nothing? It upset him and he thought that in a pinch Roger Wallace wasn't much to count on.

The night Joe met old Colonel Balstock at the Blondell's everyone was talking about the big Tammany steals and about the scandal at the Mint and a dozen other affairs to show that after all Atlanta with her talk of a little railroad fraud wasn't so bad. The old man refused to shake hands with Joe, grumbling, "You are all smeared with the same tar, every man jack of you, don't believe there are two honest men left in this town unless it's Blondell and me, and I'm not sure of Blondell." He hissed and coughed back of his shaking white mustache as if he were handling burning matches in his mouth. Joe tried to laugh it off and Blondell begged him not to take offense, the old fellow had his foibles but a kind heart, still Joe's spirits fell and he had a hard time getting through the evening, even with Lucy teasing and coaxing.

For every Colonel Balstock refusing to shake his hand there was a hanger-on glad to show he thought Joe a good fellow. Firms that stood well with the Republicans haunted the office, waiting to make more money before their chance was gone. Wheedlers with specially priced goods waited for hours and young Caldwell of the E. C. and J. O. Caldwell firm hung around getting into long confidential talks with Joe. Roger warned Joe to go slow with young Caldwell as it was well known he was a high-flyer. The warning complimented Joe, he plumed himself for being selected as a companion of Caldwell's. Caldwell's house was given preference in a last big buy of the road and the two young men went to the theater together and Joe stayed out at hours that made Grandma Fawcett anxious.

Joe called at the Blondells' less that month and Lucy worried and blamed old Colonel Balstock. Joe told her it was nothing but business and when the holidays were over he'd be a free man.

"Why what do you mean? Aren't you free now?"

"Well, yes, but you see the road will change hands, and I'll be out of it. It hangs over me, all this business."

"What business?" Lucy said.

"Oh you wouldn't understand. It's nothing." But once when he had left her, he ran back and took her tight in his arms and made her promise never to let anything separate them, trembling very much so that Lucy was worried and made him come back into the house and drink a hot toddy.

A week before Christmas, Joe dashed off a note to Catherine saying he would pick up a few little tricks for the family but they were not to call him extravagant or he wouldn't give any more. A few days before Christmas he stayed late at the office to see to the expressing of his packages and to write a letter to Catherine.

My dear Sister,
    I am sending today a small pkg. containing 1 dozen solid silver spoons and 1 dozen forks and knives. They were given to me by a firm from whom we buy. The

weight is 24.5 oz. and cost in New York $2.75 per oz.
You must be very careful about the silverware I send
you. Somebody might make it an object of theft. The box
of knives and forks cost $280. The tea set I sent several
days ago was made by Tiffany and cost $810. So don't let
anyone steal it. I want to tell you that should you ever receive a telegram signed George Fawcett or any other name
you may know it's from me and if you want to answer it
send it to the same name and take the telegram you get
to the Tel office and inform the operator that yours is an
answer so it won't cost anything. I merely tell you this to
put you on guard because sometimes I might want
to know something or someone might be sick—anything
might happen when we would want to correspond by tele-
graph. Tell Mother she must not say I am extravagant
or I may not give any more. Grandma Fawcett wants me
to send her love to all.

Your affectionate Brother

ps. I told you $100 of the money I sent to Aaron was to
buy a watch for you. I have thought since it might not be
enough. I want you to have a fine watch and if it is not
enough tell Aaron I say to give you two hundred.

When he finished the letter he was in a warm glow of
approval. He thought of the astonished happiness he meant
to bring them and it seemed worth any risk. They deserved
the best and he only hoped his luck would last. "Business
has been good," he wrote Aaron and followed up his letters
by an early visit home.

Joe was now a hero. The girls fought for the right to
sit beside him and when he talked they sat beaming in
a row opposite, watching every word, the way his mouth
opened and his eyes looked at them. Even Mem hid her
eternal buttonholes during the week he was home and

insisted on an exact account of how he came to make so much money. She could not make head or tail of it and respected her son and his knowledge of high finance. Buying and selling was the order of the day and everyone knew that was the way to make money, not by hard work, like the suits and buttonholes. But money come at in that way did not seem reliable and she must hold it in her hands before she could believe. When Joe actually put the bills into her hands that were to buy the new home, she sat there stupefied and proud and a little unbelieving. It was hard for her to show her happiness because she had no belief in the good times. They came and went again and so it must always be, she thought. But buying a house was sensible, you had something then.

Joe would not hear of a house except in the best part of town. Property on Broad Street was higher than he could go and he had to content himself with Fifteenth Street, a block away from Broad. It was a fine new house and on the shopping trips for furniture, the idea was to buy only the best. The best carpets, the finest parlor furniture, with silk damask upholstery, the best mattresses and beds. The phrase "nothing but the best" echoed in the girls' heads after they were in bed. It never really left their heads again in all their lives. The girls even began to try to walk with greater dignity to fit the new house. When the day came to move, Joe superintended everything and had the piano put in the place of honor. Late that night, although many boxes were yet to unpack, Anne and Catherine played their first duet for Joe. He sat very still as the sisters played, their fingers whisking over the keys, their heads lifted and cheeks flushed. Something about the music, its childishness, the eagerness with which they sat there, their slim necks, disturbed him, he felt tears in his eyes and angry at himself rose and walked to the window. He stood there with his back turned while Catherine sat with hands folded and Anne began "Listen to the Mocking Bird." When he finally turned to thank them, they saw the tears in his eyes and were certain he was thinking of little Nannie Ellis lying in her grave. It only made them love him more to see his feeling and in their room that night both girls added a long and special prayer of thanks for their dear and generous brother.

It took almost a week to get the new house into shape. The new carpets must be laid, curtains selected and hung and everything must be just right. In the dining room the silver tea set with its eight pieces and delicate handles of ivory and carved figures had the place of honor. Catherine couldn't keep away from it and loved to touch the silky silver, so cold and clear that her own face was reflected back at her. The tea set was the center of the house; it almost seemed as if the house had been purchased to give it a proper setting. On one side of each piece was engraved, *From Joseph*. On the other side, *Christmas 1870*. Joe tried to make believe the silver tea set wasn't much but he kept gravitating to it and couldn't help taking pride in that phrase *From Joseph*. His generosity seemed now to go on forever in that engraved silver. No matter what happened, the tea set would repeat *From Joseph*.

Nearly every evening they all sat together in the new parlor with everything spick and span, admiring, and talking about the old days in Locust Valley. The family could spend an entire evening in such simple pleasures and Joe was the center of it all, even on the nights Aaron came up from Grapeville and stood slouching on the outskirts, half smiling, his hair mussed up, feeling ludicrous in comparison to the elegant Joe.

They had not been living in their new home a week before David discovered that their back yard faced the back yard of Edwin Forrest, the great tragedian. David had only to walk into his own alley and find himself overlooking the stables of the famous actor. Each day around four o'clock he was one of a group of admiring boys, gaping, while the old actor wrapped in a great fur collared coat stalked majestically out of his house and mounting the carriage steps via a little stool, seated himself for his daily drive. When Joe heard this he was very excited and thought what conversation it would make back in Atlanta and how proud he would be to say his family lived near the great actor's house, neighbors in fact. He managed to saunter through the alley as the carriage turned out of the stables and wheeled into the main street.

It was a narrow driveway and the coachman pulled in, afraid to spatter the fashionably dressed young man. Forrest in his fur robes was staring ahead with his worn face assuming even in that carriage a tragic look, but as the carriage swerved he looked straight at Joe and seeing the good looking young man with such excited and enthusiastic eyes staring at him, he drew himself up in the grand manner and smiled proudly, as he used to smile before the beastly war, when crowds of young men rioted in New York for his sake, defending him against that lisping upstart Macready.

The smile flashed at Joe. Why, he was only an old man with false teeth, riding alone in a carriage, his best days over. Joe wished he had not seen him. But the little boys continued to hang around the stable every afternoon.

CHARMED LIVES

BACK in Atlanta he had a few days feeling high spirited as if he'd hit the town for the first time. The ride on the train had tantalized him with visions of travel and roaming around meeting all kinds of adventure. He tried to settle down to good hard work but the road had been quietly leased to the new company during his absence and the business now was to wait to see what would happen. Nobody had actually lost a job and the pay went on just the same. Ton Ferris was inclined to be a little short with everyone and he was pretty busy toadying to the new bunch and wasn't so ready to make arrangements to pay up bills that crammed into the office during emergencies.

Mr. Fawcett was definitely up on the carpet at Washington about his senatorship and Bullock was holding on at the State House with no intention of quitting. Joe began to feel that nothing harmful could ever happen to him. Papers were full of terrifying news about other people and of poor creatures being hauled from their beds. Negroes were wandering around like wild creatures or else pushing themselves forward with their uppity ways and getting lynched for daring to take their emancipation seriously and poor whites were sore and brooding for fear they would lose their jobs to Negroes now they were to be hired for next to nothing or just impressed in gangs for vagrancy. It looked bad all around and all the time the employees of the State Road were in a kind of magic kingdom where they weren't touched.

Joe began to be superstitious about luck and to quit worrying and to fancy that nothing could or would happen except lucky events. He was leading a charmed life with a growing bank account and the thought that his family lived in a fine home in Philadelphia, all paid for and which no one could take from them, made him determined to hang on to the road as long as the others did and to take his chances with the rest.

He was very different from Blake Fawcett who trusted nothing but hard cash. Fawcett on the carpet at Washington was crafty and smooth and thoroughly competent to handle the situation for all it was worth. He stayed at the

Willard, rose late and had chocolate in his silk dressing gown reading mail from home. He enjoyed letters from his fond admirers in Atlanta. He particularly enjoyed letters from Democratic renegades who for the sake of hard cash had skillfully changed allegiance. Democratic lawyers in shoals had come to the rescue of the Radicals in Georgia and for the sake of a little Western & Atlanta gold had drawn up accommodating papers and voted in accordance. V. I. Haskill was a character of this type and Mr. Blake Fawcett appreciated correspondence with him. He ripped open a letter from the gentleman as he sat in his plum colored robe, sipping chocolate and thinking rather sentimentally of his sister Estelle and her touching belief in happiness.

Atlanta Ga. March 15, 1871.

My friend,

Which is what I rise to maintain. I seat myself to state that I am in good health, "hopin that these few lines will find you enjoyin the same blessin."

I wrote you Griswold's offer. I presume you have it, 5000 cash, 5000 in 6 mo., 5000 in 12 mo. with interest.

I am telling everybody, Dems and Rads that you are *sure* to go in, that Cooper's case shuts up the Democracy and Rads will put you in on general principles.

Just send me a word. Do the skies lower? Or is the "goose hanging high?" I am going "heavy" on Morton. I say he is the second power in the government and is for you "till you cant rest." Everybody admits him to be a whale and that with him you are safe. But everybody don't imagine how much Morton wants you in.

I am just from Chatt. The W & A is in an awful fix. As I rode I prayed.

As soon as you are seated I think I shall go back. My trip helped me. I am getting hearty as a *buck* and quite *bucky!* All is well here. No news, only what you have heard, no doubt, about three Ku-Kluxers here for the penitentiary for 7 years from Chattanooga. One confessed some right smart, with more to come. A Democrat "kotch em" and has pocketed $7000 for his trouble, so rewards have done some good in finding out things.

Pass that C & Southern bill if possible.

As a Democrat, I say "I tell you" my party won't make anything out of that State Rights issue. If the Democracy want to split, let them run on the old fogy schedule. I shan't and I am not alone. With my prayers and best wishes for you personally

I am yours,

V. I. Haskill

Fawcett folded the letter and absently abstracting an elegant gold toothpick, played with it, while he opened another from the top of the pile. He appreciated letters and saved most of them. Only notes from his son George were frowned over and torn into little bits for the waste basket. Even then he occasionally dug out the pieces and carefully placing them on a plate, burned them with a match and blew the ashes into the fireplace.

He hoped George would not send him any more indiscreet memos. The fellow inherited all his lack of comprehension directly from his mother's side of the house. Why her brother was practically feebleminded. For all sensible projects he might as well be a baby in diapers.

With Fawcett in Washington, Joe had plenty of time to write home but all that spring he wrote seldom. The little band that he had equipped was in full swing and David even practiced on his flute. Hortense was not satisfied with her violin and only Catherine and Anne were really happy. David would rather play with Charley Schwartz than practice the flute and he thought more of dogs than music anyway. But by threats and promises the girls managed to get the band together for a few tunes and they kept at it in the hope of showing off the next time Joe came home.

He was a long time coming North that spring but business was very good. Mem had even given up the buttonholes and she had her hands full polishing and protecting all the fine things they now owned. The family was still admiring their new dishes, curtains, silverware, carpets and elegant parlor furniture. Aaron came up every few weeks and looked out of place in the fine rooms. But he had a bold easy way and talked a jargon of town improvement schemes and politics. He thought Joe was all wrong to get in so strong with the Republicans when their father had been a Democrat and they were a Democratic family. They could mark his words if something crooked wasn't up in Georgia and that railroad was stinking loud enough to draw buzzards away from New York even. "Watch out," Aaron said. "Someone has to pay the fiddler." And he'd sigh and shake his head and take such a satisfaction in making them all uneasy that Catherine told him in pretty vigorous terms not to worry Mem.

Catherine studied the papers and was bewildered at the stories of corruption. What kind of a world was it? She wrote Joe to ask how the railroad affairs were coming and if the new investigation they were talking up would affect him. He answered with a quick trip North, bringing the red cardinal and the mocking bird in their great cage. He also brought them a rare treat, a great bunch of bananas. They had never seen bananas before and David didn't know whether to like them or not. The bananas were hung in a little storeroom at the top of the stairs and after Joe had gone South again, the girls and Aaron soon demolished them. David decided he liked them when the bunch was half gone and coming home from school hurried up the stairs and took a quick inventory of the number of bananas left. He was more interested in the bananas than the birds but their song was clear and disturbing and the great cage made the bow window with its plants and flowering geraniums exotic and strange. He wondered what the tropics looked like and bragged about Joe and his birds and bananas to the boys at school and several of them came home with him to take a look.

Joe had come and gone again pretty quickly and his main object was to transfer all his property into Mem's name. He had admitted that the Democrats were causing trouble and while everyone expected it to blow over he wanted to be prepared. When Aaron heard of it, he snorted and volunteered that the kettle was bound to boil over sooner or later if the fire was kept hot enough, why it was a law of nature. No one paid much attention to Aaron's grumblings and he was really very cheerful that summer. He took on weight, spruced up a bit, bought a couple of new neckties and when the girls played the piano stood behind them humming loudly and wagging his head. Mem hoped he wasn't into any mischief down there in Grapeville by himself and she was glad when school was out and David was bundled off to Grapeville to be out of the way of the bad city boys and to keep a kind of check on Aaron.

Aaron was now deep in Grapeville schemes with Mr. Flemmer. Flemmer was a man of means who had lived abroad and had mixedup ideas about the Renaissance and Darwin and the origin of species and town planning and immigrant labor. He planned his town with an eye to beauty and made restrictions from the start on all the lots sold. Houses must stand back a certain number of feet, there must be so much shrubbery and so many trees. The Italian laborers brought over from vineyards were given lots in South Grapeville where the streets were not so wide and the trees were still very young. But the land was good and the houses that went up though flimsy were up to date.

Aaron boarded with a Mrs. Amy Purchant but during that summer spent a great deal of time supervising odd jobs at Mrs. Ferrol's. Mrs. Ferrol was a newcomer whose property was halfway between Grapeville and South Grapeville and had all the seclusion of real country life. She had bought the land, built the house after the English fashion, very severe, of brick, with fireplaces in every room. David was allowed to pick blackberries on her place and in the midst of the picking could hear her singing and playing the piano. Once when he thought Aaron was in town, he heard his brother's laugh and it gave him a funny feeling to be out there in the blackberry patch like that.

In the city the girls were leisurely for the first time in their lives and bought new ribbons, studied fashions and experimented with new ways to do the hair. But they kept up the serious things too and both Catherine and Anne pasted up scrapbooks of quotations that pleased them. The two older girls practiced on the piano for hours each day and Hortense mooned around and made little headway with the violin.

In June the furniture sweated and stuck to their dresses. Catherine and Hortense, both dark complexioned, turned very pale and their lips showed a white line around them on the hottest days but Anne with her fair skin and red hair turned tomato color and had to sit down in the basement kitchen with the "hired girl" to cool off. They now actually had a hired girl. A letter from the friends up-country decided Mem to ship Catherine and Hortense to Lochiel for a vacation.

These distant relatives were still spoken of as "the friends." One branch of the Trexler family had settled around Allentown and the other branch had gone west to

Buffalo Valley near Lewisburg. The relatives had traveled back and forth for seventy years and Joshua and his cousin Solomon had never parted without tears. Now the two city young ladies prepared to dazzle the backwoods cousins. But when they got there Catherine sent back word that they were not so backwoodsy as supposed as they knew something of bustles and wore overskirts. The country cousins thought the local six hundred dollar a year minister a great catch and couldn't understand the indifference shown by the city ladies. Catherine and Hortense, with the background of their fine new house in Philadelphia, enjoyed visiting for the first time in their lives and went the rounds of farmhouses being shown off and exclaimed over.

Anne sweltered in the heat, took care of the birds, practiced the piano and when the papers from Atlanta came was sometimes too stupid with the heat to wade through them. Now and then in the evening she would open one languidly and marvel at the repetition of Governor Bullock's name and the sarcasm leveled against him.

The *Sun* demanded "Where is the Governor that he is absent from the state for so long? On whose business but his own is he engaged?"

Joe wrote only a few lines asking after the birds and the music and Anne had an uncomfortable feeling that he was getting further away from them now they all were prosperous. She was only seventeen that summer and for the first time was free to read and play the piano and reflect. She was a little sad to be left behind while the other two gallivanted around the country and it seemed a curious coincidence that she should have been the one to stay home from school to help and now must be the one to stay home even during the vacations. In that mood of half sadness and feeling a little sorry for herself, she went down to Grapeville and met Mrs. Ferrol.

Oxtail

DON'T be stupid and shut your eyes and imagine that the only things in life worth while come from men and what people call romance," she used to say when she was grown and had become Anne Wendel and tried to find ways to tell her girls how best to live. "There's Mrs. Ferrol." She had only to say her name and something of the mood that must have been Mrs. Ferrol's made her raise her arm and prop her chin on her hand and look dreamy and almost like an actress, with her fine arms and red hair, and it was plain to see how important Mrs. Ferrol had been and still was.

They had read poetry together all that summer and Mrs. Ferrol had recited Shakespeare and had talked about the days when she had been on the stage and about the parts she liked to play and Anne had watched her fascinated, wondering why she was not still on the stage and what had brought her to Grapeville and why her husband had left her and the two small children.

For the first time in her life, Anne saw another person with a curiosity and an itch to understand, and every gesture that that woman made seemed suggestive of past living and was exciting to the young girl. The way Mrs. Ferrol wore her clothes and golden curls, who might not have loved her? After Mem, with her worry and drive for life, the expansive way that Mrs. Ferrol had for wasting time, for standing around in the sun and talking and rooting in the ground with fingers that loved the feel of earth and taking out wild plants and replanting them so that they grew and thrived, made Anne feel her young girlhood and the world almost more than she could stand. But just what this kind of woman did for Anne, warm and responsive child but chilled with early worries and sewing and responsibility for younger children, just what she did, with her easy standing around and her laugh coming suddenly from her in the midst of gardening as she squatted on her haunches, throwing her head back and laughing and then laughing again as if the world were the best thing that had ever happened or thought of happening, just what she did to Anne, set free a little with the new piano and Joe's wealth bursting upon them like the sun, Anne only knew years later and tried to pass on to her children.

THE AX FALLS

ANNE went back to Philadelphia that autumn loaded down with paint boxes and clippings and lists of books to read and ideas from Darwin's *Origin of Species* and doubts and found her sisters plump and brown from their upcountry visit, talkative and a little silly, especially Hortense who was puffed up over some conquest of a country youth. They were all sitting around the table after dinner and Hortense was giggling and acting nervous because she had been expecting a letter from an admirer in Allentown. The doorbell rang and she rushed to the door. Anne and Catherine followed more slowly and saw the mailman hand a letter to Hortense. She started to tear it open then gave a little scream. "Why it's for Joe."

Mem hearing them say "Joe" pushed her glasses to her forehead and came to the door. "What's that? Something wrong with Joe?"

"No, no, a letter for Joe. Do you suppose he's coming home again?" They soon decided that was what the letter meant and lived with Joe's expected visit on the brain. When a doorbell rang, one of them shot toward the door but not until another day did word come from Joe. Catherine brought the letter in and tearing it open began to read, gasped, said slowly, "Why it can't be," and to Anne's "What is it? What's happened?" she shushed and held up her hand. "Wait a minute," and read the letter through, looked at Mem and holding to the letter said, "I never heard of such a thing. Who could have done that to him?"

"Done what?" Anne said, and Mem reached out and grabbed at the letter.

"I can't understand, why, someone is accusing Joe."

"Accusing Joe?" said Mem settling her glasses.

"Yes, accusing Joe of having made away with thirty thousand dollars."

No one spoke. The girls stared at one another and felt that they were turning pale. "It's that Blake Fawcett," Catherine said. "Aaron said Joe should watch out for him."

"Let me," said Mem fumbling with the letter. But the words jumped at her. "Here," she said, "I can't make head or tail, what is it?"

"There's not much here," Catherine said. "Just that he has been accused and it's in all the papers he's sending and he can explain everything and we are not to worry."

"What papers?"

"They'll be here tomorrow, probably, we'll have to wait," but she found it hard to wait. Her hands felt cold and she wondered if she were going to be sick at her stomach. She put the letter back in its envelope and went upstairs. Her face in the glass looked pale and remote and she splashed cold water on her cheeks and rubbed them with a towel to bring back the color. She combed back her hair and looked around the room furnished with new things. It had a foreign, hotel-room look to her and she went downstairs. Mem had put the letter out of sight and David was trying to study with his head propped on his hands. Catherine sat down and tried to write a note to Aaron and covered a sheet with a scrawl of the date, August 28, 1871. August 28, 1871. August 28, 1871.

The newspapers arrived the next day and they were astonished first to find nothing, and then on an inside page an article headed in big type. CARD FROM COLONEL FAWCETT. The date was August 16. "Why this has been going on for a week," Catherine said.

Mr. Editor:

I see in each of the city papers of this date notices of the arrest of Joseph Trexler and another party, for cheating and swindling the state of a large sum of money. The fact of the commission of this act came to my knowledge sometime since, and efforts were made by myself and others to have restitution made if possible before warrants should issue, but on Saturday last, being satisfied that further efforts in that direction would be futile and for other reasons that came to my knowledge and having taken legal advice, I proceeded to swear out warrants before Judge Smith against Joseph Trexler and J. O. Caldwell testifying that I had reason to believe each one had fraudulently obtained by deceitful practises, $8000. Upon these warrants I understood both parties were arrested and waiving examination, gave bond for their appearance in the next regular term of Superior Court. One of the papers says I had them arrested for obtaining $1600 when the true amount charged was $16000. It is stated also that Mr. Joseph Trexler was a nephew of mine, a member of my family and had been my confidential secretary or clerk in the office of Superintendent of the Western & Atlantic railroad. Each of the above allegations is untrue. He is in no way related to me or to any member of my family and never was a clerk in the office of the Superintendent of the A. & W. Fourteen months he was a boarder at my house paying $25 a month. As to Mr. Trexler forfeiting his bond or leaving the city, I know nothing, I only know I told him last Saturday that he could not remain longer at my house. I acted as I thought best for the interest of the State and the promotion of justice. If I had failed to have the parties apprehended I would have been censured. So it seems, no matter what I may do, right or wrong, there are certain parties who hold me blameable. I have done what I conceive my duty in the matter and I care not who is pleased or who is displeased.   BLAKE FAWCETT

Catherine was so indignant that she could hardly speak. But it was some consolation to know that others thought Fawcett had done a terrible thing. They must have thought so or he wouldn't have felt called on to explain himself. She could see how the most innocent thing Joe would do would be misconstrued. As for his leaving the city, that was perfectly innocent, she knew very well, he had written them himself he was in Chattanooga. Anne had torn open the wrapper on the other paper and now handed it to her sister. It was the *Era* and dated August 24. "It's Joe's," Anne said.

Mr. Editor:

I addressed a letter to you a few days ago but withdrew the same on my arrival as being here I thought best to make my statement in this form. The public generally seems to be under the impression that I absented myself from the city some ten days ago because of my inability to successfully meet certain charges made against me by Mr. Blake Fawcett. It is also surmised that after having been so suddenly arrested and placed under bond for appearance, I became alarmed lest further investigations should take place. In explanation of my absence I can say that I left Atlanta with the intention of attending to some important business of my own in no way connected with the transactions that have taken place since. When I was arrested and gave the bond on the 12th and 13th instant, it was at my own urgent request, so that I might feel protected during my absence. The bond was given in good faith and my conduct in the future will clearly convince people of that fact. I am ready now, as I have been in the past, to meet, before the courts, any and all charges made against me in regard to illegal state road transactions. In the Cawkins trial several utterly false statements were made as to what I had said or done. To refute such evidence will be an easy matter when the proper time comes.

JOSEPH TREXLER

"There, you see," Anne said. She had been reading over Catherine's shoulder and as she read she was positive everything was going to come out all right. How straightforward Joe's letter sounded beside that of the perfidious Fawcett. Catherine said, "It's that Fawcett."

Mem said, "Aaron told him all along to be careful."

"It's not Joe's fault," Anne said.

"Of course not," Catherine said. She was skimming through the papers for more news. Under the caption "The City" were two little squibs. One referred to Mr. Trexler's return and said his friends were rejoiced to see him and thought undue advantage had been taken of his absence. The other was a question. *"QUERY: Mr. Trexler returned to our city day before yesterday from Philadelphia, he says. Does anyone know the trains upon which he left and returned?"*

The query made Catherine uneasy again but she said nothing to the others. They all hoped Aaron would come to the city as soon as he heard the news. Mem made Catherine write a letter to Joe and get it mailed.

My Dear Brother,

Recd. yours of the 24th this morning, very glad indeed to hear from you but somewhat alarmed at the intelligence it contained. Although we are still in the dark yet more enlightened since we recd. your papers this afternoon. I hardly know what I shall write, in fact we can think of little else. The very idea that you should be brought into such trouble. Who is that man that dares to injure your reputation? Did Blake Fawcett bring the charge of his own accord or did others force him to it? I wish you were home just one hour so that we might hear and know how matters stood. Of course to speak plain mother is anxious and desires you to lookout for yourself and your belongings. Has this fraud the papers speak of any reference to those buying up claims along the road? Sincerely hoping you will have a chance to vindicate all charges made against you which must necessarily injure your reputation. You know there are some people who once receiving an impression immediately admit it as a fact, and without making any further inquiry, would censure you. Write Immediately.

Your Ever Loving

Sister Catherine

That finished, she tried to take an interest in her scrap-book but an editorial on "Hospitality" and another on "Restraint" seemed stupid and she wondered why they had ever interested her. Mem made no comments but looked worried and indignant. During the evening Catherine or Anne burst out about "that Fawcett" who had always pretended to be such a friend. How could people do such things? This tortured Catherine more than anything else. Whom could one trust? All her resolution could not keep her from feeling chilled and frightened.

No word came from Joe for days. Aaron came up from Grapeville, stood around with his hands in his pockets, shrugged, munched cookies and trod crumbs in the good carpets and finally told them there was no use crossing a bridge until they came to it. Mem snorted at his speech and that same day began saving drippings in the big iron kettle that they had made soap in back in Locust Valley. The girls played the piano and did a few sober pieces and hymns. When a letter came from Joe, Catherine slit it nervously, almost afraid to see. There was a check inside and Joe was certain everything would turn out all right. Mem cheered up and they had dumplings for supper. Most of the money was deposited immediately and after a family discussion Catherine wrote again to Joe.

My dear Brother:

Recd yours of the 9th. What a good thing it is that you have such firm friends, those whom you have tested and on whom you can depend in this day of need. The very fact that you have so many friends must be sufficient proof to all that you are entirely innocent, but we are so glad that you have such a good chance to prove your innocence to the world. You are perfectly right and all credit belongs to you for taking every precaution so as not to leave Atlanta until all is settled. Judging from your letter the F's are indeed wading more than knee deep in hot water, if it was cold water they might freeze, but as it is they must be on the watch day and night or it might overpower them. I am so glad that you have completely outwitted them, they are beginning to learn what you are made of and will probably cease to make an effort to mould you into any other form, but that of Joe Trexler. What a mass of human beings this is, how is one to tell on whom he can rely or who are the traitors? Mother wants to know whether you are to buy or sell any property now that the property is not released, or how do matters stand, if such were the case, that you could not carry on business it would certainly be a great disadvantage to you. Mother deposited $2300 of the money you sent. With a part she means to purchase blankets and some linens for the house and settle a bill for some china she got, as mother says nothing goes so fast as money. There is the painter's bill remaining unpaid and then there is the third story front room to furnish of course we can do without this yet, but as mother does not want to spend any money unless it is necessary, she wants to hear what you say to do. David is lazy and would rather talk to Harry Fell than practise the flute. Mother says do not leave any of your *gold* behind. When you send your rifle and music box if you have any cast off clothing, send it for David. We have not become much acquainted with our new neighbors but the one below is the most inquisitive woman I ever saw she had the impudence the other day to ask Anne if the house was mother's or yours. Please write soon. Where are you boarding now?

Ever Your Loving
Sister Catherine

The letter got off that evening and now there was nothing to do except to wait for Joe to come home. They were certain he would do even better in the North, nearer home.

II. BIG FROG EVIDENCE

O N THE morning of August 12, 1871, Joseph Trexler was arrested on the warrant of his friend and patron, the Honorable Blake Fawcett, candidate for the United States Senate and former superintendent of the State Road. The charge was cheating and swindling. On the same day a like warrant was sworn to by Colonel Fawcett and arrest made against Mr. J. O. Caldwell. Both gentlemen waived examination and gave bond for their appearance in the next term of Superior Court. Caldwell was surprised and scared at this turn of affairs and before the news had leaked out got in touch with the bookkeeper of the road, C. P. McCall, and told him of his arrest. McCall scratched his little mat of hair on the back of his head and turned to his friend Major Hargreeves of Rome. "You see what I told you. Fawcett's trying to beat us."

"You can catch him," Hargreeves said. "Don't forget, he's the real piece of cheese."

"He's sly all right. Why he was in this office three days ago offering to pay off the whole amount against these two if we would hush it up. He's been making one excuse after another for months."

"How long has he known it?"

"Since June, so far as I know. Earlier probably. George Fawcett knew. He was in on it."

"George Fawcett was in on it," Caldwell said.

"This money Caldwell and Trexler pocketed was nothing compared to what went down somebody's gullet."

"I tell you McCall your move must be quick. He thinks

he'll distract the public with Caldwell and Trexler. How'd you like to be meat for the lions, hey, Caldwell?" Caldwell smiled sickishly. He felt very much mistreated. He had offered to pay back every cent he had taken, three thousand nine hundred dollars, and tell all he knew besides and in payment for his bravery and generosity, they had arrested him. He sat pouting his small red mouth trying to look dignified. Hargreeves was smoking a big pipe and he blew some of the smoke toward Caldwell. "Your story doesn't jibe with Trexler's."

"Trexler thinks he can get out of it. He's got so much on Fawcett, he thinks they won't dare go very far," said Caldwell.

"He's fooled there," McCall said. "Fawcett is sharper than he is, and I admit he's sharp. But Fawcett is going to make anything Trexler says look unreliable, do you see. That's why he got him arrested."

"What about me? He can't hang much on Trexler without me and isn't my word unreliable too in that case?" Caldwell said.

"Not unless Fawcett wants to press the matter, it isn't. Wait and see. Ain't that so Hargreeves?"

"We've got some cards up our sleeves. To begin with, get busy swearing out warrants yourself. Begin working gradually up to the big bugs. Why not take Cawkins as a starter?"

"Cawkins was in with the crowd, all right. Besides I found out he has a bank account of thirty thousand and he made something like three thousand a year as auditor. Pretty fair," said McCall.

"How's your own bank account?" said Hargreeves.

"Mine? Above board, anyhow. They can't get me there."

"They might cook up something but we'll be ready for them," said Hargreeves. Caldwell sat dejectedly and now he snuffled and looked at McCall. "What had I better do? Here I gave back every penny, I turned it over and you gave me a receipt. Now I'm no better off than Trexler who hasn't given back a cent. Is that fair?"

"Mr. Caldwell," said Major Hargreeves impressively, "have you noticed any extensive display of fairness in any of the events that have been occurring in this state for some time? If so, you have a perfect right to expect fairness now." He turned his back and Caldwell, trying to appear chipper and on good terms with everyone, took himself off.

"What do you make of him?" McCall said.

"I don't think of him at all," said Hargreeves. "But now you speak of it, I don't trust him. He's too loud with his confessions of guilt. Why he enjoys it, like the fellow at the revival who keeps on repenting year after year. This fellow is looking out for himself but even so, some of his story rings true. The unpleasant odor of truth. What do you make of Trexler?"

"Trexler wasn't thinking. Nobody has been thinking. He wanted to make money like all the rest. He admits certain things and denies others point blank. He knows enough to put the big ring behind the bars."

"There's going to be some fast running around here, or I'm mistaken," Hargreeves said.

"Let's get after that Cawkins warrant. That arrest will start the ball rolling and surprise our friend Fawcett." McCall hooked down his hat from a peg with his ruler, smoothed the ribbon with his hand and perched it jauntily on top of his skull.

Complaining loudly of the heat the two descended the stairs and paused on the way to duty to take a little liquid refreshment at a bar.

Cawkins was arrested in his home in Marietta at an early hour on the sixteenth of August charged with being connected with the State Road swindle. In the afternoon the preliminary examination before Judge Cutts commenced in a packed courtroom. Messrs. Hargreeves, P. A. Fowler, M. J. Becker and Hill & Brother lined up for the prosecution and the defense had procured Messrs. Gardner and Wills, famous criminal lawyers, and Hatcher & Hatcher. The heat was almost overpowering, though his Honor Judge Cutts and several attorneys took things very coolly. Some legal sparring was engaged in much to the edification of the crowd of eager listeners.

Major George Garnett was the first witness. He testified to a conversation between Mr. Cawkins and himself which took place at the Sassoon House some two months ago in connection with a fraudulent transaction in connection with the purchase of supplies for the State Road. He had heard it rumored that Mr. Cawkins was in some measure

CONNECTED WITH SOME OF THESE FRAUDS

and in order that Mr. Cawkins might have an opportunity to clear himself from the imputation, he introduced the subject. McCall had dined with them but had walked out afterward and was not present at said conversation. Mr. Garnett informed Mr. Cawkins that it was rumored that he (Cawkins) had received eight hundred dollars as his share of a certain transaction. At first Mr. Cawkins attempted a denial but afterwards

ACKNOWLEDGED IT,

and said that he had given Mr. McCall four hundred of the amount. Subsequently the witness had seen Mr. McCall and informed him of the statement of Mr. Cawkins as to the four hundred dollars.

An account of the trial duly appeared in the daily papers and was carefully read by Mr. Blake Fawcett, Mr. K. I. Trimble, the several witnesses, the Misses Lucy and

Lenore Blondell, as well as countless others. The business of whether or not Cawkins had accepted eight hundred dollars and had given four hundred to McCall distracted the citizens and kept them from considering the major issues. A copy of the *Era* was picked up at twelve noon the preceding day in Chattanooga by Joseph Trexler disguised in a new plug hat and a large cigar, who hastily scanned the paper, took it to the privacy of his room and read it inch by inch.

His own name had come up and its prejudiced treatment by the judge did not cheer him but at the same time it was no more than was to be expected. His position was exactly nowhere. The prosecution or the defense would use him if they could. Caldwell would save his own skin and Cawkins would play the innocent white lamb, at least until news of his bank account got on the stand. McCall was out for Fawcett's scalp and the higher-ups. It was his one chance to get in with the new administration and hold down a job. Garnett was with McCall because he knew the jig was up with Fawcett. Bullock was out of the state and probably had been expecting this all along. He was alone and what of it? He puffed hard on his cigar and tried to study the paper. He knew Fawcett inside and out and if he beat him, it would have to be at his own sanctimonious game. News of the big steals was bound to come out and when it did, his own small transgressions would be trifling. There wasn't a man in Atlanta that wasn't tarred with railroad money. If he went back now and wrote a frank open letter to the press, the kind Fawcett was so good at, admitting he had been slack about certain things and was anxious to make a clean breast of everything so that the people could judge, he would confuse a number of people and gain time. He felt happy at this inspiration and began making notes for the letter on the back of an envelope.

He studied the *Era* all the time remembering it was the organ of the Fawcett crowd. Then he sauntered out and picked up the *Constitution* in the hotel lobby. The *Constitution* was on Fawcett's trail and small fry like Cawkins were so much red herring. They announced it was clear "the prosecution was trying hard to make a scapegoat of the clerk Trexler and to invalidate his testimony in advance as he may know too much."

Joe now saw he had made a mistake to run off. But Fawcett had put the idea into his head. It had been a clever move on Fawcett's part and made him feel a fool to have fallen in with it.

His worst blunder was the promise he had given Grandma Fawcett. She had come into his room when he was packing his things and had stood there, leaning on her cane looking at him and not saying a word. Every time he saw that cane he had to remember she was using it because her hip had been broken while she was feeding his birds. The cane was all he could see out of a corner of an eye as he shut the little trunk and started strapping it. She had moved toward him then and he had looked up at her, she was trembling very much and pale as a sheet. He hadn't been prepared for her to ask him to promise not to tell what he knew about her son. She had grabbed hold of his hand, looking him straight in the eyes, and had made him promise on the Bible, on his honor, on his love for his own mother, and all those words were too much for him, she especially could not be hurt and he had promised patting her shoulder suddenly as if she had been a child. Now he couldn't help but suspect that perhaps Fawcett had put her up to it. He doubted everything Fawcett was connected with and could hardly look himself in the face for shame that he had been under the man's influence for so long. Why he had actually been half convinced when Fawcett told him that the swearing of the warrant meant nothing, it was a sort of necessary evil, a gesture to the public and behind the scenes they were still the best of friends.

For the first time he felt entirely alone and very small and surrounded by enemies. Was Roger Wallace to be trusted? After all he was going to marry Estelle, Fawcett's sister. The only thing to do was to put on a bold front and go back to Atlanta. If he couldn't tell what he knew because of his promise to Grandma Fawcett, there were others who would tell. He turned in at a bar and ordering a whisky and soda swiftly drank it. He gave a short laugh and could feel the man next to him stare with a look that bored his cheek. He deliberately laughed again and turning, said, "Excuse me, I'm afraid I laughed out loud. Funny thing, I was thinking of a joke I heard at a minstrel show. Ever go to one?"

"Why no," the man said, the stare melting. "No, I never did. Reckon I should if there is a laugh in it. The state things are in. What do you think of that outburst in Atlanta? About time things blew up. Of course New York, it's to be expected, Tammany is no surprise to me but when it hits so close you begin to think." Joe shook his head commiserating and nervously pulled out his watch and took the time of day carefully. In the act he felt the other man's stare again. The stranger seemed to be evaluating that thin gold watch and its works and chain and before he could begin on Joe himself, Joe slid the watch back and paying the bartender, left. He felt uneasy, more at the discovery in himself of a continual nervous fear than at any recognition from the man in the bar. As he went down the street he had the feeling that his clothes were no longer an asset; they were conspicuously too good and it gave his very insides a cold feeling as if he were about to be opened and examined like the inside of a watch.

In the morning his head ached, he wondered if he were coming down with malaria and decided to postpone going back until he heard the outcome of the Cawkins business.

The trial went on before another crowded courtroom. Judge Cutts spread a wet handkerchief over his hot bald head. Mr. Ton Ferris the treasurer of the road and young George Fawcett made the most stir. The witnesses agreed that there had been something peculiar about the bills in question but although their several suspicions had been aroused nothing had been done about it. It was not their duty. It was the duty of someone else.

It was not the duty of Mr. Cawkins, the auditor.

It was not the duty of Mr. McCall, the bookkeeper.

It was not the duty of Mr. Ferris, the treasurer.

Nor of Mr. George Fawcett, the purchasing agent.

In the discussion aroused by the different gentlemen concerning their duties, the case of Mr. Cawkins almost disappeared.

By skillful cross questioning the eminent defense attorney, General Gardner, managed to elicit from several witnesses the impression that Mr. Cawkins was an innocent man, imposed on by Joseph Trexler, a Yankee, and used by that person as his dupe and tool.

The prosecution, to offset this, brought Mr. Cawkins himself to the stand for a brief moment.

Fowler (for the prosecution): Now Mr. Cawkins, will you kindly tell us the amount of your salary as auditor of the State Road.

Cawkins: Three thousand dollars.

Fowler: And now, will you also be good enough to tell us how you managed on such a salary to save upwards of thirty thousand dollars in the space of less than two years.

Cawkins: By virtue of the strictest economy, sir.

Even Judge Cutts grinned as he rapped with his gavel

for order. The witness left the stand looking grave and injured.

It was a satisfactory day. A search had been made for Joseph Trexler and he was reported absconded with varying huge sums on his person. Mr. Fawcett wrote more pious letters to the papers averring his intention to do all in his power to bring the criminals to time.

The third day finished the business. The prosecution was opened by Major Fowler, solicitor general, who said the trial had been entered into with all seriousness by himself and legal brethren. He wanted everything done in a strictly legal way. Other trials would follow and the object of the prosecution was not to persecute any man or set of men but to arrive at

THE WHOLE TRUTH
To ferret out the guilty and to protect the
GREAT INTERESTS OF THE STATE
Now it is not necessary to prove the feelings of the party, and all the facts are not necessary to be proved before this Court, but, sir, we have adduced evidence sufficient to show that

CAWKINS IS GUILTY
There may be others with him; we have Caldwell's evidence as to his own and Trexler's participation and our sole wish is to punish the guilty not the innocent. Sir, he did this as an officer of the State. The defense attempted to say that

HE WAS IMPOSED UPON.
Why, sir, the idea that Mr. Cawkins, the auditor of the State Road, who, it is in the evidence, is an experienced officer, was bribed and imposed upon by this man Trexler, is simply ridiculous. Why, you, your Honor, and everyone who knows Trexler knows that this is not so—that he hadn't the sense to do it—he was only a *candy maker,* and hadn't sense enough to impose on anyone. And you can't

attribute this to negligence. For Mr. Cawkins is well known to be

AN EXPERIENCED OFFICER

and had no right to audit an account for more than three thousand dollars as that was the law on the subject.

Joseph Trexler seated on his bed in a hotel in Chattanooga read the account of the third and last day and came to the words *candy maker*. His collar felt tight and his heart began to pound. So he hadn't had the sense to hoodwink Cawkins? He forced himself to go on with the account skimming the legal sparring. Down the page his own name jumped out at him again. General Gardner talking:

. . . The prosecution talk of the man Trexler not being smart. Why, sir, he is smarter than they, for he imposed upon them just as he did on Mr. Cawkins. There is my friend, Colonel Culberson, he is smart, it is a hard matter to get around him and yet with all his shrewdness Trexler proved

MORE THAN A MATCH

for him, more than a match for the whole Board of Commissioners, and yet the prosecution say he could not have done this. One of the points made by the prosecution is that the draft was written in New York and in three days was presented to Mr. Cawkins for his audit. Well sir, that was only another evidence of the smartness of my brother Fowler's

CANDY MAKER.

He dated the draft on the 7th, waited until the 10th, just the time it would have taken a letter to come from New York here and he presented it for audit. Now, your Honor, I submit there is no case against my client.

The state rising to close the case said that there was

TOO MUCH TREXLER

and too much Cawkins together. Judge Cutts cut it short with an order to bind the prisoner for next term of Superior Court in the sum of six thousand dollars. On argument of his attorney, it was cut to two thousand.

Joseph Trexler folded the paper and went over to the glass above the washstand in his room and looked at the face of the Candy Maker. He was very pale and he hated the sight of himself. He turned away and took off his new tie. It was choking him. Only a Candy Maker. Cawkins was Mr. Cawkins but he was only the man Trexler, a Candy Maker. Both sides united on that point. There was no ground under him and he had no friends. The words candy maker didn't go with his fine suit or his tie or his manners or his gold watch. He took out the watch, fingered it, put it back in his pocket and jerked at his vest. He'd show them. His father had been better than any of them. Suddenly out of nowhere he remembered the clipping from the Allentown paper that Mem used to take such pride in:

ONE OF GOD'S NOBLEST WORKS, AN HONEST MAN

He could remember the day of the funeral, the people standing outside the Blue Church with their wreaths. What could he tell his mother or Lucy? It would work out all right. A matter of politics and candy maker or not, he would outwit them all. He was a fool to take it so seriously. Trimble was still smiling, or was the last time he saw him. Why should the Southerners think themselves so fine? Nothing except a handful of Negroes made the difference. Waited on hand and foot made the difference. He felt that he was contemptuous of them all and, cheered, smoothed his hair. He would never be able to explain the last two years to anyone, not to himself. But he kept thinking of the words in the *Constitution* about "the clerk is being made a scapegoat" and as he thought of them he wanted to cry. He felt homesick and longed for any member of his family. Even David would be a kind of comfort. He was really almost a martyr.

The next day he was back in Atlanta and was relieved that Roger seemed so glad to see him. He told Joe he should not have gone away and Joe said, "Why it was the old man's idea." Roger said he hadn't known that but the old man was full of crazy ideas lately. Joe showed Roger the letter he proposed sending the papers and when Roger approved the two went around to the different offices together. It was a fine bright day and the two young men looked happy and innocent. The editor of the *Constitution* didn't know what to make of the situation. Trexler looked like a nice young man and an honest one. He ended by growling that Fawcett would still be proved to be a really bad man. That done, he blew his large red nose very hard, complained of a draft and went down to the street. Rumors of new arrests were already exciting the loafers in front of the hotel.

McCall and Major Hargreeves would have nothing to do with Fawcett or those who sided with Fawcett. Rumors that Fawcett had tried to pay Trexler's alleged frauds if the matter was hushed up were noised all over town. McCall was said to be furious at the story that he had been offered a bribe to fix up the books. Fawcett continued writing bold letters to the papers. McCall accused him of trying to steal his books and Fawcett countered by ordering guards to stand watch over the bookkeeper's books. The town was in an uproar and the wise ones said that Fawcett had hoped by this coup d'état to put the bookkeeper out of the way. The *Era* praised Fawcett and said that certain gentlemen who had been yelling "Stop thief" might be discovered to have skirts not wholly clean.

Fawcett's friends said that he was not guilty but was being made a mere tool. It was becoming dangerous to be anything but a mere tool. No one accused Joseph Trexler, the clerk and candy maker, of being a mere tool. He was almost forgotten in the excitement about the McCall books. Fawcett exercised his judgment and appointed Harrow, the attorney general, former attorney for the road, to take charge of the books. People yelled that Harrow had no business in such a position and Harrow, equally dextrous, played into popular favor and turned the books over to a Citizen Committee. The books were found to contain numerous erasures and had never been balanced since December, 1870.

Newspaper reporters from New York hung around the Sassoon House and the Trimble bar. Fawcett was the big news. Was he involved in the steals? Intimates stuck to the mere tool theory. Reporters said this last version was impossible. Fawcett was nobody's fool. He was either completely innocent of all knowledge of the crimes or the biggest crook of the lot.

The New York *Herald* man inclined toward the latter view. He made an appointment with Fawcett, who came into his parlor with the pictures of Ben Butler over the mantelpiece and Grant and Senator Morton on the side walls and shook hands with the young fellow, inquiring cordially how he liked Atlanta and if he was being well treated. The reporter was impressed by the bland manners and the frank open look of the slight rather delicate appearing man. His hands with the ring, the cuffs with the gold cuff links, the easy gestures, made questions a little embarrassing. Fawcett relieved him by declaring himself ready to answer all questions, in fact welcomed the chance.

Correspondent: Why did you take no steps to have arrested the parties implicated in the frauds until a fortnight ago, although you knew of their offense three months ago from McCall?

Mr. Fawcett: Mr. McCall was not the person who first

told me. Months ago when I was in Washington my son George sent me a letter and stated he had discovered something he *dared not commit to paper*. I immediately returned to Atlanta and George told me of the frauds perpetrated by Trexler and others, mentioning the Caldwell bills. The next day McCall told me the same. I asked the amount. He said twenty-five thousand dollars. I then determined to endeavor to collect the money before beginning a criminal prosecution. If I could recover the money I could have the guilty parties arrested all the same. The penalty for the offense is only one thousand dollars fine and six months in the penitentiary; hence if I had them arrested then the state would have been the loser of the amount taken. McCall assumed the responsibility of pressing the matter. Caldwell came to me in tears and asked if he could do anything to avert the disgrace of discovery. I said I was sorry for him and *would rather have lost a thousand dollars* than to have heard frauds had been committed but that I could see no way in which I could help him. It was necessary to give the parties time to pay. McCall wrote me on August 9 saying he did not believe they would make restitution. I heard Trexler was making preparations to leave town and did what I considered my duty in the matter.

Correspondent: Then your delay was due solely to your desire to recover money for the state.

Fawcett: Such was my sole motive. I could have no other as I was not in the slightest degree implicated in the frauds.

Correspondent: It is stated that you expressed yourself willing to pay the amount of the Trexler fraud if the matter was hushed up.

Fawcett: It is utterly false. Caldwell asked me if I would contribute to a fund of two thousand dollars to be paid to McCall who would then resign leaving me to appoint someone who would fix up the books. I said I wouldn't contribute a dollar. *If my own son was implicated* in the frauds I would not. Subsequently I heard Major Garnett had offered to compromise the case for two thousand dollars. I never offered to pay a cent.

Correspondent: Do you not think the removal of McCall has given your enemies a weapon against you?

Fawcett: In what way?

Correspondent: I mean, to be candid, has not the removal given the impression that you dread an investigation into the frauds and desire the books out of the hands of the man who made public their fact?

Fawcett: No, I do not agree with you. On the contrary, it shows I do not dread exposure. I defy those who charge me with complicity. I should have discharged McCall sooner but I was a friend of his.

He let his head droop shaking it as if no one deprecated McCall's rôle more than he did. At the same time his nostrils opened slightly and the pupils of his eyes darkened giving his pleasant hazel eyes a curious luminous look that the eyes of animals have at night. The reporter looked at him intently and wondered if it were true that he was consumptive. He had heard that rumor also. He felt guilty to be questioning but ventured one more.

Correspondent: As regards the alleged ring of swindlers, the parties Mr. Trexler is said to have made known to the prosecution, can you tell me anything on that subject?

Fawcett: I know nothing about it. I have had no conversation with him since his arrest.

He shook his head again slowly and with sadness, murmuring, "Too bad, too bad, a great shock to me," leaving the reporter with the impression that he was really burdened with the sorrow and shock of late events. Somewhat confused, the reporter shook hands with the graceful figure and outside admitted to himself that he admired the scamp.

Entering the hotel he passed Joseph Trexler in the

lobby. He felt sorry for the boy, a Northerner and in a tight place. He didn't look guilty, neither did that other boy from Savannah, who had been arrested that morning. They didn't look like common cheats and swindlers, it was kind of ridiculous to imagine it. The higher-ups fitted the parts better. The clerks were bunched together at the desk and one called out, "More arrests, guess who?"

"Trimble?"

"Nothing so fancy. No, Ton Ferris, the honorable treasurer."

"You don't say. Who swore out the warrant?"

"McCall. Hargreeves is back of him. That little Rome lawyer is shoving the State Road robbers down to hell as fast as his legs will allow."

"Do you know what the bond was?"

"Yes. Ten thousand. Ferris said he had been holding state money, just waiting for someone to pay it to."

"At least there's some good in arrests if it brings a little hidden cash to light." He turned and started upstairs and passed young Trexler and another young man with a thin face and eyebrows that met. They were both talking.

The two young men halted in the street outside. "I don't think you should feel so hard about the old man," Roger said. "He was asking me about you only last night. He feels bad about the whole thing. It'll clear up, see if it won't. Trouble can't last forever."

"Look, across the street. Isn't that Lenore?"

"Who? Lenore Blondell? Yes, she's beckoning to you."

"Wait for me, Roger. I'll be back." Joe ran across the street to Lenore, who flushed and walked determinedly up to Joe and shook hands. "Why don't you come to see us?" she said looking up at him and smiling.

"Lucy wrote me not to come," Joe said.

"She doesn't mean that Joe, she's just frightened at all the talk. You know there's been an awful lot of it."

"You're not frightened," Joe said.

"Oh Lucy and I aren't alike at all. I don't care what silly people think." She tossed her head and flushed a little. "You come to see us, Joe. Father asks about you and so do we all. Lucy isn't the whole family. She'll be all right in time."

"I won't forget you asked me. Perhaps you'd better run along. People are looking at us."

"Let them look," said Lenore. "Just let them look."

"Give my love to your mother," Joe said.

"And to Lucy?" said Lenore.

"To all of the family, everyone," Joe said smiling and as she held out her hand again he pressed it warmly and said, "Tell your mother it will come out all right."

"She knows that; we know," said Lenore.

"Thanks," said Joe. He walked back to Roger slowly. "Lucy won't see me," he said.

"She'll get over it," Roger said. "It's all the talk. You can't blame her."

"I don't," Joe said, but he felt very tender toward Lenore.

"What do you think of Bullock staying away so long?"

"You know what they're saying? He's afraid to come for fear of impeachment."

"They're worked up enough to clap him into jail even."

"That's what scares me Roger. Guilty or not, he'll be clapped into jail and a lot more besides. Any Northerner."

"Oh, you're exaggerating. No, they'll quarrel among themselves and forget it. You'll be overlooked. Don't take it so hard."

"I'm not," Joe said.

"I've got eyes. You're thin, you don't eat and you'd better keep in shape for the investigation."

"I'm ready," said Joe.

"Good. Listen Joey, you'll laugh at this five years from

now. You'll be a happy married man dandling a baby on either knee and you'll wonder how you ever got so worried about a thing like this. It's politics, I tell you. You can't blame people for getting excited. They've seen everything turned upside down for years. But it'll blow over. You'll think back and wonder what it was all about. Joey, I can just see you, you'll be a fine father. You'll make a fine family man, you will. Oh say, Joey, you'll have to tell the girls to quit looking at you then, hey Joey?"

"You're thinking of yourself, not me," Joe said. "It's your own children dandling on your own knee, you're thinking of. Well, you have every right to be happy."

"Don't be so doleful. Wait till we are old men together recalling the good old days. You'll laugh at yourself now."

They separated and Roger walked off whistling. Joe stood on the corner fingering his fine watch chain. He had half a mind to go to the Blondells' but no, he had better wait. Besides he could not put off writing to his mother any longer. He wondered just what he could say.

TWO SISTERS

L ENORE BLONDELL did not admire her sister Lucy. All her life she had heard friends and relatives rhapsodize about Lucy's beauty and she thought she could see clear through Lucy. She had that scorn that younger sisters often have for elder ones and that belief in her ability to divine the older sister's motives. Lucy was all self, according to Lenore, and she was never more so than when she sat down and wrote to Joseph Trexler not to come to the house for a while for her sake. Lenore was certain that in Lucy's place she would have gloried in defying Uncle Minot and all the raft of acquaintances and connections who now were so quick to blame the trouble on a handful of Northerners.

Lucy cried a great deal and sat alone in her room shivering and trembling and longing for Joe. She thought what a terrible position she was in and how tragic it was that a well bred Southern girl should have fallen in love with a Yankee. A good many stories had gone around after the war about Southern girls falling in love with Yankee soldiers and how tragic it was and she now felt that she too shared that tragedy and disgrace.

Her mother and father did not interfere. They had too many other children and too many money worries. Mr. Blondell did not know which way to turn. Lenore was the only self reliant one but he wasn't going to lean on her just because she was not so pretty or so likely to marry. Besides it would take several years before she was ready to teach. He could see now what the poor whites had to put up with because they themselves very often had no more to eat than people of that kind. Blondell felt very sympathetic toward Joe and his trouble. Since he was without means himself he caught himself scheming in a way that would have made him ashamed once. Now his own plots made it seem very likely that Joe was probably involved in the trouble. Joe had a large family of brothers and sisters and who could blame him? Lucy was just a stuck-up girl with pride that no longer had any reason for being. It was silly to go on holding the head high and acting high and mighty when you were no different from anyone else. Because he was so desperate he had a good many odd ideas lately and right now he thought Lucy was a fool not to run away with a fine chap like Joe. He would like to see Uncle Minot get that slap in the face. All his life, he had hated Uncle Minot and it hurt to feel he had no authority in his own family and that Lucy would knuckle down to an old tyrant who would never loosen his purse strings for anything but windy advice. Uncle Minot had tried his best to make Blondell get into the war and his ideas and those of the rest of his tribe had parted company right then and there. He hid as a secret shame the daily fear he had had of being forced to do battle. Fortunately he had had a weak heart and had cheerfully yielded up his goods to avoid the sacrifice of a struggle he hated.

Mrs. Blondell could not tell her husband what she thought, she hardly knew herself. She didn't feel strong enough to throw off the influence of Uncle Minot. So she sided with Lucy in her pride but to Lenore she mourned and worried about Joe. She didn't see why this blow had to fall on them, not that he was guilty, why how could he be when he was like an own son to her, always such nice manners, so tender and considerate and to think it had come to this as if the war had not crushed the life out of a body and made the future look dark and dreary. Not that she was one to give in to such thoughts, oh no, but still you had to face facts. Especially with Papa so impracticable. If it kept on they would all find themselves working out in the fields, just common laborers, or else in the workhouse. You can't live on hope forever. It was ages since they had had a really filling meal. The first day she had seen Joe she had said to herself, there's a young man bound to rise in the world, he had such an air and was so interested in everything.

"That's what I like, that intense interest," she said to Lenore, "shows you aren't dead but alive to what is going on in this beautiful world, not that it is so beautiful now and I suppose it's sinful to let Lucy get involved with a Yankee boy but still it looked as if it were for the best, and who is to know? Somebody must be to blame for all this sorrow and trouble in the world. It makes it much easier if you can blame someone and put your finger on the cause, practically heals it to do that, and this terrible time, some say it's all the fault of the North and some say it's the smoke from Napoleon's guns still polluting the world and causing congestions that break out in people and I do wish they'd get a name for it, makes it so much easier. That poor Joseph, it just must come out right for the boy but Lenore you shouldn't torment your poor sister. She's suffering. I'm sure of that. I'm sure I should suffer something terribly."

The day that Lenore saw and spoke to Joe she marched straight into the room where her mother and Lucy were sitting. "I saw Joe," she said, standing with her chin in the air and her straight straw colored hair straggling from under her hat.

"What did he say?" Lucy said turning quickly to look full at her sister. "He sent his love to mother," said Lenore. "Didn't ask after me?" "Let me see, no I don't seem to remember," said Lenore, pretending to think and walking carelessly toward the table. "You're lying, I can tell," Lucy said. "Lenore answer me," said Mrs. Blondell. "Don't torment your poor sister. Is he all right?" "Yes, he looked all right and he said he was all right and I don't need any old Uncle Minot to tell me he is all right."

"It's not true. You see how she is, Mother, you see," and Lucy burst into tears and left the room. Mrs. Blondell looked reproachfully at Lenore who said, "If she really cared, why doesn't she see him?"

"Oh Lenore," sighed Mrs. Blondell, "you know so little of life. Some day when you girls are mothers you will realize how hard you make it for me. Really Lenore I think you might be more considerate of your mother." The shocked hurt tones of the mother irritated Lenore and make her feel as if she were all alone in the world. She went out to the grape arbor and saw Sophronia, one of Lucy's bosom friends, cross the grass. "Now they can have a good cry and enjoy themselves," she thought and when it was time for supper and the two girls came downstairs arm in arm, Lenore looked sharply at them for traces of their tears and enjoyment.

Mr. Blondell stirred them up with news of another arrest. "Ton Ferris this time," he said. "Lee swore to the warrant. Oh everyone is getting in on the fun. Lee says he sold Ton a switch, lathe and iron for Ferris's own use and then the railroad paid for it. And what's more Ton has a lot near the city fenced with fine timbers about the length and breadth of railroad cross ties and he has enough firewood stacked up at his home to last two years. Good thing, some pretty cold days are coming or I'm mistaken."

"What do you mean, wood?" said Mrs. Blondell.

"I mean firewood, the best, ash, oak, beach. Wish we had some here. I can't get anyone to tackle that wood lot any more. Yes, daughter, Mr. Ferris has a fine woodpile. Nothing but the best would do for him." He let his head sink dejectedly but brightened up and began rattling away a lot of nonsense that put Sophronia into giggles.

The next day the girls were disappointed that there were no further arrests but the day following McCall himself was arrested on charges of embezzling and altering the books of his office. Major Hargreeves, prosecutor for the other cases, switched to the defense. Harrow came out for the prosecution and bitter words were exchanged during the hearing between the two lawyers. The next arrest popped out of the box in two days.

THE STATE ROAD MUDDLE

The Honorable Blake Fawcett was arrested at his home on Walton Street on the warrant sworn to by affidavit under oath by Mr. McCall.

He charges that Blake Fawcett is a common cheat and swindler. That as superintendent of the Western & Atlanta he signed a certain paper, the same being a draft in favor of the Tennessee Car Company for the sum of $32,540.10 and pur-

porting to be in payment for cars to be used by the W. & A., he knowing at the time that the said company
HAD NO EXISTENCE IN FACT
and said cars were never furnished to said Road by said Company. . . .

The warrant was served by Constable J. R. Thompson and Fawcett was arrested and held for preliminary trial. He was sitting by a fire when Constable Thompson called with the warrant. His head was resting on his hand; the cuffs with the heavy impressive gold links weighed upon his wrist. He looked pale and tired and during the formal reading of the warrant, rose and took his medicine ostentatiously, carefully counting ten drops into the half glass of water. "Sit down, Thompson," he said.

"Thank you, Mr. Fawcett, but perhaps under the circumstances—"

"Circumstances? You mean that thing? Is that the best they can do? Arrest a man who has spent his life in devotion to his state? So the slanderers have the upper hand, have they? Well, thank God, Thompson, that the people of this state are the final tribunal. When the facts are before them—" He swallowed his medicine and filling the glass from a carafe of water, sipped it slowly while Thompson stood awkwardly waiting.

FALL GUY

IT WAS soon all over town that Fawcett had been arrested and Joseph Trexler hearing the news went at once to his hotel. He stood in his room looking around aimlessly and then began mechanically to pile together papers on the table. His rifle and shotgun stood in a corner in their cases. He took two suits out of the closet and looked at them, then laid them on the back of the chair but he was pleased with them and felt a little cheered. When he heard a knock at the door he stiffened, then got up and opened it boldly. It was Roger Wallace. "Here," Wallace said, speaking in a low voice, "anybody with you?" When the door was closed, he said, "Heard the news of course?"

"You mean Fawcett, yes."

"The women are upset, Estelle crying and poor Grandma just sits there and doesn't say a word. They're bloodthirsty, I tell you, regular bloodhounds and all out for blood and money. Have you been on the streets today?"

"Only to the post office."

"They are ready to tear anyone connected with the road to pieces. You haven't a chance Joey. A Northerner and all. You must get out while you can."

"You mean run away?" He was surprised at his own surprise and hoped Roger wouldn't notice his things scattered around.

"Now Joey," said Roger, "don't take it like that. It's not running away. You can come back when things get settled. But right now you can see for yourself, feeling is running pretty high."

"Roger I know what you're after. You've been talking with the old man, haven't you? And he wants you to get me to run away so it will be easier for him. I know him by this time."

"Now Joe," said Roger getting up and beginning to walk around the little center table and to pull at the chenille cover. "Now Joe, you're prejudiced against Fawcett. He doesn't feel that way toward you. He is thinking of you too when he thinks you ought to get out. He's no ogre, you know he's not, he did a lot for you. Now didn't he?"

"I thought so once but now I'm not sure I didn't do as much for him. I was a useful tool for him anyhow."

"Where do you get such ideas? You and your tools. Is everybody crazy? I never heard tools called on so much before. Everybody claims to be a tool. Who was the master mind anyhow? Crazy, the whole lot. It's absolutely the only way to explain it and I think I'm pretty bright to have hit on it. But Fawcett now, why Joe, he thinks so much of his family and all he couldn't be the kind of person you make out, he couldn't, now could he? Well shake your head if you want, but I know, I say I know that you can't decide things like that. The times are bad, we all agree, and furthermore the Fawcetts as a family are expansive about money. They don't know how to handle it, that's all."

"You're going to marry his sister, I see that," Joe said.

"That's not got anything to do with it. I tell you, you have to go. You have to. I didn't want to bring it up but Grandma came to me and told me you'd promised. You have to stick to what you told her. And if it would do you any good to stay, I'd say, stay. It won't."

"I'd like to know if it was Fawcett put Grandma up to it."

"You're crazy Joe," said Roger, biting his thumb nervously. "It's unjust of you."

"All right, it is then. What of it? But I hate to run off and let people say I'm the guilty one. They will say it."

"They'll say it if you stay," said Roger. "If you stay you'll have everybody against you. Both sides will work it to incriminate you. But if you go, one side at least will be working for you in secret. Hull said he'd look after your interests."

"Hull? Why he's liable to arrest any minute himself "

"Who isn't? He'll take care of your property. Gardner is going to take over all the cases and try to break the attachments against them. When he does, Hull can sell your stuff and send you the money."

"Sounds all right, but I hate to run off." As he said it he knew he was glad to have such a good excuse to go. It would be something to tell Mem. She would be proud of him for respecting his promise to Grandma.

"It's the only thing to do. And remember Joey, I'm your friend." He stuck out his hand and the two shook. "This can't last forever," Roger said. "You'll be coming back with colors flying, see if you don't. They will get tired soon and go off on another chase."

"I hope so," Joe said but that night when he went out on the dark streets he couldn't help looking up at the stars and wondering if he would see them over these same roofs again. He walked a good deal, afraid to step in anywhere and he planned out what he would say to Lucy the next day. He was determined to make her believe in him before he went away.

Fawcett's preliminary hearing the next morning was taken up with squabbles among the lawyers and the trial was postponed for the day, some said with intention, in order to give Fawcett more time to arrange his affairs. It gave Hull also time to call on Joe and get him started out of town.

There was no train until evening but Joe packed and left his guns and music box to be sent after him. Then he went to the house of Hull's sister-in-law at the edge of town. When evening came Hull was to drive him to the Blondells' and from there to a train on a junction of the W. & A. line north. The two men spent the day playing cards and smoking. Joe was absent minded and Hull played a poor game. Mrs. Jackson had a good dinner for them and her little girl came from her nap to hang around

Joe, pleasing the mother who said she guessed there was one young man who was fond of the ladies and the ladies were fond of him, even the little girls.

As the cards were shuffled and dealt Joe tried to realize he was going away and that great changes were taking place but it seemed hazy and unreal. He beat Hull at cards but for a wonder Hull was good natured about it. Hull was too cheerful and his cheerfulness was suspicious. Joe again went over his affairs with Hull and Hull promised to do exactly as he said and to take care of everything and watch developments. When his case came up in October term of court, what would happen? The bond would be forfeited, for one thing. "Don't worry about it," Hull said. "We are all in the same boat. It'll come out all right. I'll take care of your interests and Gardner is as sharp as they make them. This will blow over."

At seven they drove out to the Blondells'. Hull admitted as they drove along that it was lucky they had kept out of sight during the day as the prosecution would be hunting all over for Joe as a witness. "You'll be out of the way now," he said. "A needle lost in the big haystack." He felt good and began whistling, sitting with his heavy shoulders hunched and his lips puckered up good-naturedly. It was a warm September night and a moon coming up behind a row of thin larch trees looked dark red and too heavy to ascend the sky. The big Blondell house was lighted downstairs and Hull stayed discreetly in the buggy as Joe went up the path.

He sat there smoking and looking at the sky and making his own calculations, now and then one of the horses lifted a leg and stamped, the right one had a sore on the hoof that needed attention, wonder how she got that, with a nail or what? These louts of boys no damned good, none of the niggers any good any more, not even for a good crap game, the whole business going to hell that's about it and the future is out of our hands, it's a law of nature that every man must be for himself and the survival of the fittest. Anyhow, he's young, just a sapling, I'm old and Fawcett's old, we can't start again. A young fellow like that, why if I was him I wouldn't stick around when the West is full of mines and opportunities and fortunes are piling up out of nothing and every young fellow has a chance. There's Australia too, a fine place, good healthy climate, more mines. Why I'm doing the boy a favor to get him out of here, actually I'm just plain unselfish to sit cooped up in a room smelling of cabbage all day. Why does she have cabbage when Paul hates the smell as much as I do? Any refined man hates a smell. There's happy married life for you, she does it because he hates it, and so it goes nine out of ten married couples living like I don't know what. My bitch Henriette would be ashamed to litter in such an unwholesome place and there's more than one reason why some of us stay bachelors and not sour grapes either and this Joe, look at him, can have anything he wants, what he wants of Lucy Blondell with no money and nothing but a pretty face that Time takes care of, I don't know. He'll thank me some day, he'll be glad he got out of the noose, not only love, but that mess with Fawcett. That man has gone too far all along the line, makes even his friends sick pocketing the lion's share and pretending all the time he's doing something else. I never saw anyone who could fool more people, even the Governor doesn't know whether he's standing on his head or his heels. Fawcett's not helpless, not like Joe, why Joe might as well back up against a wall and let us take a pot shot at him as to linger around here the way things are. He'll thank me to his dying day and I'll take care of his interests, at least as good as anyone else would, I'll say that. Course, he's giving himself away running off, but how can he help it? He's showing his hand, why nobody will believe he hasn't pulled out the jack pot all by his lonesome and that's just what Fawcett is hoping for. Let the two of them fight it out and best man win, that's all this life is, just a continual scrap for the top of the heap and here he comes now with the whole crowd with him. I'll get down and walk around a bit.

He got down and leading the horses, hitched the team to the tree and then whistling, he pretended to examine the moon now slowly and heavily rising, all the time looking back over his shoulder where he could see figures on the porch and hear them all calling to Joe and he calling out very cheerfully, and then he saw Joe with Lucy come slowly toward him and the door of the house close slowly with the family shutting themselves in considerately to leave the young couple alone together, it might be for the last time. He put a bit of brush across the road between himself and the team and still curious could not help looking back and seeing the two dark figures and hearing her voice suddenly, not loud but painful, "No, no, no no Joe," and then in a minute Lucy put her two fists against his chest and beat him hard and cried, how hard she was crying, why it suddenly seemed as if she had come awake and for the first time in her life knew what it was all about, that she had been a fool hiding and keeping away from him and being afraid what people would say and as if now that it was too late, only when it was too late, did she understand and deny it could be true.

"No, no, Joe you can't go," and it wasn't only to Joe she was saying "No, no," it was to everything she had ever known and to herself for being a fool and for not knowing and she said "No, no," but it was no use, he put her hands down gently and then he walked back to the house with her.

Hull could see them darkly blurring with the trees and bushes and then a crack of light opened in the dark house and she was inside and in a minute Joe was lighting a cigar and saying in a strained voice, "Where are you Hull? We've got to hurry," and Hull was coming out from the bushes feeling kind of tired and ashamed for some reason and he said, "Have a cigar Joe," lighting one himself.

"Thanks," Joe said, "I've got one."

On the train going North Joe worried what to say to Mem and the girls. At Chattanooga a man in front hoisted an Atlanta paper and Joe read over his shoulder, saw

STATE ROAD IMBROGLIO

and leaning forward, his eyes straining to the fine print, picked out words running into one another."*Speedy trials for accused urged . . . it will end in farce . . . prosecution at loggerheads . . . robber clan at liberty . . .* WILL HAMAN YET REACH THE GALLOWS ERECTED FOR MORDECAI?" He wanted to laugh. There was something funny about the whole business, serious though it was. The way they would be hunting around for him and the lawyers fighting and Fawcett on tenterhooks and who would be stupid then? He was out of it, which was more than they were and if Hull could be trusted, he wouldn't lose. It would die down, that is what they all said. It was politics. If Hull tried to cheat him he had ways he could get even. He could get even with the whole lot of them if it came down to it. He'd show them and yet as he said that to himself he felt kind of sick and lonesome as if he were a child again and not sure where he was going or what would happen. When he thought of Lucy he had to get up and walk to the platform and smoke a cigar and the whole business made the train seem like a prison. He was glad when they got to Washington and he could stretch his legs and take a look around before going further North.

Mem gave him one sharp look and he found it easier than he thought to talk about the trouble. Surrounded by the family with one of the girls ready to fill his plate when it was empty and to see that the coffee was good and hot, he saw the South as unreal and he almost felt as if he had never been there. When Aaron came up from Grapeville, Catherine began at once, "Oh Aaron, it was just as we thought, that treacherous Fawcett. Why he even put Grandma Fawcett up to such a trick. She made Joe promise not to tell what he knew and of course he had to run away or that whole family might come to harm."

"What do you mean, come to harm?" said Aaron.

"Why Fawcett would have been discovered for what he is. It would have brought that family to ruin and Joe had either to stay and tell all he knew or get out. Don't you see?"

"It looks to me that Fawcett is bound to be tripped up anyhow and there wasn't much sense in Joe making a useless sacrifice in coming away, if that was why he came." He spoke in a curious skeptical tone that made Mem look up quickly and then look at Joe. Joe was listening with more respect toward Aaron than he usually gave and he smiled when Aaron finished.

"You don't understand it up here and I almost don't either. There's this big ring of swindlers and they are all protected. The government is back of them, how are you to get them? At the same time the people are yelling for justice. Something has to be done. I'm from the North and no one from up here is very safe down there in times like this. I didn't have a chance for a fair trial. Everybody told me so. Mr. Blondell said the only thing to do was to get out."

Mem's lips tightened as he mentioned Mr. Blondell and

she thought of Lucy. She was almost glad this had happened to get him away from that Southern girl. All Southern girls were lazy and designing and made poor wives.

She was so relieved by this idea that she accepted quite calmly Joe's plan to leave immediately for Canada. There was no knowing when a search might be made for him. If the revengeful mood lasted in the South he would be as good as gone in his own home. The girls flew around repacking his bag and taking out papers and letters for safekeeping. Mem got together some fine fresh pears and apples and Catherine chattered about Toronto and if French was spoken and how nice it would be to go there and practice her French. Joe talked to the red bird and the mocking bird in their great cage and felt homesick for the South and sad but quickly pulled himself out of it. After all, he was young, anything might happen and he was bound to come out on top, so he kissed them all good-by very cheerfully and they felt exactly as if he were only going upcountry to see the relatives. When Catherine went to the train with him and he had climbed aboard, they both felt excited and a little happy and she called out, "Oh Joe, just think, you'll see Niagara Falls."

At that moment both of them completely forgot that Joe was a fugitive, running away.

Oxtail

I F AMOS WENDEL had made a go at his business Anne
Wendel, who was a Trexler, might not have dug so
deeply in her past, fishing up stories for her children.
She was only one of many women not acclimated to the
Iowa town that never lost its frontier flavor. Even when
the hot winds did not blow, the streets seemed hard and
bare, the buildings squat and cut short in their growth.
But in the spring when the lilacs bloomed it was easy to
feel at home, even in Oxtail, and there were Sundays with
the children tumbling around and Amos smoking a good
cigar, reading his paper and the chicken coming browned
from the oven and the whipped cream piled high on the
cake and the long soft afternoons going into twilight so
like the twilight of her girlhood with Joe's music box making plaintive music, only now they had gramophones. The
changes were coming so thick and fast, she had to make
her children feel where they were going. With all the
many patient ways she had of working and saving and
waiting it often struck her as hard that she must still be
living the struggle of her girlhood.

Once when Aunty Blank died she thought new days
were coming. But somehow most of Aunty's money went
to Aunty's adopted daughter, a nobody Lizzie. The real
feeling Anne had felt when she had heard Aunty was dead
turned to suspicion and anger that Aunty had left her
flesh and blood so little. When four hundred dollars was
doled out to Anne, she thought that now they had some
capital and could do something.

Seemed to her as if they had always been struggling for
capital to make investments that would give them the
start they must have. But the four hundred came just in

the nick of time for her husband's business. He could show her in black and white that money put into the business would pay itself back there in a larger way than any other. What his figures could not show was that the corn crop would burn up that year and still less that slowly and surely the big businesses could crowd out little men. Already the house in Omaha had its eye on Oxtail waiting to crowd their small competitor to the wall. Even as a distributor Amos Wendel's day would soon be over. He knew nothing of this and was never so cheerful as the day the four hundred was poured into the business.

The children heard from their mother that they might as well have dropped it into the Missouri. Where were their father's hard work and honesty leading him? Sometimes Anne Wendel flushed and said, "I just wish he'd let me collect those bills. I'd show him." Once she took the buggy and two of the littler children and went out to the Babcock place and came back empty handed. "Their baby's awfully sick," she said that night and that was all.

The hot days left us stranded on the porch of evenings and we thought of back East and the lilacs and the dewy evenings with the nightingales singing, only that was not true about the nightingales. We only thought that. We just grew in the heat and the world was big and wide outside of Oxtail, bands played somewhere, white turkeys walked across fields and handsome young men ran away for mysterious reasons.

FUGITIVE OR SHORT YEARS

THE NEXT few days the family on Fifteenth Street was nervous to sounds. A doorbell startled them and once a harsh voice of someone selling something next door penetrated to the little family in the dining room and they all looked at one another in a frightened way. Aaron was very gloomy and said that it was very bad for Joe's reputation because there were always people who believed such talk whether it was true or not. "That's what comes of your highflyers Mem," he said. "I don't see what he means if he thinks he is going back to Georgia. How can he do business? This is not so easy to live down."

"Aaron you never see the point. This is different. It's politics. Joe tells you and tells you."

"Oh I know all Joe tells me but he's a boy himself. Not that I don't hope it turns out the way he thinks it will." But his voice sounded grudging and Catherine had to admit that she wasn't as fond of him as she was of Joe or even of David. Mem was only concerned lest the family become a burden on Joe. She didn't like the idea of his moving around either. "You never get anywhere by that. The best thing would be if he would stay home. What good is this fine house if he isn't here to enjoy it?"

But they couldn't get him to stay home. They had a kind of superstition about it and remembered their father's prophecy about his boy, that he would live to circle the globe. When he wrote saying he was thinking of going out West or to Australia, they were proud of him as if he were fulfilling his destiny and they were also depressed at such a scheme. Mem was crying the whole day long. She had gone the day after he left to the old tailor and had brought home several suits to sew on. Catherine was provoked to see her at this work again and thought it showed lack of confidence in Joe. He had worked so hard to make such work not necessary and now the minute something went wrong, she returned to that slavery.

"What's so bad about it?" Mem said threading needles rapidly and actually looking more sprightly now she was at her sewing again. "It's not dishonorable, is it? Somebody must help this big family. There's David to be educated. I never did count much on Aaron and as for Joe, it's not right he should feel us like a millstone around his neck. Especially not when he's in trouble." She said the word trouble as if it were a sickness, like malaria, unavoidable and liable to be slow of recovery.

She had put away all the silver and the carved wood fan and the jewelry for the girls. She was not only afraid that someone, she didn't know just who, might come and demand to take these things away, but she was also convinced they were too fine for their home. The home itself was too fine. She had said so all along but no one had paid any attention to her remarks. They were all alike, all wanted the best, just like Joe. And what did that amount to? Her girlhood had been saving and she had worked hard. She had been apprenticed after her father died to a sewing establishment. Joshua Trexler had taken her from the shop to marry her and yet she couldn't say she had not learned a lesson during those years, to save, to be patient, to wait. She hadn't cried her eyes out or moped around, she had worked and waited and Joshua had come along. What did the Lord intend that she should learn by losing first a good father and then a husband and both before their allotted time? Wasn't it patience and hard work she must always depend upon? Hard work had followed each loss, from a carefree girl she had become a sewing apprentice, from a sewing apprentice, a wife, from a wife, a widow with six children to support. Where had her husband's restless hopes carried him except to the grave? Joe was like him and she must stand there and not be able to make him see that steady ways were best. With sewing in her hands, her feet were on the ground, and she meant to stay there. Her thin erect figure, with its sharp shadow thrust far out into the next room beyond the portières, never drooped, although she sat there until nearly two o'clock.

When no inquiries were made for Joe and no one knocked at the door demanding information, and even the papers began to quit printing news about GEORGIA FRAUDS, the family relaxed and began to think it was all a mistake. When Joe's trunk came from Atlanta in the name of Ada Pearson they had a good laugh. Catherine took charge of the papers and put them in their father's old strong box along with his letters to his wife from the legislature at Harrisburg.

Mem took the clothes out to air on the line back of the house. She stood admiring the fine cloth and workmanship. In all her life she had never seen such clothes, certainly her own husband had never had any like them. She felt a sudden pang to think what he had missed, and that right now he was missing this fine day with such a clear blue sky and those tiny clouds up so high. He'd never seen the new house either with all the fine things and sheets that you couldn't have bought at that price back in fifty-nine. Why he'd been laid out in clothes that were not one tenth as good and walking toward the house, she looked back and didn't like to be reminded of the clothes of the dead that had hung on lines airing after they were gone. She rushed back and snapped the garments off the line and told herself that the sun was bound to bleach out such good material and maybe warp the seams.

They waited for news and where to send his trunk and

the first word was from Niagara Falls where he'd run into the Governor of Georgia. They were a little frightened because now it seemed no one could tell friends from foes but Catherine composed herself to write a letter and get it off at once so he would have it when he reached Toronto.

My Dear Brother,

I am glad you arrived safe at Niagara and under any other circumstances I would say that we were glad that you had met some friends from A. but in this case they might betray you, except the Governor himself, he I believe is your friend. Well I tell you when I heard how nicely you met him, I considered it as good as a feast. It must have been quite a surprise on his part as well as yours. Up to this time no inquiries whatever have been made I feel almost ready to conclude they have given up the search or made some kind of settlement. Judging from Atlanta papers that just came, *The Sun,* I mean, I cannot see that the courts are doing anything particular, altogether they act with regard to this matter as if it was mere child's play. I cannot compare it to the action of men with their brains in their proper place. On the contrary they act like men with their brains all in their pockets. This may sound very uncharitable, but how can I help saying so? I don't think that there was anything for you to fear do you? You might have stayed and no harm would have come to the F's through your staying. This is my opinion. I see by Saturday's paper that they brought poor Cawkins up again but have postponed his trial indefinitely. Aaron is very sorry things have turned out so, he says that it is doing you so much injury, your reputation you see is what he means is being ruined. "But all is well that ends well" so we will have to hope for the best, even though we be compelled to stand face to face with the worst. Mother told me the last thing this morning not to forget to tell you that she would take the suits in that she had made and would not take out anymore. She has been low spirited ever since Anne told her that she (Anne) had told you that she had work of this kind again.

Now I understand mother exactly, you see it is very plain that a family like ours will cost a good bit to maintain, and she does not like to ask you so much for your money and hence the reason why she sewed again though not so very much. What you have done for us already is more than we ever had any reason to expect, and now for our family to be a burden on your shoulders is more than I like to see. Please write soon.

Your Ever Loving
Sister Catherine

Joe had been downcast over the news of the sewing but Catherine's letter put it in a different light. He couldn't bear to think that his plans must go one step backward by all this foolishness. From Toronto the whole business in the South looked like a silly affair of schoolboys. Yet it was so dangerous he couldn't go back, at least not for a while. He gave a good deal of sober thought to the future and to the West and Australia. He wasn't going to be handicapped by that affair in the South and he didn't intend to be dodging around all his life. If he could get his money out he was ready to start in anywhere else. Capital was all that was needed to clean up untold wealth. There was nothing in the South he couldn't have just as well or better somewhere else. Even Lucy. Once he was making money, she would come anywhere.

He thought he was very sensible about his affairs and was provoked at a kind of nervousness on the streets as if someone who had just passed had recognized him. He began to think of growing a beard. He had had the family send on his shotgun and rifle and felt better with them near him. He was a little chilled by a letter from Anne in which she said they were sending the rifle and shotgun. "Don't shoot yourself," she wrote. "Remember the blue spots on your forehead." He laughed and passed his hand over his forehead and wondered if they were conspicuous enough to draw attention. Identifying marks of that kind would prove dangerous in times like this. But the next minute he was telling himself that it was all foolishness to get so worked up. They weren't searching for him. They would just fool along down there and do nothing and keep him from coming back and time would slip by. Time was the worst. He couldn't bear that the best years of his life should be spent up here waiting. At that moment it seemed that he was wasting years and not days in idle waiting and he was suddenly frantic to get away.

When papers from the South came he read them through and tried to make sense out of them. Ferris's case had been dismissed. McCall's had been dismissed. Cawkins had been brought up again and his case postponed indefinitely. Fawcett was getting out of it with an indefinitely postponed case. How did they work it? Lucy wrote him a long letter that made the blood come to his face. He felt that he couldn't stand it to be sitting idly by any more. The first letter with any real news was from Mr. Blondell and it was mostly about the Fair. Who cared about the Fair? It made Joe angry and he fumed and fretted. Blondell reported that a few little squibs had appeared in the papers. One said he had been assassinated. The *Constitution* had printed a letter from Memphis saying that Joseph Trexler had passed through that place on his way to California. Blondell did not think they would do much with the big guns but they might hurt those that did not have so much money. Joe did not know whether to be glad or sorry that his disappearance had not stirred up more of a rumpus. In a way he felt slighted that nothing more had happened. It made him feel funny to be eclipsed by a little one horse Fair. He had seen better fairs. The old Allentown fairs were better.

In a few days he heard from Roger Wallace and had to hear more gabble about the Fair. Could they think of nothing else when he was dying to know what had happened to the indictments and if Gardner had succeeded in releasing the property and if Hull were taking any steps to sell? He couldn't bear to sit here tied hand and foot and Roger's facetiousness made him provoked and irritable.

You can't imagine how happy I am to know you are out of reach of the blood and money thirsty rascals. I have been asked about you often but I never know anything. Hereafter I'll tell them you are at home in Philadelphia, as long as you are not really there. I was uneasy about you and did not send your shot gun until I thought you were out of harm's way. I think as much of you as I do my own brother and wish I could be with you again. I have missed you so much and often think of you. I hope you will enjoy yourself all the time you are gone, will have the papers sent you but you will have to pay for them for I am unable to do so. I owe you a few dollars which I will pay as soon as I am able and will have the papers charged to you but if I was able I would send them and they should not cost you a cent. Twemble resigned from the Ice Company and I was unanimously elected to manage it and will do my best to make it pay. The Fair was a poor thing but we took the medal on ice. It is reported this a.m. that K. I. Trimble is "busted" just what I expected. I won't tell anyone where you are Joe but my intended wife, I know she'll keep it. Joe I would like to tell Mr. F— where you are for he would like to know but if you say not I won't. I showed Grandma your letter but don't be uneasy, she will never tell anyone. Mrs. F— has been quite sick for the last two weeks. You will be surprised to learn that Miss Mapie Boole is dead, she died last Wednesday of congestion of the lungs. All others are well. Joe as soon as the big reward is offered, look out for me. I am going for you, will divide all I make, that would be a good way for me to get a start. I don't think they will pay much to catch you. I am the only man in Atlanta who knows where you are and I will not deceive you, you may trust me in all things, I will prove true in every instance. I beg you not to have any fears, you know who I am, now that I am not uneasy I will write often when you write home remember me to all your family and believe me to be

Your true friend

Roger Wallace

Joe put the letter in an inside pocket and alternated with feeling pleased and peevish when he thought of it. It was cheerful and the thought of Roger marrying and having everything his own way, galled him. Not that Roger didn't deserve the best and he was the only man that hadn't made a cent for himself. He was almost too good for this world. He wished he was in Roger's shoes rather than his own. No, he didn't either because he wouldn't like to have as little initiative as Roger. He wouldn't want always to be poor as Roger was almost certain to be. It took courage to pull out of that sort of poor and easy state which Roger just accepted. He was kind of proud of his initiative and what he thought of as business ability. He would get there yet and everyone in Atlanta would know of it too.

He could think of nothing but getting hold of a little capital and starting all over again. When people wrote prattling of other things, he felt irritable and impatient. Catherine gave an entire letter to pears that Mem was sending him and how they were Duchess pears and just right and she had tried to find some for him before but they were always so soft and it would be awfully nice if he could buy them some gloves if they were cheaper there as she had heard and she believed that a dozen pairs would be about right and to remember that in buying black to get an extra large size, and he might get four different colors, three of each, black, leather color, buff and green (not too dark) all in Fenian Style and the black should be 6¼ and the colored in size 6. She did inclose a letter that had come from Atlanta and he ripped it open and was excited to find it was from Hull.

He was as disappointed with Hull's letter as with the other letters he had been receiving. What was he expecting anyhow that the news he did receive seemed so flat? Hull wrote there was no doubt in his mind that they were at that moment hunting for Joe and the ice company was busted and if he could raise some money to pay his note on the ice company stock, so much the better, otherwise Hull would have to sell it for not more than two dollars and thirty cents a share. "If you can fix to pay us we shall greatly appreciate it as money is very scarce and it will pay you to hold the stock. I am watching your interests at every turn and Gardner will communicate with you through your mother."

Was that really all he had to say? Joe turned the sheet over to see if there wasn't something on the back. There was nothing and he wanted to scrunch the letter up into a wad and hit somebody in the eye with it. How preposterous for Hull to be asking him for money! What about those lots and realizing a little money on them as he had promised? Joe spent a great deal of time writing letters and mailing them first to Catherine who would remail them. He read the newspapers and re-read his letters and got nervous and his appetite failed and at night he took in a variety show or sat around the lobby of the hotel or played pool and sometimes he looked out at the same old moon and thought of Lucy and was miserable and romantic and determined to keep from getting too soft and sure that he could keep his head clear and fool them all.

He spent hours seriously reading items in the papers

that meant next to nothing to him. A rumor was going around that Francis Joseph was disposed to abdicate. There was talk of renominating Grant. He remembered hearing Bullock tell Fawcett of Grant's signing the Fifteenth Amendment with Thayer and Bullock looking on and the way he had scrawled his name without even reading the document. A man had died in a hospital from swallowing a half pound of shot taken on advice of an old woman, for constipation. Yellow fever deaths were mounting in Charleston. At Winchester, Tennessee, three Negroes were taken from jail and beaten by white men. He was frightened at some of the news about beatings and shooting. No one could predict what might happen in the South. At least in Toronto his skin was safe. He got sick and tired of being safe and was ready to burst back into Atlanta when he picked up a paper and read in bold type

GOVERNOR BULLOCK HAS RESIGNED

and Contri, president of the senate, had been installed as acting governor. The resignation had been written before Governor Bullock's visit to New York on the twenty-third to take place yesterday. That was the thirty-first.

Joe did not know if this meant he was cut off from the South for good or not. He got off letters to Roger and Catherine and waited for replies.

The family on Fifteenth Street took all of Joe's talk about going to Australia very seriously. The trouble in the South, as they called it, had changed their very lives. The girls thought of themselves as years older, actually aged by the event. They were a little puzzled and inwardly halfway disappointed that the excitement had died down so soon. They talked soberly of the future and of the unreliability of people who called themselves friends. They were convinced that Joe was bound to prove his innocence and this conversation was not yet painful to them.

Later on they were to come to a time when they could not bear to mention any of the circumstances of the Atlanta trouble but now it was something to wonder about and gave them their first real excuse to ask themselves, What is life? They enjoyed the excitement, so sure were they that in the end it was bound to come out all right. Only Mem was grim and fretted and hesitated about getting out more suits to sew as if her doing so admitted that she expected the trouble to continue forever. She had no use for Joe's talk about Australia. As if this country wasn't big enough for anyone. It was all nonsense to go shooting off like that among perfect strangers. She would never see her own boy again, they could mark her words, it would be the last time they laid eyes on their brother. But there was no use in her wasting breath, she had learned long ago that no one minded her. Hadn't she cried and told Joe again and again not to go South? What business had a boy of nineteen away from his home? But nothing had stopped him and look what had come of it.

Catherine finally wrote Joe not to go West or to Australia in the wintertime and she was concerned as to the effect Bullock's resignation might have on his plans. Joe did not know himself what the result of Bullock's resignation would be. He got the papers from Atlanta and noted that the hubbub was dying down. The legislature had met and had immediately passed a resolution denying Bullock's assertion that it had intended to impeach him without an investigation and that the people of Georgia did not recognize the results of the war. Contri read his first message to the legislature hoping there would be no ground for further reconstruction and urging investigation of the state bonds and promising sparing use of the pardoning power, free education but not mixed schools.

There was no mention of any railroad trials and it

almost looked as if the entire business was being forgotten. Joe began to feel that he was forgotten and living in a world that was forgot. He felt homesick and longed to talk to someone who knew about his past. Too restless to sit waiting in Toronto any longer he made a move toward Montreal and in the lobby of a hotel overheard two race track men talk of racing. He remembered old Ton Ferris and his talk of Saratoga. There was a glamour about the name and that kind of life and on the impulse he crossed the border and found himself in a small hotel in the dead of winter. He tried hard not to be disappointed that the big hotels were closed up. He walked past the Congress Hall and Grand Union hotels and listened to stories of the swells who were there in the summer and the flirtations of famous people and how two young people had been asked to leave the Clarendon for getting up and waltzing in the drawing room in a newfangled dance that was nothing more nor less than an embrace.

The proprietor put himself out to please but the food he served always reminded him of some greater feast that had become a legend in the town. Joe got to feel he was eating with ghosts and he himself was scarcely less real. A letter from Catherine joking him about being in or near the Rip Van Winkle country and to beware of the spirits that put one to sleep for twenty years, got on his nerves. He had the feeling that he was asleep and out of everything. He hoped it wouldn't last for twenty years.

He was so homesick he didn't care what happened and took the train for New York and Philadelphia and once the train was moving the excitement of travel and of new places and cities was on him. He burst into the Fifteenth Street house as gayly as if he'd come home after a holiday abroad. He was the same old Joe and had stopped in New York to buy a few trinkets for them all. His gayety reassured even Mem who was sure everything must be going to turn out right or he could never be so light hearted.

Catherine met David on the steps outside and pulled him into the little back vestibule. "Joe's come and you must wash your hands and look at that coat! What will he think of you? Aren't you sometimes ashamed when you think how hard he's tried to have everything so nice for us and you go right on playing with muddy dogs and going out of your way to find the roughest boys to play with?"

"They aren't either. Let go of me. You hurt."

"Hurry then, and what's this in your pocket?" She pulled and he struggled with her. "Let that be. I won't have you touching my things and that's my marble, I won it fair and square. Let me alone." Catherine couldn't keep from laughing at his red angry face and pinched his ear. "All right, but try to be a good boy while Joe is here. He won't be here long."

"Where's he going?"

"I don't know," Catherine said. "Hurry now and wash yourself." They had to get the little band in motion that evening and the reluctant David did his best with his flute, looking stout and ridiculous as he blew away, and Hortense stood mournful with her violin while the only two happy ones, Anne and Catherine, pounded at their duets or took turns accompanying the others. Joe was so pleased with them and with Mem who for once had put on her best silk dress and he kept looking at them and at the pretty parlor with a kind of longing to remember always, as if he half knew he wasn't going to see them all together like this again.

A letter came from Hull and Joe went over it several times to get the drift. He was surprised at the poorness of the spelling. Why the man was practically uneducated and yet he had been in with some of the biggest bigwigs in the

South and had swaggered around in the very best clothes money could buy. He wrote:

I have not the slightest doubt but what we shall be able to make the money out of the property, It is only a question of a little time. I saw Gardner and he is going to attac the inditment to brake the bond as soon as the Grand Jury is dismissed. He feels confident that the inditment is deficient and that he can brake it and relieve the bonds. In that event it leaves the Property assigned to Pette clear and unincumbered also your Julry [must mean jewelry]. I shall immediately put the Property on the market and force a sale of it before the State can get an attachment on it. This is the first of the Program and if it works as I expect Then Gardner will attac the attachments mine included and if he succeeds in braking them I will then step in with my other papers, I have made arrangements with a party for me to deed the Property to him I have also made arrangements with an attorney who is your friend to stand in and defend the party I sell to. The party I sell to will immediately put the property on the market and force a sale for what it will bring. I suppose you see by the papers the proceedings of the Gen Assembly I think they are fully determined to change the old laws and make new ones that will hang up the Property in law of every officer and employee of the State under Bullock and Fawcett that they possibly can get hold on. Therefore I shall force your property off eaven at a Sacrifice if it is once cleared for I look at it as just that much saved to you That is I shall force it off unless otherwise ordered by you or your mother. Do you own property on Peachtree St formerly known as the Titus property if so who has the deeds to it Jack L told me you owned it and that it had been levied on for your Taxes. I have deeds to five pieces of property including that held by Pette and the Finch property does this include all you own that you want me to operate on? There is some four hundred dollars due on the Finch property which have to be paid before Titles can be had. Write and let me know about the Titus property and if my deeds cover all and whose the property is that is deeded to me

Yours Resp

W. I. Hull

Joe's spirits went up at this letter which at least seemed to show that things weren't entirely at a standstill. Every day he read all the papers and fidgeted at the slowness. The busy way in which the family went ahead with its chores and the children to school made him feel the only idle soul in the world. Aaron came up from Grapeville with a mess of blue prints and stood around, his clothes sloppy, his eyes very blue and abstracted, listening to Joe's analysis of the South.

"If you want to get in on Grapeville—" he suggested finally.

"No, that's too small for me, Aaron. Not for me. Not with the country yawning with opportunities. Of course I must have a little capital." A little capital had become an obsession with him. He must realize on that Atlanta property. Everything he had was tied up down there. He fretted through December and in January opening the Atlanta *Constitution* read:

FAWCETT PARDONED BY ACTING GOV. CONTRI

The history of radicalism shows no more monstrous perversion of official duty than Contri's pardon of Fawcett. He gives absolution for everything and with one stroke strives to sweep out every crime from a bad man's record. His pardon on the ground that there was no chance for a fair trial due to political feeling and that ex Gov. Bullock had said he was convinced of his innocence and would pardon is just another link in Contri's infamy.

There was a column of fulmination. Joe was used to their ranting and saw only that Fawcett had been pardoned.

He walked into the kitchen where Mem and Anne were preparing schnitz for pie. "They've pardoned Fawcett," he said, "So I guess it's all right for me to go back." If Fawcett was let go he couldn't see how they could hold the others. Mem and Anne certainly agreed. At the same time Mem advised caution and Joe wired Roger Wallace. He didn't want to put his head in a sack but if Roger said it was all right to go back, he certainly would go. He was excited and happy for the first time in months. Say what you will, it was humming in the South. Philadelphia was dead in comparison and as for Grapeville, it would make a fine Old Men's Home.

When it came time to pack up his things, he shook his head over his trunk and decided to send for it later. Mem was anxious and convinced that if it wasn't safe for his trunk, it wouldn't be safe for Joe. Joe laughed at her but inside he wasn't altogether easy. He was almost being pushed back into the South by not having anything to do in the North. Philadelphia was dead and he wasn't willing to begin anywhere on a puny scale. He knew he had money in Atlanta and he was determined to get it out. He thought it was a great virtue to feel this way and to be unwilling to accept a small place in the battle of life.

When Roger wrote cautiously that he believed it would be safe for Joe to return, nothing could keep him. Roger said no more arrests had been made for months, those indicted were walking around, their trials postponed indefinitely. After the elections things might be very different as it was pretty certain that a Democratic governor would change things, but right now with Contri still in power, it was safe enough. Joe was off on the night train for the South. It would give Hull a jolt to see him.

When Lucy Blondell heard that Joe was expected back in Atlanta her feelings were terribly upset. People had told her she was beautiful for so long that it did not seem right for her to suffer. She was shocked to find that being beautiful meant almost nothing at all. She got no pleasure out of it any more. It was really no fun to comb her hair or to dress up and her life was turned upside down. Her situation seemed terrible and romantic and nothing appeared simple any more. Her girl friends were silly and shallow and when she tried to confide in Lenore out of loneliness and a kind of fear her sister's direct matter of fact way antagonized her. "If you love him," Lenore said, "what are you worrying about? What more is there to it?"

"Oh Lenore, you know there's more to it. How can we ever marry with that hanging over us?"

"It's not hanging over him in the North. You oughtn't to let him come back, it's not safe. Papa said so. If it were me I'd go to the ends of the earth for a man I loved." She looked past her sister suddenly embarrassed and shy. Lucy didn't notice how Lenore acted; she was too much involved in her own emotions. She said, "You can talk. No one knows what they will do until they are faced with it." She hoped that would make Lenore realize that she considered her advice worthless. She went on, "We aren't all alike. I happen to have a few feelings for my poor father. This family has had a hard enough time since the war without me disgracing it and making you all suffer. We've had enough suffering, is the way I look at it, and I'm thinking of my father and mother, which is more than you are doing when you talk like that."

She actually felt exalted when she talked in that way and very sure of her own good motives. Lenore just sniffed and suddenly Lucy broke down. Sobs tore out of her and Lenore looked at her frightened. So Lucy really cared. She patted her sister's head awkwardly and Lucy lifted her face for a second and stared with agonized frozen eyes. It hurt Lenore inside to see her and she suddenly felt very young and ignorant. She thought it was quite possible that Lucy was the nobler of the two and she told herself that she would do all she could to reunite the two who loved each other. Even as she made this resolve she had a great pang and a lonely feeling came over her, almost too much to bear. If Lucy went back on Joe she would stand by him, she would secretly and unknown to anyone stand by and she thought as she resolved all this that she was full of sense and not nearly so romantic as her sister.

Joe dropped back into town and no one was very surprised to see him. His friends shook hands, asked how he'd been and went on talking about their own affairs. Business was about the same. Fair had been poor this year. Joe had a vague disappointed feeling as if he had never been away. Roger and the Blondells were the only ones to make him feel he had been on quite a journey. Hull acted as if they had parted casually on the street a few days before and seemed surprised that Joe expected results so soon on the lots.

"Gardner hasn't been able to break the indictment," he said. "I'm surprised you came back, seeing you are under indictment." He stood mumbling as if hurt at something and went on, "I've been doing the best I could for you Joe. Nobody could have done better. They've made it hard for me, we'll have to wait. Times have changed, Joe, they have certainly changed."

Joe could feel the difference and he felt cramped in Atlanta. He wanted to get clear of the indictment so he could move around freely again but he wanted to move. He didn't want to stay in Atlanta any more. A new crowd was due to come into power with the elections and there was no knowing how they might play up the railroad frauds to their advantage. In spite of the rumors, Joe couldn't feel any harm would come to him. He had come back of his own free will and he couldn't see how they could get him and let a man like Fawcett go scot free.

A new legislative committee had been appointed to waste time and money in investigating and to satisfy the public demand and before he knew it he was called before them and found himself in company with some of his old cronies, Caldwell and A. S. Gorme and other business men whom he had acted as agent for a year before. He answered all questions with a frankness that baffled the Democrats and made the one Republican member of the committee pick his teeth, clean his nails and pull down his cuffs a dozen times an hour.

One day went by like the next and Joe got the feeling that nothing would ever come of the arrests. He began to think of buying up more property and of beginning a little trading. Gardner continued optimistic about his ability to break the indictments. The new crowd came in with the old crowd still amiably expecting the best. The first blow was swift. Before Joe could write the news, the family in Fifteenth Street read that he had been rearrested and was behind the bars.

When word finally came from Joe saying that his bond had been refused and that Fawcett had fled the state, Ferris had run away at midnight and K. I. Trimble was a fugitive, they were terribly indignant. What kind of hyenas were those people to trap Joe and let the guilty walk free? Catherine could hardly contain herself and had confused ideas of going South and playing the part of a Charlotte Corday. She wrote him at once, with Mem sitting beside her anxiously suggesting bits of advice bound to be useless.

My Dear Brother,
    Recd yours. It would be impossible to say how anxiously we were waiting to hear from you, especially Mother, who was worrying so, that your letter together with one

from Aaron was like a word in season indeed. Mother was so miserable since that terrible report was made in the *Era*. Your letter confirmed it in substance but then you put it in such a different light and besides you told us what we did not know and that was that "they" had actually refused bond. I must say I fear I should be very uncharitable to such. We are waiting every day for news. Do please write. David I am sorry to say was being very officious in helping to move a cart and had his fingers badly crushed between the wheels. The wounds were on his left hand, the consequence of which was, that he could not take any lessons on his flute since. What a boy! I hope no one ever prophesied that he would sail around the world. I fear he would not come back with his 168 bones in their proper place or size. Do please let us know exactly how things stand.

Your Ever Loving

Sister Catherine

He felt cheered by the little details in her letter and sure that she believed in him. She intended that he should and did not want him to know that she was afraid to look ahead and wonder where all this would end.

Aaron did nothing to cheer them. He complained that he was being taken away from his work at Grapeville and that he had said all along Joe should quit meddling with the South. The more reason there was not to alarm Mem, the more Aaron became ruffled and irritated. He acted as if he, not Joe, were in trouble. His grumbling at least had the virtue of distracting the girls and they were so busy all the time he was there pulling down shades, finding him pens, raising windows, taking out the dog Rebbie, that they forgot their anxiety. At night Mem moved around after the others were in bed, opening drawers, rocking, and tying things up in paper. The Philadelphia papers were silent about the late developments. Northern papers were getting tired of Southern frauds. In a few days they had a letter from Roger Wallace saying that they could expect Joe soon. What did he mean? They had not yet been able to decide on anything except that Aaron would have to go to Atlanta. Mem made two pairs of underdrawers for Joe and thanked her stars for some honest work to occupy her. The next letter was from Joe postmarked in Virginia. He was making the trip in jumps, probably to throw anyone who might be hunting off the scent. Tell Aaron, he wrote, to be ready somewhere to see him. It wouldn't be safe for him to stay more than a few hours at a time in Philadelphia. There was no signature. Catherine wrote Aaron and Aaron went out to see Mrs. Ferrol. She was bathing the children and came down the stairs with a bath towel around her waist. "Hello, what brings you so early?"

"Anyone here?"

"Only the children."

"Joe's on his way North. He wants a place to hide for a few days. He'll be going West probably but he can't stay in Philadelphia even for a day. What do you think of him coming here?"

"Just the thing. No one would know who he was, they've never seen him. He doesn't look like you does he?"

"No," said Aaron squinting his eyes and rumpling his mussed hair even more. "No, he's very handsome."

"So are you, and you know it. You just want me to flatter you, I know you. But if he doesn't look like you I can say he's my brother here on a visit."

"Good idea. But we'll have to see what he thinks. I don't know how serious it is and he may not even want to come to Grapeville. After all, they may be watching, for all I know."

"Why not meet him at say, Glassboro?"

"That's it. Glassboro. We can meet in front of the hotel or the depot. I'll have Catherine wire me the time and place." He was pleased with the arrangement and excited. The excitement made the whole business seem unreal. It was as if a lot of children were playing hide and go seek. Not one person in the South seemed to be acting as if he had brains. It had been a stupid mess from the start and just the kind of thing hardest to extricate oneself from. Joe's reputation was now absolutely smirched. He got a letter off to Catherine and waited for her wired reply. After this business he was ready for a good hot lunch at the Norton House and ate with relish.

The next morning he received a wire: "Hotel Tuesday night."

Joe had come home.

He had entered quietly the night before and had kissed them all as if nothing had happened. They started to talk in whispers and Joe had laughed and told them how Roger Wallace and Mr. Blondell had connived to get him out of jail. There wasn't anything else to do as everybody agreed he had no chance for a fair trial. Later on he was sure that a few thousand would fix it up all right but not so long as the Democrat Smith was in the governor's chair. At that, he wasn't so positive that if he had five thousand he could not clear himself now.

Such talk troubled Mem and made Catherine feel frightened but Joe laughed and said they didn't understand politics. Catherine went out to send a telegram to Aaron after Joe had decided on Glassboro and she looked up and down the street like a conspirator. But it was no longer just exciting, she was beginning to feel a terrible fear and she tried to ignore her feeling. She helped him repack his little trunk and take out papers and during the time they had to wait for his train to Glassboro, a letter came addressed to Ada Pearson and they had a good laugh about it. He looked at the letter swiftly, could it be from Lucy, but no it was only from Lenore. Lucy would never write to him again. The very thought of what had passed between them was too painful to think of and he moved around quickly and firmly to hide his agitation. Nothing could have convinced the family more of his innocence than the cheerful firm way in which he made his preparations to depart, the Lord knows where.

The two Trexler brothers met outside the hotel at Glassboro and Aaron nervously suggested they walk up the track. Joe said that would only make them conspicuous and boldly lighted a cigar. As they strolled around the town, Joe talked. "Aaron, you'll have to look after Mem and the younger ones. I'll start West and don't know where I'll land. I'm going to need some of that money I've given Mem. There isn't any reason for them to stay in Philadelphia, too expensive. Catherine is ready to teach next year and David can get his schooling at boarding school if not in Grapeville. If they sell the house, they can buy a place in Grapeville I should think."

"I've already thought about that. Guess they will have to come to Grapeville." He appeared reluctant and Joe looked at him sharply.

"You'll have to take care of it," he said.

"Oh I'll take care of it." Aaron was thinking what he could do with Mrs. Ferrol in the same town with his mother. It wouldn't do. Mrs. Ferrol might as well sell them her place as long as she would have to leave anyhow. "I think I've got just the right thing in mind," he said.

"Good," Joe said. "The main thing is not to worry Mem. She deserves all we can give her." Aaron grunted and felt injured because he was still troubled about his Mrs. Ferrol.

"I wish you'd come right out with it Joe and tell me straight," Aaron said. "What part did you play in all this business?"

"Do we have to go over that at this hour? I've explained until I'm black in the face."

"Don't get mad," Aaron said. "I only wanted to help you."

"Then take care of Mem, that's all I've got to say," Joe said.

"Where did you think of going first?" Aaron said.

"Detroit," Joe said. They walked around the town until a train came and Joe hopped aboard and went back to Philadelphia. Aaron felt important but anxious. He didn't know how he was going to tell Mrs. Ferrol that she would have to leave Grapeville. He didn't want to have to think about it.

At six the next morning Joe took a train for New York from Philadelphia. Catherine was the only one to come to the train with him. They weren't so gay as they had been when he went to Canada but they tried to make a joke or two and Joe waved from the window and sat soberly a long time watching the houses first huddled together then spaced wider and wider apart and at last they were among little fields and he was out of it but he could not forget his sister's face looking at him from the other side of the car window that was a little cold and misty as if a thin film of water were between them.

To put her out of his mind and Mem, straight as an ironing board forcing him to eat pears and a good dish of oatmeal until he was ready to choke, he got out Lenore's letter and slowly opened it. It was written on two sides and began *Dear Joe* and ended *Ever Your Friend Lenore.* Ever your friend. The small tidy foot, the grave bulging forehead and pointed chin, freckles and small brilliant eyes. She was no beauty, not when Lucy was present. But when he thought of Lucy, he got up at once and went out to smoke in the other car, keeping his eyes determinedly on the scene outside and fighting back a longing to cry.

The dull gray of winter was changing to a faint green. Factories and smoky houses were closing in together. They were nearing New York and he pushed Lucy back in his mind, far back.

TWO SISTERS

LENORE went to the post office every day to see if a letter had come from Joe and Lucy watched and hoped for news. She was thin and everyone said it was terrible the way she was drooping and not eating enough to keep a bird alive. Lenore felt a kind of awe of her sister. At night when the two sisters were in bed Lenore could feel Lucy shake with sobs. She would pretend to be asleep because if she so much as stirred, Lucy stiffened and held her breath. Lenore felt small and ignorant and could not understand why Lucy had not run away with Joe. She had become a different girl and talked a great deal about putting trust in God. It would make your blood run cold to hear her talk so calmly and to know that all the time she was thinking of Joe and wondering where he could be, wandering off somewhere all alone, or worse yet, in gay lighted places where people made much of him and loved him as he deserved. But when Lenore suggested that some day he could come back and stand trial and vindicate himself she shuddered and said, "No, no, I couldn't stand digging all that up again."

No one was able to console Lucy and she was a lost soul. Lenore thought a great deal about Joe and wished she could console him.

Catherine and Anne also wished to do something for their brother but there was nothing they could do except to practice hard and to see that David did not fritter away all his time at marbles. Catherine worked hard outside of her teaching hours on her French hoping to qualify as a teacher of languages some day. The house was put on the market but prices had begun to decline pretty sharply. It looked as if they would not even get their money out. Mem said she would sit there until Doomsday rather than give that expensive property away and all the talk of unemployment frightened her. They seemed no sooner to pull themselves on their feet than bad times came and ruined everything.

Aaron was provoked at the bad times coming just when he was beginning to do business in Grapeville. He and Flemmer were already busy on a seaside resort that they planned to promote in the same way they had Grapeville. Lots were in demand in Grapeville even now during the bad times but the grape business suffered. He had come to the conclusion that there was nothing for it but to bring Mem and the children to Grapeville. They could cultivate a little land, raise sweet potatoes and fancy chickens and at the very worst, have a garden for their own food.

Mem was happy about this plan. She was full of energy and hope as soon as any plan involving work came along. If they all worked hard, everything would turn out all right. Work was the one reliable thing. She fretted in the house on Fifteenth Street, covered the fine furniture with cloths and made the family eat in the basement kitchen. For her the Fifteenth Street life was finished. She even uprooted all her geranium plants and put them in pots ready to transplant to Grapeville. The bedroom carpets were taken up and rolled carefully into a corner. The family lived as if they expected to move tomorrow and months went by.

MRS. FERROL DISPOSSESSED

MRS. FERROL did not altogether want to sell her place to Aaron's mother and she was very much disturbed by the proposition. She was not anxious to leave Grapeville. She had not been a good actress for nothing and had played her part so well in the small town that no one had the slightest idea that her children were also Aaron's. They had been born in Philadelphia before she built her house in Grapeville and the boy was three years old on her first trip to the town. From the beginning she had carried everything with a high firm hand. People had even innocently commented on her boy's resemblance to Mr. Trexler and she had had the face to laugh and to say coolly, "Why there does seem to be a likeness. Well we are all related to Adam and Eve, they say." She had so composed a way, loved flowers and gardening so much and appeared on the main street with her mother, a very neat pursy old lady with clean starched pocket handkerchiefs and small curled bangs, that she at once took a place among the most respectable group in Grapeville. Besides, it was well known she had a very good account at the bank.

On Sunday couples walked or drove past her place, pointing to the house. There was considerable pride in the town about the house and grounds with the surrounding fields sown to sweet red clover. Mrs. Ferrol herself was often seen working in her garden with gloves on her fine strong hands. She had romantically named her place El Dorado and couples liked to roll that name on their tongues as they passed. "There's El Dorado."

Aaron finally proposed that Melinda Ferrol sell her place to his mother because he could not see the two women living in the same town at the same time. He dreaded what his mother's sharp eyes might see. If she should lay eyes on the boy would it be so easy to delude her? It went deeper than that, it was an actual discomfort to think of being with his mistress in the same town in which his mother lived. That his sisters had all innocently met Mrs. Ferrol and were full of admiration for her did not alter things a jot. His jaw took on a stubborn slant and he said it wouldn't be fair to him if she stayed. He would never feel at ease at her house and he would never get a minute's peace at his mother's. If she moved to Philadelphia he could see her almost as often and without this fear. Besides they were always in danger of someone's finding out.

"Is that your real reason?" Mrs. Ferrol said, slowly drawing the golden tassels of a long purple glove through her fingers.

"Why of course, what else could it be? I'm obliged to be sensible. The family has to go somewhere and if you stayed it would be bound to come out. This way you get a sale for your property and it is a good thing both ways."

"Now Aaron, I see through you. I know you better than you know yourself."

"I don't know what you mean."

"Why does your family have to come here at all? There are so many other places. But then I suppose that can't be helped."

"There's no question about them coming here. Where else should they go?" He looked at her, astonished, and she had to hide her irritation and resentment in an easy laugh. If he had only rebelled against the situation, but no he accepted it and was ready to sacrifice her for his family. Sometimes she thought men didn't feel, at least not the way women did. He didn't seem to realize what he was asking. No matter what she did, her life would be hard. She had married that blackguard who refused to set her free and sometimes she felt that Aaron was glad of it because it left him free. She had made her choice and was not sorry. What woman would want to wither away, childless, for an early mistake? No, she had children and her books and her piano and her garden and all were good. Why must she go away and be shuffled off as if she were no more than a pin?

She put him off from day to day and let him think she quite agreed with him. He never saw her any prettier than she was that spring and summer, always in some new dress and always light hearted. Toward fall he began to think it was going to be very hard to part with her, even if he did make trips to Philadelphia. He began to resent the family who were trying so hard to sell the house in Philadelphia and living on as scant an income as Mem could pare down to without starving. By October Mem was ready to quit Philadelphia even if the house wasn't sold. They could rent it and get to work and help themselves. She could not bear to feel idle and worthless. She kept after Aaron to look up some place for them in Grapeville and he had half a mind to risk it and to put the family in a rented house for a while when something happened to make it necessary for Mrs. Ferrol to leave Grapeville.

She hardly knew how she was going to tell him. She tried several times, talking vaguely about the future and the flowers and the sunset over that pine tree. She hinted that women always had it harder than men. Tears came into her eyes easily but she always smiled quickly so that he would not get tired of her and think she was a cry baby and complaining. He actually got impatient with her vagaries and swung around again in his feelings to his mother's side. He was looking out the long window in the dining room one evening. Her mother and the children were in bed. "Well I think Melinda it can't be put off much longer. I've got to get the family settled this month."

"I know," Mrs. Ferrol said. "I'll sell to her."

"What?" he said, turning around, astonished at the ease of the thing. "Yes," she said, "I don't want to, but I have to."

"What do you mean, have to?"

"Haven't you noticed anything?" she said desperately looking straight at him and blushing very much.

"Noticed?" he said, then saw the blush, got suddenly very red himself. Even his ears burned. He found himself patting her shoulder and murmuring a line that astonished him. It was out of a book he had read long ago. "I'll never desert you, darling." The phrase sounded silly and bookish but she seemed to like it. He was glad everything had worked out so easily for his mother.

Mrs. Ferrol packed up her belongings meekly as a lamb. Anne came down from Philadelphia and followed her around with admiring eyes. The two had long talks and the older woman felt a curious closeness to Aaron's sister. She wished Aaron had the intuitive understanding his sister had. As for Anne she actually felt that the house was being blessed by Mrs. Ferrol's presence.

Aaron wondered how he would feel living under the same roof under such different circumstances. He tried to put doubts out of his mind and to be practical and so long as his mother and Melinda Ferrol were never to meet, there was no use in examining what was past and done too closely. When her trunks were corded and ready to go, he went into the house and sat with her, feeling very empty and uncertain. He wanted to be at ease and comfortable but he felt like a little boy who had been thoroughly bossed by his mother. The whole idea of the family's soon coming to Grapeville irritated and humiliated him and Melinda did not make it any easier by sitting there so quiet and so uncomplaining. When the trunk man came, she followed Aaron out into the bright day and pulled his arm and cast an eloquent look up at the window of her room. He thought it was inconsiderate of her to make it so hard for him, trying to remind him of things that would be unholy enough when his mother came into the house. He was torn with being angry at his mother and at Melinda Ferrol and yet he wanted at that moment to cry, to put his head on Melinda's breast and have her comfort him. As he could not do this in the open daylight, he pulled himself together and tried to be philosophical and to tell himself that life was full of unanswered questions.

Catherine was to stay in Philadelphia that winter and board on account of her school. Hortense and Anne were delighted to be quitting the city and David could hardly believe his luck. Now he could keep as many dogs as he wanted. Aaron told him pretty sharply that he would have little time to be running around picking up stray dogs as they expected him to do a little work around the place himself; there were going to be plenty of tasks for a young man of his size. David hated to be talked to like that and sulked until he remembered that at least he was going to get out of school. No one knew just what to do about David's schooling but they agreed that for the time being he could help around home and forget it.

The house in Fifteenth Street had at last found a buyer who had paid part cash and had given a mortgage. He had also relieved them of the parlor furniture, the fine walnut with the silk damask. Catherine thought it a sin to sell it for less than it was worth but Mem could see no earthly use for such finery in Grapeville and any price was better than none. Catherine knew Joe would hate to hear of the sacrifice and made the others promise not to let the news out in any letter to him.

Letters came from Joe postmarked Detroit, Cleveland, Toledo and Chicago. He could not seem to settle down. The cities seemed to be hit with a slump and he kept moving hoping for brisker business. Men were being let out of work toward the close of 1872 and before the opening of the New Year bank failures had caused the withdrawal of cash from many savings accounts.

Old Uncle Blank took out a cool ten thousand and hid it around the house, refusing to open a door or a window if he could help it for fear the very smell of gold might waft to the street and excite to robbery. He grew fatter and fatter, spreading out like a brood hen, pinching the pennies to add to his hoard. But he continued to be fond of food and did not sacrifice his belly.

Joe was following the rumors of money to be made. As the months went by he was impatient of patient schemes; he had magnetized himself with money and followed money and the news of wealth. His letters were of great concern to Catherine. They were briefer than they used to be, told less, and cut him off from the family. She fretted to be sitting with her hands folded and unable to help him. Joe insisted that nothing could be done about the South with the present set of politicians in power and she could not understand such business. What had politicians to do with justice? With the family absent in Grapeville, she thought continually of Joe. For a young man of so much ability, so handsome, generous and good to be wandering around, never knowing when he might be arrested, was a terrible wrong. It made everything seem upside down and she turned more and more to reading her Bible. It soothed her and yet she could not sleep. Sometimes she felt feverish for hours and lay in the dark, her eyes burning and her head on fire. She told herself she was studying too hard and now that it was more than ever necessary for her to pass with a high ranking, she was continually uneasy worrying that she might not pass.

Her landlady, Mrs. Cliff, a pretty, slovenly woman, was always warning her that she would wear her eyes out. "Now Catherine, you're at those books too much, look at that line, naughty girl," and she reached with her soft finger and tapped Catherine's forehead between the eyes. "Why you'll put your eyes out with so much reading. Just wait, when you are my age, you'll see what little good it does you. The men don't like women to know too much, my dear, you'll be cheating yourself of a husband one of these fine days if you don't watch out." And she'd slide into the room and begin a cozy story of her life with Cliff, always chasing to lodges, night and day, until there was many a time she would mind it less if he were chasing some petticoat, it would show he had a more human side at least. Catherine dreaded these long aimless talks and they kept her up later than ever.

She wrote regularly to Grapeville and to Joe. She felt the full burden of the family on her shoulders, not the financial but the moral burden, to keep the girls interested in their music, to get David out of his lazy ways and to keep them all going with bright thoughts of the future.

By spring Joe had settled in Toledo. The family were in Mrs. Ferrol's house and Mrs. Ferrol was somewhere in Philadelphia. None of the carpets of the Fifteenth Street house fitted the Grapeville place and the family were living half barbarians, Catherine said, on those bare floors with strips of rag rug running this way and that. When school was out, she would see that things were put in shape, now it was all the family could do to get the chicks started, the plowing done and the hotbed for the sweet potato plants started.

The hard work seemed to give Mem a new lease of life. She felt elastic and young and hardly noticed how tired the children got working out in the fields, bending over the long rows as heel to heel they knelt to set out the sweets. Now and then Catherine felt able to afford a trip over the week end and was astonished at the strides they made. They had two snow white pigs, a pony, two dogs and a cat.

The birds hung in their big cage in the sun and Catherine stroked their heads with a finger, looking at their hard bright eyes and wanting to cry for Joe. The birds seemed all that was left of his venture in the South and the birds could not live forever.

Without actually knowing, she felt that it was over between Joe and Lucy Blondell and letters from Lenore to be forwarded to Joe made her the more certain. The more time went on, the fewer letters, other than Lenore's, came from the South. No one did anything about Joe's property. Roger was married. You might think Joe had died. Her heart shut when she thought of it. The very word died was a bad omen. She sang and played the piano for hours afterward to drive out the gloomy thoughts. But he was so cut off, so alone.

She was alone herself. She collected all of her father's diaries and old letters and began reading them. She drew a family tree with all its branches. It gave her a feeling of stability to draw that tree and to make the branches with the good fine stout old names. Her father had kept up a great correspondence with relatives, some scattered now as far west as Illinois, and she spent many an evening patiently going through his old journal book trying to trace cousins and nieces. Replies came slowly but all spoke of Uncle Joshua or Cousin Joshua and the honor they gave her dead father made Joe's trouble easier to bear.

She wrote him not to take cold, to keep warm and never to worry about the future or the past. Out of a sense of duty, she even went to see the Gerhardts on a little mean Philadelphia street, where the older girl Abby had got herself married to a little dried up shrimp of a tailor, Sam Weisel, and the younger sister, Maria, beautiful and tall, never spoke to Sam and Sam never spoke to her. The three were penned in the narrow house together, Maria issuing out into the fresh air to go to work in a big dressmaking establishment down town. Neighbors on each side never knew their names and when Maria came to die after a life-time in that house, they only knew that "the one who went to work" was dead.

In this house, Catherine let herself be persuaded to stay for supper now and then, when a mean hard little loaf and a stingy cheese made their appearance on the grayish cloth. Out in the open air, walking back to Mrs. Cliff's, Catherine felt almost as if she had gone through some penance and her heart seemed lighter. But she could not fathom why Aunt Carrie, her mother's prettiest sister, had such strange children, the one married to a gnome, the other tall, cold, hard to approach. She would stay away from the gloomy sisters for months until perhaps a note from Maria, stilted and proud, accused her of neglecting them.

Spring was slow that year. She polished her watch chain and her watch, kept her enamel earrings bright with tissue paper, spent an evening a week in going over her clothes. Her diary was up to date, the letter writing had all been done, she was going to begin to read all of Shakespeare's plays. She was sitting on the bed, half asleep, thinking of the summer and all that must be done, of her coming ex-amination, and she felt almost too tired. The back of her neck ached almost constantly, she must get a tonic, this spring weather was bad for one. How pleasant it was years ago when they were all little in the old home in Locust Valley and little lambs bounced around on the big meadow near the mill. The air smelled fresh there, not like in the city, always stale. She lay back on the pillow and then sat up quickly hearing someone stumbling up the stairs. She waited a minute and heard a knock, called "Come in!" and started toward the door.

Aaron opened the door and put his head in. He was very pale and his hair was more mussed than usual.

"Why Aaron, what's happened? What are you doing here? Is it Joe? Or Mother?" She was sure at once something had gone wrong.

"No," Aaron sat down in the chair nearest the door. "No, nothing is wrong. That is, nothing with Joe. Mother's all right. We've got several hundred chicks now." His voice sounded very flat and Catherine said again, "Now you're hiding something from me Aaron, I can always tell. You're so transparent. What's gone wrong. Did you lose some money?" She laughed, hoping to cheer him up. Why he was the kind to be affected by a mere nothing, a great baby, what would he have done in Joe's shoes?

"I was just going back to Grapeville but the train's not going for an hour yet."

"Yes, but what did you come down for? To sell some of the pigeons? Mem wrote they were raising pigeons too. Why that place will be a menagerie if you don't watch out."

"Pigeons aren't bringing much of a price now," said Aaron in a flat voice. "No, I wouldn't make a trip for pigeons." He was staring straight ahead and Catherine had a dread of what he would say next. It wasn't the family, not Joe, what was it? Perhaps Aaron himself was ill, suffering from some disease for which there was no cure. Perhaps he was trying to tell her. She felt her eyes smart and her heart pounded but she went on resolutely, "Tell me Aaron, are you sick? There must be something."

"No, I'm all right, nothing the matter at all. I guess I'd better go now, it will be train time." He turned to the door his hat dangling from a limp hand. She followed him absolutely puzzled. Well, he always was a strange one, no one could make head or tail of him. At the door he stopped, it was open now and the dark hall and stairs yawned ahead of him, a bottomless pit. He kept his eyes on that darkness and said quietly, "Mrs. Ferrol died to-night. I thought I'd tell you."

CATHERINE DISPOSSESSED

JOE DID not know what to make of the confused letter Catherine wrote him about Mrs. Ferrol. He had had his suspicions about Aaron and Mrs. Ferrol and it made him angry that his brother had not had the sense to keep his affairs away from his innocent sister. The poor child had evidently got herself into a terrible nervous state. Why couldn't Aaron take a little responsibility, instead of always standing around, absent minded, tie under one ear, never saying anything and then have Mem praise him for his peace loving disposition. Where would the family be, he'd like to know, if *he* had been peace loving? Peace didn't butter your bread or get you Fifteenth Street houses or the Grapeville house either. The least Aaron could do would be to manage his own affairs without worrying others.

It was a shame to think of all his own money tied up in the family and no capital so he could start West. He knew that with a little capital he could make money, he'd heard of the real fortunes made by '49 men and there were mines opening all the time with the same chances. It was too bad to think that he had worked hard in the South and now had nothing to show for it except a good conscience that his mother was well taken care of.

He had so many troubles of his own that Catherine's letter, with its dark brooding strain, irritated him. Lately, he got upset at little things and it made him feel almost as if he were sick to get like that. What was the matter with him anyhow? A few more years and the trouble in the South would be forgotten. A little hard cash would wipe the slate clean right now. He knew those money hunting rascals. Things weren't so bad, in a little while he'd have capital and then just watch him. He looked at himself in the mirror of a passing show window, at the hat jaunty on his head, his good clothes, the fresh tie, and had to smile. Just wait, he'd show them all.

When a letter came from Joe, Catherine grabbed it from the cold marble stand in Mrs. Cliff's front hall and took it up to her room. Her hands always seemed too cold or too hot, nowadays, and the climb up the stairs took her breath away. She held tight to Joe's letter and said, "Letters are all I have, really, they are all I have in this world." But the next minute she knew it was silly to talk like that with a mother and brothers and sisters to care for. It was ungrateful to think such thoughts.

She sat on the edge of the bed and tore open Joe's letter. . . . Business was slow, if they had money in any bank, better take it out, times were bad and banks shaky. He was thinking of going to Colorado, with a little capital he could set them all on their feet. Don't worry, he was the boy to knock the spots off the hard times. . . . She put the letter back in its envelope. He was talking to her as if she were a child and in fact what more did she know of life than a child knew? She had been living near Aaron and had known nothing of his life. She knew next to nothing now, only that night a crack had opened when he told her about Mrs. Ferrol. Now her own life seemed shallow, puttering with books and little tasks. What had really happened in the South? She felt like a nun, closed in and shut tight from the world. She was earning her living, helping the family, went to church, wrote to relatives, and while she had been puttering with the past, digging up old names, Aaron had been living.

They called it living. And a woman had died for him.

She had learned that Mrs. Ferrol had died giving birth to his child. No one else in Grapeville would know that and Aaron had had the courage to go back as if nothing had happened. Why it made her look like a kindergarten pupil. And that was what was meant by Sin. A Sunday school teacher had tried to warn them about it. "Don't give way to sinful thoughts, get up, breathe, exercise, swing your arms." At the time she had been puzzled. What sinful thoughts? Now such thoughts came in an avalanche. She got up and hastily opened the window. It was chilly and she sorted her clean laundry, after that she could write letters, go to see the Gerhardts, read the Sunday school lesson, study her French and say her prayers. She was alarmed that she could not sit still. What was happening to her? She could think of nothing except her brothers and the lovely Mrs. Ferrol that in her thoughts were so mixed up together. She stooped to touch her arms to the floor in a good healthy exercise when Mrs. Cliff knocked and edged in, holding a telegram gingerly. Catherine grabbed it, what now, had Joe been taken? It was only Aaron asking why she had not written about the room for Anne. Why she would pay him for this, frightening her so. Mrs. Cliff was still in the doorway. "Hope it's not bad news," she said hopefully. "No, Mrs. Cliff, nothing like that."

"I'm scared of telegrams," said Mrs. Cliff. "Can't bear to touch one with the poker if I can help."

Catherine had clean forgotten to do anything about Anne's room. Anne was coming to Philadelphia to learn telegraphy. Mrs. Cliff charged an outrageous price, four-fifty a week, but where else could Anne go? It would be a comfort to have her and a dread too. Lately she couldn't bear to be alone and couldn't bear company. She scrubbed herself carefully and put on fresh clothes and decided to sally out and see if she could find a cheaper room for Anne. Even the streets were not the same any more. It was as if scales had fallen from her eyes. What was going on in houses? What did she really know of Joe?

Little Anne with her round fair face and bunches of red hair coiled behind her ears came to the city and found a room on Poplar Street. She was excited, and subdued because Catherine didn't show more enthusiasm. She wrote Mem that Catherine had got as nervous as a witch and Mem had the two girls come down to Grapeville the next Sunday where she could look them over. She fussed about Catherine and mixed up a lot of sulphur and molasses that Catherine hid on a top shelf as soon as she was back at Mrs. Cliff's. There was nothing the matter with her blood. Perhaps Darwin and his ideas were poisoning the air; one of the teachers at the school had tried to tell her this but she couldn't help being fascinated by the new theories. Sometimes lately she had no desire to go to Sunday school and stayed home instead cutting out clippings from papers about duty and the home and womenly women and she found it hard to keep her mind on these things that had nothing to do with the life that was secretly going on around her.

She sat up late every night studying for the exam, as the day drew near, and even when she tried to sleep had dreams that she could not pass the exam or worse that Joe was digging a terrible hole in the ground to find gold, but at the last minute it turned into a grave for a dead baby. She woke from these dreams chilly with sweat, her head pounding, and drank a long cool drink and tried to concentrate on the far off stars but they made her feel so lonely, she could hardly bear it. She was tired out on the day of the examination but wrote furiously and brilliantly, passed with the second highest mark, and went back to Grapeville wondering why she did not feel more elated at her victory.

El Dorado was in a ferment of growing things. New

chicks came out every day, the fields were sprouting, vegetables were up in the garden. Mem was here and everywhere, her skirt pinned up, her hands rough with soil, her glasses pushed high up on her forehead. David was grumbling about school and how he should be educated. He had come to the conclusion that there were harder things than going to school.

The house looked as if it had just been moved into. Carpets were not yet down, curtains not up, furniture stood almost where it had been placed by the movers. Catherine tackled the house, pushing chairs around, moving chests, her back ached with the strain but she told herself the exercise would be good for her. She made long lists of things to be done; measure the rooms for extra carpet, send samples to Anne to match, get new window shades, screws for the rods, the cat had mange, what about a cure, match the curtains upstairs. Lists were made and lost and became vastly important, she would hunt all over for one and find it crumpled in her own pocket. But the air was good and on Sundays the sound of the church bells brought the tears to her eyes. Why was she crying? Thousands of new chicks were out, their cheeping, running and scratching ought to put life into a body, Mem said, watching her eldest daughter anxiously, disturbed, wondering, Is the girl in love?

On Sunday they stopped their grubbing and hoeing. The big calm house was peaceful to walk through and Catherine liked it better than the outdoors. But the rooms seemed to follow her around, she could not get it out of her mind that Mrs. Ferrol had lived here. Did they stand there? In that spot of sunlight? How could Aaron sit so calmly eating his dinner in this house where she had lived? Were men a different race, callous, or did they only hide their feelings and if so why? What had happened to the other children, why had Aaron hid all that part of his life?

It was Sin and Aaron had yielded to sin and Mrs. Ferrol had paid a price for yielding to sin with her own life. Her ears buzzed and she felt caught in a trap of questions she could not answer. Trust in the Lord, but her own prayers slid over her like water. Nothing seemed to penetrate her heart any more. She was all alone. She read Joe's letters carefully and felt as if he were deceiving them too. What was really going on in his life, what did he think and do? How little they knew and Mem for all that she had borne and raised these big men, how little she knew.

Every night before she went to bed she bathed all over and put on a fresh nightgown. Mem was scandalized at the size of the wash. There was no sense in being so wasteful; it wasn't as if she were a dirty girl. And they had their hands full with the chicks without making the washings any bigger.

Italians kept coming around asking for work. It was a very bad time. Aaron was busy in the Italian part of town. Many of the workmen had bought their little houses put up by Flemmer and sold to them on a monthly payment basis. But suddenly prices were not so good, the crop had been bad, some of the people could not make their payments and one of the banks failed. Aaron came home with his hat off and his necktie flying when he heard that. But there wasn't a penny of Trexler money in that bank. What Mem had was still in the Philadelphia bank and she took it out at once and when it came home in bills, she put it between bricks and hid it in the basement. It was only a hundred and some odd dollars after the Grapeville house had been paid for and the chicks started. They were all fancy bred, that was the only kind to make money with.

The bank failure took Catherine's mind off the house and herself and she actually began practicing on the piano again. She made new lists and sent them to Anne to fill out in Philadelphia. Anne was now hard at work going to the school to learn telegraphy. She came home once a month and washed and mended all her clothes. Joe seemed settled in Toledo and with the chicks growing without too many losses, their affairs began to seem brighter. Hortense and Catherine ripped up their old clothes, washing, pressing, remaking them.

They were sitting on the steps in the afternoon sun when Aaron came walking across the corner lot. He cut the corner straight over a bed of asparagus and Catherine could feel her heart skip a beat. What was up now? Mem was out with the chicks and David was playing hooky and had made an excuse to go to the store. Aaron came up to the girls, looked around, said, "Where's Mem?"

"Out in back, what's the matter, is it Joe?"

"Yes, just look at this." He tugged at the envelope and brought out a penciled strip of paper.

Dear Bro

I am in trouble here and wish you to raise $1000 (one thousand) dollars mortgage and send by telegraph to Lee & Town attys who will write a letter herewith—don't delay a moment, my safety depends on it. I won't need it all but still want to be sure

Your Brother

Joseph

Catherine stood up and looked straight at Aaron; she was surprised at her own calm, it was almost as if she had expected something like this. "Well," she said, "have you done anything yet?"

"No," he said, "Why no, I can't without telling Mem. The place is in her name. What do you think we'd better do?"

"Tell her and get her to sign. What did the attorneys say? It's about the South, isn't it?"

"No," said Aaron, slowly, "that's the funny thing, it

isn't. I can't make it out. Seems there was a mistake about some goods and the parties got the police and the police found his trunk with papers about the South. They got greedy and wanted the reward. To get rid of them at all, the attorneys need money to buy off the parties who say Joe got goods under false pretenses. The attorneys think they could clear him of that if it weren't for the South. There's nothing for it but to raise the money and be quick about it."

Catherine took the letter from Lee & Town but she couldn't understand it. The words jumped up and down. What did it mean? Did it mean that Joe was really in trouble again? Hortense had dropped the skirt she was ripping and sat with drooping shoulders looking scared. Aaron pulled a blade of grass and stuck it in his mouth, whistled and walked after Catherine over to Mem.

No one wanted to talk about Joe's new trouble. The money went off that afternoon and they had supper as usual. Toward the end of the meal Mem couldn't stand being bottled up any longer. She sputtered that it was all the South, the South was back of this, they could mark her words, it was their doings, she could see it as plain as daylight, someone was laying a trap for him and trying to get him into more trouble. Aaron did not try to argue with her. He wasn't sure himself just what had happened and had written Lee & Town to give him further details. He went out for a walk, so he said, giving Catherine a significant look, and she followed him. Outside, they walked slowly down the road, and Catherine said, "I can't believe it, Aaron, what can it be? What possesses Joe?"

"Well, we'll have to wait and see. His future is ruined. I don't see how he will ever pull himself out. It's all due to his extravagance. I've told him so again and again. Take me, what do I spend? Just about nothing. Pare down your wants and you free your life. No, nothing but the best is good enough for Joe. Why he isn't twenty-five yet and look at his clothes. The President of the United States doesn't have any better, if as good. It's all foolish."

"Well, if anyone has benefited by his extravagance, we have," said Catherine. "We can't talk. No one could be more generous than Joe." Aaron only grunted, he knew very well he never gave anyone anything and somehow his stinginess did not look so pretty any more. Perhaps he had been stingy with Mrs. Ferrol too, and Catherine at once felt awkward with her brother and began to stumble over the rough ground.

"Watch out where you are going!" Aaron called, without even so much as reaching out a hand toward her. He was a neck or so ahead of her, for all the world like Uncle Blank on his way to church with Aunty trailing after. So he had some of the old sour German in him did he? She wanted to laugh and kept from it only by walking faster and concentrating very hard on each step. She couldn't really feel the new trouble Joe had got into. "Do you think he really did anything wrong?" she said.

"Who, Joe? How should I know? I suppose not. He just got in a mess. No, I don't think he deliberately did anything at all. But wait and see. One thing is certain, he shouldn't be carrying all those papers about the business in the South with him. Why he's labeled right then and there and there's no escape. Let him send them home, I'll write Lee & Town to that effect."

They waited for more news. Nothing came from Joe but in a week a letter came from Lee & Town, Toledo, Ohio.

Dear Sir:
    Within an hour after the despatch of Mr. Virgil of the deposit in the Grapeville Bank of the money we had your

Brother at liberty and he is now well out of the reach of harm. We did not apprehend any danger from the charges against him here, for the parties to whom the goods belonged were of opinion after we had seen them, that he should at once be set at liberty, and they did what they could to that end, but his trunk falling into the hands of the police they examined all his personal memorandum and correspondence among which were divers communications from the South, and evidences of former troubles. They at once set themselves about to discover the cause and to obtain the reward for his apprehension. Your money came in the nick of time and by a little strategy on our part the police are disappointed. You may not hear from your Brother for several days but you will hear.

Say to your mother that the charges against her son here were not of a serious nature and had it not been for the pressure from the South we think we could have completely vindicated him. We have said to your Brother that the sources of his trouble in the South should be adjusted. He is too bright and good a boy to be laboring under the disability arising from that matter. We think it could be satisfactorily adjusted, though we know nothing save what he has said.

We expect to have his trunk in a few days. It is yet in the hands of the police. We will hold it until we hear from you if we are to send it to you.

Yours Most Truly
Lee & Town

When the trunk came, they took Joe's clothes out and hung them on the line to air, because he wouldn't need those good things now on the railroad construction job somewhere on the prairies, no one knew where, Western & Central R. R. the stamp said and it was just as if he had sunk out of sight. He wrote two short notes to take care of his trunk and that the rheumatics were getting him in the shoulder but nothing to worry about and came of sleeping out without a proper tent. The trunk went up in the attic and Catherine sat beside it a good half hour with half a mind to open it and find out something definite but she put it off.

No one talked about the new trouble and they tried to act as if Joe had really gotten into something that was better than hanging around in cities. Catherine thought of the trunk all the time and played the piano to keep her mind off it but it kept getting on her nerves and she would take out the key and look at it a dozen times a day. She had a feeling that the whole business could be cleared up by a look in the trunk but she was scared to find out. There was no one to talk to about it. Mem wouldn't hear a word about any more trouble and scolded at the South as if it were some kind of a great animal that could be shot and done away with and all their troubles solved forever.

The blackberries were bigger than ever that year and even Mem joined the pickers at the edge of the wood lot. Catherine waited until they were hard at work and then she went to the attic. The papers lay in a forlorn puddle at the bottom of the trunk and she fished around through the *Eras* and *Constitutions*. She didn't know what she was looking for but as soon as she saw the leaflet labeled *The Evidence* she took it out and closed the trunk lid.

It was hot in the attic. Several black wasps buzzed near her head.

The Evidence Taken by the Committee of the Legislature to Investigate the Management of the State Road. Printed on cheap paper, about a hundred pages. She turned it over carefully to put off finding out the truth. There were many clippings in her scrapbook about truth. She felt very tired, almost too tired to read the book, and she could hear the shouts of the blackberry pickers out in the hot sun. Joe would need more money soon when he left that place and David had to go to school in the fall, he couldn't hang around and be a wild boy any longer getting lazy, and they couldn't afford any more carpet, it would be better to paint the floors. Suppose the chicks died and they couldn't sell eggs, and that crop of clover looked very thin.

The wasps steadily ground out their noise, circling around her head but she put up a hand and brushed at them. They might have been flies for all the attention they got. *The Evidence.* She opened the first page, turned, kept on slowly turning, her eyes quickly taking in a page. There was no mention of any Trexler. None at all.

THE CARTERSVILLE & VAN WERT R. R. SUP-PLIED WITH CROSS TIES, MACHINERY, IRON, ROLLING STOCK BY OFFICERS OF THE WEST-ERN & ATLANTA

BOARD BILL FRAUDS AT CHATTANOOGA

HOW RENTS WERE PAID BY THE ROBBER CLAN

BOGUS NAMES ON PAY ROLL

ERA BOUGHT WITH MONEY OBTAINED ON FRAUDULENT BILLS

OVER FIFTY THOUSAND TO ATTORNEY

FORGERIES IN THE NAME OF A. S. GORME

MEDICATED PAPER USED BY EMPLOYEES OF THE W. & A. AFFECTED WITH HEMORRHOIDS

THE CALDWELL FRAUD, DIVISION OF PRO-CEEDS AMONG ROBBER CLAN

"Some time in November Trexler came to me and said he wanted to make his mother and sister a Christmas present and also wanted a shot gun and rifle for himself. He got me to order a lot of silver tea sets, knives and forks, fine shot gun and rifle amounting in all to about this bill. After I had ordered them he came to me and said he had no money to pay for them unless I would make an account of this sort which I did and handed to Trexler. None of the goods mentioned in this account were ever sold or de-

livered to the W. & A. This account is not receipted but Trexler paid me afterwards for the goods I ordered for him."

She could hear the voices coming nearer from the blackberry patch and under the very window, David whining in the heat, "Look Mem she's eating my berries, make her eat her own berries," the voice dragging like his bare feet in the dust into the kitchen, and the others murmuring and following and over her head the big black wasps, how many now, why five as sure as I'm alive circling around like buzzards. She reached her hand up, brushed the air, turned a page, the page crinkling and her heart sounding so loud, ticking away and the wasps buzzing, and one ear cocked, what if someone should come up the stairs? Hurry now.

"A few days previous to Dec. 7 Joseph Trexler came to me and said the road would be leased and that he wanted to make some money out of it, that all the officers of the road had been doing the same thing for some time and that he did not see why he should not. I told him I had no objections to his making money and that I would like to make some if he could tell me how. He told me he knew all the officers of the road were making all the money they could before the lease would take the road out of their hands."

"Cath-er-un! Cath-er-un! Where are you?" And the voice mounting from the first floor to the second. She's looking into my bedroom. Just sit still and wait. "Cath-er-un, why don't you answer? She's not up here Mem."

"I told Trexler if he would suggest some way to make some money I would go into it and suggested the best plan would be to order a lot of goods from New York and charge double for them and he could have the bill paid. Trexler said the goods would not have time to reach here before the lease and he asked me if I had any friends in

New York whom I could get to make out a bill for a large amount, that it would not be necessary to deliver the goods as he could get the bill paid anyhow.

"I rejected the proposition and refused to listen to it. This conversation took place a few days prior to Dec. 7th. Trexler kept after me about it and threatened to withdraw the patronage of the road from our house unless I acceded. I finally gave in and made out this bogus account for $5995.40. In order to give it a colorable appearance, I drew a draft for the amount in favor of the house and signed it McGraw Grant & Co., dated from New York. I took the draft and account down to the W. & A. R. R. depot about the 10th of December and presented the draft which was drawn payable at sight to N. P. Cawkins, the Auditor. Cawkins said he had no money then in the treasury of the road with which to pay it but accepted the draft to be paid in thirty days from date."

"Cather-un! Mem, she must be down with the chicks." Hortense's voice going out the side door, now the screen door slams, she's crunching down the path, that shale is noisy for a path, Mem is going too, and David calling, "Wait, I'm coming, gosh these stones hurt my feet, they burn them up. Oh wait."

"I took the draft and went away, leaving the account at the office. I did not hear anything until the latter part of December when the lease was made. Trexler came to me and said we had better get that money. I told him I had nothing more to do with it, as it was in his hands and that he would have to see to its payment. Trexler told me he had seen I. P. Ferris the Treasurer who had told him there was no money in the treasury of the road but that he (Ferris) could get it by borrowing from the bank and that he would have to have $525 commission. Trexler asked me if I thought it worth while to pay it and said he supposed Ferris wanted to make something out of it which was the

*reason for the large amount. I said I had nothing more to
do with it but if he could get it paid it would be better to
do so even by paying that large amount.*

"*That was the last I heard of it until some days after
when Trexler handed me $2,000 as my share. I asked
Trexler how he got the money without having the draft.
He stated that that did not make any difference but to let
him have the draft, and he would hand it to Cawkins. I
gave Trexler the draft and supposed he had given it to
Cawkins. Trexler also said he would have to pay James
Miller $1,000 for certifying to its correctness, which
amount Trexler afterwards said he had succeeded in cutting down to $900.*"

"Cather-un! I don't see where that girl has gone. Did
you ever see the like!" It's Hortense coming to the house
again. I'll have to go. She pushed the papers into the
trunk, shut and locked it, hid the key under the brick by
the window, as she got up she reeled. Why I'm dizzy from
the heat. The wasps reeled and whirred around her following her to the attic door. She hurried down the stairs
and came out on the terrace. The sun blinded her and her
hands shook as she shielded her face.

"For goodness' sake, where have you been? Oh Mem,
here she is, of all things. Well, didn't you hear us? We
were shouting loud enough to raise the dead."

"I was in the attic looking for those curtain rods and I
guess I must have fallen asleep."

"Lazy girl, lazy girl, lazy girl, goes to sleep in the morning, goes to sleep in the morning," yelled David, picking
his way over the hot shale with his bare feet. Mem came
up the path with four fresh eggs in her hands. She looked
sharply at Catherine, at her flushed cheeks and dazed eyes.
"Where were you?"

Catherine repeated her explanation; it sounded silly.
Mem shook her head. "You might get sunstroke up there

in that heat. I don't think the rods were ever put there anyhow." During the meal she kept a sharp eye on Catherine who could think of nothing to say, ate next to nothing and was scolded by Aaron for not paying any attention to him when he had asked twice for the salt.

There was no chance to go back to the attic that afternoon. At night when the rest were sound asleep Catherine lay stiff in her bed staring up at the ceiling where the trunk in the attic stood. Even in the pitch dark she could see the trunk and feel it hanging over her like a great stone. Her bed lay under it and she had bad dreams and woke up terrified in the dark that, thick and heavy, seemed to move slowly down upon her.

She prayed earnestly and the prayer took the terror away, tears came and she cried quietly sobbing into her pillow. Joe, Joe, where was Joe? What had he done? She could not rest until she read the entire report but even now she was telling herself that one man's testimony wasn't to be swallowed whole. Perhaps he was one of those who had tried to get Joe into trouble.

As soon as she thought of this, she grew quiet in her bed and felt so calm and happy. It was growing gray outside, she could see the dark outline of the cherry tree and fell asleep. But waking brought back the question of the trunk again. She could hardly wait until breakfast was cleared off the table and Pony had been hitched to go to the store. Mem was going herself and by a little suggestion, Hortense decided to go with her. That left only David and he would be outdoors on business of his own. When Pony had turned the corner, Catherine was halfway up the stairs.

The attic was cooler but the wasps had increased. A little cloud of them buzzed around one of the topmost rafters. She went over to the trunk, opened it and dug out the report. Her heart at once started its clump, clump, clump and her hands trembled. She was angry at herself and sat for a moment with her lips tight pressed. Then she turned the pages hunting for the name of Trexler.

Trexler. On all those stones at the Blue Church and in the old Lutheran graveyard. The plain straight gray stones. Trexler. Here lies a Trexler. Honest, peaceable Trexlers.

"to the amount of $1,153.20 and which is for white lead, linseed oil and strained lard oil is entirely false. None of these goods were sold or furnished to the W. & A. R. R.

"Before this account was made out, Trexler came to me and said he thought he ought to make himself a Christmas present of a fine gold watch, and got me to go with him to jewelry store and examine their stock. He said there were none there fine enough for him and wanted to know the best make, and he was told the Jurgenson was the best. There were none in Atlanta and he got Lawshe & Haynes to send on to New York for samples describing the kind he wanted. This was done by telegram. An answer was received stating that the kind he wanted could not be had. Just then I told Trexler I could get them and he told me to send on and get two as he wanted to make a friend of his a present which I did and he got me to make out this bill for $1153.20. The watches cost in gold $450 each. Trexler collected this bill, paid for the two watches and made me a present of one of them."

Was Pony coming back already? She straightened up, startled, hearing a steady clump clump as of his heavy hoofs through the soft dust of the road. Looked out the window. The green lawn, the clover field, the neat garden to the left, the hens cackling over their new laid eggs, and no buggy in sight. She leaned out against the solid window sill and could hear the clump in the wood tick against her cheek. Why it was in her, that steady clumping, her own heart. She lay very still, sprawled along the floor looking out, her cheeks burning, her head pounding in the heat.

The wasps wove back and forth above her on the rafter and swooped down toward the window. She reached up and brushed the air, letting her arm fall back against the frame of the window. Something sharp pierced her, a wasp had stung her. She sat up rubbing the itchy place where a red swollen patch began to spread unevenly. It hardly hurt her. She wondered that she did not feel it more. The trunk lay open and the report was still in her hand. Should she shut the trunk and never go near it again? It would be wise to do that. She began slowly to pick herself up but she could not leave the report. Not yet. Trexler. The name of Trexler.

"The account for $5995.40 presented to the W. & A. Dec. 7 was bogus."

She brushed hastily through the balance of the report. Would no one say a word for Joe? There was no time to hunt carefully, now she heard the wheels of the buggy grind on the gravel and Pony snort as he neared his own stable. She slammed the lid shut and tidying her hair went downstairs.

"What have you been up to?" Hortense said. "You look like a sleepwalker." Mem was coming in the door loaded down with bundles and looked at her, it seemed to Catherine, curiously. They would all know what she knew. It must be written all over her. She tried to distract them with questions about the shopping but her voice sounded high pitched to herself and silly and she was certain the others were watching her narrowly. Soon they would demand to know all about it. What would she say then? They must never know. The papers must be burned. But she was treating it as if it were the truth and wasn't this just a sample of the treachery Joe had told them about? For all her pains, she still knew nothing.

She followed the others to the kitchen, and in her uncertainty fumbled with the dishes making mistakes, as she set the table. Everything looked slightly bloated to her as if warped with a kind of mist that floated between her eyes and the things she saw. She looked sharply at the birds and the red bird set up a whistle, followed by an imitation from the mocking bird. Poor birds. Poor birds in a cage. Mem, why don't we let these poor creatures out? But she mustn't say it out loud, they would look at her in astonishment as if she were sick. "Why what is the matter with Catherine?" they would say.

She put herself to work after they had eaten, getting Anne's laundry packed in the wicker basket to go to the city. Anne's buff lawn waist was torn on the shoulder, perhaps she could mend it with threads drawn from some of the scraps. David came in complaining loudly of the poison ivy. He had been secretly scratching himself for two days and it had burst out in large violent blisters with the heat. They got him to wash himself carefully and to sit quietly out in the side yard with his feet on an extra chair. The birds chattered in the cage over their empty seed cup. No more seed, she must remember to tell Anne to send more. She stood over the ironing board finishing one of Anne's petticoats, and the heat from the iron rose to her flushed face.

Two ceilings separated her from the trunk and she tried hard to think of the list to go to Anne, of little items to send for, to keep from running up the stairs again. The dark hot attic was two floors above her and even in the kitchen she could feel the trunk like a hot magnet drawing her up through the very ceiling. Twice she put the iron down and ran up the stairs, her hand on the attic door. But that was weakness, no she would not give in, it was like a vice, it did not show strength of character. She ran down the stairs again and found a great brown scorch on the ironing board. After the clothes were packed for Anne, she hunted up pencil and paper. Now for the letter. Now write her the list. Let's see.

Dear Sis:

Your buff waist is torn, perhaps you can mend it from thread of the scraps you have. Get some Swaynes Tetter Ointment. David has the poison ivy very bad and what is worse than all it is in the most delicate part of his body. I think the salve will be good for him. Enclosed find money for it and also for a bottle of birdseed. Please send right away as the birds have no feed. Also send my black belt which I must have left in the drawer at Mrs. Cliff's. The ingrain carpets we had in Fifteenth St. were not big enough and we sent a sample to Lippincott's to match, now they say they have none to match, ask them if this cannot be matched in New York. I hope this won't inconvenience you to attend to this for I would like to see some room with carpet in and we cannot afford to buy new carpets. When you go to Lippincott's ask them where you can get the nails to fasten the Patten Fixture to the window frame. I think it is a wire nail about 2½ inches. We cannot have the shades finished unless we have those nails, it seems we can't get them in Grapeville. I wish you would get two dozen of them and send with the bird feed. Please tell me all about Mrs. Cliff when you write and also tell me how the fun terminated and was the party that I know in it?

                    Yours in haste,
                                    Catherine
    Don't forget the carpet.

Now that the letter was done, all the details were off her mind and the house again seemed vacant of all but the trunk. She dressed and decided to walk down with the letter but the basket would have to wait until train time tomorrow. The streets were drowsy with the heat and people lounged in doorways. What was wrong with her, what was wrong with them that they did not know how dangerous it was to stand around and smile like that while the very earth cracked under their feet?

And when she was home again and the supper dishes were finished and the others sat around in the twilight, she could not sit still and walked to the road and back again. When it was really pitch dark and they were all going to bed, she suddenly could not bear the thought of her bed with the heavy darkness pressing down upon her weighted by the trunk over her head. She made Hortense sleep with her and in the night woke sobbing aloud in her sleep with Hortense sitting over her shaking her and saying, "What's the matter, Cath, are you sick, don't wake Mem." She quieted down and lay very still but her body felt cold as ice, as if it did not belong to her head, that was hot and seemed apart from the rest of her, like a balloon that would cut itself loose from the earth and rise and rise. But the bed was rising instead, it seemed to waft them gently up and then to fall like a wave. She was scared and did not dare call out, she prayed again and blamed herself for her little faith.

It was plain to everyone in the morning that Catherine was sick. Mem made her go right back to bed and stood over her scolding her for having studied too hard. Catherine lay very still and did not answer but two tears came out of the corners of her eyes. Mem's heart stood still at the quiet of those tears and she hastily went down to the kitchen. Perhaps the men of the old days were right when they said learning was not for women. Was it a punishment to have let Catherine study so much? She was certain it was the studying and she told Aaron that nothing was to blame except those examinations.

With Mem or Hortense in the room Catherine could see no way to sneak up to the attic to the trunk. She had to get out the papers and burn them and have one more look and she made a dozen excuses to get the two to leave her alone. When she shut her eyes tight and pretended to sleep, they tiptoed out, and she got up and rushed up the steps of the attic. She knew the page, she had to see once more.

"shown conclusively that the late superintendent was a bad man and utterly unworthy of the trust confided in him . . . he not only defrauded the people of their money but the demoralization of his example was felt throughout the social, business and political circles in which he moved."

Fawcett. That was Fawcett. A bad man. She had the papers squeezed together and into the fireplace and still no sound from below. She put a match to them and they gave a puff as the draft caught them. Now she could get into bed in peace but as she started to do so the fear that a paper might have dropped or been forgotten made her toil up the attic steps once more. She stood on the hot boards of the attic and tried to stoop to look again into the empty trunk but wasps buzzed around her head, they passed in and out of her eyes and bored into her hair. As she stooped, she fell, with the wasps all about her and she screamed out in the sudden darkness.

Oxtail

THE STORY of Anne Wendel's life and time was unfolded as much or more in things unsaid as in those told her children. There's Catherine's death. We, Anne Wendel's children, never really knew how Catherine died. That thick emotion our mother felt was all we had to go by. Where did her life end and why? They called it brain fever and when we were older, in the detached way of the curious we looked up that term to find its symptoms and to see just how the young girl had suffered. Fever, delirium and then unconsciousness. An infection, started at a tiny point, perhaps the tonsils or the ear, leaking to the brain itself. To the minds of those who saw her die, brain fever was a disease caused solely by worry and anxiety, and she left that burden on them and especially on her brother Joseph. This death was to those left behind a remediable death, that is one that they fancied might have been avoided like death from starvation. They felt they knew the circumstances that had done this girl to death and guilt was always with them.

This guilt made it impossible for the two Trexler girls when they married to show the whole true Catherine to their children. When they talked at all, they told separate stories, Hortense out of her own need for some special romance, that Catherine had died because she had loved and expected to marry a man already married, and Anne that her sister had studied too hard trying to pass her examination. Neither sister would have breathed a word against their brother Joseph, and about his death too they kept a mysterious silence.

What mattered was the way these mothers talked of the dead, giving to death a tragic romantic quality almost more to be desired than living. What had these two wanted so much that they had died, before their time? Action, an intense will toward something and then death. Violence was in death and in living. Violence was in the walls, in the house next door, where the inventor read his Bible and his wife sick of his idle praying walked with her unborn baby and fell down in the streets, was brought home limp and swollen, carried between her house and ours. Violence was under the kitchen floor when suddenly one night the old woman let out a wail for her dead son, the news just then arrived that he had been hung for a murderer in Utah, and all the walls looked fearful to us. We went out into a wild night with the wind bending the branches of the box elder trees and stooped to look through the basement window where she sat on a chair rocking back and forth in pain, holding her old belly with crossed arms, wailing. When would it hit us or would it steer off like the cyclone?

The meaning of these deaths had to wait. Later to all four children it had a different meaning, dependent each upon our different ways of living. And the way that Amos Wendel was finally licked in the early lifetime of the two younger children, I was one, and in the later girlhood of the two older ones made a difference that was important. The two older girls had beaus, a settled way of life would soon be theirs, but the two younger girls were raw and unsettled in their way of living. Then, this material of Anne Wendel's telling reënforced their struggle and as the débris of bills and worries climbed higher around them, a kind of anger surely mounted in them, still helpless children, who did not want to die.

W. C. R. R.

WHAT country, W. C. R. R. Hell on wheels moved and crawled, tents, a shack or so a mile to the rear, cook wagon, gamblers, tools, men, following track of stakes in the ground as the road was leveled and tightened mile after mile over buffalo grass country. Where we at now? Who wants to live way out here? The path of suckers leads but to the grave. What about the gold fields? One nugget for every grain of sand. You're eating, aren't you? Look out for your watch. That's good, I ain't owned a watch, Christ where would I get a watch? Be lucky if you don't come down with typhoid out here. Water no good. This is the third crew on this man's road. Shut up, men are cheaper than water, any day. Besides the lakes ain't far from here, can't you smell them at night? The breeze comes from the big lakes, I just wake and smell that lake smell. Lakes? You're crazy, this here outfit is nearer to desert land than lake country. W. C. R. R. W. C. R. R. W. C. R. R.

Where we going? West by east, the ship without a sea. Be glad of sleep, be glad of a pipe, where are the big cigars now? Be glad I'm young. I'll get even, I'll show them.

Hello. The mail. The stinking pouch in the hot sun, now then Johnny don't crowd, here you are Jim, hello what's wrong with the young fellow? Heat? Water? Trexler sat down suddenly on the clay bank holding a letter in his right hand. "What's matter?"

"No," said Trexler, "I'm all right."

"Take it easy, easy now."

"I'm all right," said Trexler getting up, obviously not right.

"Bad news, maybe."

"My sister," said Trexler. "Dead."

W. C. R. R.

August 14, 1873

Dear Bro,

So you have put our poor sister in the ground. Oh but this is cruel. The only misfortune that ever befell us. We never knew what affliction was until now, and how I shall ever be able to do without Catherine I can't tell. I, like you, have continually kept the welfare of our sisters in view. I expected that sooner or later we would place them in a position that would become them better than that in which they have been taught to consider themselves. We have good sisters, and although the most promising one has been taken from us, let us for the sake of the one that is dead, still strive to do all we can for the remaining two. I am sure Catherine is not lost to us forever yet we must learn to live the rest of our lives without her. Very few meals were eaten by Mother and the six children that the thought did not pass through my head, "How much longer will we be permitted to seat ourselves at the same time?" Now indeed one is missing and how are we to bear to sit together again? As I said before I must leave here, but I can't make up my mind to go anywhere and unless the climate affects me more I shall remain until the cold weather closes the work. If I stay I am to have a tent of my own then I can sleep warm and comfortable. The rheumatic pains are in no way serious. Love to Mother and all, while you are all together and can console each other remember I am alone and in ten fold more grief than you can possibly be—For all of you can comfort yourselves that you soothed and tended her to the last, but I, I never knew she was sick until she was three days deep in the ground. Oh had I only known it in time so that at least I might have seen her buried. But it is too late, too late.

I received two bundles of papers, on one was written "Vacation! Will send more soon, Catherine." I can never read those papers, they will remain folded as they are. Write.

Your Bro.

BALL AND CHAIN

LETTERS from home followed the slowly moving W. C. R. R. No one reproached Joe and no one told him about his trunk in the attic and Catherine found in a faint beside it. He read their letters over and over and saw through all the little details about the garden and the chicks and the birds their efforts to put heart into him.

For the first time in his life he was homesick and lost his appetite and only managed to drag through the hard work. What was he doing here? Where was it leading? This kind of thing could get him nowhere. He felt as if he had fallen down to earth with a hard bump and all his optimism about a quick road to fortune was silly.

Two things were necessary for that, one capital, and the other, to get rid of that business in the South. In hard times like this, the country was full of people glad to earn five hundred by turning him in. He would be safe nowhere. If he went home and put the chick business on a paying basis, he could raise money to buy off the South. With the South bought off, his property down there would be automatically released and could be sold; the proceeds would provide the capital for a real investment. He could go West and speculate in supplies, perhaps clean up like that fellow Mills and a dozen others, who with a few thousand dollars had made millions in shovels, picks and grub in '49.

He wrote home suggesting his plan and Mem at once came back with an urgent letter to please come home. Of a sudden she developed pains and aches, complained she was too old for the hard work, had attacks of headache which never really let up until Joe was once more under the same roof. Aaron was skeptical of the scheme. He was afraid someone in Grapeville might have heard of the reward and that Joe might not be safe even if people were told he was a hired man, but then, where was he safe? At least here he was doing some good.

Joe went at the chicken business in a scientific way. During December and January he made many changes in the houses and figured on paper a big increase in their output in the spring. He and Mem argued the merits of different birds and Joe came out strong for the Plymouth Rock as opposed to the Leghorn or Asiatic. They were good sitters, though not hard to break up; good mothers and had good plumage, beautiful to look upon, in fact the Plymouth Rocks had all the good qualities that can be produced in a fowl. He decided to put in prime selected birds from Upham and Corbett strains, hens weighing eight or nine pounds, cocks ten or eleven pounds each and eggs for sale at the hard times prices of thirteen for a dollar and a half. They would get the brooders started early and have several thousand chicks by March.

He was up at half past five every morning, building the kitchen fire, putting on the kettle, feeding the horse, the cow, two pigs, tending to the chickens, and by the time the others came down coffee was on and he was standing by the flowers delicately watering the heliotrope and rose leaf geranium and pinching a dead leaf from Catherine's favorite, a bleeding heart. No one spoke of Catherine, her very name stuck in the throat but the birds received more attention than they used, because she had cared for them and the plants were kept almost too moist with frequent waterings. Mem had locked away her watch and chain, her earrings and brooch, and Anne had gathered all her papers together, her diary and her scrapbooks. One scrapbook recently started on a University Female Institute Catalogue she decided to add to, first clipping an orange label for the outside on which she wrote *Treasures*.

> To mortal man great loads allotted be,
> But of all packs, no pack like poverty.—Herrick

Poverty is the test of civility and the touchstone of friendship.—Hazlitt

The only fence against the world is a thorough knowledge of it.—Locke

Of all the agonies of life, that which is the most poignant is the conviction that we have been deceived where we placed all the trust of love.—Bulwer-Lytton

What is past is past. There is a future left to all men, who have the virtue to repent and the energy to atone.—Lytton

Have courage to cut the most agreeable acquaintance you have when you are convinced that he lacks principle; a friend should bear with a friend's infirmities but not with his vices.

Mean spirits in disappointment, like small beer in a thunderstorm, always turn sour.

All that poets sing and grief hath known of hopes laid waste knells in that one word "alone."

But one false step, but one wrong habit, one corrupt companion, one loose principle, may wreck all your prospects and all the hopes of those who love you.

He that loves Christianity better than truth will soon love his own sect or party better than Christianity, and will end by loving himself better than all.—Coleridge

Anne read the little clippings over and over and wondered if it would not be a good thing to show the little book to Joe. So many of the clippings seemed to have had Joe in mind. That one about the false step and the unprincipled acquaintances. What could that refer to except the South?

Anne was boarding on Poplar Street and came home every other week for Sunday. She could tap out the Morse code on the kitchen table and give any message David could think of in code. He began to think it would be a fine thing to be a telegrapher and to go all around the country, particularly out West. On the days she was home Anne took David in hand and she told Mem they would have to send that boy to school. Catherine had urged the same thing and that was enough for Mem. She couldn't bear to send him among complete strangers and hit upon Lewisburg where so many of the old friends were. They could have the boy for Sunday dinner and in case he was sick, watch over him. Besides she wanted another good cow, in fact they could use two and sell the milk and if she went up there with him she could select the cows and have them shipped to Grapeville. It was practical all around and the boy must have schooling. Joshua Trexler had emphasized the need of giving the children education more than he had food and who was she to say it was not right? With much brooding, she had come to see it was not too much education that had killed Catherine, no it was worry about the family, about Joe, that had made it seem so desperate to her girl.

David was her last chick, she put a great belief in him and determined he should have every chance. The other children treated him as if he were thoroughly spoiled and were always teasing and laughing at him but in her opinion David would show them all. He was her baby.

No one made any plans for Hortense. She was a thin gangling girl with great sad dark eyes and she tried hard to work into the family but she always felt outside, she did not know why. Catherine had been first and now Anne had stepped naturally into her place and was looked up to and loved by all the rest. Joe always consulted Anne and even Aaron called for Anne when he could not find his tie. No one paid much attention to Hortense and no one ever had paid much attention to her. She felt sickly that winter and read all the symptoms of different diseases in the big Patent Medicine Book with the colored plates of ulcers and boils. Sometimes at night when she could not go to sleep, she cried quietly to herself and wondered how they would all feel if she died too; they would be sorry then and wish they had appreciated her. Even if she didn't always have her nose poked into a book, she had her qualities and that time she and Catherine had made a trip to Lewisburg, she had been popular and Cousin Amos had taken her to a camp meeting and had treated her as if she were really grown up. Men didn't like women who were too clever and Anne would wake up some day and find herself on the shelf and wish, too late, that she had been just a womanly woman.

Anne was sometimes impatient with Hortense and her ailments and told her if she took a glass of hot water before breakfast and a good brisk walk afterwards she would be all right. Hortense said it was easy for those who were well to talk but Anne had no patience with her meechy ways and thought if Hortense would keep the darning basket empty instead of leaving it all for her to do on her days at home, she would be healthier. But toward the end of her day home, she would feel sorry for Hortense and her long face and manage to laugh her out of her troubles. Anne felt that she owed it to Catherine to be good natured with her sister and every time she felt like saying a cross word to her, she hunted through the papers instead for a poem or a good clipping to put in her scrapbook *Treasures*.

Since the family had moved to Grapeville, the church had been neglected. The feeling that people in Grapeville might know why they had left Philadelphia, that they might find out about Joe, made them shy of going about much. Mem did not like this state of things and since Catherine's death grumbled at Hortense and David to go to Sunday school at least. Anne made excuses to stay away. She said she was afraid someone might ask her embarrassing questions about the hired man, but she was glad to have an excuse to read the book she brought home from Philadelphia.

During the week she read almost every night until closing time at the Mercantile Library. The list of books found among Catherine's papers had been added to and whenever she came across an article referring to books she copied it faithfully. Are you deficient? Are you deficient in taste? Read the best English poets such as Cowper, Thompson, Pope and Coleridge. In imagination? Read Milton, Akenside, Burke and Shakespeare. In reasoning? Bacon and Locke. In sensibility? Goethe and Mackenzie. She took down all the names and read everything she could lay her hands on, muddling her mind with all sorts of ideas and trying hard to fit them to things that she knew. She longed to have someone to talk to but Hortense was useless and Joe did not think she should read Darwin. All that had happened made him want to believe in the simple old faith of his childhood. How else explain the tricks that Fate played? One must accept Destiny. Once he accepted Catherine's death and that nothing could change it, he felt calm and resigned and able to bear it.

When Mem put on her best cape and tied the strings of her bonnet on Sunday afternoons before going to Catherine's grave with a geranium blossom, a few sprigs of heliotrope or a fern, Joe left the house that he might not have to see her walk up the road alone or with David and the girls. He busied himself with the chicks, scattering the feed bitterly. He was her brother, and he could not go to her grave for fear of comment from people who knew him as a Hired Man.

Even in his own home, he was not himself, not Joseph Trexler, but a Hired Man. When the others came back from the grave they had that quiet calm refreshed look that he remembered so well in his old Quaker grandmother just home from meeting. They spoke softly to one another and no one teased David all evening. Their gentleness removed them from him; he felt hard and cold to be so shut out. He could not help his resentment at being cut off from his sister and alone. While the girls set the table, placing the plates softly, he sat by the window, hunched and dark. The flesh seemed to drop from the fine bones of his face, emphasizing the nose and high cheek bones of his father and Catherine. Anne could take in his feeling at a glance and she had a way of touching him on the shoulder, lightly, and he could feel the hardness melt out of him and the flesh come back on his bones and his eyes quit burning. After the evening meal he picked up the book Anne had brought back with her from Philadelphia for him.

He wanted only travel books. He had a book now about out of the way places and there was a fine description of the island of Sicily. He could easily imagine himself on that island. He was not sure that it was not his duty to write a letter to Lenore or Roger as if from abroad, saying he was sending the letter with others to his sister to re-mail. If word got around in Atlanta that he was out of the country, he might be able to move around with less danger. The more he thought of it, the better he liked it as a practical plan. If the authorities quit looking for him in this country he would certainly feel safer. And Lucy would feel badly when she read that letter. Even when he was at work in the field, the temptation to write that letter came upon him so strongly that only by inwardly composing it could he go ahead with his work.

"The blue water of the Bay of Naples, the deeper bluer skies, the sky above an old volcano's head streaked faintly with red like blood and underneath the long buried cities."

He could see the paper of the letter, a thin crisp blue, the ink, and Lucy's hands reaching out for it to take it from Lenore, then her face bending over it and dropping tears. The idea was so refreshing that strength seemed to go into his very bones and he swung the hoe sharply as if it were a pick in the ruins of Herculaneum and Pompeii.

He made himself half sick with work. He fussed around the chicks, following the directions with a patience that drove even Mem half crazy. She began complaining that he was a regular driver for work and would see them all under the sod if this kept up. Whole days at a time, the scheme of making money from the chicks seemed so easy and so practical that he almost felt as if he were already putting the receipts in his pockets and had taken the train for the South to buy them off. He could not get it out of his head that a few thousand dollars could clear him for life. And what was a few thousand dollars? What had it been to Fawcett or any one of those men? Without that money he was held up in everything he wanted to undertake. He might as well have a ball and chain on him.

Money was power and power was freedom. It was all right for a fellow like Aaron to talk about paring away your wants and securing freedom. Freedom for what? Freedom to do without, that was about it. Aaron could live and die knowing one spot only if he wanted to. Joe sat figuring on little scraps of paper with a stubby pencil each night after supper. His features would sharpen and strain over minute characters. Mem would feel uneasy at his intentness and urge Hortense or Anne if she was home for a little music. But no one had touched the piano since Catherine's death. Her music stood on the rack and was carefully dusted. Anne promised herself each Sunday to play the old music and break the spell but she got as far as the keys and no further.

The music box that Joe had had in Atlanta came in handy now. Its funny little tunes repeated monotonously had the same soothing effect as the whistle of some bird. Joe's pencil would stop, then begin drawing aimless circles, finally his face that had looked so drawn took on color and life, he would leave the room and they could hear him bounding up the stairs, two steps at a time. A few minutes later, behind a cigar he would be laughing at them, his face softened and lazy, teasing David back of the smoke rings he was so mysteriously and perfectly blowing.

In January, Mem took David to Lewisburg and they visited the relatives, stuffing themselves with sausages and pies. Mem bought two of the best cows in the county and arranged with a drover to take them as far as Montgomery County where Aaron would come to ship them. David settled down in the school and wrote home regularly. He complained that the lessons were hard and that he had paid out six dollars for books and that with some other items left him only three dollars and forty cents. They were pinched for money that winter and Joe watched the brooders anxiously.

David was glad to be by himself in Lewisburg and to feel important. He strutted a little among the other boys and pretended he had come from Philadelphia instead of Grapeville that was not worth boasting about. He was not very popular with the boys at first and some of the town boys even called him Fatty and made him mad clear through. On top of that a dollar disappeared from the bottom of his trunk and he went straight to the principal with the story and told him there would be a lot of ground torn up if he did not get his money back. He wrote a long virtuous letter home describing the bad boys who swore and stole and added a pious injunction that they were not to worry about *him,* he had not come to the school to mix with bad boys but to get an Education and be a sensible man. Mem was very pleased with this letter but Anne and Hortense snickered about it to Joe who laughed and said the little scamp certainly knew how to get what he wanted. He frowned a minute later and said he was afraid David would need some watching as he grew older and if he was settled in some business when David finished school, the best plan would be to have David with him where he could watch over him. Mem said it looked to her as if at least one of her sons was going to be careful with his money and David was smart enough to draw up neat little accounts of his expenditures.

Blackening Brush	35 cents
"	15
1 Box collars	40
hair cutting	15
2 linen collars	40

$1.45 out of $5.00

Mem was so pleased with the account that she did not get upset at the item of the collars which according to Hortense was quite superfluous. The boy had no business to spend his money in that way when his sisters were going without their very shoelaces to get him an education.

If one of them so much as reproached him he knew how to get around Mem. There was always some dark tale about a regular Rough, the worst boy in the school who had over two hundred conduct marks and was told not to go downtown for a week as punishment and who had actually run away from the school instead. Anne wrote to him regularly trying to give him good advice and David answered her solemnly asking what her opinion was about boys going with girls, most of the fellows had girls but he believed it was a practice that distracted a boy from his studies. Anne wanted to laugh at him, why he was a regular little Jesuit, but she only added a postscript to her letter, telling him that he was quite right and should leave the girls alone and not to forget he was being sent to school, at some sacrifice, to study not to play and get into mischief.

By May, they had hundreds of Brahmins, Buff Cochins, Plymouth Rocks and Leghorns and the runs were lively with little bouncing balls of yellow fluff. Buds were opening, trees were green and there had been just the right amount of rain. The family sat outdoors in the early evening and during the day Hortense rambled over the place. The fear that Joe might be found out had bound them up all winter, now they began to feel easier and relaxed with the warming sun. Everything promised a hopeful summer. The fields were a thick green, the pony whinnied to get out and the cat had kittens in the woodbox back of the kitchen stove. Anne skipped a Sunday home and Mem said she didn't see how she could find an excuse to stay cooped up in the city when it was spring.

No one knew why Anne had not come home and she was ashamed to tell them. She could not bear to admit to herself that she had fallen in love. It was not right to care so much for a man who was practically a stranger when Catherine could never care for anyone again. Her feeling of loyalty to her sister was to shut herself up in wax and then she reproached herself for being so unkind to Catherine's memory. Catherine would want her to be happy, and half suspicious of her right to be happy, she was happy.

Anne had met John Gason at Mrs. Cliff's. He was boarding there and had the identical room that Catherine had lived in. When Anne learned this she could not help being interested in the young man. Something seemed to melt in her and make a friendship with him inevitable and almost holy. Besides he was a stranger. He was an Englishman and had only an uncle and a half dozen cousins in the city. He was in the jewelry business and his hands were long and fine. There was something about him that reminded her of Joe. He had the same pleasant manners and an air of being someone, he dressed well and read good books. She was relieved to learn that he knew many of the authors she knew. There were so many really curious coincidents, his staying at Mrs. Cliff's, having Catherine's very own room, his likeness to Joe, and the discovery that they both went to the Mercantile Library, that it was no time at all that they seemed to have known one another always. Outside of her brothers, he was practically the first man she had ever really talked to about anything except the weather. And she did with him what she could not do with anyone in her own family, she talked about Catherine.

The sympathetic way he listened, watching her very lips move, touched her to the heart, she could feel herself get warm all over, up to the very eyes, her voice stopped and she became confused. What was I saying? Oh how terrible to stop in the midst of telling about Catherine, what a terrible thing, and she felt suddenly cold and full of horror at her callousness. But her sudden change only made John Gason the more considerate and kind to her. He had hardly known her two weeks when he bought her the first present, the cunningest little pair of solid gold opera glasses, very tiny and when you looked into them, you saw a picture of Henry Ward Beecher on one side and the Lord's Prayer on the other. It must have cost quite a little even if he did get a reduction on account of being in the business. He gave her his card with elegant lettering, *John Gason,* and the word *Jeweler* down in the left hand corner. When she opened her pocketbook to get a little change, she saw the card and blushed and wondered if, in case of an accident, they would find the card and send for him. Before long, he presented her with a splendid *Vicar of Wakefield* in lavender and gold with handsome engravings and a long poem *The Deserted Village.* Mem did not approve of the presents. She put on her glasses and peered at the gifts suspiciously. She could not understand why her children allowed themselves to be distracted from the business of life by knickknacks.

The presents were carefully wrapped in tissue paper and kept in a drawer upstairs with a carved fan of Catherine's and her silk basque with the little brown ruffles.

Hortense became very restless at the sight of the presents and began teasing Mem to let her go to the city and learn to be something. So far Anne's telegraphy had come to nothing. There were more telegraphers turned out by the school than there were positions. Anne took a position at Gould's store, instead, and sat in a dark cubby hole, adding up figures in a big dusty ledger and copying from sales slips into the ledger. When she had paid for board and room, there was not much left out of the six dollars but she stuck at it and kept hoping soon to get a better position. Nothing now would have induced her to stay at home in Grapeville.

On Sundays she frequently went home and listened to the family gossip, how Rebbie had caught another skunk and would not come out of the barn even to eat he was so ashamed of himself, Pony had got a nail in his foot and the red bird was molting. Joe was working himself to a bone but he was very hopeful and had a long talk with Anne about giving up her work at Gould's and helping him that summer with the chicks. He was positive they could clear up a lot of money and as soon as Smith was out of office in Georgia settle up down there. Roger had written, always addressing his letters to Ada Pearson, that there was no hope so long as Smith was in office.

No one in Grapeville had really had a close look at Joe. He never showed himself on the streets and some thought it was funny that the hired man at Trexlers' did not go to town on Saturday night. He was certainly an unsocial fellow. Aaron had wind of some talk off and on but nothing to amount to much. He was anxious at the slightest hint that people might be noticing Joe. When he saw Babcock, the sheriff, twice driving by the place and slowing his horse as he neared the house he went to Joe and told him of his suspicions. Joe laughed them off and said Babcock wouldn't have sense enough to scent anything.

They were sitting at supper on a Saturday night and Anne had come home from the city. Joe was facing the windows that looked toward the road. A door with glass in it looked in the same direction. It was not a clear view to the road on account of trees but Joe put his knife down and held his fork in his left hand and then put it down very softly. Anne was sitting opposite him and saw the pupils of his eyes tighten. Mem looked up and moved sharply, startled by Joe's listening. Joe picked up his knife and fork and cut his meat. "Act natural, all of you, Babcock is coming. Leave it to me."

Aaron said, "Shall we say you aren't here?"

"He's seen me. This afternoon. He was driving by. Keep quiet all of you."

Babcock and the other fellow were coming across the lawn and saw the family seated near the window eating. They descended the few steps to the area and came up to the door. Aaron got up and wiping his mouth on his napkin, opened. He looked inquiringly at Babcock.

"Evening, Mr. Trexler. I'm sorry to disturb you folks but it's my duty. I guess I better have a few words with *him*," and he pointed a long finger at Joe across Aaron's shoulder.

"Certainly Babcock, but I can't think what you'd have to talk with him about."

"*He* knows, and you know too, come now, no use us pretending. It just makes it hard for the women. He ain't no hired man and you know it, he's your brother and come to see him close up he's as like your sister, I mean the one that passed away last summer, as two peas. Now he's wanted and you know that, too, no mistake about it. Now don't you?" And he spread his legs apart and stared belligerently and triumphantly at the silent family. Joe quietly folded his napkin.

"Come now," said Babcock, "don't make it hard for your family, come now, it's not up to me to let you go, but the law, if you're innocent you can prove it I expect at the proper place."

Aaron said, "If you'd mind your own business Babcock, instead of snooping around—"

"This is my business, Mr. Trexler, for which I was duly elected by one of the biggest majorities ever known in these parts. I tell you I made that fellow Skelton look pretty small. He couldn't find a hole to crawl into. Well, come now, it's getting on and my dinner's getting cold. I'll take you up to my place tonight and tomorrow we'll take a little trip together and no one the wiser. I believe in being considerate of the women, that's the way I look at it."

Aaron started to open his mouth but Joe took hold of his arm and pinched it. He looked straight at Babcock and smiled. "Many thanks, Mr. Babcock, for being so considerate of my mother. If you'll allow me I'll change my clothes and be with you in a second. I wouldn't want to disgrace you with these old clothes. Don't blame the officer, Aaron, he's only doing his duty; he's got the law on his side and I'm not sorry this has happened, I've wanted to clear up that Atlanta matter for a long time. Give me five minutes, Mr. Babcock."

"Take your time, Mr. Trexler, me and Booth here will wait outside just to keep an eye on the place, matter of formality, hope you'll excuse it ma'am," and with a bow to Mrs. Trexler, he turned his back and sauntered outside with the satellite Booth.

Joe moved toward the stairs, saying quietly, "Aaron come up while I change." The two went up. The mother pulled her work basket toward her and quickly sorted through a bunch of socks, mated two and ran her hand briskly through for holes. Her cheek bones had taken on a bright metallic flush but she said nothing. Every few minutes she peered out at Babcock who was smoking and looking tranquilly through the glass door at her. She clucked angrily and shaking the socks, went up the stairs after the two men. The girls were petrified by the beady stare of Babcock who was amiably attempting to fascinate them with blowing smoke rings. Anne began clearing the table but she moved clumsily and in a minute Aaron ran down and said, "Here, take Joe's tie up," and handed Hortense his tie from a rack by the little mirror on the wall. She took the tie and went up the stairs. It was darkening outside and in the kitchen very gloomy.

Aaron lit the lamp on the side table and the one on the wall by the stairs. He was whistling light-heartedly. Mem came down the stairs and with her back to the glass door said something to Anne. Joe came down running and called, "Come in, Babcock, be with you in a second."

Babcock tapped his pipe, put it in his pocket and he and Booth stepped heavily into the kitchen.

"Right cold these evenings," he said, rubbing his hands cheerfully. "Looks like frost."

"We don't want frost now, Mr. Babcock," said Joe. "Spoil the fruit."

"I'd like to take a look at those papers, Babcock," said Aaron. "I want to see if they are in order."

"Right you are, Mr. Trexler, here they are, all legal and no mistake about it."

"Well I want to be sure it isn't just a trick," said Aaron. "There's a good deal of doubt about this case as you probably know." He reached for the papers and moved toward the light on the table by the wall. The girls moved behind him leaving the stairway open near Joe. Joe stood carelessly tying his tie and pretending to look at his shoes. Babcock, impressed with his good clothes and his air, excused himself as he passed in front of him and went toward Aaron and the light. "Here you are Mr. Trexler," he said, fumbling with a sheaf of papers and selecting one.

Mem had moved over toward the door and appeared to be clearing the table. Booth, grinning and picking at his teeth with a splinter of wood, closed in behind Babcock and gaped over his shoulder. The minute the group bent over the table, Joe turned and in a flash was on the stairs. He took it two at a time and halfway up, Babcock let out a roar. The two girls closed in on him and penned him behind the table. The last look Joe had was of Babcock's red face over his bulging vest, the jaw dropped in amazement. Then he ran.

He made for the woods. It was dark but he knew every inch of his ground. He could hear Babcock roaring and bellowing and wondered how long they could trap him in the kitchen. In the few minutes upstairs the plans had worked out in his mind. A whisper to the others had been enough. How quiet they had been and how quick. He was full of admiration of them. They were like animals, wary, and ready to jump at a whisper. If he had a five minute start, he was safe. Babcock would thresh around in the woods, bellowing and helpless. He took his tie off and ran, pushing aside the blackberry bushes at the edge of the timber, and came out on the dark road. He could hear shouts and then a dog barked and a shot went off. He began to laugh and running, still laughed, shaking with a kind of nervous laughter. That pig of a Babcock. He'd get even with the South for this. Circling the cranberry bog he made toward the cemetery and its white stones stood out like guideposts in the darkness. To the right Catherine's new stone was alone and he slowed as he passed. He was as near now to that stone as he had ever dared to get. It seemed to stand in darker ground than the others but the bark of the dog sounded nearer and he ran faster, planning as he ran how best he could get across the Delaware.

When Babcock howling like a stuck pig shook Hortense and Anne off from his legs and arms, he rushed to the door and shook it. Mem had locked it. "Where's the key? I'll have the whole kit and caboodle arrested for defying my law, see if I won't," and he kicked at the door. Booth had been pinned to his chair by Aaron and he now struggled up and came to assist Babcock. The two, clumsily kicking, knocked in the lower panels and the upper glass. The splintered wood ripped Babcock's trousers as he squeezed through, followed by the skinny Booth. Aaron unlocked the door and followed. Mem and the girls stood in the area, listening, as Babcock threshed and bellowed through the woods. "They'll never get him," Aaron said. "He's too fast for them, now why in thunderation don't you girls do something for your mother? Get busy somebody and make tea." They came back into the kitchen and stared at one another. Mem sat bolt upright and drank three cups of tea and although it was very dark now, she lit a lantern and went out to the chicken runs.

It was a black night and toward morning it began to rain a little and the first drops plopped loud and ominous on the trees around the house. Only Aaron slept; the two girls lay in their beds, stiffly, shivering and dozing and Mem lay in hers, now cold, now hot. Toward morning every bone in her body ached and with the beginning of the rain she got up, hunting blindly through her tears for a handkerchief. When she found a big one belonging to one of the boys, she blew her nose loudly and furiously, and the noise calmed her. She put her clothes on briskly and went out into the yard through the heavy wet grass to the chicken run. The first rooster's crow was bugling as she opened the gate and the chickens rushed toward her, scratching and pushing, their bright beady eyes circled with the buff feathers.

At six, when the rest of the family came down, they found Mem sitting by the table, breakfast ready, and Mem with her glasses on, stiff and upright, pretending to read an old Grapeville *Courier*.

They had to wait three days for news from Joe. It came through David who had received it at Lewisburg. It was in a tiny envelope addressed to Anne and written in pencil on a sheet of paper taken from a drug store counter advertising Wistar's Wild Cherry Balsam.

Dear Sister,
    Please take charge of my trunk and take out all papers and letters and a little box of jewelry everything in fact

with writing and put it safely away. I am not sure that
Babcock did not have you all arrested for obstructing
"his" law, judging from the way he roared and howled
through the woods. Grave as the situation may have been
there was something about it really comical, what I can't
say, but still it has given me amusement from the moment I was on the stairs until now. I am sadly needed at
home and it is too bad that this has happened but no use
to lose heart. I am confident when Smith is out of office
a few thousand and probably less will make it all right,
with this in view I worked hard at the chicks that a part
of it might be made up, but never mind. Had some trouble getting across the Delaware first to Bayside then Stowe
Creek and back again and at last had to go the whole
route over again and come to Pennsville and came over
this morning. Have not concluded where to go have
thought some of Australia as I don't think I can stay
safely and contentedly in this country and unless I can do
this I cannot make much money but if I can be content
I can surely make money. Laying off and only making
board and expenses don't do you see, if I wanted to do
that I could find a place in the U. S. Am resting here and
will give my address in the next. Chicks must be kept
clean and I would not keep the Buff Cochins and Plymouth Rocks any longer than a good chance presents and
not over winter nohow. Will write.

Yours

There was no signature. It was some years before he
dared to sign his name again. He would put an initial *J*
to letters but never his name. Joseph Trexler disappeared
on this side of the Delaware in May of 1874 and Victor
Dorne put on his clothes and waited in Waynesburg, Pennsylvania, for his sister from Philadelphia who was bringing
clothing, two hundred dollars and papers necessary if he
should want a passport. But a passport now seemed a dangerous thing to apply for and he decided to go West.

Jacob Clark, the hotel proprietor, kept a sharp lookout

while they sat in Joe's room talking over plans. How did Joe work upon Jacob Clark to make him willing to run around peering and whispering for his safety? It was a puzzle to Anne. There he sat on the bed, telling her again how the chicks must be kept clean, and to be sure to keep his papers under lock and key, and she knew that everything he asked would be done, why he could wrap them all around his little finger. Why had the South been so hard hearted to him? Now he must go so far away, where wild Indians were waiting to scalp white men. When she told Joe her worry, he yelled with laughter, and said, "Why don't you know Denver is a big city, with theaters and people of fashion? And I'll go there first until I see what is ahead of me."

He was so gay about it that Anne did not have time to think that she might never see him again. It was only after the train was out of sight that she let that thought come into her head, and in that day it was considered cold hearted not to have let this fatal thought come into the head of those who traveled and those who were left behind.

Hortense took a great satisfaction in writing the details of the escape to David who was all agog for news. She lamented that the whole town knew the story, it had been in the papers and though no names were mentioned everyone knew who it was. Their troubles never seemed over. Wasn't it awful that Joe should have been obliged to leave them just now when they needed him so much on account of having a thousand chicks?

David found it hard not to tell a few of the boys about the excitement and he referred darkly to Indians and the West and said that he might be quitting school next year and going West. Some boys laughed themselves sick at Indian Dave, as they now called him, and cut pasteboard arrows to pin to the back of his clothes. He got very indignant at the insults and always reported them immediately to the teacher. "You just wait and see," was his answer to his tormentors and he repeated this so often that he gradually shut them up. They began to believe him and talked among themselves about how much better it would be to light out and go West than to stick here grubbing away at worthless books and sit shivering in prayer meeting every Wednesday night. David did not tell Mem of his ideas and he was careful to report every penny he spent in a neat little account with ruled lines showing cash received and cash expended. He was a great comfort to Mem and at his first suggestion that his third suit was worn out completely and he was forced to wear his best clothes during the week and his second best around the place for baseball and exercises, she at once ordered goods for a new suit. If his money was running low he wrote plaintively about all he meant to do for Mem and the girls some day, how he would buy them a new buggy and see to it that they didn't have to work so hard, ending, "What about the money, can you send some soon, my shoes are about wore out and I am almost walking on my stocking feet."

Mem never seemed to see through his wheedling. She took her youngest very seriously and was convinced that he would be the staff for her to lean upon in her old age. The girls were ashamed of her for forgetting how much Joe had already done for them but she no longer counted on Joe. When she talked of the future, she talked about David.

Aaron was a liability rather than a support. His plans were all for the future. Mem had loaned him a thousand dollars of her money that had come from Joe for his projects. It was very easy for Aaron to take money and hard for him to pay any back. Even when he had it, he put off parting with it. He was very touchy too about being asked to help out with expenses at home. For one thing he was hardly ever there. He had a sofa in his office downtown and nearly always slept there. He could not tell anyone why he did this and he would not admit to himself that he was uneasy in the house where Mrs. Ferrol had lived. It was easier for him to pretend that he often worked late at night and it was too far to walk home. He ate most of his meals in restaurants and when Mem began grumbling about her cow not having been paid for yet, he felt injured and sat down and wrote a long letter to Joe. Mem would not let him put a foot inside the door without beginning on her troubles. She never spoke of her anxiety for Joe but she harped day and night about the cow and the place and the responsibility of the chicks. In many ways she was a changed woman. She talked more and complained continually. All that she had never said about her terrible grief at losing her daughter and her anxiety for Joe went into feverish worry about David's laundry, the cow, the chickens and the way she was left high and dry with all the responsibility of everything on her hands.

The girls could only sit and take it. They knew what was back of her continual grumbling but it did not make it easier. Hortense often complained of headache and won the right to stay in bed in her own quiet room all day with a handkerchief moist with camphor on her head. Money was scarce and the girls did without new clothes. Anne gave all she had to Mem for David and was almost ashamed of the expensive presents John Gason bought her and hardly had the heart to display them at home. When he bought a beautiful pair of green kid gloves with tiny tassels and clasps of gold she was almost glad that they were flatteringly too small for her. Now she could keep them hidden with her other treasures and not make Mem feel bad with such elegance.

Spring that had come on so bountifully seemed to wither in June. The women rattled around in the shell of a house empty of menfolk, and Aaron only showed up on Sunday in time for the roast. He was thin and uneasy and after dinner they could hear him walking around and around upstairs whistling in a thin pipe and stopping in one place so long that it gave them the fidgets to imagine him up there, his hands in his pockets, his shoulders slouching, his blue eyes staring nowhere.

Joe wrote Aaron a sharp letter from Denver telling him he should pay for Mem's cow and make her feel better. She had given Aaron a thousand dollars and if he couldn't pay for her cow, he must expect her complaints. Later he would be able to send something but it looked to him that Aaron was the one to assume a little responsibility about the family. His cold note astonished Aaron and he paid for the cow without a murmur. He was bothered about Joe and thought if he could be cleared of the trouble in the South, he would certainly make money. He wanted Joe to make money and he wrote Joe suggesting that he, Aaron, write to Smith. It made Joe laugh. He always thought of Aaron as dreamy and impractical but nothing he had ever done seemed so wild as this. Why there was no chance of anything short of five thousand dollars until Smith was out of office. He wrote Roger Wallace to jog Gardner and try to get him to dispose of the real estate. Now more than ever, he felt the need of capital.

The new country excited him. He was farther west than anyone of the family had ever gone. His own father had never crossed the Mississippi. He had come that far, but no farther. Along that stream up toward the north, Joshua Trexler had taken his hazel branch and his curious animal sense of what was good and what was bad in wild land, and he had settled more than one colony of German immigrants fresh from the homeland after '48. He had said, here is fresh water, and here is good soil, and he had struck his staff and they had taken his word and made their homes and flourished.

As he had crossed the Mississippi, Joe had looked down at the rushing water. This was the dividing line. He was going farther than his father had gone and he would never cross that river again without twenty-five thousand dollars to give his mother. The size of the sum pleased him. If it took him ten years he would get that money. He owed it to her. Perhaps he could find gold the way his father had found pure water, with a kind of instinct. Gifts like that ran in families and only got lost through lack of use. He wondered if his father had lived, would he have been a success? He had died at a critical time, when machinery was coming in, roads were opening up and the country changing. If he had lived, he might have been considered far seeing and wise. Dying was his one mistake. Joe told himself he would not die, he would live and not fail.

The fat farm lands on each side of the track were solid and promising. There was no end to the richness of Kansas farm lands and Joe counted as many as ten men in one field. These fields made the Eastern farms look puny and sterile and not worth monkeying with. He was in the land of the future, where anything is possible.

He stopped off at Kansas City and was taken back by the talk of hard times. Hundred acre farms couldn't be mortgaged for a hundred dollars. Storekeepers shook their heads and grumbled about mortgages falling into the hands of Eastern capital. Joe did not want to listen to such talk, he wanted to believe that there was enough for everybody and after all, weren't the plowed rich fields a sign of real wealth? As the train left Kansas, farm lands turned to rolling grass country that spread like an endless lawn from sky to sky. Now and then dark specks on the prairie moved nearer and nearer and turned to herds of buffalo racing alongside the tracks, sometimes parted by the train, hurrying and jostling, frantic not to be left behind. Sometimes antelope, nimble and graceful, stood quite still, ears erect, mild and astonished at the snorting train.

The unending grass, the soft empty prairie, was like the Old Testament country of Joe's childhood. A great happiness was in him. Train passengers talked easily with one another, made friends and exchanged life histories. At the stations where the train stopped for lunch, those with money in their pockets got off and, joking, went in a body to the lunch rooms where they were waited on by Chinks in dirty white aprons. Those left on the train opened their pasteboard boxes and dug out the dried remains of bread, cheese and small twisted apples.

At night, Joe and a young fellow from St. Louis stood on the back platform and talked about the theater and fortunes and going around the world and seeing life in Australia and what was the meaning of the hard times and once near midnight they saw not two hundred yards off in the moonlight a herd of buffalo racing along, swiftly and mysteriously to disappear.

III. THE BADLANDS LEAD
TO DEADWOOD

P ROFESSOR PENNEY was a small mild man who in the home had practically no say. He had been brought up by a New England mother of stern stuff and had fallen into the hands of just such another who saw to it that he made her his wife. He was fond of flowers and spent a great deal of time in his laboratory working out chemicals to detect mineral deposits. He had studied the layouts of every mine in existence and knew the Virginia City and Washoe mines as well as a farmer knows a crate of eggs.

The human element bothered him and he liked to get hold of someone more timid than himself and talk of the human side of mining. Hearst and Haggin, mining nabobs of the Coast region, knew him as a reliable man and when news broke that a small discovery party of hunters and trappers had stumbled into the Black Hills via Poorman's Gulch and had found gold in the streams, these gentlemen had been quick to tip off the Government at Washington to send Penney at the head of an expedition to find out if it was really going to be worth while to scrap with the Indians.

A few miners loaded with hundred pound packs had got the scent before Penney took the trail out from Cheyenne to the north. They had skirted the brassy rim of rocks and the sunken gulch with the black burned out trees, dodging Sioux varmints who were shooting at sight to protect their hunting grounds. The reservation of the Ogalalla

Sioux and the Brulés spread over miles of Nebraska and Dakota territory and enclosed the entire Black Hills region. The Indians went to the Hills for lodge poles, arrowheads and to hunt the black tailed deer, the white tailed deer, the elk and the antelope. The egg shaped group of hills rising like a raw knuckle out of the plain was sacred to the Indians. The lightning and thunder were born in these hills, the iron earth rattled with terrorizing storms. It was their land and they wanted no whites smelling around. Red Cloud called on Sitting Bull, Crazy Horse, and Two Moons to help drive out the prospectors. Things began popping in Washington and it was not considered worth while getting into a scrap with the Indians over a few freebooters. Politicians traded on not molesting the poor Indian. The first group of miners, traveling on their own, risking their own skins, had no sooner scooped up a little wealth than they were herded together and driven out by the United States Cavalry troopers.

The way was cleared for Penney's expedition of practical mining engineers. Penney had nosed out a little information from the sulky First Discoverers on parole in Cheyenne and found that most of the coarse gold and nuggets came from up Nigger Gulch way near the northern limit of the Hills. The crew began on French Creek without much promise but over the divide at Spring Creek several bed rock holes showed ten dollar diggins, that is a man working a string of six sluices with fair fall and ample water could make ten dollars a day. On Bear Butte the hard rock miners found good pay prospects. The granite, rotten on the surface, hardened with depth and showed considerable free gold. Penney and his men followed the line of least resistance, his nature was that, trained and bred in the bone; where such a line gave him the minimum trouble and he followed that line, down the creeks, going downstream, and when they came to Whitewood, they unhitched the teams and snubbed the wagons down the steep slope and followed the creek along its least resisting line, downstream, striking a few caves of beauty but of no mineral value.

If Professor Penney had not followed his nature and his nose and had, instead, gone upstream to the fork of White-wood and Deadwood creeks he would have stuck his pick into the richest gold strike of the whole region. A mere quirk in his own nature prevented him from being the intermediary between the quarter billion dollar Home-stake Mine and Hearst and Haggin, who were however just as ably served later on by the two Manuel brothers, quartz miners, and Hank Harney, tenderfoot.

Professor Penney cheerfully following the line of least resistance cleared out of the Black Hills with his reports and his samples and his mild bulging eyes, pleased at his efficiency, and he paid off his men in Cheyenne and went to Denver where his story broke, setting every adventurer in the country by the ears. For even though Penney had laid hold of no giant deposits he had found enough to make every man with red blood in his veins look around for a horse, a gun and a stake.

The Government now ordered out all the rag and bob-tail miners, and soldiers went in to pull those out who resisted. The Sioux pranced catlike around the rim of the Black Hills and took pot shots at every hat that came into view. The Hills were outlawed, and a stream of adventurers began slowly to ooze in to Cheyenne from Denver and points further west and slowly worked into the Hills, bribing the soldiers. Hearst and Haggin sat down to wait. "Patience," says Haggin, "is the foundation stone of success."

Professor Penney gave his story to a nice young fellow on one of the Denver papers and went on with his work of testing minerals with acids. The reporter threw up his job and with a map of his own pricked like the Professor's to show the most likely deposits, set out for the gold country.

Joseph Trexler, reading the story the day the news broke, pulled out of the combination grocery-bakery fifteen miles south of Denver, gave his hen, then setting on a nice half dozen eggs from Jersey that had traveled in a box wrapped carefully in flannel, to his landlady, strapped his guns together, counted his little wad and turned north toward Cheyenne.

A year of it had been enough for him. At the start, the Boston man who wanted him as partner had made what looked like a good proposition. The amount to be invested was a thousand dollars, each man to furnish five hundred, Joe to do the work and Sumner to tend to the store. The business was good for thirty dollars a day, on paper, with a sure profit of 30 per cent and not much expense outside rent which was only thirty-seven per month. Nothing much else offered. Peddling garden truck in the mining camps was uncertain. Wages all along the line were smaller than he had expected back East. The big profits you heard about back East weren't in wages, that was certain.

And they hadn't been in the grocery and bakery business. Joe had gone back to the bakery end and had tackled the bread making but the heat of the ovens made him weak with sweat and afterwards in his chilly little room the bed felt cold and damp and he took to having one cold right after another. He found himself doing all the work and Sumner taking it nice and easy in the store, chinning with the men and yet drawing the same profits. But he wasn't one to go back on an agreement. He stuck it out and wrote to the folks that things were going fine.

They had dug up five hundred dollars for him to use as his share in the business and he swore he'd more than treble that within a year. When he pulled out of the business, the thirty dollar a day sales had dropped considerable because one of the mining camps that had been the biggest purchasers had shifted up the line. He was glad to clear out even at a sacrifice. Anne had written that she was afraid the postmaster at Grapeville had got wind of where he was and he began to be nervous and jumpy. Business had not been brisk for some time and he stocked up on blankets, warm clothing, cartridges and a supply of army ration. Following the Denver Pacific Railway on a long legged bay he headed through Fort Collins and Greeley toward Cheyenne.

Miners, outfitters, tinhorn gamblers, fly by night adventurers, male and female, milled in the streets of Cheyenne and chattered about Black Hills gold and Indians on the warpath and Custer's Seventh Cavalry and their matched iron grays, flea bitten grays and roans. Soldiers strutted around the streets and got first servings in the eating houses. At night Joe rolled up in blankets at the Mammoth Corral after a good hot meal at Dyer's set out on tin and stoneware at four bits. The Corral kept filling up with a four horse team from Boise and California Joe Miller, famous trapper in buckskins riding a cayuse, who had quit wolf poisoning on the Bitter Root River to answer the call of new diggin's, trailed in followed by three pack animals. A young fellow with white eyelashes and a hard shell derby, soft white hands and a continual smile, drifted in toward morning and sat down on a wagon tree with a lead flute in his hands. At the first sign of life from the rolled blankets he piped up with the plaintive "The Heart Bowed Down." The fellows began cursing him out but he smiled and screwed up his eyes in the white lashes and went on picking out a tune.

Joe fell in with two men from Idaho and they decided to start for the Hills that night. No one was paying any attention to the soldiers' warnings of shoot to kill. The valleys of Red Water, Belle Fourche, Bear Butte, False Bottom, Spearfish, Hay Creek, Rapid, Castle Creek, Spring and Alkali were outlined with knives on every table that presented a surface a knife could cut into. Gold was here and here and here and Blaine said he had heard the Silver Creek area gave the richest promise.

It was late November and the thermometer was dropping fast when Joe and his party crashed through brush and dead timber following their crude map to Silver Creek. Some half dozen others were there before them. Cabins were going up, and the men were taking turns at bringing in game for the winter. Blaine, tall and bony, boasting perpetually of his practical mining experience snooped around up and down the canyon, wrinkling his nose over the gravel, taking up hatfuls to smell, taste and patiently wash until his hands turned blue and his nose seemed to lengthen and grow transparent as an icicle.

"I don't like the looks of it," he told Joe, drawing him apart and talking in a low theatrical whisper. "Now you see the way she lies, two far from rim to rim and all this gravel, for all we know, is a wash-up from recent rain storms. I'd lay a bet that bed rock is ten feet deep below the surface." But in spite of his pessimistic talk, two fellows higher up were washing out gold every day, and before January a thin wispy fellow from Kansas found a nugget worth twenty-three dollars and at night sat by his fire guarding his claim with his Winchester.

Prospectors in Palmer's Gulch were digging a drain ditch and claims in the vicinity were going at a dollar and a half. Joe took a chance, and he followed Blaine around staking three hundred foot claims above and below Discovery on Silver Creek and he took a chance on a hard rock claim in Bear Butte Gulch. If there was gold here surely he would get in on it. He was one of the first and the other sixteen men felt just as he did. The earth was freezing fast but they could poke down below the grass roots and pan pay prospects. Blaine said that if the place was properly worked it was bound to yield rich returns. But he wasn't satisfied with the placer stuff.

Joe could see with half an eye that placer mining wouldn't last forever and that if there was real riches it would be in the hard rock mining. At night he couldn't sleep and lay thinking over the lay of the land and what different miners had told him. The earth under his feet was crammed with gold and no one knew where to begin.

Coxey on the claim below threw down his pick and quit. His grubstake had given out, his shoes were rotten, he coughed all night. He said he was through with mining forever. He had followed it around from Nevada to Colorado and now here and so far as he could see it was nothing but sweat for the most of them. About the time he found something, he would have to sell out for a song to some bloke who had more money than he did and all because you have to have more than grass in your belly. By God he'd quit this time before he was hauled off in a box or shot in the back and Blaine shrugged at Joe and said, "You see, the fellow wonders why he never gets anything but the dirty end of the stick. Why look it, the dirty yellow squirt can't stick at it. Has to have a full belly or he whines. He's got as much chance as we have hasn't he and we have as much chance as the next. It's every man for himself and let the best man win."

He whistled cheerfully and Joe made a good pot of coffee to eat with the venison that night. Inside, the cabin was warm and cheerful, they had plenty of wood piled higher than the cabin outside, they had enough venison to last until the thaw began, they had tinned stuff and they still had coffee. What more did a fellow want? Every day they kept their hands in with a little digging when the ground wasn't too solid and they rocked out a little dust.

Joe's knuckles were black and stiff and bled under the nails. He had to quit work and sit by the fire nursing his hands, reading an old copy of a Denver paper with a long description of Ireland in it. He read that article a dozen times and wished he had gone abroad and was now wandering around among the ruins of Italy or with a band of adventurers on some big excavating job among lost cities. Now that the excitement of getting into the Black Hills was over the long wait until spring was almost more than he could stand. Most of the men felt the same way and for something to do talked about scrapping with the Indians and cleaning up the country. Joe wrote letters home to pass the time and told Anne when she had occasion to write South, to say he had gone abroad. He actually felt as if he had gone abroad after he wrote that, and lying half asleep in his bunk that night composed a long letter about the Bosphorus and castles by the Sea.

Near Christmas letters came in from the outside and a box for him with Fassnacht cakes and a dozen eggs carefully packed and only three broken and a jar of strawberry jam and three Jersey pebbles which he held in his hand turning them slowly over. One for Mem, one for Hortense and one for Anne. He knew they were meant to remind him of the old home but they were Jersey pebbles and he never wanted to see the place again. He put the pebbles on a ledge back of the stove, a little dissatisfied with Mem and the girls for sending them to him. Now that he could no longer send them presents, he didn't want to be reminded of it by their presents to him.

Even the old music box, carefully wrapped by Anne and packed with the rest of the things, reproached him. Anne had actually reminded him of her loss by writing with some sharp instrument in the brass rim inside the box, *Good-by Old Friend, Anne, 1875*. He stood it on the table and turned it on and the old familiar tunes made him happy in spite of himself. He remembered the day he bought it in Atlanta with Roger Wallace laughing and joking with the clerk and saying that unless that box were the best money could buy it wouldn't be good enough for Joe Trexler. He unpacked the rest of the box and set out the food so that the other fellows would get a taste of it when they came in. His hands had kept him in the cabin pretty closely lately and the cold had come down so fiercely that card playing was about all the occupation anyone could take up. Near the bottom of the box was an envelope and in it a note from Anne and another in a plain envelope.

Joe went over to the fire with the plain note. It was from Lucy. The cold was coming in the one window with the flour sack covering and the light from the fire was all he had to read by. He was provoked at himself for wanting to put off reading Lucy's letter. Someone might come in any minute. He could hear them outside the door swearing at the damned sons of bitches who were too lazy to shovel and only sat around on their hams waiting until someone else did the work so they could cash in on it. There was no law to keep anyone from filing claims above and below theirs, but after they had done all the ditch digging to wash the stuff, these other bloaters come along and cash in on it. Joe stuffed the letter in his pocket and he carried it around for two days without looking at it. Perhaps she was married or happy or perhaps she would accuse him of having made her wretched and God knows he felt guilty enough, not of doing her harm, no he had no guilt there, and wasn't she the one to blame, after all for not having had sand enough to stand up for him? Lenore would have, that was the difference between the two girls but you couldn't blame Lucy, no one could help the way they were made. Finally after two days he sneaked the note out of his pocket one late afternoon when he was on top the ridge where he could practically survey the whole country.

Do we still trust in God? Or have we forgotten all? I forget! No, not until this heart shall become cold and motionless can I forget or cease to love you. God knows best and knows why it is our hearts should suffer and be separated. Oh, will it always be so. But thy will be done. Trust in God Joe. O Joe, forgive me, forgive the pain I have caused you. God only knows what I have suffered. No one will ever know. Forgive me for the sake of what we have been. I will not trouble you any longer for I can scarcely hope you will receive this. Goodbye, I can never forget or cease to pray for you. Trust in God, Joe. I am the same today that I was over three years ago.

L. B.

His hands shaking, he put the note back into its envelope and stuffed it in a breast pocket. Perhaps some Indian shooting from the ridges behind might get him and they would find him lying with that note. He would like to be buried with such a note and go under the earth with words like that. He oughtn't to be glad she was suffering, but he was. No one would ever know what he had suffered. His own family least of all. They had been brought up that way and sometimes he thought of all of them going around with their own hard stones of trouble in their chests. He was hard and tight inside of himself now and there was nothing to do about it. At least Lucy was living in a world with tablecloths and linen and clean blankets and her hands weren't cut and bleeding. It didn't go below zero in the South. If she was miserable he was a thousand times more miserable. She had friends and a sister to console her. He wanted to read the note again; why it was like poetry. He hadn't washed his shirt in weeks and his socks had holes in them and what would she say if she saw him with a beard? How had he got into such a fix? What terrible thing had he done to be thousands of miles away?

If anyone thought he was going to feel guilty about that business in the South, they were fooled, no man in his shoes could or would have acted differently. He wasn't going to take the blame for it and yet here he was, actually taking the blame, half frozen, with a gang of crazy devils who all lived and ate together and shared together and never asked a question and were more human than any of those damned bloodthirsty stuck-up Southerners who thought themselves so highly civilized, had any notion of being, or than that sneaking Jersey constable knew how to be, in a million years. And Lucy was a million miles from understanding what it was all about, and so were Mem and Anne. None of them could know what it was about. He didn't himself. He was in it, square in the midst of it, and he knew as little as the next.

If he died and went straight to Hell he couldn't feel further away from home or Lucy. The note in his pocket made him feel almost as if he had died and he made up his mind not to read it again.

Oxtail

WHEN Amos Wendel finally failed in business, the attic was the hardest spot to tackle. The two younger girls helped their mother all they could with the job of packing and they thought it was about time some of the old papers were burned instead of cluttering up bags and boxes. Somehow they began to read one old letter and then another and for hours they sat there piecing together the dead and gone. Papa's failure got a little faint with all the other failures and successes and the deaths and births crowding in the heat and dimness of one small attic room. When Victoria came to Lucy's letter, she handed it to her sister and they read it and re-read it.

"I can never forget or cease to love you."

Had it been true? "Poor Lucy," Victoria said. Pity was easy. Lucy was no doubt dead. Uncle Joe was dead. Their mother's wedding dress wrapped in the blue cloths lay at the bottom of the trunk. In five hours they must leave that house for a smaller home. The two girls had come to burn, now they wrapped the old papers together, tied them and dusted their hands. They knew the papers would go with them and wondered how far.

Anne Wendel came upstairs as they started down. Her apron was torn and dusty and when she saw them she began, "What do you think Papa is saying? It's awful to think of. He's down there talking about being a night watchman. With all his experience saying a thing like that. It's at the jewelry store. He'd only get fifteen a week and he says nobody wants an old man, he can't expect more." Her lips trembled and her eyes begged that they stand by her. The girls were tired of pity, they felt suddenly impatient with their mother. It was too much, year after year, the little disasters.

Victoria said, "That's better than nothing, Mother, we might as well face facts."

"Oh but a watchman," said Anne. The girls began hauling down the bags, bumping the steps and heard their father come to help them. He was brazenly cheerful smoking his pipe, and said that if they knew what was good for them they'd burn half the trash and make an end of it.

THE DEAD AND GONE

Anne had taken charge of all of Joe's private papers the year before and she had kept them religiously under lock and key. For some time now she had been accumulating a secret hoard of her own that was kept locked up in the drawer of the old chest. When the letter from Lucy Blondell came asking her to send the inclosed to Joe, she had quietly steamed it open over the teakettle after the family was in bed. She itched to know what was in that note. She told herself she ought to look at it in case it was lost in the mails. Her conscience did not hurt her because everything that she did lately was subordinate to her pain at being alone. John Gason had been gone a year and for many months she had had no word from him. Everything she saw seemed a clue to that silence. Lucy's letter must tell her something she had to know.

When she read it, she felt a great light-heartedness. It was true then that time was nothing. Lucy said she was just the same and three years had passed. She reproached herself for grieving that no letters had come, as if love were not strong enough in itself. The letter made her feel that she was not alone, Lucy and Joe probably and if they, why not John Gason, loved in spite of time. Surely love meant more than Hortense tried to make her think. It wasn't a bargain counter, you write me, I'll write you, you love me and I'll love you. He would come back to her, she would not let herself be shaken any more. Hadn't he said that he was going to Australia with his uncle and weren't there many reasons why letters might have been lost? Perhaps he was lying sick somewhere, not just forgetting her as Hortense wanted her to believe. Hortense's sound practical ideas were so much poison. Perhaps that was the way to get a husband but it had nothing to do with love. Lucy with her beautiful pale face trusting in God wasn't practical. But she had what Anne wanted, belief. Trust in God, Lucy said, but Anne couldn't do that. She sometimes wished she had not read all those books and lately she had tried to pray but it was only foolish. Her prayers seemed to be going in a great funnel up into the sky and when she looked at the stars and thought of her prayer wandering around among them, in such a universe, it made her ashamed. Poor Lucy, oh Lucy, she thought, we both know what it is.

And as it was very late she tiptoed softly to the chest and having copied the letter, put that copy in beside her letters from John Gason so that she might have something to look at and to reassure her in the long days to come.

PRISONERS ALL

PRETTY DICK, banjo player at the Gem Theater in Cheyenne, rode in from the north and told the boys around Silver Creek that he had seen a buckskin trouser leg filled with gold dust in a miner's cabin on Deadwood Creek and was riding to Cheyenne to dig up money to buy up a claim. The whole gang quit work overnight and packing up tools and what grub they had set out for the new diggin's. Joe, Gilly and Blaine were almost the last to leave. Parties coming in camped near their cabin and they itched to get on before all the good claims were grabbed up.

Thirty cabins had gone up in January on the flats above the branching of the Whitewood and Deadwood creeks and by March there were over a thousand tents, wickiups, spruce and fir lodges. The ground was thawing out and the waters of Deadwood Creek were red from iron ore washed down from the sluices above. A sawmill got going and Joe joined a long line waiting to buy lumber at seventy dollars a thousand for the sluice boxes. Trees, newly cut, fell into the streets in the path of the roaring bullwhackers engineering their load of stoves, picks, shovels, grub and ammunition.

Harney with his wagon crammed with fresh apples packed in bedding and straw sat hunched on the box gently clucking and moving slowly through the crowd that gathered like magic around him begging to buy. That night he had his pockets pretty well lined and boasted that now he could grubstake the Manuel boys. "I'm no millionaire but I aim to back them boys to the limit. They're sure enough quartz miners and know pay streak from a gravel bed which is more than some can say." Joe listened to Harney and the Manuel brothers and anyone who was a sure enough miner. He didn't know just where to buy a claim and they were selling high, twenty-eight pennyweight was a price.

The land was so jammed up with timber it was hard to get at. A few were doing purty good at sluicing from the whipsawed lumber still heavy with gummy sap. It took a strong current to get results. The roots and brush had to be wrenched out to get at the gravel underneath and after he had nosed around a little, Joe came to the conclusion that there weren't a dozen claims east of town doing more than pay expenses.

The stuff was in the ground or water, though, and he and Blaine struck a pay streak that had the hard luck to run off the main creek channel and go to the left some eighty-five feet. They started in tunneling and hoisting and after weeks of back breaking work they rigged up a track and little car to take the gravel back to the creek to wash out. The Manuels and Hank Harney were on a knoll behind their claim. They were making cuts as it was cheaper to do than sink a shaft and it cost enough at that what with steel, explosives and grub. Those boys were in a tight pinch and pounding the rotten quartz for a grub-stake. When that didn't bring in enough, Harney took his team and cut cordwood and sold it from door to door.

Joe and Blaine could look up at the Manuel boys hacking away and Blaine was all for sitting down and taking it easy, God Almighty he wasn't as young as he once was, but Joe just said, "All right you sit down, I'm going to keep on for a bit." He couldn't seem to let down except at night when it was too dark for anything else and then he was so tired it took a few drinks to get him waked up and feeling human. The place began to look like a town with its flimsy shacks, about as durable as lemon crates, and after Joe had a few drinks in him he got a lot of fun out of Main Street with its gambling tents and saloons where there wasn't a drink you could name they didn't hand you.

Women were scarce as hen's teeth and yet every now and then a pretty girl, young and kind, drifted into the cribs back of Main Street. When the theatrical troupe came to town, the girls in the show looked especially good on the stage. Now and then fresh girls came to town and some of them got married. It was only later, in the eighties, when the wild freedom of the camp tamed down, the Pinkertons came in and machinery took control, that the girls began shooting themselves in the early morning above the Gem Theater and Dance Hall. In the beginning, it was All Promenade to the Bar and girls in purple cow handkerchiefs stepping up and the night of one dance the belle of the ball wore a black velvet dress with all the cow brands of the ranches of three states embroidered in gaudy colors over the skirt and tight basque. The men worked hard at mining at the start and at the end of the day liquor was better than grub. They were a hopeful lot, not a man there didn't expect to strike a bonanza.

Along about May the Indians began stirring up trouble along the edge of the Hills. The Hills belonged to them and they began to see the white men were in to stay. Miners from up Nigger Gulch way and from French Creek came in with their tongues hanging out, ready to drop. They hated to take time to fight the varmints off and were scared to go away from their claims for fear someone would jump them. It would make you laugh to see some of the sights when the Indians started shooting. A man didn't know whether to run and get jumped or stay and get shot. News came in that soldiers had chased a band of Indians and massacred the whole lot except one chief who rode without stopping for two days with his squaw and baby. Blaine said, "It makes a man ashamed to hear that kind of business." There was a loud mouthed storekeeper near by and he spoke up and said, "Do you want to be killed? We're developing the country, ain't we? We need protection, don't we?"

The bull trains kept out of the Hills and a scare went around that the Indians were planning to starve them out. Men quit mining and stood around talking about the Government's not being on the job and taking care of them after they had risked their skins to settle wild country. Now that it was certain that the Hills were rich gold country, there was no sense in delaying in driving off the savages, that never did a lick to develop anything. A good deal of talk went around that a petition should be made up to go to Washington and some of the men who were more pushing, and had an eye on building the town up as a nice paying town enterprise, got together and drafted a memorial to send to Congress to urge for the speedy abolition of the Indian title to the country they were now occupying and improving.

During the scare there wasn't an ounce of food for sale and Joe went around offering one hundred and twenty-two dollars in gold, all he had, for a twenty-five pound sack of flour but no one would take it and a man who was known to have two sacks of flour slept on it every night with a Winchester beside him. In about ten days the scare broke and flour was for sale but Joe kept his gold and went down to the new Rapid City with an eye to getting in on some kind of speculation. He was all for the new town that was bound to grow into a city by and by and it was great to be living in country that was springing up overnight.

He felt proud and happy even though the gold hadn't begun to fall into his hands the way he thought it would and after he had gotten in on some Rapid City property he wrote back home that Rapid City was flourishing and Custer had fallen.

BANKER IN EMBRYO

WHEN David Trexler read that Rapid City is flourishing and Custer has fallen he felt he could not bear to stick in that stupid school any longer. He was now nearer home, at Bennet Square School, but he was not sure he was learning anything. There were too few teachers and only Mr. Shortcrow really took an interest, the other fellows would never bother to explain a problem and if you asked, you got called to order. Besides there was never enough to eat, just enough so you wouldn't starve. The fellows stole from one another and swore too and he didn't believe that they were the kind of boys he wanted to know. He needed a new hat and it was a shame to send him only a new band when he had asked for a new hat, why his hat looked the worst in the school, even Sneak Thompson had a better and everyone knew that Sneak's father paid for his tuition with butchers' meat.

The next time they sent him eggs from home, he would sell them and he bet if he sold them to the boys he could get more too, Mem said they were four cents apiece now but he would charge five. After all he ought to have something for his trouble, hadn't he? He had sold one of the little mince pies Mem sent for twenty cents to Ray Lodge and if he had had more pies he could have got rid of them all but Mem would be angry if she knew he sold his pies.

Anyway he was going to get out of this school and go West. Last year when Joe had been in Colorado he had said he would send for him but now that he was in the Black Hills he had written Mem not to let David come by any means. Treating him as if he were a baby. He was good and sick of it. All he was good for was to run errands for them and take care of their letters for them. If he wasn't responsible, they wouldn't have let him handle the mail that way. It was risky business, wasn't it, getting letters from Joe and forwarding them under another envelope home and then he mailed all of theirs to Joe too. He was pretty sick of always having to ask for every penny and then when they sent a measly dollar have them tell him that money was pretty scarce in that quarter. As if he didn't know it was scarce, he ought to, the way he just about went without a cent of spending money.

There weren't many boys would stand it the way he did, without a murmur, but they never thought anything he did amounted to anything, oh no, not even when he walked all the way to Wilmington with some of the boys and back again and they were nearly dead from such a trip and he had expected when he wrote that some of the boys meant to walk to Philadelphia even if it was thirty-six miles from Bennet Square that they would tell him to go in on the bus but they never even suggested it and instead Hortense came out to see him. He found out it cost a dollar and a half to stay all night at the inn so she only stayed a few hours and went on home but at least she could see with her own eyes that the school didn't feed the boys any more than chicken feed and she promised to see to it that eggs and pies went to him every week. Hortense looked awfully pretty and a couple of the boys joshed him about her until they heard she was his sister when they were solemn and respectful and they had better be or he'd show them.

Money was so scarce that Mem paid his board bill at the school every month instead of by the term and sometimes when she fell behind Mr. Shortcrow would look at him in such a way that he couldn't think of anything except that the bill wasn't paid. He was sick of boarding school and when he went home for Easter week he told Mem that he wasn't going back to that school another term. The whole family went into consultation and Mem had a long talk with old Dr. Felton who said that the best thing for the boy would be the drug business. He had a friend in Philadelphia who ran a drug store who was on the lookout for a bright apprentice. David wasn't very enthusiastic about it but he had nothing else to suggest except going West with Joe and Mem wouldn't hear of it.

The discussion about the drug business and how little money they had just about spoiled his vacation at home although the girls and Mem put themselves out cooking all his favorite dishes. Aaron was hardly ever there and they turned themselves inside out making apple dumplings and cookies for the man of the house, as they called him. He began swaggering around, telling them what he'd do when he got going and they took him seriously and listened and by the time he went back to Bennet Square he felt he was just wasting his time in such a place.

He told all the boys that he wasn't coming back and was

going to a pharmaceutical college in Philadelphia next year and had a place as an apprentice in a drug store already promised him. The boys couldn't do enough for him and there was a good deal of talk about what kind of things customers would buy and how he would feel when a woman came in and asked for constipation pills. Then some of the fellows began thinking up things to ask for and they all got to squealing and yelling and carrying on so that Shortcrow sent that ninny assistant to tell them if they didn't quiet down he would forbid their going into the town at all until the end of the term.

David was quite the man for the rest of the term and when Joe sent a little box with real honest to goodness gold nuggets, he could hardly contain himself. He was the center of a crowd six deep all wanting to look and "Let me hold 'em in my hand just a minute, come on Trexler, let me," and he let some of the fellows that had shared their Christmas cake with him hold the nuggets but most of them had to content themselves with looking while he rattled the nuggets in his hand and then let them lie on his spread palm to tantalize the boys and make them sick to be in a stupid baby school while all the time real men were fighting Indians and leading a wild exciting life full of adventure.

After the way the fellows had treated him during those last weeks it was kind of a drop to go back to Grapeville and although he was to start in learning the drug business in the fall, they put him to work milking the cow and fixing the fence and weeding the garden. If he hadn't kicked he would have had to pick blackberries just as if he were a regular baby. He whined and teased for a plug hat and even the girls had to laugh at him, why he wasn't sixteen yet, but he swore that fellows he knew had them and besides he was big for his age, wasn't he. "Big around, you mean," Hortense said, and he was so mad he never showed up until dinner time and then he wouldn't speak to any of them and had to be coaxed to eat his dumplings.

Money was scarce as hen's teeth and they talked all summer about where the money for David's tuition at the pharmaceutical college was coming from. Any minute Joe might strike it rich and it was tantalizing being always on tenterhooks about what might happen.

It had been a hard spring and the chicks had not done very well but there was plenty to eat. The girls never went anywhere so it didn't matter so much if they didn't get new clothes. They had never stayed so close at home as they did that summer and Hortense teased all the time about making another trip upcountry to Lewisburg to see the relatives. She had been just a gangling girl when she had made the trip before with Catherine and now that she was really grown up she was sure she would relish being shown off and taken to camp meetings. She wrote religiously to Cousin Amos's two sisters and now and then he wrote a note to her and she always answered at once.

Mem said if anyone went upcountry it ought to be Anne. She was looking peaked all summer and kept shutting herself up in her room while Hortense fairly raved about the way she was letting herself get all scrawny and thin over That Man, who had never intended to do anything but Dupe her. *She* could see with Half an Eye and it was too bad Others did not have her sense of discrimination. She could hardly contain herself sometimes when Anne went upstairs and shut herself in, she had a kind of gnawing feeling as if she were left out and alone in the world without a soul to care.

David was so absorbed in his own affairs he was no consolation and Mem would only worry if she tried to confide in her. Besides, what was there to confide except that she felt like an empty pit inside of her all the time and at night had crying spells that kept her awake and tossing for hours.

The house just seemed cursed that summer, what with the nervous tension of always expecting good news from Joe and none coming and Anne always expecting a letter from that Gason and none coming and Mem always expecting something to turn up and nothing turning up and David just taking for granted that if any money came in, he'd be the one to get it, and Aaron so absent minded that half the time he forgot to wear a necktie. It just about set her crazy and when Anne wasn't reading Gason's old letters, she had her head in some book and got up from it looking all of a daze as if she didn't have half her senses. The birds got on Hortense's nerves and she had half a mind to open the cage door and let them out, only Anne would carry on so. Anne was for saving everything, she wouldn't let anything be thrown away and some of Catherine's clothes upstairs, it was a sin and shame the way the moths had been allowed to get into them, just hanging on to them.

Toward the end of August Aaron actually helped Mem to dispose of some of the chicks and he even went so far as to pay her for all his laundry and Sunday dinners. It was quite a blow and Mem was sure he must be sick but they were awfully glad for a little change. Mem wrote the Gerhardts to ask if David could board with them and what they would charge and she got back a vinegary letter from the oldest one, Abby, saying that they couldn't do it for less than three dollars and a half a week.

Aaron said, "If David gets three-fifty's worth of grub in his stomach at that house I'm much mistaken. He'd better lay in a winter's supply of something to chew on if he doesn't want his inner organs to wither up on him." Mem said that at least the Gerhardts were Christians and it would be better for a young boy to stay with them than to be thrown on his own somewhere. David didn't like the idea a little bit and his heart sank down to his boots when he saw Abby and the way she kept that house. They were sitting down, he and Mem, in what she called the parlor and actually while she was talking she was switching around with a dustcloth and apologizing about just taking up the roughest, and how the place was a sight, although you couldn't see a crumb anywhere.

Sam Weisel came in just before supper and didn't cheer a body any, he was such a gnarled sour looking fellow with great hawk eyes that went through you as if you were a piece of cloth. His shoulders were stooped too from squatting all day at the tailoring as if he had a hump. At about seven o'clock Maria came home from work and her face was so pretty and fresh that David cheered up and thought that now things would certainly brighten. But it was a dreary evening meal. Mem had taken the train back to Grapeville and Sam Weisel never opened his mouth. Abby kept brushing imaginary crumbs from around her plate and Maria talked only to David, turning her face pointedly away from Sam. It began to dawn on David that she was deliberately ignoring Sam and when Sam also turned his face from Maria the thing got more and more mysterious. In the week that David spent at the Weisels', he never once heard Sam or Maria address so much as a word to one another.

He brooded about it and in a long talk with the senior apprentice at the drug store where he put in his time when he wasn't at the school, he asked what could have passed between the two to account for such a silence. The senior apprentice was a very romantic looking fellow with wavy hair and professed to know a good deal of the world and all about Women and he told David that in his opinion, Sam Weisel had more to him than appeared on the surface and like as not had made some kind of a proposition to his own sister-in-law. David was horrified at this idea and he kept being haunted by it and after he got to bed had awful thoughts about Maria naked and Sam Weisel chasing her that made him feel just sick and terribly ashamed of himself all the next day.

When his week was up, he quit the Gerhardts', the food was too slim and he couldn't stand Abby always after you with the dustpan. But what got under his skin the worst way, was Sam and Maria never speaking to one another. He took a room near the store and tried hard to save a few cents every week so he could take in a minstrel show. He sent his dirty clothes home for the girls to wash and got his socks darned that way. All the technical Latin words of the drug business pleased him and he liked to show off by dragging in allusions to his profession. The first day in the store was pretty discouraging and he wrote a sad letter home that night describing the sixty dozen cologne bottles he had washed and stamped. "Oh, if I only had an acre of ground to plow," he wrote and felt the tears about ready to fall. Never had the good earth seemed so good now that he was forever chained to a dark basement washing bottles. The worst was, riches seemed far away, with the senior apprentice only getting a hundred and twenty-five dollars a year and board.

It was quiet in Grapeville and Hortense began talking of going to the city to learn stenography. As nothing had come of Anne's telegraphy, Mem saw little sense to this plan. Aaron was no help and talked of running for sheriff or pound master. Mem was sure that Mr. Flemmer had been a bad influence on him. It was known Flemmer was an atheist and gave talks about geology and how we came from monkeys.

They just managed to scrape along all that fall and once when things were so bad they didn't have a dollar in the house, Anne sent her pin with the two diamonds in that Joe had given her and told David to raise some money on it. He walked around, kind of scared and feeling as if he looked suspicious, and at last got up nerve to go into

Johnson's and see what he would give him. The mean old bugger wouldn't raise it any higher than twenty-five dollars and the rate of interest was outrageous but there was nothing for it, he had to take it or leave it, so he took the money and the ticket and went off with the smell of stale clothes and mothballs and dirty socks stinking in his nose. He actually felt abused to be up to such a trick and raged to himself at the way things always were, never a cent of money and he never felt so pinched and poor in his life.

The hours in the store were long too and already the senior apprentice had made several rather serious mistakes with the prescriptions because he was so worried about not passing his exams and there was practically no time for studying. But David did manage to go down to Grapeville that Christmas and Mem had been cooking for three days as if she expected a raft of company. He tried to be appreciative but he felt gloomy all the time and conscious that his trousers were tighter than they should be and his sleeves too short. They had not heard from Joe for weeks and Mem made the girls get out the silver tea set that hadn't seen the light since Catherine had hid it in that funny place in the trunk upstairs the week she died. They got out Catherine's knives and forks, too, in the rich leather case all lined with purple velvet and everyone kept bright and chipper and tried to remember old jokes and talked about the days up in Locust Valley but the silver was awful and Anne kept coughing and having to go to the kitchen. Then she got a regular fit of hysterics, laughing in a crazy way that sent the chill down your spine.

He was actually glad to be back rolling pills again and cracking jokes with old Gibson, the senior apprentice, who was worried sick for fear he'd given a woman the wrong kind of a dose. All their funny conversations, about what kind of a woman do you think that is, when one had just left the store, and Gib's funny stories made up on the spur of the moment about how she was sick and tired of her husband and was carrying on with a fireman, dried up. Gib looked sour all the time and talked darkly about the whole damn business being a squeeze for your life.

David was fairly driven to go to the Gerhardts for a little recreation but there he found the same curious business between Maria and Sam Weisel and he was sorry he had come. He kept looking from one to the other and imagining things and he was glad when he got out of the house. He made up his mind that as soon as he was through school he was going West, there wasn't a chance for a man in this dump and he certainly didn't mean to be kept down all his life. Joe finally wrote after Christmas with good news that they had found gold and were in high spirits as they had been almost two thousand dollars in debt, with no cabin and winter coming on. He had shifted quarters, given up Rapid City and was trying his luck on a new site at Bear Butte. His chief concern now was a young friend from Illinois who was down with the mountain fever and fared and shared as he did. If it took all he made that winter he meant to take care of him. Sometimes it looked as if the poor boy wouldn't live and then again, he thought with good care he might pull through.

The only reason he had not mentioned David's coming there any more was his fear of his exposure. There were enough examples before his eyes and yet he had thought he could manage David and he would be making five dollars a day but now thinking back over it, he wouldn't have risked his presence there for fifty dollars a day. But times were changing and it would never be so rough in the Hills as it had been that summer, respectable women and children were coming in and the turbulent element would never reign there again.

David almost boiled over to be treated like a baby and as if he needed watching and when he went home the Sunday after, he sulked and said it looked to him as if some people considered everybody first before they did their families. He had always understood that a man's first thought should be for the family. Anne and Hortense laughed at him and Anne teased and said he was just jealous of the Mountain Fever Boy and not to mind that he'd get there yet with or without Joe. He poohpoohed and when Hortense said he was red as a turkey cock he got furious and slammed out of the house saying darkly, "You just wait and see, wait and see," but he didn't know himself what he meant by those words.

TWO SISTERS

LUCY BLONDELL could bear never hearing from Joe much better than she could bear seeing her sister receive letters from him. It was not only a thorn in the flesh, it was being nailed to the cross to see the satisfaction Lenore got, with her plain face and freckles, getting letters from a man who had been out and out in love with her sister. Not that Lenore ever crowed about it or showed her triumph but even that would have been better than her constant consideration that made Lucy always feel as if she were an invalid who had no hopes of getting well. Such people as Lenore were too amiable for this world and sometimes Lucy just wanted to scream. She had times when the only relief she got was fancying herself screaming herself hoarse. How they would carry on if she did such a thing. Like as not, they would send for a doctor and before she knew it, they would have her in a strait jacket. She went around feeling as if something was bottled up in her and it gave her face a curious sly secret look that actually frightened the family.

They talked about poor Lucy and encouraged her all they could to have a good time and go out to parties and she had plenty of chances, no girl had more, because say what you like, suffering only made her prettier and her skin got so fine and so white it was heavenly. Lucy wouldn't have anything to do with any of the young men near her own age and when she did let herself go anywhere with one of them, out of boredom, she always was mean and insulting and fairly shamed her own family, like the time she stalked upstairs in her party clothes after young Marsden came to take her to the Peabody dance and came down in her old clothes and just laughed and said she had changed her mind but Lenore could go if she had a mind! Father and Mother felt terrible and Mother took him out on the porch and had a long talk with him and came back all cried up but nobody reproached her and that was what scared her. She pulled herself together and said she wouldn't do it again and was sorry and even wrote a note to Marsden but she hated her family with their soft compassionate faces, all standing around, condoning her.

Sometimes she thought she would marry one of the boys hanging around, just shut her eyes and choose one of them and marry, to get away from her family and their sympathy. When she had a bath and afterward took care of her nails, she got a real pleasure in sharpening them and whittling them to a point and polishing them hard and brittle. Once, when her own pet kitten came around whining and crying and begging for something, she had hit him a hard box over the ear and sent him spinning. Nobody had said a word to her but little Clare had set up a howl, you would have thought the child was killed. She was ashamed of herself and the kitten wouldn't come near her for days but she finally got a good piece of meat and tempted him with it and before long he was up on her lap again, purring, and had forgotten all about it. She never could abide that cat again with his meek forgiving nature.

If she so much as tried to take a walk of an evening, and there were times when it seemed as if it would be a blessing if she could run, if she could just race along that dark evening road and fancy herself running into Joe's very arms, but no, sure as fate, Father would come out of the house and pretend to be smelling the sunset and if she so much as started out, he would be there, looking after her, leaning on the gate with that terrible anxious look that she just despised. Only when she was alone in her own bed, and she had quit sleeping with Lenore and had demanded a room of her own since she overheard her sister tell Mother that it was terrible the way she cried sometimes, shaking the bed with sobs, did she feel any kind of happy peace.

It was actually a temptation to go to bed early and shut the door and she would have locked it, only someone had taken away the key. Once in bed with the sheets tight around her body, she could let herself go and imagine what she pleased. Alone in the dark, nobody could bother her or stand around pitying her and she could lie there warm and almost happy and press herself hard against the bed with her arms stretched out like a living cross, oh she was crucified on the living cross of the Lord and then the tears would pour down her cheeks like the warm blood of Christ. She took a great comfort singing hymns and could sit all day playing the piano and singing "Jesus Lover of My Soul" and "Home to the Mountains."

Even when she knew it got on everybody's nerves, she kept right on playing as if possessed, longing to look out of the back of her head at the way they must be signaling one another in despair. There was a kind of contrariness in her that just seemed to delight to keep on playing like that to torment them. But no one said a word to her and

on Sundays when the relatives would come to call and sit
around the parlor munching spice cake and drinking up
all the best wine, if she'd come down the stairs and stand
in the doorway, they would all stop talking and there'd be
such a dead hush, you could hear a pin drop. She knew
very well they had been talking her over again. She just
longed to burst out laughing and say something terrible
like, "Well go on, go on, tearing me to pieces, aren't you,
having a good time feeling sorry for the poor girl, just go
on and kill the mouse, you cats," but instead she always
went around saying nice cool things and feeling that if
somebody didn't do something quick she'd drown in that
well of pity.

If only someone would come along and order her to do
something it didn't matter what, she believed she would
fall on his neck with gratitude, but nobody did. They were
all scared to death of her and wouldn't even say boo. Ever
since she was a little girl people stood around saying, "Oh,
who is that lovely child, did you ever see such hair, just
like spun silk but look at her complexion my dear if
that won't set the world on fire, wouldn't you give your little finger to have her skin," and she had just taken for
granted that she would be worshiped.

No one had ever crossed her until Joe came along and
he had acted bored when she tried to assert herself and
act high and mighty. The night he was late coming for
her and she had sulked he had paid no attention to her
all evening and across the room she had seen him laughing
and talking with that Geraldine Thompson as if *she* hadn't
a right in the world and were not at that moment injured
at the way he had treated her. It scared her because she
knew in a minute that some other girl would snatch at him
and perhaps she'd lose him. What a fool she had been to
think that the only way to lose a man was through some
other woman. What good did her good looks do her now

and what lies people had told her about chaining men with her beauty. If she was as homely as mud she couldn't be more unhappy, in fact Lenore who was plain was happier. Not that she thought so much of the letters Lenore got from Joe, all filled with descriptions of castles in Sicily and references to Odessa and Constantinople and while she was tantalized by the thought of his traveling around in gorgeous places and going to embassy balls with the most beautiful women in Europe flocking around, still the letters didn't sound as he talked. There was something stiff about them and even all the references to friendship and kindness and loyalty that Joe put in didn't fool Lucy, not for a minute. She could see with half an eye that those letters were intended for her more than for Lenore. When he wrote in one that he guessed he was by now pretty well forgotten in Atlanta and only ancient history, it was like a direct message to her and she went to her room and wrote her heart out.

But it didn't change matters because as long as that dreadful business was hanging over his head, what could be changed? What a little thing it would be for somebody like the Governor to write on a slip of paper a few words, everything would be cleared up, Joe wouldn't have to be on the other side of the world. She could imagine herself telling all her friends, who took such delight in pity, that it had all been a mistake and that Joe had been completely exonerated. There was talk going around about some of the fugitives coming back and standing trial and she got awfully excited and said it was foolish to stir up all that trouble again and then she had burst out crying because it seemed so hopeless. Lenore had been all ears and eyes and probably went right upstairs and tattled to Joe because she never got an answer to her note at all but toward spring, she got a blank envelope with three feathers in it of some bird with the loveliest colors and a single line on a sheet of paper, *"Forgive and forget."* She turned the envelope over trying to see where he was now but it had the Grapeville, N. J., postmark as all his letters did and she knew he must have sent it first to his sister so that the Atlanta authorities could not possibly trace him. She put the three feathers with their long slender pointed ends like arrows in a box at the bottom of her dresser drawer and she felt that something simply must happen soon. She could not bear to go on living in the same house with Lenore.

Lenore and her mother were always holding low voiced and secret consultations as to what could be done about poor Lucy. The girl wasn't getting over it at all and things did look hopeless. Father said there wasn't a chance of Joe's getting cleared of that mess for years and Lucy herself got hysterical if it was suggested that Joe might come back and stand trial. Lenore said that Lucy had inflicted a good deal of pain on Joe and they ought to think of poor Joe as well as poor Lucy. As Lucy was so stubborn and wouldn't hold out a string of hope to Joe about the future, the best thing was for them to forget each other. Mrs. Blondell just rolled her eyes and moaned and said it showed how little Lenore knew of Life or she wouldn't talk like that and Lenore didn't answer but she thought to herself that she probably knew as much about it as any of them.

The whole household was being sacrificed to Lucy and it even looked as if Lenore could not go back to the seminary the next semester on account of so much going out all the time for pretty things for Lucy to wear so she would cheer up and forget. Lenore had never been so anxious in her life to go on at the seminary. She was eaten up with a desire to learn everything and she felt when she was studying that in some way she was making herself a better friend to Joe who always wrote of such intellectual subjects and of things he had read and seen. His letters were wonderful and she couldn't resist reading portions of them to the girls at the seminary. They didn't know of course who the letters were from and teased her when she insisted they were from a *friend*. He couldn't write about the most ordinary thing without making it seem somehow exceptional and exciting and cultivated like that letter before Christmas from Belgium where he talked about wanting to go home to Grapeville for Christmas on account of all the grand things his sisters and mother would be preparing for that day, the fowls, the little speckled shoats, the unusual firmness of the trout, the delicious venison, the gages, pears, grapes and apples all for him and the cakes made in the same little molds that associated themselves with the Christmas of his childhood by that little band of dear ones all watching and waiting for the return of the "Rover."

Why it made her own mouth water to read about it. And some of the things he wrote struck like a shaft in her breast. She could read beneath the lines and see where another could not. That passage about friendship, how many times she had taken the letter out and read and re-read it. It was all right for Lucy to have that superior look when Joe's letters came and the way she could shrug her shoulder and just dismiss everything was a caution but Lenore sometimes hated to have Lucy touch those letters. She wanted to wrap them up and hide them where Lucy couldn't find them, not if she looked a million years. She had read the passage to Margaret Gower because she was a sympathetic person and Margaret had felt about it just as Lenore did.

Just now I ask myself how many friends of my youth whose names and faces are still familiar many with whom intercourse has been more or less constant, could I approach without some reserve or embarrassment and rely upon now as then; to how many could I write and devote more ink than business or the ordinary civility of mere acquaintance is entitled to, without feeling that early friendship has been absorbed by more congenial agents? I do not impugn the motives, which are governed by individual tendencies, yet there seems to me something pathetic in contemplating the fact that human nature from childhood to the grave is ever bent upon taking advantage of the present; amid the struggling and jostled, few indeed can calmly decide whether friendship is merely a convenient and clever word or the impregnable fortress of confidence, trust and reciprocal joy. Hastily glancing over the past ten years of my career, and that takes me back to my teens, of all the young friends made during that interesting period there remain but two of the masculine and one of the feminine gender, the others having been, by reason of various circumstances and pursuits, estranged. There is no sentiment in me which provokes grief and regret so quickly as the loss or absence of those whom I learned to regard and honor without an effort; hence viewing the subject in this light with the statistics 3 to 10 as a basis, you will observe that I have reason for alarm, lest at the end of a few more years the most ingenious mathematician would fail to make that sanguine x yield more than a significant ?. I trust that such a result may never be attained. I meet firmly the rapidly approaching year praying that the friendship that breathes, lives and feels, may endure.

Margaret Gower agreed that that passage was a Classic and Lenore knew it was more than that, she could see it as a proud appeal to her friendship not to weaken and totter like Lucy's but to be strong and prevail. It made her proud and happy to have Joe write like that and nothing that Lucy could mutter about those letters could shake her. Lucy could be jealous of her getting letters from Joe if it pleased her but all she was doing was trying to be kind to him and write to him when Lucy had as good as refused. Lucy was just contrary and a great trial but she could bear it, she could bear anything so long as she was of some use to Joe. Oh she just wished she could take all his troubles on her own shoulders. It made her weak all over just to think of the happiness of bearing Joe's Cross.

She begged so hard that at last Mr. Blondell said he would find a way to let the poor child go back to the seminary when she had set her heart on it but there was very little money for any extras and she tutored the younger classes to help pay for her tuition. There was no shame to that, not with the very best families in the South all poor as church mice but it was hard on her health and her skin got awfully yellow and tired looking that winter. About the only relaxation and pleasure she had was getting letters from Joe and writing to him, not that they kept up a very regular correspondence and the letters were few and far between but she lived for them and envied him his capacity for Experiencing Life. The school seemed awfully little and close and sometimes she actually felt as if she were shut up in a box.

She and Margaret Gower sighed and talked about the free life men had and about how nice it would be to travel around and See Things. Margaret said that even that would tire and it sounded so sort of learned that Lenore wrote it in a letter to Joe. Afterwards she was sorry because he wrote back:

You imagine I tire of the beautiful and interesting? No, no Lenore. Those who seek a cosy fireside to peruse a sketch of some lovely land, those who can satisfy their desires by viewing a picture, those to whom travel is irksome instead of exciting, are they who soon tire and a miracle is necessary to infuse them with interest. But I am an enthusiast. I climbed the perilous peak of Teneriffe until blood oozed from my lips and great globules formed along the arteries that I might for a moment behold a world of solitude. Oh how solemn and grand. I worked for months in the ruins of Herculaneum and Pompeii as well as a short time on the Tiber that I might supply my mind with information of an interesting nature. Being thus constituted, I never fail to appreciate the beautiful neither does the good escape me.

Margaret Gower had to admit that there was no answer to that and all that day they both felt awfully small and isolated, as if they had been swept up on a desert island, where nothing ever happened. Margaret Gower talked every day about Joe and had to hear over and over again about the way he looked, his hair and his eyes and his nice manners, so considerate and charming, everybody loved him. The two plain girls were transformed by their talk and would come down the stairs to the meager supper arm in arm, with flushed cheeks and excited eyes, and Margaret loved to hint in talk with some of the older students about Lenore's friend, who was terribly interesting and had traveled all over the world. They both agreed that it was a regular education to write to Joe and get letters from him and Margaret said that it was the best thing that had ever happened to her in all her life to be allowed to see the letters Lenore received from her friend.

THAR'S GOLD

THEY got a cabin up just in time before the cold set in and Joe fixed up a good bunk with the best blankets in it for John Huber who was a pretty sick man. There was a regular run of mountain fever in the camp all that fall and winter and people began talking of laying out a permanent cemetery because the raw graves gave one the jumps. The saloons did a good business and it got to be quite a habit to walk in and get the news and a few drinks. When Handsome Harry, the best stage driver in the district, came down sick with the fever everyone chipped in and did the best they could for him and the girls at the Gem took turns nursing him but it wasn't any use and he went out very characteristic with, "No, boys, I'm on the downgrade and I can't reach the brake block."

Joe got the best of everything for John Huber and when he began to mend was as pleased as if he'd raised the fellow from the dead. They rocked out enough gold that winter to keep stocked up on grub, but Joe wasn't satisfied and planned to go somewhere else as soon as spring broke. The winters were terribly trying with the gold frozen in solid so no one could get at it and everyone nervous for fear someone would get the jump on them.

The Manuel brothers and Hank Harney were mighty hard up and had strained their credit so much that they finally offered the storekeeper who had been helping them out a proposition to put his name on the stake for a hundred feet. That made the storekeeper an undivided owner of one fifteenth of the Homestake Mine for one sack flour, one two pound can baking powder, coffee, sugar, powder and fuse and a few other necessaries amounting to around ninety dollars. The storekeeper was kind of scared that he would never get his money out but he had been helping the boys out and hated to turn them down. On number 2 below Discovery they had taken out a hundred and fifty thousand dollars in three months and the fellows took turns guarding the claim with a Winchester night and day. An example like that kept everyone keyed up to pretty high expectations and it took months of hard weather and hard work to thin the place out. The loafers, and those who lacked gumption, quit and left the field clear. Joe got hard and stringy and no one would have known him in that beard. He had to laugh at himself giving Huber so much good advice about laying off gambling and disciplining himself with a little work every day.

For days at a time the snow came down in a blinding storm and all anyone could do was play cards by the stove or read the old books again and Joe got a lot of fun out of writing letters to Lenore Blondell about life abroad and castles in Sicily and the coastline of Ireland. It was as good as a trip to let himself go and he was pleased at his style and thought it quite literary and even began to have ideas for poems. When Lenore's replies came he always wanted to sit right down and answer but restrained himself as an immediate reply would have been a dead give-away. He hoped she would show his letters around, not only because it would throw anybody who had ideas of claiming a reward off the scent, but also because he wanted his enemies to think of Joseph Trexler, the little candy maker, as riding high on the waves.

There was something about Lenore's devoted replies and her complete belief in him that made him feel a little hard toward Lucy. He even felt aloof from his family in Grapeville and got tired of letters which were always about raising money for David's this or that. Anne did not write often and when her letters came they worried him and reminded him somehow of Catherine. When he wrote her he always addressed the inner envelope to *My Anne* and he was very tender to her and often talked about how nice it would be when they could be together again.

By spring Joe and Huber had paid off their debts and Huber invested in a white Stetson and had a pair of tony cuff links made for himself out of Black Hills gold nuggets. Joe kept trying to get enough ahead to send something to

Anne, but grub was high and his first shipment of gold was held up on its trip to Cheyenne. Within a short time, eight holdups roused the fellows who were grubbing away on their diggins and a warning was tacked up alongside the bloody vest of Johnny Slaughter who was shot off the box as he drove down Split Tail Gulch one dark night. Persimmons Bill got it in his brand new corduroy coat and a few others like him were sent spinning to Hell where they belonged and it began to look as if the place were settling down. Placer mining was giving out and slick gents with long cigars came in and put up at the best hotel. Most of the boys were stuck without a little capital and since the first shipment of ore to Denver a few months back, there was talk all along the line about Eastern capital coming in.

The Manuel brothers were still holding out on what they calculated to be a rich claim and galena ore along Bear Butte Gulch showed rich promise of silver, copper and gold. Expectations went higher and higher and Chinese put in truck gardens. The Big Horn Store was doing a thriving business and Joe began to wish he had followed his first hunch and had gone in for town speculation. It was too late to back out now and when spring came he went to work on a new stake near Galena and began to think there was really something to it.

For one thing, he was part of a group of miners, all of whom were pooling what they had and had staked out a large enough area to be tempting to capital. They had come to the conclusion they couldn't do anything alone. A few had gotten rich but when you contrasted them to those who had barely made a living the showing wasn't so impressive. The spring nights were wonderfully sweet scented after the hard cold winter but nothing compared to the mocking birds and all that warm heavy sweetness in the South. The birches and aspens began to put out tiny green shoots and showed up pale and springy against the dark pines and spruce. A school had started and Henrico Livingstone threw stones at the children as they went by thinking they might jump her claim. More than one head cracked after the long hard winter and the night poor Shartrell came around cackling and said he'd opened a vein of rattlesnakes that he expected to get rich quick on, it made your blood run cold. The poor fellow never did get it out of his head that he was a rich man and had struck a bonanza and he was just about as content with his snake claim as some of the others were with their open cuts.

John Huber was getting very discontented with the hard pick and shovel work. He hadn't saved up anything but he kept at Joe to set him up in the saloon business. He was drunk more than half the time and had crying spells when he talked about his fine upbringing and what he had degenerated into. Joe said he was willing to set Huber up in any kind of business but the saloon business but Huber wouldn't hear of it and pointed out that of all the businesses that was the surest way to get rich. The men all talked about getting rich and the town went right on growing and it actually got a little opera house with a company of players that put on *Jane Eyre* and *Still Waters Run Deep,* all high class stuff. Huber was great for the theater and hung around hoping he'd be called on to take part, but Joe couldn't seem to feel easy with the theatrical people any more.

He had to admit that he was changed and felt more at home sitting in the cabin writing letters to Lenore than he did knocking around. Not that he didn't like a good stiff drink and the girls weren't so bad once you reconciled yourself to them but his mind was always somewhere else. The only thing that could get him really roused up about the Hills would be a big strike. He was bound to hit it any day but the waiting around and the monotony got on his nerves.

Now and then Anne sent him papers from the East and he had to smile at the way the papers ran on about the exciting life in the mining camps and the gambling and shooting. You'd think a man was popped off every five minutes to hear them when actually only about seventeen men were shot up in a year, this last year, and if none of the shooters were convicted, well, that was a more private business than say stealing a horse, on which a man's fate depended sometimes. The Black Hills were beginning to be a pretty good place for lawyers and a number of fancy brands came pouring in from the East, especially after news went out about the Manuel boys' selling their claim to big capital. They finally sold out for sixty thousand dollars to Hearst and Haggin and cleared out so fast toward the East no one ever saw hide or hair of them again.

The capitalists straggled in and business began to hum. The whole character of the place seemed to change overnight. The Pinkertons came in and hired out their guards to defend claims and everybody began to be suspicious about everyone else. Before, one man was as good as the next and if he could shoot straight was sure of defending his own. Now the Pinkertons just stirred up trouble and to make business for themselves hired people to cross and crisscross claims that all the old timers knew were marked out. There wasn't an old timer on the spot that didn't go a little crazy and just long for someone to buy him out and those who had no ore to show practiced a little judicious salting to trap the wealthy nabobs who had so much money anyhow that a little thrown away on a salted claim couldn't hurt them none. A new slick bunch of men began coming into Deadwood with tony clothes and money to hire miners to dig for them. The old timers didn't know whether to like it or not and some of them grumbled pretty loud but the storekeepers and saloonkeepers said it was fine for business and showed that the town was catching up with civilization.

There was not a spot in the Hills where you couldn't hear the whistle of a saw or stamp mill and the swamps and thickets were cut through with roads. Riding along to Galena, Joe liked nothing better than to let the old nag out and then to bring her up suddenly and hear the whine of a mill somewhere in the brush. The place had grown up so quick that it sometimes gave him the shivers and he had a panicky feeling that he was being left behind. Men came in and struck gold and sold out and he was still there, nothing much ahead, with so many irons in the fire that surely one of them must get hot.

SNARE AND DELUSION

JOE always wrote as if something big was about to happen. It seemed to Anne that something like that would happen and lift the whole family out of the rut. His letters just kept them in a quiver of expectation and it made Anne feel very bad when David got so snooty and asked if it were not about time Joe was finding out whether or not it was going to pay him to stick in that place. Just because David was earning his board and not a cent more, he was always writing home, "What about sending me a dollar?" or, "I've had to borrow fifty cents from Howard, what about sending me a little money?" He seemed to think he was an authority on Getting Ahead. He would have to do more than wash out sixty dozen cologne bottles in a day to prove that to her, not that he wasn't a good boy but he was ungrateful to Joe and acted as if the girls just lived to give him a start in life.

If she lived to be an old old woman Anne was sure she could never forget those years, waiting for something to happen and waiting to hear from John Gason. Not that she really expected to hear from him seriously until the May of 1877, that being two years from the time he had sailed. No, she had made up her mind that suddenly a letter would come and that would be all there was to it. But nothing came. She humbled her pride and wrote his cousin in Philadelphia who answered at once that he was as much at sea as she was. The cousin seemed to think Gason had gone to Australia and there the trail ended. She read and re-read all his old letters and could not see a sign of anything but love. Something must have happened, he must be dead, and it was easier to think of him dead than indifferent. The family got on her nerves and she couldn't help answering shortly Hortense's silly remarks. There was nothing she liked so well as walking by herself, just to be alone with the stars at night. If she walked a little past the Tracy place she was as good as in another country. The sky with its stars was over the whole world, over Madame Canutson that Joe had told her about, the woman who drove the bull train in the Hills and rocked along on the empty prairies with her baby in a bed made in the oven of an iron stove she was bringing in to some miner. The sky was over John Gason, wherever he was, living or dead.

When spring came, it seemed as if the trailing arbutus under the leaves made everything worse and half the time Anne was on the verge of writing Joe and begging him to let her come out there with him. She was a good cook and wouldn't mind roughing it. What were they doing now in Grapeville but roughing it, with half the time not fifty cents in the house and Mem worried and David always after them to make him some pants or a shirt. If they didn't do it right on the dot he went ahead and spent a dollar for a shirt that they could have made for sixty cents and kept the difference for themselves. With money so hard to come by, wouldn't you think he'd be more considerate? No wonder Mem was so put out with the boy.

Try as they would, nothing brought in the money and for eight pair of pigeons they only got two dollars and that was considered high. When they took home clothes from the tailor to sew, the three women kept at it four days until eleven at night and got only a dollar and twenty cents for their labor. They could have cried, they were so disappointed to have such a dribble for their hard work. Why it wasn't seven cents a day for each of them and made them feel so helpless. What could they do to get some money when such hard work brought them not enough to buy a little bread? They were just at everybody's mercy and had to sell the sweets for less than it cost to put them in. Nothing seemed to pay and yet they were at it from morning to night.

Hortense kept begging to go to the city to learn stenography but there wasn't a penny in the house to give her for the tuition to say nothing of the board. Anne felt she could not even be spared to try to find another job like the one at Gould's and whenever she spoke of it Mem burst into tears.

The turkeys were great pets and if Anne got far enough away from the house with them following after her, she felt a real peace and then there was Pony with his nice disposition, why it just soothed your heart to stand near him and feel his old soft nose rub along your face as if he knew what was wrong and wanted to comfort you. It wasn't as if they had real friends in the town, because they had started off on the wrong foot, you might say, on account of Joe and being so sensitive about him. But the Derrs were nice people, very plain, even though he was a cousin of a President. Leah Derr was refined and read the papers but the old people worked like horses and ate the plainest food. When Anne stopped to dinner with them, they all crossed themselves except Leah and she sat very straight and looked out the window with bright and bitter eyes, that as plain as day showed her scorn for that kind of monkeyshines. Leah and Anne had many a good long talk together and when the old folks were in bed the two would stand at the Derrs' gate and wonder about the stars and the many worlds spinning around in the sky and Leah said that with so many worlds there wasn't any sense in thinking. God could care for every sparrow. The two talked about the future and agreed they would probably be old maids. When Anne was alone, she could not bear to think of that agreement, she knew it was a lie and could not think of life all alone. But her heart sank never hearing from John Gason. She would carry on long conversations with him in her mind and these made her forget how hard up they were and how all the time they seemed to be glued to the place in Grapeville for the best years of a girl's young life, with all that she had to give to love going to waste and drying up and souring on her so that if something didn't happen to save her, she would be an old woman with nothing to look back on but the price of sweets and the bird feed running low again.

In the summer David went up to Bethlehem to call on Aunt and Uncle Blank after all these years and took her a bottle of cologne. It was nothing fancy but even then he didn't dare give it in Uncle's presence for fear of some kind of outbreak. He also took her a box of the best Havana cigars. The Blanks were the same as ever except that Aunty was very gray and time seemed to stand still. He was actually glad to get out of the house and a good deal offended that no one had shown the least curiosity about him and the great strides he was making. Aunty did take him aside and ask in a hurried way about Joe and her lips kept quivering but he didn't go into details and thought it showed very bad manners not to ask him about himself.

It was a treat for Mem and Anne to have him at Grapeville in the summer and he was very good about the place and actually plowed up two lots for potatoes. Anne laughed till the tears came to her eyes at the funny stories he told about Abby, and Sam Weisel and Maria not speaking, and the things Gib told and when he said he wasn't going to let old Trudel impose on him the way he did on Gibson, Anne said, "That's the boy. Don't you do it, David. That's the trouble with Aaron. He just lets Flemmer ride over him."

"Well nobody is going to ride over me, not if I know it, no siree bob, if there's any riding to be done, I'm going to do it." David actually condescended to get his flute out and he and Anne had some good duets with Hortense chiming in rather feebly on the violin. When David left in the fall, the house seemed too forlorn for words and the girls both felt sick and were troubled all the time with colds and pains. That whole winter nothing happened. They made a sled during the big snow and it turned out a regular joke, something between a coffin and a dogcart, but Anne and Hortense got into it and drove to town. Coming back, the wind was so sharp they couldn't stay on the seat and got down in the straw and let old Pony find his way home alone. It was the event of the season but when it was nearly spring good news came from Joe saying he thought he had something pretty good and actually sent them a hundred dollars. They were working on a silver claim now and believed that silver was the metal of the future. He might even come East the following year and they were all to cheer up because good times were coming.

The girls were jubilant and Anne felt some of the heaviness in her heart that was always there, on account of no word from Gason, lighten. Hortense planned to go at once to Philadelphia and begin on the shorthand. She said she hated to leave Mem and Anne alone with all the spring work but Anne was actually glad of it and welcomed the chance to work until she was ready to drop. She could not bear to see the days go by and no word and sometimes had a queer frantic feeling as if she would begin running and never stop.

Hortense wrote home very regularly and helped David buy the cloth for his new suit, all out of Joe's money and they picked a nice pattern for eleven dollars and got a tailor to cut it out for something around four dollars and what with findings coming to about two dollars and seventy-five cents David had an outfit very cheap. They got the goods and Mem and Anne sat up half the night working on it because the sweet potato plants were ready to go in the ground and they didn't dare take the time off in the day to sew.

Hortense shopped around for herself. She was always wanting a pair of cheap shoes or a new this or that, not that she spent more than a few cents, and no one could look more stylish on less. She washed out her own stockings and handkerchiefs too and pressed the handkerchiefs in a big dictionary so the landlady wouldn't see how few she had.

Poor little Rebbie was poisoned after she had been gone two weeks and died in spite of everything and it made Hortense feel so bad as he was like one of the family and had been through so many changes with them, the ups and the downs, had lived on Apple Street and gone to

Fifteenth and when Anne wrote she had planted a tube-rose on his grave she was really comforted.

Hortense worked hard at her shorthand but thought it was very difficult and she and David went out to Chestnut Hill a couple of Sundays and talked about the times they used to go there years ago and both felt very old and mature and like crying.

Back in the boarding house, Hortense had a good cry about Rebbie again and wrote Anne not to tell her if anything should happen to one of the birds, she didn't think she could bear it. Afterwards, she went downstairs to have a long confab with the landlady about ways to dress the hair with a braid wound around the head real high and a couple of puffs behind and a curl or two reaching to the top of the collar. She went right back to her room and added a postscript to her letter to Anne to please send some of her combings to make up into curls.

Anne sent the hair off promptly and it seemed to her she was always running errands for those two in Philadelphia and washing clothes for them. After the sweets were in the ground, they could take it a little easier but the strain of waiting for a letter from Gason was there all the time, it was like a part of her body and with her night and day and the first thing when she woke. When she was looking for a letter from Gason so much, the last thing she expected to get was one from Lenore Blondell, saying that Joe had written her she must come next summer and visit his sister and there was nothing she would like better because Joe was her greatest friend and everyone in that house loved him, her mother like one of her own sons, and even she who had hurt him so much, Lucy, and did Anne know that Lucy was married, poor girl, she had suffered more than need be and had a really wonderfully considerate husband who loved her for her very sorrows and worshiped the ground she walked on. Anne felt her heart almost stop beating and didn't know why it upset her so. It seemed all wrong. "I will love you always," Lucy had said, and now she was married.

When Hortense came home on a weekend she found Anne looking drawn and pale. She had a long confab with Mem and the upshot was that they made some excuse to get Anne off to the city and leave Hortense at home. Then the two got a pair of scissors and went at the lock of the chest but it took a screw driver to open it and Hortense took out all that Gason's letters and burned them up.

Anne saw what had happened when she came back and cried and carried on and said, "You've always been jealous of me, always. You were mean about him from the very start and for all I know have hidden letters that came." Hortense turned pale but kept her voice down, "Accuse me if you like, you'll thank me some day. I never touched a line that man wrote to you and you know it. I'm only thinking of you now when I burn those things. I'd rather have you hate me than to see you waste away reading that stuff over and over." Anne blazed all over but she kept her mouth shut. She quieted down and turned pale and trembled so that Mem was frightened and wished they had kept out one letter at least. She and Hortense did not speak for days and it was a long time, perhaps never, that they were good friends.

All that summer she was very thin and quiet and it was a bad year for business. The papers were full of strikes and how the rioters in Pittsburgh had gone wild tearing up mattresses and carrying off sewing machines and shrimp and looting everything. David was pretty scornful at what he called the mob but Anne was very quiet and said they were all too poor to talk like that. It was easy for her to understand how a person might be driven to do such things. There were times when she thought if she could only find a rich person's pocketbook or a diamond ring, she wouldn't give it back, even if she knew the owner because half the time those people didn't give you anything but a thank you or some stingy reward.

David was always thinking of himself as the owner of a big drug store and actually the boy was funny. Anne didn't know what she would do if she didn't have him to laugh at. He was no hand to manage for himself and always wheedling for a little money and of course as she never had any, it meant she must try to get it out of Aaron and that was like drawing nails out of a solid oak beam.

Hortense was taking her time learning shorthand in Philadelphia. It did seem funny to have her there when if one of them was to earn money it might as well be Anne who already knew telegraphy and something about keeping books. She began to see that Hortense had just gotten to the city to be away from the hard work and to find romance and wondered why it was she should always be the one to stay at home. There were no more sweet letters to comfort her and when she thought of them turned to dust forever, such a stab of pain went through her that if anyone had asked her her name at that moment she couldn't have told it. She knew most of those letters by heart and after she went to bed would say some of them over and think how Hortense hadn't been so smart after all.

Once, when she was at Aaron's office begging for fifty cents for David, she picked up a little book and began reading. It was all about God and against him. She had felt for a long time that if there was a God, he was against her and now it did her good to read hard words about him. When Aaron came in, she lifted her head and blushed and he fussed with his papers and came nearer. "What have you got there?"

"It's a book I found," Anne said.

"Hm-m, yes, well it won't hurt you to read that. It'll do you good. I'm surprised you are so interested. You girls ought to read more of that stuff. But not in here. Anyone come in?"

"Some woman," said Anne indifferently. "She asked when you'd be back." "What'd you tell her?" "In an hour I said," and Anne turned and looked at him but he was the same, absent minded, fumbling around in his pockets.

She wished there was someone sympathetic to talk to, but David would only act virtuous. It did her good to know she had been right about David when she finally brought up the subject one Sunday and he got indignant. "Who put such ideas into your head? What would Mem think if she knew? How do you expect to get along thinking like that? I'd like to know who made the world if God didn't." Without giving her a chance to answer he stalked out of the room and she burst out laughing.

But whether it was the new ideas or cheerful letters from Joe sending occasional small sums that certainly kept the wolf from gnawing the doors from the cupboards, Anne felt as if something nice might happen at any moment and even Gason might suddenly present himself at the front door.

With Hortense and David in the city there wasn't a spare penny for anyone else. David could tease the last cent out of Anne with his funny letters always headed some crazy way like Plaster & Pill, Inc. or Patent Medicine Co., or Fish Town, and then he was such a martyr with his airs of being dragged to the depths because he had no soles to his shoes that she hadn't the heart to let him suffer. Hortense pretended she was pining for the country and wrote asking for Kate and Omily and Baby and Pony but she always seemed very glad to take the train back on her visits home and she hated dishwater on her hands and creamed her face with a lotion every night. She laughed at Anne and her old fashioned way of sticking to oatmeal water but say what you please, Anne's skin was nicer.

By winter Hortense had not yet mastered shorthand and as there was no money, she came home and the two girls put in a long dull winter trying hard to make the good walks and the crisp air last through the day and they tried hard to keep up with the piano and the violin. Sometimes it did seem aimless and when Aaron at last let Anne try to make a few collections for him, she seemed to take on weight and color overnight.

One day when she was alone in his office straightening up, she pulled open a bottom drawer and saw a bundle tied with wide green tape. Before she knew it, she had it open and there lay a pair of woman's gray shoes and some baby moccasins. Without being told, she knew whose shoes those were. It made her tremble and afraid for a minute to be alone. She wished she had been to John Gason what Mrs. Ferrol had been to her brother. She thought she never could feel quite the same about Aaron again but there was no way to talk to him. She thought about him and about Joe and felt very tender about her brothers but she didn't cry any more alone in bed. She lay tense and waiting and impatient with the poverty that kept her in Grapeville wasting her best years.

In the evenings she read books from the Mercantile Library and tried to think she was laying a solid foundation for her life. There was so much to learn and she was so ignorant. She tackled the books with a kind of feverish vengeance and underlined passages. If it hadn't been for her brothers out in the world, living, these years would have been a vacuum. But one or the other was always making things lively. Deadwood was wiped out in flames but Joe wrote not to worry, all he stood to lose was two hundred and fifty dollars.

David was dissatisfied with his place at Trudel's and wrote complaining letters every week. Hortense went to the city and came back reporting that his face was pale as putty and she believed he was secretly taking that arsenic for pimples on his forehead. Anne wrote him trying to work in a sermon against such a practice but he came back hotly with a denial. "The idea, as if I didn't know better. I only tasted the stuff to see what it's like. If you want to know what's making me pale it's this basement mixing Trudel's rheumatism specialties. Anyone would get pale as a potato sprout down here. And he leaves me no time to study. I'm going to blow up to him. I won't stand it. If I fail to pass my exams because he hasn't got an assistant and leaves me so much to do, he'll hear from me."

The day that David actually got his courage up to tackle Trudel the old man gave up going to church to work over the problem. He was so upset by David's spluttering that he even promised an apprentice. David felt he had won the battle and had to tell somebody. He went over to Sam Weisel's and strutting up and down their parlor, told about the terrible ordeal he had been through.

"I told him that I had not passed the examination solely because of his leaving me in the store alone and that he had no right to do that. I gave him to understand that he could by no means get the best of me. I don't know what the sequel will be but he can't get the best of me. I shall make him suffer and there are more ways than one to kill a cat. Isn't that so Sam?"

Sam grunted and Abby looked uneasily at the carpet which he was wearing out with his unnecessary strides but Maria laughed and said, "It would be a good thing if we all had more fight in us. I work in a room with a skylight you can hardly see through, with the gas sputtering all the time but no one dares complain. It isn't right. I often think it isn't right."

"Well I won't put up with it," David said. "He knows he's licked. I won't swallow it."

"Poor people have to take what they can get," said Abby primly. David suddenly wished he had not come. He hated to be reminded he was poor and dragged down to the level of that stupid Abby and Sam. Why didn't Maria and Sam speak to each other? Sam was filling a short pipe and tiptoeing down to the basement to smoke it. He was such a coward, how could he have made a proposition such as Howard had hinted at? It made David uneasy and he took his leave and spent the rest of the day wishing he had gone to see that little girl Howard had introduced him to called Pet, the one with the brutal husband, who had actually played in a variety show and knew all the latest song hits.

By the time another winter came on Anne had begun a little knitting business that according to the agent would net her a nice tidy income. Mem was skeptical about its making much money and it proved to be just another swindle because the machine had to be paid for in installments and the goods turned out did not begin to pay for the machine.

Hortense answered a number of ads by mail in her best handwriting but when they found out she had no experience, the salary was so small it wouldn't have paid her to go into Philadelphia to live. She was determined to get out of the rut and made up her mind that if nothing else turned up she would spend the winter living off the Union County relatives. She could pay them a nice long three month visit and by that time it would be spring and anything might happen. David suggested that Anne and Mem go along and then they could shut up shop and save some money.

Hortense got herself ready and was off the very last of December. It wasn't long before she was reporting back the time of her life and how much all the friends made over her and how each one insisted she come to stay with them. Cousin Amos Wendel was home for a vacation and had taken her to Milford to a camp meeting and she was going to spend most of her time with the Wendels on account of Alice Wendel's not being well. The poor girl had caught a heavy cold and seemed to be fading away. Everyone tried to be cheerful and pretend she would get better but Hortense was sure Alice didn't think so as she talked of being quite ready to live or to die.

During the three months that Hortense spent in Lochiel she talked so much of Cousin Amos and Ed Barber that Anne and Mem would not have been surprised if she had had something to announce when she came home. But she had nothing to say except that Amos Wendel and Ed Barber were the best friends she had ever had and such gentlemen, not like the rest of the country people.

She looked very blooming and Anne caught her cutting out recipes for wedding cake that she pretended were for the friends in Union County.

IV. LITTLE TRADER
WALKS OUT

T HE YEAR 1880 saw each member of the Trexler family make a new start in life after what seemed almost a decade in the hard cold ground. Hortense went to Lochiel and swished around among the rustics. She talked continually of Cousin Amos and Ed Barber and wrote several times to each of them on her return and when they did not answer at once, she got moody again. Not that there was much time for moodiness because David was actually graduating from the pharmaceutical college the first of March when Hortense was finishing her visit to Lochiel. It was up to Mem and Anne to provide him with decent clothes and they made him a pair of pants and a couple of shirts. As he had no money as usual, Aaron dug down and handed out what was needed.

David's letters home had been suspicious for several months. He was always complaining of no time to write. His new place was no better than Trudel's but gave him more rather than less time to himself. The owner didn't know B from a bull's foot according to David and anyone hearing David talk would think him the whole works. Keeping track of his seventeen pipes and smoking them according to ritual seemed to be the boss's chief occupation. But it was David's frantic demands for money that mostly made Anne suspicious. When he wrote that he didn't intend to smother in the damned Fish Town any longer and was going to St. Louis if he had anything to say about it, Anne made up her mind to go to the city.

His handwriting was more sprawling than it used to be and looked suddenly to her eye thoroughly unreliable. When she went up for commencement she found David in a state of flurry. His mind was made up and he was ready to go to St. Louis.

"You can't mean it David," Anne said. They were in his room the night of the exercises as he struggled with his collar button getting very red and not looking at her.

"I certainly do mean it. I'm not going to stagnate here. Why what chance have I? Ten dollars a week and board. I can get twice that in St. Louis."

"How do you know you can?"

"I've had the offer. Here you go, talking against the one opportunity I've ever had. All the family is against me. You'd like me to rot here for ten years. Not much." He actually turned on her and looked ready to cry. He was working himself up and she could see it. "David," she said, "you can't fool me. You feel mighty guilty about something, confess now."

"You see? What did I tell you? Suspicious of me. No confidence. Ask any of my friends if you don't believe in me. They do. No wonder I want to get away. But I've no time to waste, I tell you. I've had an offer and I'm all packed up. If you want to know, there's no backing out now." He wormed into his coat, complaining all the time of the shiny seams. Anne stood up and shook her head. She was worried sick with premonitions of some hidden motive. For one thing, when he was in the washroom she had opened his drawer and saw a woman's handkerchief that just reeked of perfume. She felt she ought to do a little more searching, for Mem's sake. "If you're ready, why don't you go downstairs and let me fix up a little? We've got plenty of time and you haven't even asked me if I wanted to wash my hands."

"I didn't think, Anne, here are towels and there's the

wash room, around the corner. Don't be long will you."
The minute he was out of the room she pulled open the
drawer again. Nothing there but that handkerchief. Nothing in the other drawer. She went in his closet and quickly
felt in the pocket of his other coat. A note, folded into a
cocked hat.

"You dear boy, he's out of the way and all is safe. Come
around ten. Your own Pet."

Anne was so angry at the idea of David's letting them
sacrifice themselves for him and now throwing himself
away on some worthless little chit who was leading him
to ruin that she nearly pulled the rest of his clothes apart.
But she found no more notes. Under a coat that had
fallen was his traveling bag and opening it she was horrified to find it fully packed. She ran her hands through
the contents and at the bottom in a white envelope were
two tickets to St. Louis. When the door opened, she didn't
hear it and kept looking at the tickets.

"What are you doing Anne with my things?" It was
David. She faced him with the tickets in her hand.

"What are *you* doing, oh David?" She couldn't speak,
she was so angry and horrified at his treachery.

"That's my business and I never thought that my own
sister would be a prying sneak."

"That's just enough David. What are you, I'd like to
know, sneaking off to St. Louis with some silly woman,
with a name like that, deceiving your poor mother who
has worked herself to the bone to see you through school
so she could get some help. Now she can go to tailoring in
her old age, I suppose, oh David, how could you?"

David turned pale and said she wasn't a silly woman
but a poor creature tormented by a brutal husband and
he was only trying to save her.

"Oh David," Anne said, "how can you talk like that?
You know better. To think you'd be the very impersona-

tion of deceit and falsehood, with poor Mem after all her trials depending on you. And for what?" The sister got very dramatic and began calling names, said David was just puppyism victimized and for a little pseudo romance had been willing to wreck all their hopes, until David was near tears but still inwardly determined to get away from such a family. Anne actually wormed Pet's address out of him and he was relieved to have her take it on her shoulders. She went to see Pet and had a long talk with the little fuzzy haired creature who lisped and said she certainly never never would do anything to hurt her poor Davy. When she learned he hadn't a cent in the world and a mother to support, she was very angry and swore she would see him no more.

She wrote long high flown letters to Anne for weeks afterward and David was very chastened about the whole proceeding and took his two tickets back. He could hardly bear to think that the plans he and Pet had made to team up together in a little variety skit were over for good and he sang the two songs he had learned, "Down at the Heel and out at the Elbow" and "Empty Is the Cradle, Baby's Gone," with great feeling all by himself as he washed in the morning, wondering how he could ever go on with the drug business which he hated and didn't see how he could ever stick at and make good.

There wasn't a more miserable member of the class of 1880 than David and he almost wished he were an orphan without a responsibility in the world. Joe wrote holding out hopes for him in the Black Hills or he would have gone on in a frame of mind that might have ladled out paregoric instead of soothing syrup.

When Joe made a flying trip East on business David gave him a regular song and dance. He was determined that his brother should find a way to get him to the Hills. "There's nothing for an ambitious fellow in a town like this. The East is dead. Why I couldn't do any more than save a few pennies in a lifetime here. I want to help Mem and give her things and of course I never hope to be the hero you are to Mem and the girls but I ought to do something to pay them back for all they've done for me." He wasn't sure that he wasn't overdoing it but looking sideways at Joe he could see him kind of smiling but taking it in.

"No," he went on, "there's only one statue on the pedestal at old El Dorado, and that's not mine. I'm not cut out to be adored." Then he took Joe to a wine shop where a few young bloods recognized him with a patronizing lifted finger and Joe said, "The Hills would make a man of you David. But don't think it's easy. It's not all the romantic junk you read about."

"I know it. I'm not such a child. You were as old as I was when you went South, weren't you?"

"Yes," said Joe looking sour and hard around the mouth. "The Hills are rough, I don't know how you'd stand up but you can try. I'll do what I can." The two brothers shook hands on it, feeling secretly antagonistic to one another, David jealous of Joe's age and good looks and elegant manners and Joe bitter about the soft life David had had at his expense. The family trooped down from Grapeville to see Joe who brought them presents fit for a king and excited the girls by telling them he was going down to Washington to see Lenore Blondell and her mother. The girls had gotten very fond of Lenore Blondell in their thoughts and they sniffed a match and hoped for it. They could see that she was just the one for Joe, much nicer really than the beautiful but fickle Lucy.

If Joe had not met Agnes Mason on his trip to New York before he went to Washington, he might have changed that part of his life. He might even have kept from going insane about ten years later.

In their later years the Trexler girls, Anne and Hortense, used to wonder what it was their brother had ever seen in that Agnes Mason. At the time he married her they carried on as if it were his funeral. Agnes Mason had all the worldly attributes of success but the Trexler girls were romantic and they had grown very fond of the idea of Lenore Blondell. They had their brother's word for it that she was the purest and most unselfish woman he had ever known and that he did not marry such a creature put a small worm of doubt about the human race into their brains.

Agnes Mason had a kind of torturing way about her from the first and she had a way of flattering him with her attentions and her reminder of all the past glories of the days in the South, the swaggering politicians and wine and riding on top of the world. He could see that time now for what it was, but he liked the way it had made him feel, on top, and prosperous and powerful. The Mason family were a big bunch of New York promoters with their fingers in a dozen parts of the world and a hard and knowing way of disposing of peoples and fates with a flick of the thumb. They were what Joe wanted to be if he was to get ahead and he knew it and he took a final flying jump at that kind of thing before going down. He never had it in him to be a topnotch successful man, but he liked the shine of it and the spectacle and he couldn't separate himself from it.

Agnes Mason was the fly paper that trapped him even in his inner secret life that should have belonged to himself. She could dress like a queen and act like one and in her company, Joe forgot all the old bakeshop and the

little candy maker days and the jibes of the Atlanta lawyers and he felt good. Before he knew it, he had got himself incriminated with her, he had said things he wished
unsaid and cursed himself all the way down to Washington.

Once in that town he felt a little better because when
he saw Lenore Blondell he knew he did not love her. He
knew too that she loved him and this made him feel terrible and at the same time happy. He wished he could
really offer marriage to her but she was so plain that she
surely would not expect it.

Lenore Blondell and her mother had given a great deal
of devotion to his affairs and told him that time had only
gone to show that he had had nothing to do with the irreg-
ularities charged and that the prosecution had resulted in
the efforts of those who wished to escape by combining
against him. That night he took the two women to a theater and did everything for them that was fashionable and
tender and he made a great deal of them but he did not
speak and that was what Lenore wanted. He could see her
wanting it and it hurt him and irritated him and made
him want to run away.

Just before he left, he told her that he wasn't worthy of
a really fine woman and his life was too hard to share.
Lenore would have spoken and said that she had a hard
life already but something in his eyes stopped her and they
parted the best of friends. In all his life Joe never had
such another friend and in all hers, Lenore Blondell never
had such another. This very act of his in making it easy
for her allowed her always in herself to believe he might
have cared if things had been different. As for Joe, once
he was married to Agnes Mason, he yearned for Lenore
and wondered what crazy madness had carried him away
from her.

In New York he wasn't as happy as he had expected to

be in the company of Agnes Mason and in fact he was hardly civil to that lady several times. He bought an enormous brooch of black enamel and pearls for Lenore Blondell and back in Deadwood wrote a very blue letter to Anne that he didn't think he could ever content himself in the Hills again. He wished too he had not seen Lenore because now he could not write those long intimate letters he had enjoyed writing so much and even after a letter from Agnes Mason on heavy fashionable paper came, he did not think of writing such an intimate letter to her. Affairs at the mine were going slowly and he wished he could sell out and go somewhere else.

David was a changed boy to all outward appearances after Anne's discovery of the St. Louis plot but actually he was only more secretive. He didn't see Pet again because she was really angry at him to propose such a scheme when he was no better than a pauper. He found other girls to call on and even had a few "fast" friends who were not likely to move in the same circle as his sisters. He was determined to get on in the world and thought he knew more about it already than his brothers Joe and Aaron.

He took naturally to the proper things, went to the Academy of Music to hear the Germanic Orchestra and liked the xylophone solo the best. He even went to see *The Vicar of Wakefield* performed at the Museum with free tickets but could hardly keep awake during the evening and decided that "art" was naturally dull. But he was obliging as ever to his sisters and went to great trouble to market the pigeons and the sunflower seed and to sneak little samples of sweet oil for them when he went down to Grapeville.

For the first time he found he had more in common

with Hortense than with Anne whom he feared since her discovery of Pet and the two of them went for walks on his trips home and talked darkly of the future. A whole summer went by in the same plodding way and David thought it was a sin and shame that Joe did not exert himself more and find a store for him in Deadwood at once. He was certain that Joe could afford to buy a store if he wanted to. Anne said, "You are pretty young for a store of your own."

"I'll never know more about it than I do right now and I won't be a clerk all my life, not me," he said. He had an arrogant way about him that made Anne want to burst out laughing. Even when there wasn't a cent in the house he was talking grand about his drug stores. It made her tired too that everything they had should drain out to the boys and the girls get so little.

She was almost pleased to get an invitation from the friends in Union County to come and visit that winter even if it was because poor Alice Wendel was very ill. It gave her the feeling as if she might have a little life of her own and some importance of her own. She had listened to David's woes for so long that it would be a relief to hear someone else's. At the Wendel home she tried very hard to be helpful and sympathetic and the city girl with her bright red hair and blazing eyes put a kind of life in them all. She couldn't help being excited at their admiration and it gave her a funny feeling to feel happiness in a house of death. Amos Wendel came home to be with his favorite dying sister and even he could not help feeling a kind of happiness on account of Anne Trexler. Sometimes Amos and Anne would be the only ones up, keeping watch in the big sitting room with Alice's bedroom door ajar. They would whisper together and talk about their lives as children.

One night after a very bad day for Alice they were sitting silent for a long time and Amos began telling about his old dog Bull. This dog had saved his life when he was just a little fellow still in dresses. The dog had dragged him out of the brook and had stood over him licking his face. Well sir that dog fell sick when he was about nine years old, not more, no he was nine that winter. He lay out on the ice of that very brook, dying, and his father said now Amos he's your dog, you'll have to take care of him. The boy could hardly make himself do it. He got the ax and went out and then he saw old Bull wagging his tail at him and the tears nearly put his eyes out. He just shut his eyes and let the ax swing and he hit hard so as to make sure, and old Bull was really dead. He took him out and buried him but he never forgot old Bull.

When he finished the story he was a little ashamed of his feeling and wanted to laugh but he looked at Anne and she was crying. His own eyes were filling with tears, he didn't know if it was old Bull or poor Alice or Anne herself who made him so soft. Both of them were awfully aware of the dark night and the lonely room with no one around but themselves and poor Alice, quietly dying on the other side of the door. It didn't seem right to be in love in such a house but Anne knew she did love Amos and he loved her. When she took her hands down from her face, he could see it in her eyes and they were both a little shy. Anne got up to look at Alice and then she came back again. The big clock was ticking. She could feel the new happiness bubble up inside of her out of the desert of the old, and she knew she really loved him, not like the other, not so wild perhaps, but maybe better.

Everyone in the house knew without being told that something had happened between Amos and Anne and in a way it made it all the harder for poor Alice. In those days, many a family was wiped out with consumption and in the Wendel family, not only Alice but, suddenly and awfully, the plump Clara came down with the disease. They called it quick consumption in hushed tones and had to stand by and see it lick the flesh off her bones. The poor mother with her satiny loops of hair over her ears, and her sober dark dresses and her shyness, had to see her girls go. Something of her terror went into Anne and it made her love for Amos more solemn to be born in such awfulness. She had gone upcountry with the sadness of six years of waiting for John Gason and it seemed right to her that she and Amos should find each other in a house of death.

After the two girls were laid away, a brief three weeks apart, no one would hear of Anne Trexler's going home. Amos began talking of the necessity of getting back on the road again and he planned to go to Baltimore for the McCormick people around the first of the year. He and Anne went to visit with all the Union County friends who remembered Joshua Trexler and Catherine and all the old timers. Amos began to look better than he had in a long time for the traveling was a hard life and he was naturally skinny. When relatives told him how fine he looked, he was half ashamed to look so well with so much trouble in the family and he knew Anne was the reason. Every time she had a letter from Hortense he felt guilty, remembering the camp meetings he had taken Hortense to and the fooling silly kind of things he had said. He remembered too that he had not answered her last letter and in a burst of friendly feeling and desire to have her feel kindly toward him he wrote her that he hoped to be in Grapeville to see them all before he went on the road again. In a painfully short time an answer came and he read it guiltily.

Dear Amos,

Yours of Dec. 6th received and I confess that I had been
storing up many ill feelings against you as day after day
went by and no signs of either you or any message from
you but when I heard of the death of poor dear Alice and
of the serious illness of Clara and shortly afterwards of her
death I felt nothing but sorrow and pity for you all. No,
no, little did I think when I bid Clara goodbye that I
should never see her again on earth, I even had hopes that
Alice might grow strong and healthy again, but then they
are so much happier now, it would be wrong to wish them
back; I sometimes think (when things go so different from
what I *long* that they should) how much happier I might
be if I were laid away in some quiet nook, I should then
at any rate be loved and mourned for, and that would
be a comfort. Anne in her letter was wishing for snow so
I hope you will have snow so that she can have at least
one ride, tell her please that Ella Roberts was married
today, to that Mr. Garrett from Phila. who with his
mother lived in the house next to Gardner's, they went off
to Phila. with the 3 o'clock train, and that the "old gent
and lady are in their glory." It is lovely tonight, too nice
to stay in the house, Mother and I are alone, and I feel so
lonely I wish I were at Lochiel or that Lochiel was here
but there, I'll just stop wishing or else I'll find myself
wishing for everything and everybody. Now will you write
to me very soon and will you come and see us very soon
too? If so, I'll leave your name where it is (but where I
came so near taking it off) among the list of the few
friends whom I hold in very dear esteem. with the hope
you are all well, I'm

Yours Truly

Hortense

Amos was very pleased with the letter and sure that Hortense had quite forgotten the long buggy rides but Anne
sobered when she read it and shook her head at him and

decided to let Amos's attentions tell their own story rather than say anything outright about the engagement.

Anne's engagement broke ground for a regular upheaval in the Trexler family. David immediately said he was going to Deadwood with or without Joe's help. Joe wrote him that if he could get nothing in Philadelphia to suit, to come ahead and he would forward a hundred dollars. Hortense set out at once for the city and took a job at six dollars a week with Mr. Fouse's insurance office. She was slow at dictation but Mr. Fouse was all consideration and full of homilies about every day having something to teach us. David began buying his outfit and anyone would think he was going on the grand tour from the quality of the goods he bought. Mem actually cried to see him so extravagant and was filled with all sorts of forebodings about him. She told him he must save some of the money Joe sent for his fare to give her as they were never so hard up. She and Anne took out another lot of suits and worked desperately at them for wages that were a crying sin but money they must get, at whatever price. The hero was finally packed off for the West with the solemnest of farewells and he made all sorts of good resolutions to help his dear mother and his dear good home.

THE BANKER AS A YOUNG MAN

April 2. Left the store, paid a visit to Norristown and saw Bessie, went to Grapeville.

April 11 to 20. At home.

April 21. Left G. for Phila saw Pet for the last time and also Mother Calhoun. Ella was booked from night until morning at the same hotel and for the *last time* parted friends but no more.

April 22. at 8th and Fairmont at 7:10 A.M. Farewell. Went to Weisel's, accompanied to Market depot by Hortense and a last goodbye to my dear sister and my dear good home.

April 23. 9:30 A.M. arrived at Chicago went to Commercial Hotel took view of city.

April 24. Sunday went to Lincoln Park, Academy of Music, and saw Moody & Sanky.

April 25. Left Chicago at 12:05 on C.R.P. & P.R.R. for Council Bluffs, crossed the Mississippi River at Sunset. Goodbye East, How do you do West. Arrived at Davenport for supper there saw a curious picture of innocence in the shape of a pretty female but accompanied by a Gentleman but who leaves her at Des Moines. After many hesitations I am finally tempted to speak to her &

April 26 at 9 A.M. at Atlantic take a seat beside her and find she is quite interesting going to C. B. a pleasant journey ah! indeed very pleasant across the country to C. B. lose sight of her though during excitement at Bluffs—fortune again favors me for as I am ready to start from Transfer at C. B. I see E. L. alighting from the flatboat and coming towards me. The rest is as a dream, enough.

April 27. Arrived at Sidney, took dinner with E. L. The wave of her Kerchief at the departing of the train made me long for a repetition of the journey. But alas! The best of *Friends* must part; and so it ended. Remained at Railroad Round House that day wrote to my dear Home also a card to Hortense.

April 28. Left Sidney at 9 A.M. for Deadwood, ah, I'll never *no never* forget that ride across the Prairies the first 50 miles were quite refreshing but alas, as everything else, it grew monotonous and when night came all passengers wished themselves anywhere but where they were, as for myself I forced a little "Comedy" on the "Seasick" crowd and thereby drove off that weary feeling which is bound to overcome you when riding all day in a "Buss" which had a bad imitation of Springs made of leather. Though we were riding night and day it apparently had no affect on the outside world except an Antelope who would lazily endeavor to escape our rifles, at all events the Sun rose the same as usual and set too for that matter, nothing happening to prevent. At night we were brought into a tent, it was about 11 P.M. and owing to the Horses having got on the Prairie we were unable to go farther until morning for the horses we had, had traveled 20 miles, so we got out our Blankets, but no sleep that night, the air was cool and damp & we finally went into the log cabin where the Hostler lived. I'll never forget that night, how the old man agreed to give us *two* cups of coffee all around if I would only sing another Song (Coffee, by the way, was 25 cts a cup) of course I went through all I knew and the Stable men thought for sure I was some traveling circus and made me promise to stop there if I came back that way.

April 30. Nothing much of importance that day except that we finished up the homemade "Dutch cake" which the gentlemen from N. Y. liked. Also had a good dinner at Jenk's, best outfit on the road.

May 1. Sunday 5 A.M. arrived at Rapid City took breakfast at Hotel Americanie and resumed journey arrived at Crook City at 4 P.M., fooled a poor Jew on a dinner, finally took one at another Hotel and soon we were on our way to D. arriving about 6 P.M. Met Joe at the Postoffice, took me around town after supper, stayed all night at Deadwood.

May 2. *Strange things have happened very strange.* Take breakfast together and then in a spring wagon leave for Galena find a nice comfortable cabin, take a look at the mine. Am put on the Payroll without any particular work to do. Write to Anne.

May 3. Hear more about Agnes and finally tell of our Poor Mother at Home. Satisfactory Resolution. Promise to do all in our power to help support our Home. A— a second consider-ation, extreme kindness shown in J.

May 4. Get a thorough soaking in the rain in going to mill for slats in the evening. Do some writing for Joe. His eye is bad.

May 5. Write to Hortense.

May 6. Go to Deadwood to look over a drugstore. Of all the walks from Galena to Deadwood beats the bugs. Stop at Over-land Hotel. Can't agree about position in regard to salary. Won't take less than $80 and they can't afford to pay a first rate man. Engagement therefore postponed. Don't care a fig either. I didn't come out to this country to work for nothing.

May 11. Stormy day, lots of snow and rain. Have a talk with Dr. Babcock and in the evening, "take in" the "Notorious Gem."

May 12. A visit to the graveyard among the tomb stones was the following. Wild Bill was a Notorious Villain.

Epitaph of Wild Bill

Wild Bill
J. B. Hichcock
killed by the assasin
Jack McCall
in
Deadwood
August 2, 76
Pard we will meet again in
the happy hunting grounds
to part no more
Goodbye
Colorado Charlie

As seen in Deadwood May 12 by me. This notorious assassin it is said has killed upwards of 15 men, and at one time the most vicious of murderers.

May 13. Returned to Galena.

May 22. Worked ½ day in the tunnel.

May 23. At the mine a part of morning & all of afternoon. Such work! A rare treat (?) indeed, to haul *bricks* up a steep embankment.

May 24. All day at the mine, repetition of day before, only as Beecher says, "a little more so," but in this case it was a good deal more so. Heaven save the mark! I never expected this *Slavish* work and from a Brother. But it shall all pass without a murmur. I will stand it as long as I can without injuring myself. I probably have not yet seen the worst.

May 25. All day at the mine. Photo of tunnel taken including Myself.

May 27. All day at mine. A horrible exercise at the wheel barrow.

May 28. Joe went to Deadwood, I remained at cabin in the morning, at the mine part of the afternoon being called there to attend to business that was *neglected* by those hired.

May 29. Letters received from Rudolph, M. A. C. with cabinet photo.

May 30. Commenced at Ditch on Ruby Gulch.

May 31. All day at ditch.

June 1. Continued with ditch, hottest day of the season.

June 5. Came to Deadwood in hopes of getting the position but no success, can't pay a competent clerk.

June 6. Terrible hailstorm, cyclone and a Run for Life. One woman killed, another leg broken; narrow escape.

June 7. A look at the ruins, a lucky hen's nest in a shattered shed, found a novel, "Bessie's Six Lovers" and a two foot Rule on the mountains.

June 8. Went to a church sociable, a good time, introduced to quite a number of ladies, escorted Miss Rodgers home. Prettiest little girl in the Hills.

June 9 to 12. In Deadwood, made a trip to Lead with Joe.

June 17. A ramble over the Hills. Heard from home.

July 3. "A" arrived in Deadwood.

July 7. A pleasant ride to Lead City and a pleasant call on the Damsels.

July 11. Attend a sociable and Dance, immense time.

July 14. Papers from Phila. Another ride on a spirited "Nag" and a good time.

TWO BROTHERS AND THE BLACK GAMBLER

ABOUT this time David quit keeping a diary but he wrote home a great deal and grumbled that his hard experience at the mine would never be forgotten. Ever since his first letter from Sidney on his way to the Hills he had something to say against everything and everybody. He was horrified at the rough stories and relished them and sent a twig from the tree where thieves were lynched to the girls. Joe wrote that David lacked bottom but was a good boy and a help around the house, milked the cow, made butter, cut wood. Aaron said, "Now Mem, it will be good for him. He's been babied too much, that's the trouble." Mem grieved for him as if he were dead and wrote him appealing letters in upcountry German reminding him that *mir hast du* and promising that if he were not married in two years she would come to live with him. He complained so much that Anne wrote Joe she hoped he wouldn't let David rupture himself and she did hope he could work into the drug business after he had gone to the trouble of learning it.

If there was ever a time when Joe wanted less to be bothered with a sprout like David, it was at that time. He had his hands full with Agnes Mason who was taking advantage of his eye trouble to come to Deadwood. She had been almost glad that he was suffering, it gave her an excuse and she went against her entire family in making such a trip. The men of her family never rightly forgave her and went against Joe in their dealings, not that they prospered, either, because gradually they also lost out in their Black Hills holdings and were almost as helpless as he. There was nothing to do with Agnes, once she was in Deadwood, except to marry her and Joe was relieved in a way to have the problem solved for him. But before he came to the actual marrying, there were several months of dallying, David acting sulky and babyish and Agnes proving herself a fine hand to handle him. She could coax and wheedle him and came to act as a go-between for Joe and his brother. The two brothers couldn't come to grips with one another and David was either complaining to Agnes and putting up his story to her or he was writing to his sister Anne. Joe too carried on his tussle with David through his sister. In the suspicion the two brothers had of one another, they used this roundabout way to find out one another's wishes.

David hardly set foot in Deadwood before he began complaining that he hadn't come out there for nothing and he wasn't going to work for a song. When Joe gave him work in the mine, digging a tunnel, he groaned and acted as if he were being slowly tortured but the money still meant very little to him. He soon lost what he made at the races or at faro. Joe took a hard turn when he learned this, he was as hard toward David as if he had never sinned in just that way. He came down heavy on his brother and bitter and said he wouldn't do a thing for him until he could prove he knew what to do with his money.

Poor Anne was frantic with the complaints of the two and the difficulty of knowing what to advise. But when David turned down a drug store proposition at sixty dollars a month as being not worth his consideration, all her sympathies went to Joe. She wrote David she never heard of such a business and any clerk in Philadelphia would have jumped at the chance.

David was up in the air when he got that. The idea, as if he weren't always trying to better himself, but when a paltry sum like sixty dollars a month would no more than pay his expenses and allow him twenty-five dollars besides, he was not taking any of it. As for Joe helping him, well, he would certainly rather be his own boss. He wasn't ungrateful to Joe, oh no, he knew it was his money had gotten him out there and Anne was mistaken if she thought he expected too much from Joe, he might have once, but not now, no, his eyes were pretty well opened. Joe was simply extravagant beyond his means and that wasn't excusable even though someone else did benefit by it, it certainly wasn't *his* way of doing business, no sir. Now that he was there he would stand it as long as his health lasted but if anyone ever earned three dollars a day he did, up at seven and at it until twelve, then at it from one to six. At that he was gaining weight, had put on five pounds, slept well too, but like the dead. That was no kind of a life but he'd put up with it. It was hard though, at the hands of a dear brother. Oh it was hard to get up in the mornings but they had a nice garden started behind the cabin and they were watching the onions every day helping them to grow. He did wish he were back home eating strawberries and he couldn't see why Joe couldn't buy him a drug store so he could start in making some money. But he wouldn't say another word, nobody was going to call him an ingrate, no siree.

All the time, he was teasing Agnes about wanting a drug store and she actually began to talk around Joe and his prejudice against helping David in that way. Joe had a deep distrust of David who made him sick with his baby-ish whining and his narrow prejudices. He didn't intend getting into an argument with David and he talked it over with Agnes and told her she might intimate to David that Joe might buy him a store but only under certain conditions. He and a young fellow named Madison would buy the business, David's name might appear in the business but he and David would draw papers that he didn't own a toothpick, was simply acting as Joe's agent, clerk in short, and was entirely dependent upon Joe for the place and subject to discharge at a moment's notice. He would be allowed a living salary, no more, until Joe had become convinced he was capable of conducting business for himself and then he could buy Joe out at cost whether he had the money or not. Joe was surprised when he heard what a row David made at this proposition.

"All right, now I know what my own brother thinks of me," David said to Agnes, pushing his hair back and firmly marching up and down the kitchen. "I know now, all right. I've suspected all along but I hate to think blood is so thin. He doesn't trust me. Can't trust me with a paltry thousand dollars after he gets me out here in this God forsaken hole. All he wants is to keep me down and humble me. Why if I'm to be a clerk why not be anybody's clerk? Why be my brother's clerk? Is this what I left home for? I certainly never thought to see the day when my own brother would do less for me than he does for strangers."

"What do you mean?" Agnes said. "He sent you money

to come out and he's willing to help you, but you know yourself he heard about the gambling—"

"Gambling," said David, almost beside himself. "Why the idea is ridiculous, besides why should he hold that against me when his very partner and best friend is called the Black Gambler?"

Agnes's face got dark and angry looking when David brought up that name. "That's all over. He was just a poor fellow Joe was helping."

"Poor fellow nothing. I guess I heard him say right in front of a couple of fellows, and Madison was one, that he would do more for Black John than he would for his own brother. How's that? And that fellow wanted Joe to set him up with a saloon. After that, how does he dare talk about my gambling?"

"You don't know what you're talking about David. Black John is nothing. He's nothing." Agnes got up angrily and stood in front of David and he quailed at her and said, "Well I didn't mean anything but it's true he's always helping others."

"And it's true he's always helping everybody but himself. I'm sick of it," said Agnes. "Just sick of it."

"Trouble is Joe is too extravagant," David said. "That's not my way of doing business."

"You shouldn't talk about it, all Joe's family have profited by his extravagance, I guess," said Agnes. She could have throttled David with his silly baby face. She hated all that tribe. As if she did not know that they were opposed to his marrying her. He was holding off for just their sakes, afraid his mother would carry on when she knew. When she had a chance to talk to Joe alone she made him feel that his family were using him shamefully and that David would probably make trouble sooner or later. Joe's eye was bothering him, he was tortured with fear of blindness and in his misery and desire for quiet somewhere, married Agnes.

He did not have the courage to tell Mem at once and this Agnes held against him. She began rummaging in his private papers too and when she found letters from Lucy and Lenore Blondell, she read them and was bitterly jealous and venomous. Now she blamed these women for any mood of abstraction Joe might have and she nagged at him to tell his mother. When Mem heard the news she almost fainted and Anne in a burst of feeling went upstairs and wrote with shaking hands to David, "Farewell to all our hopes, Mother can go back to tailoring in her old age, oh that he should marry and just to get a nurse, we are in tears and trouble." No one wrote to Joe and Agnes wormed David's letter from him and read it with pretended smiles.

At night when she was alone with Joe, she began, "If you think I'm going to stand such talk from your sister, you're mistaken."

"I don't know what you mean," Joe said. He was taking off his coat and turned toward her with his arms backward in the sleeves.

"David's letter. I saw it. The way she carried on. You'd think they owned you, hand and foot. Don't they want you to have a life of your own? I'd like to know what they expect of you, to live like a monk all your life and turn every cent over to them? I won't stand for it. You've got to write them."

"Don't Agnes." Suddenly he couldn't stand her voice and her anger. He had never seen such anger. It frightened him and he felt he could never get away from it. Oh why had he given up Lenore with her tender and gentle ways. He felt guilty to have her flash suddenly into his mind as he stood looking at his wife in her ruffled nightdress. There she was, not Lucy, whom he still adored, but

Lenore, who adored him. "Don't Agnes," he said. "I told you before we ever married about Mother. She can't help it, she's old fashioned and she's worked hard enough to expect something from her sons. They'll get over it, especially," he added with a sinking heart, "when they see you."

"They'll never see me. I won't let them step a foot into my house after the way they act. *I'm* not the one, Victor, to begin this feud, just mark that. No, I was all smiles and kindness but now it's begun, I'll stick to it, if that's what they want. I'll not relent either. I've my pride too."

"It's not a question of pride. They don't know and were excited, can't you understand?"

"I understand only too well, only too well."

He was putting his coat back on now. "I'm going out for a little walk. You'd better go to sleep." Suddenly he couldn't get into bed with her. He needed fresh air, to breathe again. She braced herself against the pillows her eyes blazing fury. Why she hates me, Joe thought, she really hates me. With all his affairs at sixes and sevens, Agnes's outburst was the last straw. He felt shaky for days and tried to keep away from her. She held out for days, hard as nails, and then made him admit he was cruel to her in a melting scene which left him ashamed and weak. How long would it last? He had a cold sinking feeling that it would last forever.

In a few weeks he had a kind and loving letter from Anne asking him to forgive her for her haste, they all loved him so and if he was happy, that was all that mattered. He wrote back that none of them must worry for a minute about things they said to one another and he felt very happy and secure in his sister's loyalty. He couldn't keep from feeling irritated at David. The fellow was a prig, with his talk about the villainous country and the lawlessness and the gambling. But with all his talk, he wasn't against sneaking out to the race track and risking what he had on the races. Joe gave him a good dressing down for it and David had the satisfaction of his pride and silence. But he boiled inwardly to have Joe, the most extravagant person he had ever known, who risked money here and there on old holes in the earth that wouldn't yield a tin spoon, carry him over the coals. Joe talk to *him* of extravagance! The very idea. Why the way he ladled out money to good for nothings like Black John was a caution.

Joe gave him a look that might have knocked him down and went out and walked around half determined to pack the cub away that very night. Suppose he did give it to John. Whose business was that? Was he to have his family meddling in all the concerns of his life? He had given up enough for them and had life in the Hills under an assumed name to pay for it. It was carrying things too far to have a sprout try to dictate to him. He loved his mother and sisters but sometimes he was tired of thinking of them, worrying about them and the money that was needed. It almost stopped him to know how hard they worked, how they toiled year after year, the girls without the advantages he had set his heart on them having. What had the struggle been for? By the time he made money, Mem would be gone and the girls too old, perhaps old maids or married to worthless men. He was afraid to face that day when they should be beyond him, or should not need him. Sometimes he dreaded even more just to have Anne pass out of his life, married and happy.

No wonder the men were grumbling in the mines. But he couldn't afford to listen to all the newfangled ideas and it would be his duty to fire the men who talked too big. He hated that job, it put him on the outside, and he couldn't say he was on the inside with the promoters of the mine. He was just nowhere. By this time he could see the stock was watered and he wished he could pull out and save himself. But they wouldn't let him, he had the confidence of people because he had been an early prospector and then he wore good clothes. A good dummy. No wonder he liked to have the boys touch him for a little help. He had to feel he belonged somewhere. Benny Agnew was more than worth it, why he was glad to soak two hundred dollars in a lot of boots and shoes that would set the fellow on his feet.

David hearing of it almost frothed at the mouth. You'd thing the boy's birthright had been gobbled away from him. Joe let him froth. David wouldn't understand about a fellow like Benny. All that David could see was that the fellow had maybe gambled and whored to say nothing of working himself to death in icy water panning gold and lying out on hills at night. David and his nice girls from the church made Joe sick. Why the fellow actually went to prayer meeting and simpered around as if he were doing something devilish when he took the girls home. But he was a good one with songs, you had to give it to him, and energetic as the devil when it came to showing off like the time he got up the benefit for the schoolteacher who didn't get her salary. The house had been packed and he sang his little songs with the true touch. He should have been an actor.

Joe was actually relieved when, the drug store proposition falling through, and the mine work giving out, David decided to take himself off. He told the boy that experience would put some sense into him, nothing else would, and smarting from the words David prepared to depart. He signed up with the Robinson outfit to do a surveying job for the Government and he headed for the Judith Mountains near Fort Maginnis in company with a man named Stinson. The two fellows had a horse apiece and a pack animal and David's horse, Macduff, proved pretty good. Stinson had five hundred dollars from Joe to sink in a prospecting hole somewhere in the north and with this last grievance, David pulled himself together to discover his own true nature.

He was on his own at last and he looked around him and began his trading career. The soldiers at the fort were loaded with flour but had little money for gambling and whoring. David bought their flour dirt cheap and sold it to prospectors not fifty miles away at 400 per cent profit. He felt good about his sharp deal. It just showed he could take care of himself. Well, if a man didn't, nobody else would and it was all a question of the survival of the fittest.

FROM his marble days up, David Trexler was a trader and his sharp deal with the government flour put his foot on the first rung to fortune. David had all the characteristics of the successful man, the sentimentality about home and mother and the necessary shrewdness to see just how far a dollar in that direction would take him. He had the good sense never to be too generous with the women folk, never buy them fancy tea sets or encourage them to dictate to him. His way was wise and his end would prove it.

After all, look at Joseph, his exact opposite. Choose your way to die. Joe died penniless and mad and David was surrounded by thousands of dollars' worth of floral gratitude and lay in full dress suit regalia with a red rosebud looking like a gentleman while hundreds marched past him for a last look. The widows and orphans may have been disappointed at his will but not his own widow or orphan. He was a man who had saved wisely for a lifetime, never tipped more than a dime, and knew how to shoot the works in the right direction. This may not seem the right place to mention David's death, certainly an event that did not take place for some fifty more years, but it is a moment when for all practical purposes he is walking off this scene.

He has started on the ladder up and we are interested in those who are fumbling for the next rung down. Contrary to superstition the big mass are and have been for some time past more concerned with a way down than a way up. David in his way up kept his family always in mind because when he was to become really successful he would be interviewed by papers and would say that he had lived by his mother's precepts.

He was really a loving fellow, also, and there were times when he suffered from the career he had chosen. He took out his love for his fellow man in Rotary in his old age but he never got over his sharp ability to trade. He could send his sisters a ten dollar bill with the air of bestowing a fortune and get gratitude to his dying day. Even Anne Wendel was grateful to him and called him her dear brother.

He was always concerned about the welfare of his poor relations and always knew when to be a sort of Napoleon to guide their destinies. Of course in little practical matters, he used his right of judgment and it is a curious fact that although he amassed considerable he never actually parted with more than a thousand in a lifetime to his sisters and Anne's husband passed peacefully into bankruptcy without more than a hundred or so thrown that way. But the test of this man's genius and fitness to reach the peak he finally reached was the way he handled Anne's brash attempt to get him to help her in payments on her house. She had finally tired of years of rent and persuaded herself and Amos that they could gradually pay for their own property instead of enriching a landlord.

Where had Anne got this obsession to own a home? It was all part of a fine American tradition and one deep in her blood. A good many people have sacrificed a great deal of freedom for this worthy end. Anne started on her home buying, was happy at the house, solid and good, of sound construction, built some thirty years before when houses were still built with something heavier than lath, she had the thing going and then hard times, Amos's business falling off, the two younger children needing more. She wrote frantically to David. David was firm with her, told her—although two thousand miles away—that she was foolish and had made a foolish investment, offered to buy her a lot but what she was to use for a house he didn't suggest, and dismissed her.

Even then she was not crushed and kept the house, white elephant though it was, for years. But that's not all of David. Let's show David now we have him. There's the endowment he made for education at his death too small to do much more than perpetuate his name, and there are his sister's two children working their way through college the year their uncle bought the big Cadillac and took a trip to Death Valley.

THE STUFFED MOCKING BIRD

AFTER Joe promised Mem to get rid of his Escondido stock and give the money to Mem she was halfway reconciled to his marriage but she could not get it out of her head that her boys belonged to her for all time. Anne sometimes wondered what Mem would say if she knew of the numerous women hangers-on that Aaron had, who on one pretense or another found their way into his office. She hated the clandestine form Aaron's life was taking and yet she could not blame him when she thought of the high handed way Mem had always acted.

With Joe married, the girls longed to get into homes of their own. Anne tried to be patient and wait until Amos Wendel got out of debt and he talked continually about all he could do if he could only lay his hands on a little capital. She didn't care if they didn't have a stick of furniture if they could be together. Hortense took a gloomy view of life following Anne's engagement. She was always giving little digs at Amos and Anne knew very well it was sour grapes and she tried to be patient with her sister who was always having crying spells. Hortense had lost her job with Mr. Fouse on account of the hard times that were on top of everybody again, not that they ever seemed to lift from some people.

Selling insurance for the Odd Fellows made her feel a martyr and she had to travel around and sleep in hotels where the mosquitoes bit her to death. After one night in Newark like that, she crawled home to Grapeville and let herself be babied for days. She was more and more a difficult subject to handle and Anne sighed thinking of her and tried not to feel guilty about having gotten Amos for herself. Hortense had a way of making her feel to blame for her troubles and pains and headaches that multiplied as Anne's wedding day drew near. The sight of Anne making her wedding clothes was more than she could stand but she bore up under her sufferings and went to the city to peddle insurance again.

No one ever knew how she happened to meet Mr. Ripley. He certainly wasn't a man anyone would have picked out for the tall and handsome Hortense. He was at least two inches shorter and he had a dark foreign look and an enormous black beard. The beard was particularly conspicuous as he was beginning to be bald. He was very little older than Hortense but he might have been an uncle. Anne simply couldn't believe it when Hortense said they were engaged and would be married very soon. It almost looked as if she were doing it merely to be married first. Anne tried to talk solemnly to her but Hortense only looked hurt and cried and said she guessed she knew her mind as well as some other people. Still he was a pleasant fellow and very talkative and everyone tried not to notice how much jelly he ate on the first afternoon of his call.

Mem was pleased with him and said he would make a kind husband but Aaron shook his head and said he couldn't see any sense in Hortense's racing into marriage, when she was half sick into the bargain. Mr. Ripley was in the grave monument business and was said to be one of the very best engravers in the field.

In spite of Hortense's rushing ahead with her plans, Lenore Blondell was the first of the girls to be married. Anne and Hortense had often talked of poor Lenore after Joe's marriage and what a shame it was he had not married Lenore instead of that Agnes Mason. It almost looked as if Joe had a real weakness for fashion and finery because from all reports Agnes Mason had little else, she wasn't a beauty and she didn't have a very good disposition, according to David, who by the time he left Deadwood was ready to believe that everyone there was against him and ill natured. The girls had really begun to think of Lenore as a doomed old maid in spite of her lovely nature, and when she wrote she was going to be married, they were enough in sympathy with her to send the letter on to Joe and to hope he would be good and sorry.

Lenore herself felt no triumph in her marriage. When she heard that Joe had married, the news came in such a way as to half console her for her loss. Anne wrote that poor Joe had been taken advantage of by a designing New York girl who used his illness as an excuse to go to Deadwood and nurse him and compromise herself so that Joe on his honor as a gentleman had to marry her. Lenore believed every word and saw nothing except Joe's goodness. She had never expected happiness for herself really; she was so used to seeing Lucy admired and herself in the background. Her place in life was to help others be happy and bitter pill though it was, she tried to swallow it.

Sometimes she flashed out in rebellion, but as the years went on, the flashes were far apart. It seemed almost an act of Providence that the pastor at the church she attended should be a widower. Of course it wasn't the same as a husband all to yourself and he was much older and had children but he was so kind to her and the only person she had ever known outside of Joe who had ever noticed if she was tired and needed rest. She was comforted to have someone to look out for her and could not see why she should cry so when she was at last going to have the great blessing of wifehood and motherhood.

The nearer the day for the wedding came, the closer she felt toward Anne Trexler with whom she had carried on a correspondence for some time. It seemed as if she had to see her before she changed her way of life. Not that she expected to be changed afterwards, but it was just a notion she had, she felt she must see Anne and often at night she could not help feeling nervous and much afraid. She wrote long letters to Anne to calm herself and poured out all her hopes and fears, sometimes laying her tear stained face on the paper as if it were a living friend.

"Darling Anne," she wrote, "if you only knew how I love you," and it comforted her to be able to say that to the sister of the dearest friend she had ever had. She hoped to be happy in her new life but told Anne it would take great strength of mind and character to go through with all she would meet. The poverty of a minister's life alone would be hard but she hoped she would bear it and stand all that was required of her. Anne tried to be gay in her answers to Lenore and they consulted about clothes. Lenore was going to have her black silk made over with the velvet basque and then she had a new light blue cashmere wrapper and a white nun's veiling wedding dress. She herself would have preferred to wear a traveling dress but Robert wished it and she would do her best to please. Their wedding journey would be to Richmond where his new church was and where she would have the pleasure of fitting up their cottage to suit herself.

The family at Grapeville hardly knew what to expect from Lenore when she finally married and her first letter came. Their presents to her had made her so homesick, she had some little word to say about each thing, the wreath from Hortense, the autumn leaves from Anne and the wine and lunch cloth from Mem. How she wished she might exchange some of the silver cake trays for linen. Callers were coming constantly and Robert was very good to her. He had given her a horse and buggy for a wedding present. "He is very kind to me and very anxious to have everything just right," she wrote, as if ashamed of all her fears and much happier than she had expected and with a brighter future.

As Anne was three years older than Hortense, she felt

she had a right to be married first but Hortense turned out to be the first bride. The week before the wedding the mocking bird was found dead in its cage. Hortense found him with his toes curled up and carried on as if it were one of the family.

"Now calm yourself," Aaron said. "I'll get him mounted for you. He had to die sometime, think how old he was."

"That's just it," Hortense blubbered. "We've had him so long, he's like one of the family and all the animals are dying off, Rebbie and old Pony." She cried and made herself half sick over that bird. The way she acted made Anne feel very fearful of the marriage. She didn't believe Hortense really loved Milton Ripley or she wouldn't carry on like that about a bird. She wouldn't feel so terrible to be leaving the old home. The stuffed bird was solemnly packed with the wedding outfit and Anne could have cried to see her sister married with no white dress, no fuss, and the bride standing so slim and pale with those big dark eyes just haunting her. But nothing could stop the girl and Mem had no eyes for anything except that a very fidgety daughter was getting married and it would do her a world of good to have children to worry about.

Anne's preparations for her own wedding were mixed with reports from the bride who had gone to her husband's people in New England. Nothing was right, Milton's mother killed the good meat, just fried it to death and they had fine white bread that looked nice but soured in her stomach. She should have brought some Graham flour. When Anne wrote that Amos had fallen sick and they had to postpone the wedding for another two weeks, Hortense answered that she had had a frightful dream that a letter had come with a deep black border. She supposed it was her stomach, and had made cinnamon bark tea. How could one expect not to have a constantly coated tongue when there was hardly ever any fresh fish or meat? And that old lady with her interfering ways was driving her crazy. She couldn't do a thing without comment. The other night when she had tried to take some hot water upstairs for her wash, Uncle John said, "What do you want the hot water for?"

"Oh I like to drink a little," Hortense said, but she was so mad she could hardly see. Then in the morning just when she was getting on the bed to take the wash, the old lady stood the slop pail outside the door and she had to get up quick with the water trickling down her leg. "I'll take care of that later," she said and the old lady just stood there with her little beady black eyes squinting all around the room and her big hoops rustling under her dingy black calico dress.

"No, I'll get the slops now," she said darting into the room.

Hortense made up her mind that now was the time to assert herself. "No," she said, "Milton will carry the pail down when he comes home this noon." And she firmly shut the door in the old lady's face. But the contest left her all in a tremble. How could she expect to get well and strong when she had such things to contend with? But it was true as Mem and the doctor had said, that she was gradually getting better after the nervousness of the marrying wore off. But there were times when she felt she couldn't stand on her feet and it took all Milton could do, to get her up and cheerful.

One Sunday night she got her guitar and they sat in their room while she tried to strum a little. It only made her homesick.

"I wish I knew what Mem and Anne were doing. I wish we were there tonight," she said.

"Well then, we'll go there," Milton said. He was lying across the bed and he said very cheerfully, "Close your eyes. Now we are at Camden station. All aboard for Grapeville, Millville and Cape May." Then he worked his arms and legs and chugged like an engine. She had to smile in spite of her dolefulness. "Next station, Grapeville. Look, there's Anne, why Anne how are you, you're looking fine and how is Amos? That's good. Come Hortense here is the carriage, well I guess there is room for everybody, here we go, see, there is the house through the trees, well I see you have some new geraniums set out, Anne, doesn't that look fine, there's Mem waving her handkerchief," and the poor fellow went on making up pictures for his drooping wife who sat tearfully holding her guitar and looking up at the stuffed mocking bird that sat in the most conspicuous place in the room on the shelf over the bed, where a fat Bible had been taken away to accommodate him.

Joe did himself proud and sent a handsome bedroom suite to Hortense from one of the finest furniture houses in New York. To Anne he sent a handsome period chair, the walnut wood carved by hand and upholstered in the finest silk damask. With it was a pair of elegant vases. Anne was very proud of her presents, although they were much too grand for their humble beginnings and even Hortense roused to enthusiasm over the suite which created quite a stir among the relatives at York.

David, who had penetrated to the Coast with a buckboard and a couple of horses along with several young surveyors, was now established in Oregon and reported to be getting ahead. He proved it by splurging for Anne's wedding and sending a handsome necklace of California gold, the locket set in pearls. Anne was proud of her brother's gifts but not surprised that Aaron contented himself with a promise to take care of Mem. The girls were concerned about Mem, now suddenly left alone, and Aaron had more or less grudgingly agreed to take up his residence with her, getting her a good girl to help on the place and retaining his own right to spend a night or so as he pleased on the lounge in his office.

In her wedding dress, with the real orange blossoms that Amos had paid ten dollars for and for which extravagance Anne had pretended to scold him, she sat down and wrote to her two brothers so far away, her heart very full, and for the last time she wrote in her little diary that she hoped to make "him" happy forever and ever, while on the back porch in his white vest Amos churned the ice cream for the wedding feast and felt there was nothing that would ever be too good for Anne.

With the fuss and importance of the wedding, Joe and his ailing eye were forgotten. No one wanted to forget it but they had gradually gotten used to the idea that Joe's eye was in bad shape. He had made one trip to Indianapolis not long after David had started to the Coast and the treatments had relieved it. It might get better or it might get worse, the doctors said. It might be snow blind or it might have been injured by flakes of quartz in the mine. The two brides did not want to be reminded of the eye and were certain that it would get better.

There were days when Joe could not stand the light and had to sit in the darkened room with Agnes fuming at one little thing after another with no rest in her body. With his eyes closed he could hear her, he could feel her everywhere like a storm. When friends came to inquire for the eye, he could hear Agnes talk to them in a honey sweet voice and she seemed to him a dozen different women, none of whom he knew. He was afraid of the stranger and anxious to do anything for quiet. The old family failing of anything for peace kept his mouth shut and trapped him in the darkness.

He was almost glad of his burning eye to be in the dark.

Agnes had no pity for his eye, she was so on fire with pity for herself. Over and over he tried to tell her about Lucy and Lenore and his relation to them and made the fatal blunder of making them loveable and loving women. At last he gave up trying to explain his life. Why should he? What new jailer did he have over him? Could he never be free? She would never call him Joe, always Victor, insisting sometimes to his own face that that was his real name. If she had her way he would never be able to go back to himself and become Joe Trexler once more. Her very voice calling him Victor, as he sat in the darkness, sometimes made him dizzy as if he were not sure himself who he was.

If his affairs had only gone a little smoothly at this time, everything might have been different, but at this turning point, everything failed. Jack Barnes in Atlanta, who had finally gotten Joe to have his mother sign over all the deeds, had sold the land and the family in Grapeville waited for days for the money. Roger Wallace, appealed to, wrote that he was sure Jack Barnes would let them hear from him soon as he was a gentleman but that was the end of it. The gentleman walked off with the cash in his gentlemanly pants pockets and Joe was tied hand and foot. Newspapers sent by Roger Wallace to cheer him up and show Roger's perennial interest in him only blinded him with rage. All the people implicated at the same time with him were back in their places. Bullock had been cleared in the trial and Ring at one time under indictment for fifty thousand dollars was now spreading his name all over the page as superintendent of the Southern Georgia Railway with de luxe cars to New Orleans.

Every mistake he had ever made jibed at him now in his blindness and aloneness. Perhaps he should have stayed on in Colorado, but the chances had looked slim and slow. With fortunes popping all around and men in Colorado, in Virginia City, in the Black Hills every now and then going half mad with finding gold and all of them expecting it, every minute expecting it, who could blame him for not being content with humble pickings? Only the meanest spirited could be content. He had seen men make big strikes and make fortunes but most of all he had seen men dig and work and freeze and then sell out to the big Easterners for a mere mite because they couldn't hold on forever. Even now he thought that that new hole near Butte ought to pay. He had made a mistake to let go his share in the Smuggler, it was paying good. Everything he touched turned to tin, it was worthless. He had lost his luck and in the darkness, his lack of luck seemed terrifying. He had heard success stories so long and had played the same game that the winners did, and even now, if his eye just got well, there was a new rumor about some Colorado fields he must look after. If he could just wash his hands of the Escondido. All these mines were overvalued. Someone in New York got the money and very little even seeped to the mine for machinery needed. Why there were mines that actually were nothing more than holes in the ground and yet they were selling stock.

When he opened his eyes in the dark room, red rings spun and whirled in the darkness. The furniture gradually came to life and he liked to sit and think of himself as a little boy before his father died. He got so his only comfort was thinking of himself as that boy saying his prayers on his knees before his little bed. But as the eye got better, he forgot the little boy and as soon as he could bear light, was out looking over his papers and checking up on his different prospects scattered over the West. Quick changes of heat and cold hurt the eye and quick changes in Agnes hurt it too. He was almost glad when the doctor told him that he believed he should get expert attention.

He wired back East and made arrangements for the best care that money could buy. Suddenly he was frightened and horrified to think that he might lose his eye and go around with an empty socket. The fright pulled him together and he actually made a good trade with a pair of horses in the mood that was on him. Suppose his good eye should become infected also and he became really blind? He wanted to get away from Deadwood in a hurry, almost afraid that it would happen and he would find himself blind in Agnes's hands. Anne promised to come to Philadelphia from her new home in Pittsburgh to see him and the promise made him feel so much better that he cheered up, actually got excited about a new enterprise and in his mind made lightning calculations as to the probable profits if it turned out well.

Agnes consented to remain in the Black Hills and Joe made the trip East. He never crossed the Mississippi without a pang remembering his promise to send twenty-five thousand dollars to his mother or never cross the river again. He had had to give up that promise but it wasn't too late yet. The Black Hills were thinning out but he had heard rumors about diggins in Colorado that might prove themselves any day.

He found the wait in the offices of the New York doctors very tiresome. The treatments made him irritable and impatient. He was almost relieved when they told him they must take out his infected eye for fear of endangering the sound one. It was no time to be finicky about a socket but it gave him a creepy feeling, all the same, as if he were suddenly looking at his own corpse. His new glass eye was a perfect match and pronounced by all the family in Grapeville to look as good as his own. They were so loving and so bent on keeping him cheered up that he was glad he had gone through with the operation.

Anne looked prettier than he had ever seen her and he

felt left out in a terrible fashion. Nothing that he had ever bought her or had been able to do for her had made her so pretty or so content as the love a perfect stranger had given her. He told himself he was a warped nature or he wouldn't feel that jealousy and he knew within himself that if he had married Lucy or Lenore he would not feel that way. Now that it was too late, he saw Agnes as she was and with his one eye, he sometimes felt that his whole brain had been sharpened to realize his mistakes. He was really overburdened by this feeling and said to Anne, "Nothing seems to turn out right for me, but if it hadn't been for that early trouble in the South, I could have made a fortune."

"You're still young, you may make it yet," Anne said.

"That's right," he said and in a minute it seemed to him that he might yet make a fortune. All the tales of men making money just as they seemed ready to give up came to comfort him. He had heard rumors in New York of money, money. Big deals were going on, combinations were being made, a thin shanks of a little man was cornering everything in oil, some of the railroad men had cleaned up and others were only trying to think of a scheme to spur immigration to the West, open up homestead land, get settlers so that freight might bring in the money, and it made him sick with disgust to read all the cheap news about the West, with its lies and its exaggeration luring the young with notions of glamour and dash and romance. He riled about it to Anne.

"But it's so," she said. "You don't see it because you are in it."

"I see it but I see a lot more besides. Hard work, harder than any Easterner, even the poor ones, know about. Heat and cold and hardship. The gambling and shooting, that's incidental. But it reads like the whole show back here."

Anne couldn't tell him that even the hardships seemed

romantic to people who did the same thing day after day. She was getting tired of her little place in Pittsburgh with Amos out on the road so much. She longed for her first baby and for new opportunities. She and Amos were already talking of going West themselves. Everyone was doing it. Railroads were telling of the big opportunities, and rates were never so low. She didn't know why, but she was a little ashamed to tell Joe of her ideas. He knew so much and was so wise. In all the world there never was a brother like him. But when he left, the details of her new life took up all the time, letters passed between them less frequently, when she thought of him it was with a pang of remorse that she did not write oftener and allowed herself to be so absorbed by her new life.

It wasn't only her new life but the panic of '84 kept them all scratching. Prices dropped and farmers had their mortgages foreclosed. Amos's work suffered and there was no call for road trips because few farmers could afford new machinery. Aaron's business did not suffer so much, people around Grapeville were more willing to sink their little savings in real estate, now very low in price, when banks were so shaky. Even Mem's hens went back on her and ate more than they were worth. Eggs went to eighteen cents a dozen and Anne began to plan seriously to go to Grapeville to have her first baby.

The news that Anne was going to have a baby set poor Hortense on fire. For some time she had come to the conclusion that all was not right with her marriage. That Anne should become a mother first, when she had married first, convinced her that she was doomed to be the unhappiest woman alive. Girls brought up the way they had been knew little enough and she had always considered that good girls were different from bad ones. Her married life was teaching her terrible secrets, she had to wake up to her body and to cravings that she thought were wrong for a good woman to feel. When poor Milton could not make her happy, she resented him and after the news of Anne's condition came, she wrote long and frantic letters to Anne. Now she was not even sure that what had happened to her was at all what a wife should expect. Perhaps, just once months ago, it had happened and what a fool she had been to use her wash afterwards. She burned up with frantic desire and envy of Anne. Poor Milton, consulting doctors, was advised to have an operation that might help him. Hortense hardly thought of him as a patient. She was the patient and she must get well. Why she was getting all ugly leading such a life.

Milton went to Springfield for the operation and left Hortense alone in the old home. Milton's mother had been persuaded to go on a long visit to relatives near Harrisburg, Pennsylvania, and Hortense cheered up once she was boss of the kitchen. Alone, she brooded and tried to sew and tried to read to improve herself. She could hardly wait until Milton came home again. It was late spring and the house that the Ripleys lived in was near a river that during the spring freshets swelled its banks and caused trouble. Heavy rains came down the night after Milton left. Alone in the little sitting room with the walls lined with the old books belonging to Milton's father, she thought about the old man and what an unhappy life he had led with his wife. She might be Milton's mother but she was an old witch and had spoiled the life of everyone around her. Her tight nagging nature was in the very room, in the hard round tidies on the chair backs and in the stiff portraits of "her" family. It was enough to drive a person crazy and Hortense began to accuse the mother for the weakness of the son.

The heavy rain on the roof did not frighten her. She was used to sounds of wind and rain and not afraid to be alone. Late at night a neighbor rapped loudly on the door and yelled in that if the rain didn't let up there would be trouble in the morning but they would warn her in time. Hortense thought they were all too excitable and a lot of old fogies but the creek roared in her ears after she was in bed and helped her to get asleep. In the morning the water was high and limbs of trees, whirled and washed down with the flood, caught against the bridge. She stood looking out, idly curious, fascinated by the violence. Old Mr. Barnham yelled at her four times before she heard him.

"What's that?" she said.

"Flood's coming, better run for it, get to Timothy's place on the hill and you're safe."

For a second she had a notion to go upstairs and let them all run around by themselves. But one look out was enough. A wall of water was rising and soaking into the basement. She got into her coat and looked around to save what she could. The mocking bird was on top of the bookcase where she had brought him down to keep her company while alone. She grabbed him up and had just time to run up the stairs and throw him into the attic where the water couldn't rise. She was out the front door before the water came in and lodged with neighbors for the next twenty-four hours. Her conscience began to hurt her that she had not thrown some of Milton's father's books to safety. She could have tossed them up the attic stairs. Milton set great store by them but it was too late now.

Milton came home the day Hortense went back to see the damage. He was pale and shaky, had a new awfully timid look and complained it felt as if everything in him was falling out. They went to the old home together and looked at the wreck. It was a sight. Carpets were covered with mud and slime a foot deep and the books were ruined.

"If it had only happened when I was here," Milton said.

"What could you have done I didn't do? I did the best I could. There wasn't time for anything."

"I wasn't finding fault," Milton said quickly. "But the books. He set such store by them and they are worth a lot too."

"Now could you expect me to lift those heavy books when I am so dizzy all the time and not strong? I thought of them but there was no time." She didn't tell him she had saved the mocking bird.

"I know that," Milton said. "I only wish I'd been here. I hate to see the old Bible, muddy like that. I wonder where we better begin." Hortense felt she didn't have the strength to begin anywhere but she pulled herself together and brought the mocking bird down to his old place again. Milton had been told to take a month's rest but he had to dig right in.

The whole business upset Hortense so much that it was decided she should go down to Grapeville. Anne was to be there when her baby came and the two women could have a good visit. Hortense thought that now she could find out just what should happen if you wanted a baby. She left with an admonition to Milton to take good care of himself but he was very tired. He had to stir himself about a new job and it was with very little confidence that he applied at Springfield as a foreman in a big monument works.

Anne was six months gone with child when the sisters met and it almost broke Hortense's heart to see her. She hated her own flat figure and burned up with resentment against Milton who was drudging on alone in York. He wrote in a few days that he didn't feel competent to take on such a big job and had heard of something else in

Springfield that would give him experience and make him feel able to go somewhere as foreman later. Hortense worked herself up to a pitch over his letter and lack of gumption but she quieted down after her outburst and wrote him that he was quite right and ought to be resting for a while anyhow as the doctor said, and not rearing and tearing around and getting himself all unfit again.

The two sisters had good long talks and Hortense thought she would break in two with agony at what she had missed. She thought that if Milton's operation just came out all right why then there was still a chance for happiness in the world.

The struggle to make a living was hard upon them all and they talked a good deal about their most prosperous days when Joe had showered them all with gifts. Sometimes it was painful to talk of Joe, he wrote seldom and they both sensed that his wife had not turned out well. For one thing she had written a very insulting letter to Mem when Mem had urged Aaron to write Joe that she would like to visit her son. Agnes had written without consulting Joe and had told Mem that they did not have accommodations for any guests and besides Joe had given up enough of his life for his family.

When Joe heard that Agnes had taken things into her own hands and had written his mother in such a fashion, he hated her. He turned white and for days could hardly bear to speak to her. She was sweet as molasses and tried to smooth things over by telling him that he was a poor imposed upon boy and she meant to save him in spite of himself. There was something about her in such a mood that worked powerfully upon Joe. He was lonely and now that all of the family were getting along without him, he felt cut off from them and from everyone. It cut him to hear that Lenore Blondell had a little girl and Lucy two sons. He wondered why he did not have children and not having any, he felt as if he were cut off from Agnes. What else had they in common now that she had turned to such a spitfire against his people? He couldn't talk of the old days, she burned up at the very mention of them. Everyone who liked Joe or paid attention to him was an object of suspicion to Agnes. She wore him down with her jealousy. But in company she made a very striking appearance and put on her good manners along with her good clothes. As a child she had grown up in a family of racy adults, stockbrokers and promoters, and now that she was actually married to Joe, she turned loose some of their language upon him. He had never heard a woman who wasn't a whore use words like that and with such fury. It frightened him and he dared not admit that she had the upper hand.

The business at the mine was making him frantic with worry, he again faced the future stripped of every cent, and to begin over seemed to crack his skull. The trouble with his eye had receded back into his head, sometimes he felt that the empty socket was a bright bulb pressing somewhere on his brain. When he tried to make out reports, he got shaky and his hands actually trembled. What was happening? Something like panic took hold of him, and then for days he would feel a terrible lassitude, he could hardly crawl around, did not care if the sun shone, did not wonder where she was or if she might be prying into his own personal belongings.

The bad times lingered more than a few months, and before Anne knew it her first child had come and her second was on the way. She was glad to stay at Grapeville as long as Amos must be so much on the road, and they wrote to each other constantly letters more ardent than in their early days. Their debts oppressed Anne but she was full of resolution and they talked of going West. The papers were full of it and the railroads were paying out big sums for publicity to induce people to take trips West and to settle up country so that the freight might come pouring in and make money. Amos went around singing:

> To the West, to the West,
> To the land of the free
> Where the mighty Missouri rolls down to the sea,
> Where a man is a man, if he chooses to toil. . . .

and they both thought of the East as hopeless and worked out, just as David had, when he shook off the dust of Philadelphia and headed for Deadwood.

David was plowing ahead in the West and had moved to Roseland, Oregon, where he was actually buying his own store. He bragged in all his letters of his prosperity and of the farm he was purchasing on the side and now and then he sent a little money to his mother and dazzled his sisters with a five dollar bill at Christmas. Aaron took it philosophically and said "Well, what is it all for? Nothing is more futile than money or fame," but both the sisters in letters to each other thought it was a little of sour grapes.

Before Anne's second baby came, Hortense surprised them all by coming through with an announcement that she too was in the family way. Anne often puzzled where Hortense picked up such vulgar expressions. The news only brought another long series of complaints and gloomy forebodings. Hortense fainted several times a week, those veins around the vagina were all gnarled up and blue and she didn't think she would come out of it alive. When her time was near she figured it couldn't be until the full of the moon and Mem decided to take a quick trip up to York to help her out. The baby was a boy and so homely that Hortense burst into tears at the sight of him and made them take him away. The poor thing's head was all warped out of shape and he was about the worst color of a baby Mem had ever seen. But Hortense tried her best to do right by him and when the nurse said the baby should be first to go upstairs for good luck, she made the woman carry him up to the attic floor so that he would be looking up all his life and not groveling around in the dirt.

As the child got a little older, she perked up and took an interest in her son and pronounced him all Trexler, his blue eyes and fair hair had not a whit of Ripley in them. Mem pronounced him a fine strong child who tried to sit up before he was dry behind the ears. The young mother drank a good deal of porter to get back her strength and Ripley was so excited by an heir that he negotiated a partnership and went into the monument business on his own with a Mr. Allen.

They got up some good prospectuses with pictures of the elegant monuments, quite the latest thing, "of beautiful white bronze, molded and cast from refined zinc, every monument subject to the same process that gives to silver its well known frosted or satin finish which is crystallized into changeless beauty to last 4000 years." Ripley was very pleased with the descriptions which he had helped to compose and began to suspect himself the possessor of talents that were as yet dormant. But the business did not flourish. It only served as another subject for Hortense's long wails of despair. As she wrote to Anne, when one goes in business without a penny, one must nearly starve and go naked just to keep what money comes in, in the business.

Anne was in a state of worriment herself and let Hortense's complaints roll over her. Amos had decided definitely to go West and on the advice of one of the salesmen at the McCormick house had picked on Oxtail, Iowa, as a thriving place, just on the boom. An Easterner whom he knew had started up an implement store and wanted someone to go in with him. The young couple decided to take the plunge and said good-by to the East.

Nothing in the new town pleased Anne Wendel but she kept her disappointment to herself and thought she could put up with anything so long as they made a good living and were able to give the children a fine education. The house they rented was half of a double house, the other half occupied by the owner, a nasty old man, who was always trying to look in her windows and was continually fumbling with his fly. She hated the dark rooms and the mudhole in the back yard, the kitchen with not even a sink but it was only temporary, before long they would be able to move to a better house and where there would be a yard for the children to play.

The Wendels lived in that house ten years. Two more little girls were born in that house and it was to that house that Joe came for the last time. But in the beginning Anne had no idea it would be like that. The whole tribe of Trexlers were born optimists and it took another generation to see the dark side of the rainbow.

Even Hortense moved around from one New England town to another and had hopes of something better turning up. When she was eaten up by her own inner misery and the disappointment that blasted her life with her husband, she still hoped that they might make a good living and keep their heads up. In these years, the two sisters wrote often to each other but seldom to their brothers. David was getting very prosperous and was going to marry, Aaron had his head in his own business as usual and Joe hardly ever wrote any more. He seemed in many ways the least known of the brothers.

What had really happened in the South? They didn't want to think about it any more. Even the memory of that year in the fine house in Philadelphia was painful. It had given them ideas and now it would be always a little hard to scrub and rub and be content with the ends of things.

Sometimes in the evening Joe would shut himself up in the room he called his office and try to write to Anne or to his mother. He sat there with the sheet of paper before him and his hands sometimes felt completely nerveless, he couldn't make his fingers close around the pen. He had strange tinglings up and down his body but as soon as he began to think of something else his hand would grow strong again. If he stayed in that room long, Agnes was certain to come tiptoeing and he could almost feel her behind him, looking through the keyhole. Then she would tap and make her voice sweet so he would open. She spent all her energy making out what a martyr he was to his family and how he was continually imposed on.

"Nobody but you would stand for it, but you're so soft, why if you hadn't been, you could have had anything you wanted. You were here in Deadwood, one of the first, why didn't you get in on the big deals? I tell you if I was a man, I'd show you. It's just wasted on some people and here I am a miserable woman, I'd give anything to just be in a man's boots. You let them all impose on you, that's it, and you could have got out of this mine deal in better shape, don't tell me. Then the way you treat the men, why they're just ignorant brutes, you should work them not stand around talking and encouraging them to think they are as good as you are. You know what Elder said? I overheard him. He said you weren't enough of a driver, too soft, and what was needed around these mines was a little gunfire. You've heard the way they carry on, they actually have an organization and talk about bigger money and conditions. What's the matter with conditions? Is a mine a conservatory? I never heard of such foolishness."

Her talk turned him sick. He ought to take a whip to her, she was that kind of a woman, but he didn't want anything to do with that kind. The colder he felt toward her, the more she lashed him with her tongue. Out of misery, he would collapse and try to make love to her. But it was an ordeal to get into bed with such a woman. He never knew what it might turn out to be. She could make a perfect kitten of herself if she wanted to and with his eyes shut, he let her coax and soothe him and sometimes he had hopes everything would yet turn out right. Was it actually true that his happiness with such a woman depended on making a big strike? If the money was rolling in, she would respect him, he knew it in his bones. Well, she came from a family like that who sucked up money from the very ground and anyone who couldn't do it was weak and a coward. Her style meant very little to him now and yet sometimes when they went out together he couldn't help feeling something of the first pride he had felt in her when he saw the superior way in which she carried herself. Times were not nearly so prosperous in the Hills and a good many accidents in the mines made a lot of discontent. Even John Huber, who appeared and disappeared with the years, came back and talked a lot of loose anarchistic talk.

"That kind of talk won't get you anywhere," Joe said one night when the two of them walked off toward Poorman's Gulch.

"What does your kind of talk get *you?*" John Huber said. He had been two years in Colorado and had come back full of ideas Joe called "buggy." But the way he said that, with his head back and his eyes blazing and his pipe tapping on his hand as regular as if it were a stamp machine in the mines, sunk into Joe. He poohed and said it was all foolishness and cutting off his nose to spite his face but John didn't kowtow to him any more the way he used to. He didn't beg Joe to set him up with a saloon either. He was just as bad a workman as ever, couldn't stay put, but he was steadier in himself and a great hand to argue. They had a good hot argument that night about what it was all about and although Joe disagreed, some of the things that John said sunk in. There was fight about those fellows he couldn't help but like. Damn the South. Sometimes he had visions of himself back in the South telling them what was what. He hated himself for skulking off like that, but what else could he have done? He couldn't bear the thought that the men who had got him in the hole were strutting the earth back in Georgia while he was still Victor Dorne.

Even little things went against him hard. He felt as if he would fly apart when the cow got out and walked away or Agnes played too persistently on the organ. He was more particular than ever that things in the cabin should be nice and made Agnes use the best china and silver every day. When he warned Anne and Amos against coming West and they ignored him, he felt cut off completely and alone. So his advice was worthless, was it? He took more and more to Black John and silent and moody, let the fellow talk, the very sound of his voice was soothing. Here was a man who owed his very life to him and time had not made him forget. He had a lingo that was foreign and new to Joe.

"Damn it John, where do you get that talk? It's dangerous. You'll have to keep your mouth shut around the mine. At least while I'm superintendent. Instead of stirring up trouble why don't you go out and get yourself a prospecting hole and work it? Look at the chances around you. I'll stake you."

"What good will that do? You staked yourself and you got a high sounding title. Superintendent. How much else you got for all your hard work? Damned little else. Listen, I'm putting what stake I got in *men* after this, not the *ground*. You can't buck those big fellows and you know it. They're using you. When they get through, they'll throw you out."

If anybody else had said that kind of thing, Joe would have punched him but he kind of laughed and felt sore and tired. He didn't know where to turn with the worry and fret. He had the mine and he had his wife to contend with and the two were splitting him wide open. There was trouble all the time with the men at the mines too, grumbling, and the anarchists' trial in Chicago was working them up all out of proportion, Joe thought. He thought it was a bad thing to give so much publicity in the papers to those anarchists but he read every word about them himself. Even Aaron back East got worked up about them. He was all in sympathy because they were atheists and so was he. Their silent defense was a big dramatic thing to people working for a living.

Black John and a bunch of men at the mines were going to refuse to speak on the day they were to be "murdered." Joe tried to talk him out of it and was a little afraid of trouble. When the day actually came and he passed Black John on the street and said "Hello John" and John just kept his trap shut, it got under Joe's skin. He almost envied the dozen or so men who stood together in their silence, refusing to talk. It got on everybody's nerves and made the day seem like a long funeral. They were guilty, weren't they, throwing bombs, terrorizing society? But when John Huber consented to talk he made Joe feel like a little boy. He tried to tell him it was a cooked up charge and the only reason the men had been killed was because rich men were afraid of their ideas.

"Such talk won't get you anywhere John," Joe said and he tried again to reason with the fellow. At night he walked alone and he kept thinking of words that Black John had said. It was bad enough to be puzzled about the mine without getting a kink in his brain over those notions. But the notions stuck and when the papers came out with news about the anarchists, he took them to his

own little office and carefully locked himself in. He had
had another quarrel with Agnes that evening and his eye
hurt. He spread open the paper and read mechanically
the speeches of the men, now dead.

"I believe that the state of caste and classes, the state
where one class dominates over and lives upon the labor
of another, and calls this order, yes, I believe this barbaric
form of social organization with its legalized plunder and
murder, is doomed to die and make room for a freer society."

The second he read those words he felt in his bones they
were true, but the next he was saying it was idealism, you
couldn't take a lot of rattlesnakes and expect them to coo
in a bird's nest. But the words seemed to stick in his very
skin. When he got up and walked around the room, they
were as alive as human voices. Sometimes lately he thought
he heard voices and he had gone to the window but no
one was there. He went to the window now but it was
quiet outside. In the house he could hear Agnes playing
on the organ. When he went back to the house she would
complain that she had only an organ while he had bought
his sisters the finest piano money could buy. He stooped
to the paper again.

"There will come a time when our silence will be more
powerful than the voices you are strangling today."

What day would that be? He suddenly remembered the
fiery little one-eyed man down under the sidewalk in the
bakery days who used to roll pie dough and mutter. Now
he too had only one eye. It would be better not to try to
rise, to stay down in one's beginnings, where there was
company and kindness. On top, somebody was always waiting to do you. He got up and went to a little cupboard for
some brandy. Suddenly his knees felt very weak. In the
door of the cupboard was a little glass and he looked at
himself, he needed a shave and his glass eye mocked him

with its quiet unwinking stare. Clever of them to make a little flaw in it so it would look more real. For a second his own face looked strange and he felt dizzy. Then he took a drink and turned off the light. When he opened the door to the room where Agnes was playing, she stopped and half turned. From her profile he knew she would grumble.

"Here I am," she said, "trying to get a tune out of this rickety thing. It's good enough for your wife but I'd like to see one of your sisters try to use it. Why you wouldn't stand for it."

"Stop it," he said. He seemed to get tight all over, his jaws hurt to open as if he had lockjaw. "Stop it and never talk that way again. Never."

"Why the idea," she began, flabbergasted.

"Never again," he said. "Never to me." He wanted to say that what she had to say meant nothing. He still had ringing in his head the dignity of the dead men's words. They rang there without even completely communicating a meaning. Old phrases from the Bible came to him. He wondered what these men had believed in. Not God. God was of no use to them. Nor to Aaron. But when he thought of the world without God he was very lonely. The one good thing he had was remembering saying his prayers at his father's knee. The world had been before him then. Well, he had been on top of the heap, in Atlanta, only it had turned out a dungheap, God damn their souls. He carefully took out his glass eye, it burned him like a glowing ball. But the heat was still in his head. As he tried to move to cool his head near the window, all the blood in his body seemed to rush to his empty socket and he stumbled and fell.

THAT winter the boys at the naval encampment began dying like flies. The two younger Wendel girls were holding down jobs and they lived out near the university where they could see the lights from the encampment at night. They took long walks and talked about the lonely gobs and the war and wished they could save some money to get away, it didn't matter much where. The war and revolutions breaking out gave them the frantic feeling as if trains were rushing past them. Anne Wendel was back East with Uncle Aaron helping him to die and when the funerals began to scare people, it looked as if the world were doomed. It was hair raising to hear the Chopin funeral march far off, thin and awful as a bird's cry, in the midst of dictation. If you went to a window you saw the first hearse with its escort coming slowly like something in a nightmare, and then the second hearse. Day after day the hearses came and could not stop and the line grew and people got into a panic as if a plague had fallen. They had to cut out the parades and the flute music but the boys went right on dying, only now they rushed them to the train and sent the boxes home.

The dying and the big friendly Armistice Day and the knitting and buying stamps and war bonds made many people feel very mean and at the boarding house where the Wendel girls lived there was often quarrelsome conversation at the table and some sharp talk went back and forth. The Wendel girls were sick and tired of all the talk and of their reading and of the time they now felt they had wasted trying to get what had seemed education in a college. They had strained for it and when they got it, it was nothing. They kept more and more trying to get nearer to something that seemed what they called real. Nothing around them seemed very real. They couldn't understand why Papa didn't see where his bread was buttered and give up his foolish boss notions. He was only a workman loading trucks in a warehouse but he still liked to think he was a boss and wrote the girls about the time he had getting work out of the lazy men. He was at it early and late all that winter, saving his little wages with great pride, living alone, eating his meals cooked by himself, some fried eggs, some fried potatoes, some coffee, sitting down to his paper late at night, tired and glad he was still working, though old, not just on the shelf, making a nuisance of himself at his children's expense. The Wendel girls were provoked at him because he still kept on being Amos Wendel and they often talked about how tragic it was that their mother too went right on hoping for a little capital. Perhaps Uncle Aaron would leave her a few dollars but she would only spend it on her children.

The letters going back and forth that winter were sometimes full of old memories because Uncle Aaron was a great hand to remember now he was dying and the Wendel girls liked to read these scraps written by their mother at night when the night lamp was turned down in the sick room and she could let herself go and relive some of her girlhood. Once she sent Victoria some old papers that had been in Uncle Aaron's office about Joe, because Victoria had really been named for him. The Wendel girls poked through them and came on a yellowed newspaper with an account of the Haymarket Riot and the hanging of the anarchists and their silent defense.

It was raining that afternoon and very quiet in the girls' room. They shivered reading the words of the dead men that leaped at them alive and vigorous after so many years. Seattle in wartime seemed dead. The words carried over the years, they suddenly wondered what that paper had meant to Uncle Joe and they began to talk about him and to feel that the paper had a relation to themselves. Here they were, two girls, alive and greedy for more living, and the one was barely married to a boy in France, waiting for him to come home and scared that he would be brought home in a basket like that story in the paper. The other ran a mimeograph machine all day and looked out the window and watched the heads of people walking and cars go by and all the world seemed moving but herself. They had great laughs at their funny situations and wondered what all the strain of trying to save money to get to college had been for and what the few years there had done for them. They didn't want to end like Catherine and poor Joe, because in their thoughts this dead uncle was not the successful man who had bought silver and fine clothes but a man who had pretty thoroughly failed.

When the unions called a general strike in Seattle, the Wendel girls wished they were part of it. They read all the papers and got in fierce debates at the boarding house and through talk more and more sympathized with the strikers. They had to laugh at the silly talk about how all those people had earned such big wages and had spent it like water on foolish jewelry and knickknacks. When the housewives began filling the bathtubs with water in fear the dam would be poisoned or blown up, the Wendel girls almost wished something would happen. They got a kick out of walking to work and seeing the other boarding house people try to get hitch hikes. Everywhere people fitted themselves for a siege, old ladies congratulated themselves on their hoarded sugar and tiny stores did a rushing business in candles and old kerosene lamps. The whole place was scared yellow and the little necktie clerk grumbled that he was not a workingman but in a different class with his empty head behind the necktie counter.

Now in their bones the Wendel girls felt alive and as if they had a clue to living. They were ready to burn all the old papers but Victoria said it would be a shame to do that to poor Joe. They argued every night with the boarding house people and wished they were on the inside of the strike and got excited about all the news of troubles and wars in the world. Under the dead crust, something was ready to rocket up. Ole Hansen the brave mayor posed as a hero and papers over all the land praised him for being a strike breaker. The fighters went back home and things simmered down. Snow came down that winter and Uncle Aaron was slow in dying.

The Wendel girls went on mimeographing and the one Wendel girl helped in a mail order drug business that did its biggest business in rubber goods and French specialties in the lonely ranches of Montana. They just plugged along and waited. Spring was coming. The boys were coming home. They were slated to lose their jobs because wages were going to drop and many an employer would be happy to see his name in the list of those who had given a job to a returned soldier. For a few weeks while cheap girls were fired for cheaper men, everyone would be very patriotic. There was soon going to be nothing for the girls to do but to move East with the coming of the summer.

V. DEATH CLUTCHES ME BY THE EAR

W HEN his sister Anne got a letter forwarded to her from New Jersey and inclosing a letter to Lenore Blondell in Joe's hand, her eyes seemed to freeze in her head that he had forgotten she no longer lived in Grapeville and that Lenore had married. But it was a sensible enough letter only very religious and the writing shaky. In a day, news came from John Huber that Mr. Dorne had been sick but was better, should get away for a change. David came through with a handsome offer to come West and stay at his home for as long as Joe liked but by the time the letter reached Joe, he was better and writing badly with his good hand. The other arm was a little numb, that was all.

He used his sickness to pull out of his mine trouble, but it was a loss to him. He still held on to a little stock, just in case. Time seemed to drag and he went back and forth to Colorado and listened to a lot of talk and got worked up over some schemes that didn't seem to pan out. The days just piddled along like that, while he waited to get his real strength back, and the night they gave the banquet in Deadwood to some big guns from the East he was on hand and scheduled to make a speech. The liquors and wine were the best and every man there was in the finest clothes and looked prosperous. This was certainly the right crowd to make a man feel on top of the world. The meal was served on fancy Dresden china and the best

Havana cigars were passed around. It was like the old days.

Joe sat next to a Henderson of New York and talked about race horses and listened to a few dirty stories that convulsed their corner. Henderson thought it was a fine dashing kind of life but a new era was on the way and they must get a stronger control of the situation. Machinery was expensive and capital took such a risk, it must secure itself. He wasn't a slave driver but everyone knew that what was best for capital was in the long run best for labor.

The talk, buzzing of voices, the wine, the good food, the feeling of success, loosened everybody's tongue. Joe as the only prospector present was to make a speech and he went over it in his mind. He had been uncertain what to say but now anything that came into his head sounded good. Not since the days in Atlanta had he attended such a gathering and the old urge for money and power made him feel ten years younger. It wasn't too late yet, not as long as there was life. And he was only forty.

Now the head of the Chamber of Commerce rose to speak. He was a man from Ohio who had come out five years before and had a good hardware business. The wine made Joe's eye feel burning hot and he decided not to drink any more. He was a little worried for fear he would get sick again but he steadied himself with a long pull on one of the best cigars he had ever tasted. He looked around the table. The amount of capital assembled probably represented a cool fortune, a couple of cool fortunes because that fellow Henderson alone was worth quite a fortune. He rolled the cigar with his tongue and tried to keep his mind on Nolan's speech. Just words, capital, the rôle of capital in the development of civilization.

Suddenly, "I do not intend to speak lightly of the prospector. Rather I would pay him tribute. He is the

Columbus in civilization, tracking the wilderness as Columbus did the sea to discover a new world. He finds and tells the public, others come in and possess the land. They who bought the Comstock mines and manipulated their stocks have grown rich and gained seats in the Senate Chamber while the discoverer died poor, alone and friendless. Such lives have not been a failure." The voice paused with an unctuous swallow from a glass of water.

Joe knew his turn was about to come and suddenly he could not think of a word. A blank shut down on him and he looked around at strange faces. They were all rich and he was the only one who had been in the Hills in the beginning. He would die alone and friendless and poor, the speaker had said so. They were all smiling about it, their smiling well fed faces blurred and came toward him. He pushed back his chair and got out. One of the men followed him. "Anything wrong? Can I get you something?"

"Nothing," Joe said. "I'm not feeling well. I'll walk out." When he felt the cool night air, he braced up and his head cleared. They were so many Blake Fawcetts, waiting to trap him, but he knew better this time, they wouldn't get him. Wanted him to do their dirty work, like as not, and then leave him holding the sack. He walked automatically past Huber's boarding house, but all lights were out. He wanted to talk a blue streak to someone, it would clear his head. God, his *life* needed clearing out. Where could he go at this hour?

There was a little narrow street leading up the hills and he followed it. It wound past the house of the Chinaman who ran the bakery and made cakes, and had a tiny wife in rich bright silks like a jewel. Once he had had tea in their house and the memory of their gracious ways to one another made him begin crying. Tears rolled down his cheeks into his mustache. He would write a long letter to

Lenore Blondell and tell her about the peaks of Teneriffe but suddenly going back down the hill he remembered that she wasn't Lenore Blondell any more, she was married, had a little girl and did not need him.

Hortense and Anne wrote troubled letters about Joe's shaky handwriting and that he sometimes talked as if some event a way back had only just happened but again, he would write such good sensible letters, he must be all right and only subject to nervousness. Hortense was too steeped in her own wretchedness to take a rightful notice of the troubles of others. The little boy did not help any in such moods and she often felt as if she were a thousand miles from everyone she loved or who cared for her. The less she saw of Milton at such a time the better. He could feel it too and when such a mood was on her, left the house and stayed away. Oh she couldn't help herself, she cried and prayed that she might not feel so hard toward him but it did no good.

Tomorrow she might be herself again but today she felt as though there never was a woman so sadly disappointed and unhappy. Death to either one or the other seemed the only thing to set her free. Oh if she might be forgiven for the many many wicked thoughts this life had made her have. She often thought she would not care if he never came back to her alive, she would be released then. It was sinful to think such thoughts and sometimes she wondered if she was in her right mind because she had such sinful thoughts, but five years of such a life would completely change a far sweeter disposition. She pitied the boy and often he was the means of breaking up those crying spells.

That very morning she was sitting on an old trunk in

the attic having a cry all by herself and whether he heard her or why but he came pattering upstairs fast and into the room with "Oh Mama don't cry, don't cry, Milton be good boy, wipe Mama's face with dress," and then he took her hand and wanted to show her everything, his carriage in one corner and some seashells, which made her want to cry more because they had come from Sea Isle where she and Anne had gathered them together. But she tried hard to be cheerful and admired everything. She must not yield to this weakness and spoil the boy's life and maybe change his disposition forever. Now he was as happy as could be and everything was play. She thought and hoped he would take after her in being fond of birds and flowers. He was always finding some little flowers or often some nice white clover heads he'd bring for her to pin to her dress. Perhaps some little thing would happen to break her from her gloomy mood. A nice sweet rain might fall or a letter come or she might pull herself together and write to Anne or Mem down in Grapeville.

Anne did not have an easy life herself but Hortense's letters fairly scorched her with their misery. She tried to think what it must be like to have a husband like that, but it would be too awful. The only thing was the worry about Amos when he had a long trip to the country to set up a binder and one of those terrible thunderstorms came on. She had fears that the horses might run away or the buggy overturn and once it was past ten before he showed up soaked to the skin. But she never let him see her fear, and always had something good and hot for him and dry clean clothes. The best part of the day was when they could have their meal together and look in at the children sleeping.

She believed they never had lived with so much wondering about the weather, and sometimes on Sunday he'd borrow the store team and drive out and point out the corn, so sharp and delicately green, oh if the weather just held up. The days in June might be good days and then July with fine growing weather, you could hear the joints in the stalks snap and grow, but if August was hot and dry with those bitter dry winds, everything shriveled up, just burned out and it meant another bad winter with everything dear and the bills unpaid. With the two babies and all her work to do, she had little time for thinking out plans but it did seem as if the place in Grapeville was getting to be too much for Mem and something should be done.

Something should be done, the brothers and sisters wrote back and forth but the hardest to move was Aaron who was on the spot. Finally he stirred himself and found a man to rent who would work the land and Mem decided to visit all her children and perhaps stay in Oregon. She hoped within herself to stay always with David and he had written her, in a mood of showing off and of long promised generosity, to build her a cottage next door to his own.

She had the worst luck for the sale. Everything went against her. A storm the night before blew down that wisteria vine and it lay in the area when she came downstairs in the morning. The cherry tree had split in two and the cow got a crazy fit and wanted to go visiting. She behaved so ugly all day that she did not bring within ten dollars of what she might have brought. The cow went for twenty-six dollars, the horse for sixty-nine, the carriage for twenty-eight, the hatrack for eighteen, the sideboard that Joe paid so much for eighteen, and the bedroom furniture with all the hand carving for forty-one dollars and a half. "Such is life," commented Hortense, when Mem, battered with the worry and work, went to bed at the Ripley's house on the first day of her visit.

She spruced up again in a few days with that terrific energy that dwarfed her children, and made bibs for little

Milton, poked into every corner of the house and engaged Ripley to carve a monument for Catherine's grave in Grapeville.

Nobody could have enjoyed the long train ride to Iowa more than she, with her tight little black bonnet and her trim round black silk cape and the gloves that looked always too large on hands that had spread with work. She stayed with Anne only long enough to spoil the children and to make them forever homesick for doting. When she got to David's he met her with his wife and two babies and she had her days full criticizing his household and all that went on within it.

He was prospering, no mistake. As the mother of such a paragon she had to make all the pies and pushed the two hired girls into the background. Her letters to her daughters were full of complaints of the lazy girls who put the lousy eggs to cook in the coffee water and had their closets and clothes full of moths and for all she knew nits as well. It was a sin and shame for them to live off David the way they did and Ella was too easy going. Just the wife for David, Anne thought, who knew that any other would have a hard time of it.

To distract Mem from her faultfinding, Ella took her to her own class of painting and in two weeks Mem was equipped with paints and brushes and had turned out a very fancy painting very true to life of Mount Hood in a halo of pink clouds. Everyone was astonished at her age but she boiled on with her constant urges and made rag rugs and painted china and pierced every room she sat in with the thin uprightness of her person. Poor Ella felt fat and lazy with Mem around and suffered everything and cried to herself when David had snored himself to sleep but she respected His mother too much to complain and put up with it as best she could.

David, keeping his ledgers with a penny precision,

thought that no one could accuse him of not being generous considering the money he was paying out for his
mother's keep and all, but there was no use building that
cottage she talked about now, lumber was too high and
wages too and besides there was the house that Ella had
inherited, not more than ten blocks away and even though
it was by the river that was just an old woman's objection.
The river was perfectly healthy, everyone said so, and the
house going to waste, he couldn't rent it so late in the
season. He could see with half an eye the two women
were too much in one house, he would have to put Mem
where she could be her own boss in her own kitchen and
she was always saying that she didn't intend to live with
her children, she must have her own house and die in her
own shoes. What a woman, he could never regret that Ella
had so little of her energy, actually it was peaceful to get
into bed with a woman like Ella, a great big soft easy going
cushion.

All the talk about lousy eggs and hand painted china,
and Hortense moaning because she was yellow as a quince
and if things didn't change within a year Milton must
make other arrangements for her and the child, put Joe
out of their minds because lately he had an uncomfortable
way of troubling them all. Sometimes just a word left out
or letters in words usually so carefully spelled and dates
gone crazy, turned Anne cold. She would sit with the letter
in her hand and that night make some plan with Amos
about going out to the Hills to see Joe and didn't he think
that Joe was just nervously exhausted. But Agnes stood in
the way of anything's being done about Joe.

Mem had actually stopped off for two days on her way
to the coast and Agnes had refused to allow her trunk to
be taken upstairs. The two women had faced each other
and Mem had refused to untie her bonnet strings. Only
when she noticed Joe suddenly very white with a nerve

near his mouth twitching, did she untie the strings and sit with the bonnet in her sparse lap, her cheeks very red and her eyes full of tears. Talking in the old German they used to use in Locust Valley, they shut Agnes out and the devil woman, as Mem ever after called her, flung out of the room and did not show up again for hours. But she sent Mem a handsome ring of Black Hills gold after she was gone and Mem took every one of Joe's words that Agnes was sorry to heart and wrote Joe not to worry but she grieved that her son was trapped with such a creature. Her grief had some joy in it as it seemed to restore her son to her.

IN DAVID'S HOUSE

SOMETIMES when she did the dishes and hurried through the children's washing, Anne thought that perhaps that woman might die and quit tormenting Joe's life. She could wring the clothes and think such thoughts with the clothespins ready in her mouth but Agnes was always in fine health. It seemed as if always at the back of her head Anne had the thought that something was wrong with Joe and the idea that he was in danger came sharply to her at night when she woke to see if her little girls were warm and covered.

She was relieved when Joe actually consented to pick up and spend some time with David in Oregon. Everyone wondered how it would work out with Agnes the kind she was but she could be sweet as pie when company was around. Alone with the family she made trouble enough, grumbled continually, never lifted a finger to help and insisted that Joe's name was Victor not Joe. She even embarrassed them further by insisting on going to a restaurant to eat when the mood struck her. It wasn't as if it was New York, the town was so small, everybody knew everybody's business and poor fat Ella sobbed that people would think her cooking was wretched if her own sister-in-law had to eat out. Mem was constantly at Joe to leave his wife and David came out at last and said Joe couldn't expect any help from him unless he was willing to leave that vixen.

There was no place for Joe to turn. When he tried to take a walk, Agnes went with him and muttered all the way about the bumptious manners David had. "Why he's glad to see you down and out. Don't think it isn't giving him a great consolation to have you eat bread out of his hand. A man of spirit wouldn't stand for it. He offers you the farm to live on. What's that? A place without a single convenience. Am I to die in a hole like that and worse, lie buried for years where I never see anyone? There isn't even a cookstove in the house he's so proud of, an old fireplace with regular up to date pots and pans, oh yes, I can see myself cooking there. Not much. If you haven't the spirit to refuse, I have."

She could hardly bear it to see Joe in the midst of his relatives, she felt cruelly left out. Once she was sorry for the way she was forced to act and went out in the kitchen and offered to make some nice fried cakes for Ella. Poor Ella was so pleased, her plump face flushed scarlet, and she ran around getting the ingredients together as happy as a child. But the good mood did not last long. Mem had only to begin a conversation with Joe in her outlandish German to put Agnes in a black mood again.

David took a kind of secret satisfaction out of his hospitality to his family. They had all called him a baby and now here the baby was supporting the whole kit and caboodle. He was glad to heap coals of fire on Joe's head and hoped Joe would remember his own refusal to buy him a drug store in the old days. He took his burdens as he took his bank account, seriously, and kept track of everything with a feeling of competence. In bed at night he would keep poor Ella awake talking it over.

"I told Joe I wouldn't put up a cent unless he gave that she-devil up. And I won't. I guess it's about time I made a few conditions myself. He tells Mem he will give her up, that's all talk, he only does it to pacify her and keep her quiet. Oh I tell you I remember my father's story some of these days. Mem used to tell me as a young boy about his grave responsibilities and especially about that brother, that Jacob, what a handful he was. Don't tell me Joe hasn't some of that blood in him. And between you and me, Ella, Agnes may have a reason for her bad temper. Has it ever occurred to you? I know for a fact that women used to trail Joe around, why they wrote him letters that used to make the blood rush to Mem's head. And presents even they sent him. Oh that fellow has had a life and for all we know his sins have merely come back to roost."

"Well he isn't at all like you Davy, I'd hardly know you were brothers."

"Oh we aren't alike. I never had time to cut such a swath." He hoped Ella would never hear of Pet and the St. Louis episode. It would be better to keep that chapter closed. "No, he and I are cut out of the same cloth perhaps but a different pattern."

"I should think so," Ella said.

"Still the doctor says that so far as he can tell this trouble isn't caused by what we feared, you know."

"You mean?"

"Yes, it isn't caused by *That*, not that I'd have been surprised with the life he's been forced to lead, those mining camps and all. But the doctor says positively not."

"Well that's a relief anyhow."

"Oh we have to be thankful for that much. But I wonder what the poor fellow is going to do," and he lay on his back feeling warm and comfortable and glad that Ella was just the plump easy girl he had hoped for.

JOSEPH'S COAT

I N DAVID's house Joe actually gained weight and felt better and once toward spring heard about some new silver mines in eastern Oregon opening up. He was on fire about the business and looked like a boy for about an hour. "Why you can't tell, David. It might be a handsome thing. I've got to get there and look it over." But he was too tired to go and finally concluded after several family conferences and advice from Aaron that he would move his belongings out to Roseland and stay on the farm for a while, at least until he was properly cured again. The devil woman never said a word during the confabs and was quite alarmingly acquiescent to all the plans but she would not let Victor go back to Deadwood without her. The two set off together, to ship Joe's belongings, and the fine china and silver actually were packed and expressed. After that came a long silence.

Anne worried to Amos and Amos tried to reassure her that Joe would be all right. "He's run down with the life he's led. Fellow who was in Deadwood ten years ago was in the office yesterday."

"Did he know Joe?"

"No, I asked, but he said it was a hard life. He used to prospect but he quit, said you never got in on the big money anyhow."

"I don't care about the money if he is all right," said Anne. But she couldn't stop worrying. She had a terrible guilty feeling about him as if they had done him some wrong. Sometimes she tried to console herself with thinking about all they had tried to do, given him help when he needed it, stood by him. If they hadn't always been so poor. That was the crime, poverty, and always trying to struggle up.

But even with the preparation of years of shaky writing and missing words and tales of Joe's run down condition, it was a terrible blow to get a letter from the State Asylum at Yankton, South Dakota:

"Victor Dorne has been committed to this asylum by his wife and friends of his have given her address thinking she might be interested."

When his friend John Huber wrote, saying that Mr. Dorne could no longer remember names or faces and thought he was living some twenty years back, even then Anne was unwilling to believe it was true. He was suffering from a little breakdown, Agnes had done this cruel thing to him. Black John had written that his wife wouldn't have Joe around after he could no longer remember who she was and as her people were influential, they got him put away.

Influential? How many times influential people were to hurt him and do him wrong. Her insides seemed torn up and she walked around with the letter trying not to cry. She must control herself not only for the two children but for the baby on the way. She could hardly wait until Amos came home and she could arrange with some neighbor to take care of the children while she made the trip to Yankton.

She was determined to go herself. All the way on the train she looked out at the flat rushing country and tried to think how she would get him out of that dreadful place and he would soon be all right again. She could feel the child in her and she kept as calm as she could and even in her pain for Joe, she felt the strong pride of having it. When she reached the asylum she was sick at heart at the dull place and waited in the room while an attendant went to fetch Joe. She stood up as she heard footsteps, holding herself proudly, waiting with a terribly beating heart. Then she saw him. His shoulders stooped, his face looked a little swollen and his once immaculate suit had a spot on the lapel. One button dangled from a thread.

Tears gushed from her eyes. It was true.

They got him down to Oxtail and now all the family buzzed to get Joe finally taken care of. Aaron took a train from the East and Mem took a train from the West. The plan was to keep him in Grapeville with Mem. Joe himself was easy to manage and sometimes he was fairly good and once Anne talked with him about the time when they were children and he said, "If you have a boy, name him for me." She was touched that he had noticed in his misery and promised, "Yes, Joe, for you." But the next minute his gaze was off again and on the morning he left, his clothes seemed much too big for him. Anne had taken the spot off his lapel and had tied his tie and sewed the button. He stood with his eye clouded and the glass eye for the first time looked conspicuously bright. As he went down the steps she pressed her face close to the window pane and before he got into the hack with Aaron he turned and saw her. She made herself smile, the tears prickling her eyelids, and then the hack started up and they were gone.

Even in Grapeville he got no peace. Mem made him nervous with her demands that he remember as he used. She refused to allow her son to be insane. When Anne heard these things, when the quarrel between Aaron and David began about the money it took, when Agnes refused to give up Joe's clothing or any of his possessions, then she thought of him as already dead. "Let him die," she prayed as she prayed that her baby might live and have a strong life and not suffer. She had horrible dreams of him and suffered lest they might hurt her unborn child. Aaron wrote Mem was feeding him too well, he was fat and ruddy, but refused to go to bed at night and gave considerable trouble. They would all be worn out soon. Once Joe wrote her.

Grapeville N J 1881

My dear sister Anne,

I am glad to have an opportunity to write to you I trust you are well and have not negleted to put your Trust in the Lord Jesus

Your affectionate Brother Joseph

The lines running uphill, with wrong date and a misspelled word were the last she ever had. It was 1896, gold had been pouring out of the Klondike for several years and the feet and hands of many eager men had been for some time frozen.

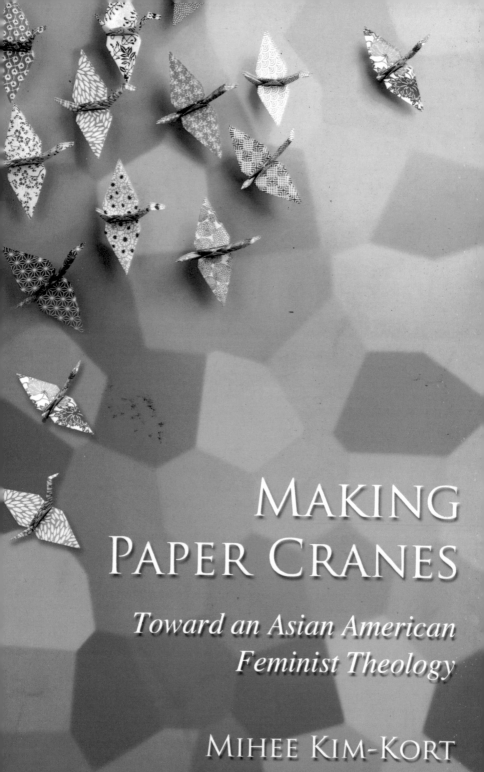

MAKING
PAPER CRANES

*Toward an Asian American
Feminist Theology*

MIHEE KIM-KORT

MAKING PAPER CRANES

CRANES

Toward an Asian American Feminist Theology

MIHEE KIM-KORT

CHALICE
PRESS

ST. LOUIS, MISSOURI

Bible quotations, unless otherwise noted, are from the *New Revised Standard Version Bible,* copyright 1989, Division of Christian Education of the National Council of the Churches of Christ in the United States of America. Used by permission. All rights reserved.

Scripture marked NKJV is taken from the New King James Version®. Copyright © 1982 by Thomas Nelson, Inc. Used by permission. All rights reserved.

Cover and interior design: Scribe Inc.

www.ChalicePress.com

PRINT: 9780827223752   EPUB: 9780827223769   EPDF: 9780827223776

Library of Congress Cataloging-in-Publication Data

Kim-Kort, Mihee.
Making paper cranes : toward an Asian American feminist theology / by Mihee Kim-Kort.
    p. cm.
Includes bibliographical references.
ISBN 978-0-8272-2375-2 (alk. paper)
1. Asian American women—Religion. 2. Feminist theology. I. Title.
BR563.A82K56 2012
230.082'0973—dc23
2012019270

Contents

To my parents, Yong and Son, who pushed me out of the nest so I would journey courageously and creatively

To my husband, Andy, who journeys with me with the utmost compassion

To my miracles, Desmond and Anna, who inspire me to work toward a better world

Acknowledgments

The word *acknowledgment* certainly does not do justice to the gratitude I feel toward so many who have been a part of this journey. I would not be who I am today without the inspiration and support of the cloud of witnesses. I am who I am because of your faithfulness to the Good, and how you have been Christ to me throughout my life.

Thank you to all those at Chalice Press, who worked on a difficult manuscript with painstaking care and attention. Thank you for giving this work a chance.

Thank you to those organizations that shaped me: The Young Clergy Women Project–an incredible resource, but more than that, a community of sisters near and far who have been a light, and an immeasurable influence on my vocational identity. Thank you also to the Pacific Asian and North American Asian Women in Theology and Ministry–a group of women ministers and scholars who are changing the world with their work.

Thank you to Rev. Dr. Grace Ji-Sun Kim, a mentor since 2008, and a woman, pastor, mother, and teacher I aspire to be like in my own life. Her wisdom, her grace, and her loyalty are profound, and I am better for knowing her, even for such a short time.

Thank you to friends over the years–in college and seminary–who continue to journey with me even now, and especially Rev. Erica Liu, who from the first moment of our friendship embodied passionate and courageous resistance. Thank you to seminary professors Dr. Mark Taylor and Dr. Brian Blount, who provided me with a space to find my voice.

Thank you to family on both sides of my hyphenated last name: Tom, Corrine, and Sarah Kort, and my parents, and especially my brother, Joseph. Finally, again, to the most precious in my life: Andy, Desmond, and Anna–my life, my light, my loves.

Foreword

By Grace Ji-Sun Kim

"PENISENVY"!

I write this on the blackboard on the day I cover Feminist Theology in my course, *Theology from the Underside*. I ask the students to read it. Most students read it as "penis envy."

The way my students read this phrase seems to reinforce how Sigmund Freud has deeply influenced our societal perceptions of men and women. According to Freud, "penis envy" refers to the inner desire that women presumably wish they were men. For some time women adapted Freud's teachings and actually believed that a penis was they all desired inwardly

Margaret Atwood believes otherwise. Atwood stated that it was not "penis envy" that women had, but that it was rather "pen is envy. It is not that women want to become men, but that women have always wanted to write their stories and influence literary discourse, which then affects how society thinks, understands, and conceives reality. Women have wanted to make a contribution to society in addition to being mothers who raised their children.

For much longer, women have recognized that the pen is mightier than the sword. There is power in the pen. The pen gives power to those who possess it, own it, and use it. The pen is the medium used to convey ideas, stories, knowledge, and meaning. There is an awesome power in the pen.

So it is that women do not envy the penis, but rather envy the pen. Throughout much of history, it was men who wrote stories, shared thoughts, and recorded events. Their stories have influenced how we interpret historical events, biblical stories, and theological understandings. Men have theologically monopolized the ecclesiastical enterprise. Women have longed to write their stories so that they can also shape the world's present context, the past, and the future in all spheres of life. There is strength and empowerment in being able to mold and shape people's thoughts through the writing of narratives, biographies, stories, facts, fiction, and theology.

I strongly believe Atwood is correct, and it should be our perspective on women needs to shift towards the realization that women have something to say that is valuable, and more than that, necessary. This understanding makes Mihee Kim-Kort's book all the more important for our time and within theological discourse. In her book, she shares her own personal stories and narratives, which nudge us toward an Asian American feminist theology.

Asian American feminist theology is still at a very nascent stage and only emerges in the aftermath of Christianity's involvement in colonialism.[1] Korean immigration to the United States occurred in three major waves. Political exiles were living in the United States as early as 1885, but the first significant wave of immigration was to Hawaii (1903-05). This can be described as immigrants concerned with either the Korean political situation or interested in Christianity and the Christian churches. The second wave was after the Korean War (1950-53), and involved a more heterogenous group, consisting of wives of American servicemen, war orphans, and students. The current wave began as a result of immigration reform through the 1965 Immigration Act[2] in the United States. These immigrants are contending with a multitude of issues, including cultural and linguistic differences, parent-child stress, and changes in roles, especially among women. They are also coping with cultural conflict in norms and values, a healthy identification in a predominantly white society, and varied levels of acceptance by both the majority and other minority groups already here.[3]

With this historical backdrop, *Making Paper Cranes* takes us on a theological journey that explores, reflects, and contributes to Asian American feminist theology discourse through engaging literary, historical, and sociological sources. Most importantly, Kim-Kort writes from her heart as she finds herself in the statistics and dates of these literary, historical, and social narratives. She opens up her life and shares her journey, in theological terms, from Korea to the United States, and through artful ways, Kim-Kort tugs at our heart through a theological narrative rooted in the genuine fragility of life told honestly.

Kim-Kort's book adds richness to the Korean immigrant history as Asian American feminist theologians remember, recall, and retell our stories. Much of her stories are experiences she recalls with clarity, spontaneity, and integrity. She candidly shares her own personal struggles growing up as a Korean child in America. Many of the stories, both hers and other Asian Americans, are difficult to digest at times as they become our stories. Many Asian Americans can personally identify with the experiences of sexism, racism, prejudice, and subordination she confronts in this writing. Kim-Kort provides valuable insights into the woundedness, pain, and *han* that exists within many immigrant women. Despite the particularity of all these stories they become the life stories of all of humanity as we see a glimmer of ourselves in them.

It is only when we all enter into this journey that we begin to understand, welcome, and embrace those who are different from us, for then we recognize our sameness in them. As Kim-Kort manages to open up our own personal wounds, heartbreaks as well as joys, miracles, and wonders, we are invited to examine our own theological journeys and enter into this wonderful enterprise of theological reflection. Her deliberate methodology and the use of compelling metaphors and images potentially can be appropriated by others in their own reflections. But again, the most important piece to this process is clearly an uncanny willingness to share one's life story. She does so, and brings a compelling new voice to this nascent theology. It is moving, heartening, enlightening, and joyous to read a fresh new voice in theological discourse in general.

Theology is biography and biography is theology. As people engage in writing their stories, they are writing their theology. Life is, indeed, a theological journey. It is the stories of God's participation in our lives and our participation in the life of God. These stories are passed on throughout church history and have enhanced our perception of God.

Kim-Kort builds on the theology of the first wave of Asian American feminist scholars and challenges us to move forward to the next stage. She writes from the faraway spaces of her heart, thereby exposing our minds and hearts to the goodness of God and a world where we coexist in beauty, love, and peace. Kim-Kort engages with Asian American feminist theological writers such as Chung Hyun Kyung, Grace Ji-Sun Kim, Anne Joh, Kwok Pui Lan, and Rita Nakashima Brock and wrestles with their voices, building order to develop her own distinctive voice within the academy.

As Kim-Kort writes, we recognize the power in her stories. They are constructive, refreshing, moving, endearing, and embracing. Her poignant and provocative words challenge us to continue the journey toward a liberative world. And she shows us, how, yes, "pen is envy," and that once we take a step forward to reinvent the normative expectations of our gender and culture, then we invite all to write their stories of grace and redemption too.

Prologue

Making Paper Cranes

Memories, Stories, Legends

I know. It's a bit cliché, making paper cranes–especially an Asian person doing origami. I remember when my mom first taught me how to make a paper crane. We sat at the kitchen table, took regular white copy paper, folded the paper over in a triangle so it made a perfect square, and creased the bottom so that we could carefully tear it off and discard it. After that, it was fold here, open here, bend here, fold again . . . and then, wow! Amazing. Blow gently into the bottom so that it puffs out a little, fold one end a little so it has a beak, and there–we had a perfect paper crane. For the longest time, this picture of my mother and me connecting over such a simple but magical object has stayed with me. I can hear her voice as she tells me, almost wistfully, "If you make a thousand of these little creatures and put them in a box, you can make a wish that will come true"–or was it, "get a long life of good health," or maybe, "find a lot of luck." It was definitely something like that. I couldn't remember if it was Chinese, Japanese, Korean, or all of the above until I googled it and found a wide variety of information about it on Wikipedia. Wherever it came from doesn't ultimately matter. It remains in my mind as a rare, lovely moment without any barriers between us.

This little tradition with my mother faded away as I grew older, but the memories of it have come back in recent years as I try to make sense of my place in the world. The memory is compelling to me–this image of my mother and me creating something together, the act of making the paper crane, and then the image of the origami paper crane itself. My connection to my mother is essential in this journey of discovering who I am, emotionally, psychologically, and theologically, because she is my family and has had the most influence in shaping me. I have other "mothers," too, the Asian American women in this country who have bravely told their stories. They have had a hand in molding me, too. Similarly, the very act of making paper cranes—the process of making something delicate and lovely out of the intersection of creases—speaks to me of the journey one takes in becoming whole (though at one level I am cognizant that it may negatively perpetuate the stereotypes associated with Asian Americans). We humans, no matter what season, need some flexibility, some bending and folding. While it seems to make little sense as a work in progress, the end result is an exquisite creature. Finally, the paper crane is a symbol of the crane itself; it is a story of something in reality. In particular, the paper crane holds various meanings mythologically, and the narratives, the beautiful legends associated with it are intriguing. The paper crane invites me to enter into it as metaphor for sorting out my own story, and hopefully, the larger story, too.

I love poetry and the play between words and space. Specifically, metaphors are useful in the way they allow me to engage my life artistically as a person of faith in a particular context as an Asian American and a woman. Because I grew up with rigid structures and strict grammatical systems, I have only recently begun to allow myself the creative expression of poetry through which I am tentatively, but more and more openly, writing about my journey of faith as an Asian American woman. During these past many years, I have been blessed by a number of meaningful intersections with other people of color who share in the struggle to be fully received as persons of worth and dignity. The bold formulations of their own experiences have unlocked whole worlds for me.

In these most recent seasons, I also discovered a new freedom that allowed me to acknowledge a poignant chaos within me, which was the result of a phenomenon I call "collisions." Growing up in a mostly Anglo, suburban, homogenous neighborhood, I avoided any conflict with others as much as possible. I generally tried to "keep the peace." After college, these collisions increased in number and were inescapable as I sought constantly to be reconciled to myself and others, especially those who came from different regions of the country or world, those who had different ethnic backgrounds, or those who were male. The power of these collisions was overwhelming and led to something I call "fragmentation," which is a disjointed state, like being in the middle of a pile of shattered, broken puzzle pieces. Most importantly, as a person of the Christian faith, I realized I did not have a theological framework with which to address this fragmentation *as an Asian American* woman. Very little in the Church spoke specifically to the Asian American woman's experience. Thus began the slow birth of this project, which I believe will be a long delivery process: writing and journeying toward an Asian American feminist theology.

The metaphor of collision resonates in me as a potentially expressive piece of the experience for Asian American women in its connection to the fragmentation that occurs in daily life. By *collision*, I mean the ongoing encounter of stereotypes, expectations, standards, and conflicting worlds that leads to fragmentation. In verbalizing the beginnings of an Asian American feminist theology, I emphasize the necessity for theological work to be rooted in the dynamic play and conversation between Scripture, tradition, and experience–a theology of the body that stresses the embodiment of faith. I believe a dialogue between these salient experiences of Asian American women and other theological perspectives will help determine how this conversation can point us to a fresh space to live into and out of God's whole redemption, which I explore further toward the end of this book.

In this project, I investigate experiences unique to Asian American groups, including immigrants and their descendants, but focus primarily on the experience of the generations of Asian American women who are children or later descendants of immigrants. I acknowledge that the story of Asian American women is incomplete without including the history of all Asian immigrants, men and women. I further acknowledge that the cultural tendencies I discuss are broad and, as in any circumstance, there are numerous possibilities for exceptions, the gray in-between cases among all Asian Americans, like Asian adoptees and the children of interracial marriages. These basic patterns are a jumping-off point, and for me, necessary for beginning to dialogue about this experience. I hope to do my best in attempting to avoid overgeneralizations and keep everything descriptive rather than prescriptive. In terms of labels, for the most part I will use the phrase "Asian American," which will potentially include people of East Asia (China, Hong Kong, Japan, Mongolia, Korea, and Taiwan), Southeast Asia (Cambodia, Laos, Myanmar, Thailand, Vietnam, and Malaysia), South Asia (Bhutan,

India, Maldives, Nepal, Pakistan, and Sri Lanka), and the Pacific Islands (Polynesia, Melanesia, and Micronesia), though not all stories will include all groups. Even these geographic labels are incomplete, but I try to include as much territory and as many people as possible. Finally, as the more pertinent resources do in their writings, I interchangeably use "European American" or "Anglo American" to refer to the dominant culture in the United States.

Ultimately, my vision is to be a part of the community that is articulating a theology that liberates Asian American women to live as whole, free human beings with a distinct voice and story, and then to empower Asian American women to be active instruments in changing the status quo. Utilizing the image of the crane in the first chapter, "Flight and Migration: The Asian American Journey," I focus on the social history of Asian Americans (both men and women) in general in the United States, beginning with the first waves of immigration. I offer a brief engagement of the political and cultural issues that Asians faced in America as well as stories of their engagement of church and faith. The main point is to communicate the stories of the ocean crossing that begin in the mother countries and continue in this country, as well as to begin to understand the distinctive experience of racism that characterizes Asian Americans' journeys.

In the second chapter, "Fidelity, Prosperity, Longevity: The Asian American Woman," I focus more specifically on Asian American women and the types of oppression they experience in North America as rooted in gender issues. The double-edged sword of racism *and* sexism stifles the lives of Asian American women, so for them to achieve any level of fidelity, prosperity, and longevity (themes associated with the symbol of the crane), it is important to name the phenomenon that threatens the identity development of those in this community.

In the third chapter, "Fight, Struggle, and Survive: The Asian American Woman's Resistance," I attempt to illustrate the possible ways of talking about how Asian American women navigate these negative social forces in terms of *compartmentalization* and *assimilation.* A preliminary description may be helpful here: I identify *compartmentalization* as an intentional separation between two different worlds–namely, the Asian culture and the dominant culture, while acknowledging the need for both. I define *assimilation* as systemic identification with the dominant culture and rejection of the Asian culture. These categories are by no means scientific or exhaustive, but introductory. This chapter also includes stories of feminism,

Asian American feminism, and specific stories of resistance enacted by Asian American women, both within and without the church.

The book takes a theological turn starting with the fourth chapter, "A New Flock: Currents from Asian and Asian American Feminist Theology," which engages the Asian American feminist community (e.g., Rita Nakashima Brock, Kwok Pui Lan, and Wonhee Ann Joh), looking in particular at the themes that are often raised for discussion in their projects.

The fifth chapter, "Freedom Songs of Long Life," is my own creative (constructive) attempt to lift up another theological perspective out of the Asian American feminist project. The metaphor of song speaks to poetic narrative, and "threshold" is a potential space in which this song is present. Here, I engage the content of this song–the experience of fragmentation, which I define as a deconstructive but potentially reconstructive process that examines the forces that impose certain identities onto Asian American women. I believe it is a process that can lead to compartmentalization or assimilation, but my hope is that there is potential healing in connecting and creating out of this fragmentation.

The sixth chapter, "Food for the Journey: A Third Space and Threshold Theology," explores ways for Asian American women to journey intentionally by embracing the concept of a third space. In other words, the third space is an attitude, transformative and often subversive, and it allows for a way to work toward changing present circumstances. Threshold theology continues in the same vein by permeating that perspective. The third space can potentially be a threshold–more than a holding place–and a dynamic place of possibility and hope.

The epilogue, "A Thousand Cranes: Everlasting Wishes," looks with hope to the future at other possible projects and where the journey might take this community of Asian American women.

Finally, as a matter of clarity, I want to explain that I choose to identify myself and this endeavor as "Asian American" rather than as Korean American, though that is my specific ethnicity. I recognize that *Asian American* is a vastly broad term, as the term *Asian* includes all possible countries between Japan and India, Malaysia and Taiwan farther south, the Philippines, and the Pacific Islands. This term encompasses ethnic groups like the Hmong, Laotians, and Hawaiians. The range of languages, traditions, and cultures is hardly containable in one term. Moreover, the dominant culture in this country has had the tendency to ignore the rich diversity of Asian groups, which has resulted in the creation of a singular, negative, and often destructive stereotype of the numerous Asian communities. Yet I make this move intentionally to be as inclusive as possible, so I might address the basic issues that impact the group(s) of people who are lumped together in this category; how people in the United States view Koreans affects how they view those of Japanese, Chinese, Indian, and Vietnamese descent. No doubt an interconnectedness exists in our experience because of our current social location in North America, whether or not the groups historically agree or get along with each other.

I believe that the most effective route toward giving any of these groups a voice is through establishing a genuine unity–not homogeneity–rooted in the tension of acknowledging a similar reception by the dominant culture while simultaneously encouraging the distinctions of each Asian cultural expression. I want my identity and my work to be in solidarity with all the Asian groups represented in North America and all around the world. Eventually, I hope my work finds expressive solidarity with peoples that experience any kind of oppression and marginality as a *liberation theology*.

This work is important to me. It has been formative in my own understanding of embracing my identity as an Asian American woman of faith. I recognize I do not develop this work in solitude but in constant conversation with others by sharing in their communities and stories. That means this project is, and perhaps will always be, in constant process. By no means do I claim that I am any kind of authority or that this project is comprehensive; but at the very least, I hope it is a beginning, meaningful sketch. There are little pieces, memories, and stories all over the place that I'm still trying to fit together to make sense of me, my family, and my community. I desire this to be a space where I remember, create, and make some more paper cranes alongside others in this field and in other disciplines. I am increasingly inspired by the rapidly growing number of Asian Americans who are making new patterns, breaking out of boxes, and allowing their stories to take flight. I want and need to be a part of it, too, for the sake of my family, and especially for the sake of my daughters someday.

1

Flight and Migration

The Asian American Journey

Bird migrations are easy to spot during any season, above all during those transitions from colder to warmer weather or vice versa. The exuberant sound of these creatures is irresistible. During my walks on any quiet hiking trails, whether in Colorado or in Pennsylvania, I cannot help but pause, look up, and follow the V-formation cutting those slow, dark lines through the sky like fighter jets going in slow motion. I have always wondered what the world looks like to them from that lofty distance, especially at that methodical pace. Do they look up, down, or straight ahead? Do they have to stop and ask for directions, or do they take the same airways, so it is familiar to them? Do they take a lot of bathroom breaks? Do they deal with a lot of strange weather? Do they enjoy these flights?

Many people, too, are prone to migrations of a sort, maybe in the form of vacations and weekend trips. For instance, I have friends who enjoy bed-and-breakfasting on the coast or backpacking across some unusual regions. But at times we face bigger journeys involving new locations, new jobs, or new homes. When I was growing up, my family was privy to both. We moved around a lot, trying to find a spot to nest, in a way, from Seoul to Colorado Springs to Denver, then back to Colorado Springs, all over Colorado Springs, and then to Princeton. But we also very regularly went on vacations that took us away from our ordinary lives. During the hot summers, we traveled to places even hotter than our Colorado home, exotic places like Las Vegas and California. We took long journeys across deserts, through mountains, and over wide, open spaces, all within our family van, where I read my Judy Blume books, my brother played with his toys, and my parents listened to cassette tapes of church services and sermons in Korean. We would pause at rest stops for meals. My mother packed an icebox full of things like *kimbap* and sandwiches. We would eventually get to our destination, whether it was the Grand Canyon, Circus Circus, or the Hoover Dam, and take hundreds of pictures.

That first journey that my parents took across an ocean would mark all of us forever. I often wonder what it must have felt like to step onto that huge, formidable mechanical bird clutching a few suitcases with me asleep in their arms. How did it feel being on a plane for so many hours for the first time ever? Did they stay up to watch the in-flight movie, restless and uncertain about what was waiting for them? What was it like to say good-bye to their families indefinitely? They left everything. Unlike those who throw everything off and don't look back, they did look back—and still look back often. It would be something ingrained in me, too, this looking forward and looking back at the same time, as I made my own migrations.

Racism: Beyond Black and White

In my high school and college social studies classes—the US history classes—I recall studying the arrival of European immigrants in the New World seeking out religious and economic freedom. I was shocked by their baggage—unheard numbers of African slaves, including men, women, and children. I learned that this was just the beginning of a system of oppression in this country. A complicated society developed, including a web of interactions between African American descendants and European American descendants. The result was inexplicable economic exploitation, cultural marginalization, and physical oppression of millions of Africans and African Americans. Despite the power of the civil rights movement, the residue of these earlier circumstances—that is, the establishment of this country at the costly expense of African and African American lives—remains in the minds of many people today. Both overt discrimination and subtle forms of racism, as reflected in debates over welfare, classism, and unequal employment, are constant reminders of the consequences of this severely entrenched system in our society.

Yet, while understanding this part of US history and present-day culture is obviously important, I was and still am affected by the lack of time given to understanding the histories of other immigrants and their experience of this system of race. Since an understanding of race relations has often been packaged as a black and white issue,

I never believed I, or any other nonblack person or community, had ever been or would be impacted by discrimination or prejudice based on race. It was literally a black *or* white issue. But as I have grown older, despite the reality that all power and race relations have come to be seen within this framework of subordinate/majority dynamics,[1] I have become more aware of the complex, not-so-black-and-white dynamics involving race in many relationships. Specifically, I have realized how this dynamic is unique to the experience of Asian Americans. I simultaneously realize that as an Asian American woman, although I am affected by this system of viewing race as a black/white paradigm, this discussion on race must go beyond black and white to become relevant to the increasingly diverse nonblack communities in this country.

Growing up going to mostly Anglo schools in Colorado, I got along with anyone and everyone. My close friends were Anglo-American and African American, and I had one Latina friend. I had a few Asian American friends, but in terms of those who were non-Anglo, there were only a few of us. I never received any overtly violent gestures of racism but there were those typical cliché moments when a kid would chant at me in an annoying, singsongy way, speaking gibberish and asking if I understood it, or our class would get a new student who happened to be Asian but Chinese, and the teacher would ask me if I spoke Chinese and if I could translate for them. Every so often there was a breakdown of groups, whether for kickball teams at recess or for projects in class, and though I remember watching groups of white kids sit together immediately, and the black kids slowly congregate together, I would look around, wavering, trying to feel out where I felt I belong the most. Some days I made my way over to the white kids, and I felt like I was joining the cool kids group, the ones who had everything. Other days I felt rebellious and thought that sitting with the black kids, who were also cool in their own way, suited me the best. But neither group ever made more sense to me, and I vacillated between both.

The acknowledgment of the not-white-or-black factor is becoming increasingly more a part of Asian American experience. Frank Wu's *Yellow: Race in America beyond Black and White* offers a refreshing, yellow-in-a-black-and-white-world perspective. He writes that "race matters," and moreover,

> words matter, too. Asian Americans have been excluded
> by the very terms used to conceptualize race. People speak
> of "American" as if it means "white" and "minority" as if it

means "black." In that semantic formula, Asian Americans, neither black nor white, consequently, are neither American nor minority. Asian Americans should be included for the sake of truthfulness, not merely to gratify our ego. Without us—and needless to say, without many others—everything about race is incomplete.[2]

No doubt, Asian Americans are caught between two unaccommodating worlds. This experience of being unable to find reception from either community, while constantly being identified as the "Other" is arguably most visible within the Asian American (though now experienced by many other groups today). In addition, Asian American communities find themselves as the scapegoat for problems that arise out of complicated race dynamics and result in violent confrontations between groups. For instance, in New York City in 1990, tensions ignited between Afro-Caribbeans, African Americans, and Korean Americans because a Haitian immigrant charged that she was beaten by the manager and employees of the Family Red Apple Market in the Flatbush section of Brooklyn after a dispute over three dollars' worth of groceries. As a result, the store owner was arrested and charged with third-degree assault, while Flatbush residents, members of the December 12th Movement, and others began a daily vigil of demonstrations that would last for almost a full year. The city did little to respond to the numerous assaults on Asian Americans throughout that year. According to Helen Zia, a prominent journalist, "to many African Americans, Korean stores and the material success of Asian communities in general represented their economic disenfranchisement at the hands of the white oppressors and their Asian surrogates."[3] Hence African American communities would often identify Asian Americans with European Americans, while Asian Americans are often relegated to some ambiguous minority status by the dominant culture.

This type of continuous marginalization from both sides creates a difficult-to-verbalize experience for Asian Americans, so space to articulate another aspect of the race paradigm becomes necessary. To initiate this discussion, it becomes absolutely crucial to examine the primary elements of the Asian American experience, which are described by numerous Asian American journalists, lawyers, and activists as the "perpetual foreigner syndrome" and the "model minority myth."

Perpetual Foreigner Syndrome

A little more than a year ago I was dismayed by a statement my father made to me when we were discussing the hardship of interracial marriage and multicultural ministry: "Your mother and I have lived in this country for twenty-five years, but we still feel like foreigners." It had never dawned on me that my parents did not feel accepted or viewed as Americans. When my father surprisingly disclosed their feelings of rejection, any romantic notions about a thorough acceptance from those around me disintegrated before my eyes. Images of various moments from my past flashed in my mind— words, interactions, and even subtle (and not-so-subtle) looks that revealed to me this sad reality. Based on my race, the Asianness of my face and skin tone, my inability to easily recall simple American idioms, and my usual preference for Asian foods, I have always endured the question of whether or not I am a foreigner. At least my English is without any Asian accent. For my parents, even though they have resided here for more than half their lives, it is a different story. Like me, they are naturalized US citizens and while they speak English well enough, since it is "tainted" with the Asian lilt, they are seen automatically as foreigners.

This recent revelation has helped me to understand my own feelings of frustration at my awkwardness in trying to field questions about my identity. When I look back, I remember countless introductions followed by the question, "Where are you from?" If I did not satisfactorily respond with the name of an Asian country, the new acquaintance would insist, "Where are you really from?" This would spiral down into some kind of guessing game. Even worse, I encountered many times the supposed compliment that my English is so competent and the question, "How long have you been in this country?" These questions perpetuated the feeling that I remained outside, and therefore, not truly a citizen.

The aforementioned are some of the surface characteristics of the perpetual foreigner syndrome: We are figuratively, and even sometimes literally, returned to Asia and ejected from America.[4] Though citizenship is legal, ethnicity tends to override it, which further perpetuates the foreigner image. Thus while ours is a citizenship based on consent, not descent,[5] this citizenship continues to be illegitimated because the descendant of Asian Americans finds himself or herself from a different shore, and indeed from an "obviously" foreign and alien place. What needs now to be part of this analysis of the perpetual foreigner syndrome is the basis of this foreigner image. The roots of this image are multifarious and require an engagement of imperialism, colonialism, orientalism, and both the relationships between Europe and Asia and the relationships between the United States and Asia. Rather than examining every possible origin of these images, I want to explore a particularly insidious but strong manifestation of these roots, which is found in the early stereotypes of Asians revealed in the social history and literature about Asian immigrant communities in the United States.

Much can be gleaned from literature of the specific historical context of Asians within America. This literature potentially points to ways the perpetual foreigner syndrome is connected to other sources and contexts. But specifically, the categories for Asians and Asian Americans, as revealed in the historical and social context of the United States, have served as a way for non-Asians to contain the unfamiliar, foreign element of those who are of Asian descent. For instance, as Elaine Kim, a professor and avid sociopolitical activist at the University of California at Berkley, carefully describes,

> There are two basic kinds of stereotypes of Asians in Anglo American literature: the "bad" Asian, which includes the sinister villains, brute hordes, uncontrollable, and those who need to be destroyed, and the "good" Asian, which are those who are helpless heathens to be saved by Anglo heroes or the loyal and lovable allies, side kicks, and servants.[6]

In both cases, the Anglo-American portrayal of the Asian person serves to function as a dichotomous template for the Other, further perpetuating this relationship, and basically describing the Anglo as a contrast to the Asian–that is, as "not-Asian."

> When the Asian is heartless and treacherous, the Anglo is shown indirectly as imbued with integrity and humanity. When the Asian is a cheerful and docile inferior, he projects the Anglo's benevolence and importance. The comical, cowardly servant placates a strong and intelligent white master; the helpless heathen is saved by a benevolent white savior; the clever Chinese detective solves mysteries for the benefit of his ethical white clients and colleagues.[7]

The Anglo is at the center, while the Asian (and presumably any other non-Anglo) is present for the sake of establishing the Anglo identity. A common thread running through these portrayals is the formation of permanent and irreconcilable differences between the Chinese–or, more broadly, the Asian–and the Anglo, differences that define the Anglo as superior physically, spiritually, and morally. These initial images serve to affect a dualistic relationship between whites and nonwhites, in this case those of Asian descent. This sense of the Other as viewed in the person of Asian descent further maintains the necessity not only for apprehension but for appropriation in the forms of conquest, control, and manipulation to the advantage of the dominant cultural group. This critical approach to understanding the dominant view of Asians in North America finds deep roots in Edward Said's *Orientalism*, in which Said defines *orientalism* as "a Western style for dominating, restructuring, and having authority over the Orient."[8] In this case, *the Orient* encompasses not only those residing in the countries considered the Orient but also those scattered in diasporas around the world. He further purports that Western knowledge about the East is not generated from facts, but through imagined constructs that see all Eastern societies as fundamentally similar, all sharing crucial characteristics unlike those of Western societies, and in essence this knowledge establishes the East as antithetical to the West. "Such Eastern knowledge is constructed with literary texts and historical records that often are of limited understanding of the facts of life."[9] The impact of these images, for the most part of the Asian as foreign, is oppressive at various levels as evidenced throughout history; it has resulted in everything from different work conditions and housing policies for certain Asian groups to the forced internment of Asian Americans during World War II.

Presently, although an enormous amount of work has been done to try to dispel these stereotypical images through the dedicated activism of Asian Americans in local communities, cities, colleges, and universities, these images continue to haunt today's generations of Asian Americans. Magazines like *Asianweek, aMagazine, KoreAm*, Web sites like *Asian Nation, 8 Asians*, and *Bamboo Girl*, Asian American coalitions and organizations, and the slowly growing number of Asian American actors and actresses, musicians, writers, and bloggers like "Angry Asian Man" (http://www.angryasianman.com) continue to actively contribute to the movement to counter these antiquated images by vocalizing outrage, raising awareness, and resisting through other deliberate acts. Nonetheless, it is necessary to diligently fight the disturbing reality that Asian American representations, whether through general stereotypes or literature or media images, continue to be more believable than a real person, as though it is easier to know Asian Americans through representation than through reality.[10] It remains increasingly efficient to interact with predictable images rather than flesh-and-blood people who may actually have more in common with the rest of humanity. Again, these representations conveniently put the Asian American in a specific role within a very limited relationship; moreover, they provide an avenue for the non-Asian person, whether intentionally or unintentionally, to maintain a secure status quo wherein they are active agents, and the Other is nothing more than a passive canvas.

One issue of enormous significance to the Asian American community that has an effect on the status quo is the discussion on affirmative action. This is an example of an issue that does not precisely fit into the black and white paradigm. Moreover, it is related to the perpetual foreigner syndrome in that it raises practical ways to counteract the consequences of these stereotypes. According to Wu, though it is not a perfect solution, the intention behind affirmative action is equality and integration.[11] The hope is to begin to counter the disequilibrium that has occurred for hundreds of years in American society, mostly in those spheres of life that are affected by class and economic status, race and culture, and gender. Wu continues: "Affirmative action is the applied component of the commitment to work toward achieving a society that not only happens to be racially diverse but also strives to be egalitarian and inclusive."[12]

Thus affirmative action is about membership and genuine inclusion for the Asian American community, as well as other groups, into larger society. It tries to transform the nature of the larger society and the terms of membership. Concerning the other options besides affirmative action—that is, color blindness and meritocracy—Wu writes that these are illusory ideals because color blindness requires color consciousness or it becomes impossible to discern itself,[13] and meritocracy is arbitrary because merit is based on the standardization of certain expectations that do not take essential contextual and circumstantial aspects into the fullest consideration. While the point here is, again, not to assert that affirmative action is the best or most comprehensive course of action, I do wish to highlight the implications of this discussion, that is, the need to recognize and dialogue about these unavoidable social realities of marginalization lived out at numerous levels that are connected to the perpetual foreigner syndrome.

Tokenism is another specific way the perpetual foreigner syndrome is manifested in relation to issues surrounding affirmative action. I have often appreciated the opportunities that were most likely the result of affirmative action efforts, ones that I believe I would not have acquired because my ability or talent might have been downplayed because I look like a foreigner–like someone ignorant of how certain things are done in this culture and unable to fully communicate in English. And yet–perhaps this is part backlash and part natural consequence–I have often found myself the "token," whether it was the token Asian or token Asian girl. It seemed I was a good placeholder in those endeavors for diversity, more like a trophy that expressed the group including me was now truly progressive and sensitive to the role of minority cultures in society. Again, my ability or talent, my perspective and voice were downplayed because they were not necessary; just my being Asian and foreign was good enough to belong to the group.

There is a connection between the perpetual foreigner syndrome, tokenism, and the phenomenon of a sort of evolution of this Asian American stereotype into the "model minority myth," which provides a glimpse into another dimension of this story.

Model Minority Myth

My father often tells me stories about my kindergarten year. I was a fairly typical five year old who loved making chocolate-covered pretzels, finger painting, playing tag during recess, and especially being fidgety during naptime. At the end of the year, there was an awards ceremony to recognize the students who were the most successful throughout that year. During this time, my father worked late nights to earn extra income for the family, so he woke up on the morning of the ceremony to a phone call from my teacher reminding him to come to school so that he would be able to take photographs of his "special daughter." He laughs when he recalls this story because he did not have time to shower, he was fairly disheveled when he arrived at school, and he forgot the camera, but he came just in time to see me receive a bright blue ribbon that said "Top Student" (only two students out of the kindergarten class received this award). Another parent graciously took a Polaroid snapshot of me in a ruffled pink dress awkwardly holding a large ribbon. This moment was somehow meaningful to both my parents because they felt this would be the beginning of great achievement in my life.

Growing up, I fulfilled the prophecy of the model minority: I was an overachiever in the areas of math and science, often a year or two ahead of my classmates. In class, I was overtly quiet, hardworking, and (the most important) I was polite to the students and teachers. Wu describes this phenomenon, writing that the phrase "You Asians are all doing well anyway" summarizes the model minority myth, which is the dominant image of Asians in the United States. As a group, besides being intelligent, gifted in math and science, polite, and hardworking, we are seen as being extremely family oriented, law abiding, and successfully entrepreneurial.[14] Asian American historians write that this portrayal began in the mid-1960s, a time of massive racial upheaval. The term was first used by the press to depict Japanese Americans who struggled to enter the mainstream of American life and to laud Chinese Americans for their remarkable accomplishments.[15] According to Zia, as this new stereotype emerged on the American scene, Asian Americans became increasingly the object of "flattering" media stories. After more than a century of invisibility alternating with virulent headlines that advocated eliminating or imprisoning America's Asians, a rash of stories began to extol our virtues. Thus the model minority myth was born.[16] This label filtered into college textbooks where it further promoted this image of Asian Americans as minorities who "made it" in this "land of opportunity."

Yet the rewards for the model minority are less than desirable. In a speech presented to Asian and Pacific Americans in the chief executive's mansion in 1984, President Ronald Reagan explained the significance of their success. America has a rich and diverse heritage, Reagan declared, and Americans are all descendants of immigrants in search of the "American dream." He praised Asian and Pacific Americans for helping to "preserve that dream by living up to the bedrock values" of America. Reagan emphatically noted, "The median incomes of Asian and Pacific American families are much higher than the total American average."[17] In the view of other Americans, Asian Americans vindicate the American dream.[18]

My parents certainly had their version of the American dream—the familiar house, cars, television sets, and 2.5 kids. We'd have BBQs on hot summer days, Thanksgiving dinners with extended family, and a backyard so we could run around. But the core of their dream would always be centered on what my brother and I could achieve someday. To them, having a home, employment, maybe even a relatively flourishing small business, and a good connection to the church was good enough for their ultimate achievement, but of course—as any parent in any culture—they wanted more for us. Their dreams, they would often tell me, were for us, and we heard many times that they "sacrificed and came to this country for us," and they "came only so that we would have better opportunities," especially during those moments I did anything remotely disappointing. They really believed in what we could accomplish, because, unlike them, somehow we would truly be Americans. And yet their language would always be almost tainted with something more, a competitive edge and a dash of bitterness or even resentment; sometimes it seemed they wanted us to be so American in terms of material success that we would be more American than Americans. We would surpass Americans in their own country. So when I did well in classes or excelled at the piano, I was fulfilling not only my parents' expectations but those of the dominant culture, too.

Ronald Takaki insists that in their celebration of this "model minority," the pundits and the politicians exaggerated Asian American "success" and in essence created a new myth. The comparison of incomes between Asians and Anglos failed to recognize other variables that affect income, like the regional location of the Asian American population. For instance, statistics indicate that the family incomes of Asian Americans actually indicate the presence of more workers in each family, rather than higher incomes.[19] Moreover, Asian Americans experience patterns of income and employment inequality, as evidenced in their absence from the higher levels of administration. They experience the "glass ceiling"–a barrier through which top management positions can be seen but not reached no matter how diligently they pursued it. The benefits of the model minority image remain largely superficial and mythical.

My father worked for the same computer company in the finance department for almost fifteen years. He was bright, a quick learner and, of course, a hard worker. He earned his undergraduate education in the United States and went on to get his MBA. Yet he was never promoted for a higher position beyond managing a small office within the larger department. Of course, he never complained or spoke up but kept his nose to the grindstone. He always believed that somehow it would all even out and that the end result would be fair. He eventually left the company to go to seminary, so there is no way of knowing how it would have turned out.

The stereotype that Asian Americans are all "doing fine anyway" obscures many realities besides income and employment, including the real diversity of personalities, ambitions, and talents of Asian Americans. At some level, this myth presents its own quandary: "Should Asian Americans accept, if not embrace, this 'good' stereotype as an improvement over the 'inscrutable alien enemy' image of a previous hundred years?"[20] Since Asian American "success" has emerged as the new stereotype for this ethnic minority, often the reaction toward Asian Americans' opposition to this image has been confusion. After all, these are positive qualities, desirable and honorable attributes, especially relative to the stereotypes as highlighted in earlier literature. While this image has led many teachers and employers to view Asians as intelligent and hardworking and has opened some opportunities, it has also been harmful. Asian Americans find their diversity as individuals denied or limited to specific arenas of life. Many feel forced to conform to the model minority mold and encounter extreme pressure from all sides if they do not fit this category. They want more freedom to be their individual selves, to be "extravagant."[21]

Again, we must note that reality is more complex than the simplifying metaphors that shape the public discourse about the Asian American experience. The model minority concept is not without its virtues; historically, it has helped turn around the negative stereotypes of Asian Americans and enhanced a positive image of Asian Americans. The model minority is usually empirically consistent with Asian Americans and with their advantageous position relative to other minorities if not always to Anglos.[22] On the other hand, discrimination, which finds its roots in the influence of these stereotypes and images, still inhibits the progress of Asian Americans and the basic survival and progress of other minority groups in the United States. This occurs because this standard, as allegedly exemplified by the model Asian Americans, is in fact a standard propagated by the majority culture of the dominant group. Rather than positively impacting all minority groups, it sets up a divisive wedge between Asian Americans and the other groups. Before they were the economic wedge to distract labor unrest, they were refashioned as a political and social hammer against other disadvantaged groups.[23] Thus Asian Americans have become pawns, a "teacher's pet" community, a group resented for their success, who are also targets of violence and hatred by other groups, yet still not even accepted by the dominant culture. This sets up an oppressive, catch-22 dynamic where Asian Americans are caught in the middle.

Since these stereotypes operate as authorities in place of history and literature, they in turn aggravate race relations.[24] These images, whether negative or "positive," end up dictating the conversation and setting up reference points for understanding people. In actuality Asian American success has become a race-relations failure.[25]

Thus many Asian Americans have begun to work to dismantle the model minority myth by seeking out occupations in journalism and law, as well as becoming writers, literature professors, and artists. Moreover, these Asian Americans are breaking the mold by becoming more active in their local communities and addressing social and political issues, especially those concerning efforts to improve race relations. For Wu, the model minority is a stock character that plays multiple roles in our racial drama. For Asian Americans to participate as viable members in society, this myth should be rejected for three reasons:

> First, the myth is a gross simplification that is not accurate enough to be seriously used for understanding ten million people. Second, it conceals within itself an insidious statement about African Americans along the lines of the inflammatory taunt, "They made it; why can't you?" Third, it is abused both to deny Asian Americans' experience of racial discrimination and to turn Asian Americans into a racial threat.[26]

Thus "declining the laudatory title of model minority is fundamental to gaining Asian American autonomy."[27]

Continued work in the deconstruction of these images will lead to freedom in Asian American identity development as well as the potential for improved interactions between these minority groups. It will take off the shackles that prevent them from having greater agency not only in their actions and decisions but also in developing their very personhood and community identity. The disassembling needs to happen not only in the loaded perceptions of the dominant culture; it needs to happen in the minds and spirits of those oppressed who perpetuate the system by being silent or avoiding the issues. No doubt, this work requires acknowledging what has happened in the past by honestly looking back, and a bold articulation of the injustices and problems, as well as looking at what is before us in the present, connecting the stories, and creatively imagining solutions as we journey forward.

*   *   *

My family has traveled back to Korea together just a handful of times. To visit their respective families for various reasons, my parents have gone back once or twice by themselves. It is incredibly expensive, and of course, the flight is so long. It just isn't the most appealing in terms of actual travel. But I really do love it. The first time our family took part of the summer vacation to spend time with our family in Korea was after I finished fourth grade. It was like waiting for Christmas morning; I was feverish with excitement and didn't sleep a wink. I can still remember the early-morning drive to the airport in Denver, and then the layover in San Francisco, and then boarding the final plane to stay up the rest of the night watching *The Never Ending Story*. All I remember about the movie is the scene with the boy sitting on top of the pink dragon-labrador creature flying through the sky, perhaps traveling to see his family, too, or maybe to simply go home.

I sat next to my mom, who was giddy like a young schoolgirl. When she was awake, she kept trying to get me to at least try closing my eyes, but she ended up falling asleep pretty soundly for most of the time, looking very much like the girl I saw in black-and-white photos from her album. She lay curled up on her side with an airplane blanket tucked under her chin. My brother and I played games, but he fell asleep, too. My father seemed like he was asleep for most of the time; he woke up only for the meals and promptly went back to sleep. It was as if he were trying to take advantage of having more than eight hours of sleep at a time, catching up on the little sleep he normally got because of work. He probably still felt the usual stress of everyday life, paying the mortgage, and traveling with two young children, but the worry that normally cut lines across his forehead, etched permanently, had melted away, and I could see peace in his face as he snored quietly.

My eyes eventually turned bloodshot as I kept them pried open the whole time, so my mom put Visine drops in them to make me presentable when we arrived in Seoul to be picked up by my father's older brother's family. I just didn't want to miss a single moment. When we finally got off the plane, I found myself drinking in every sight and sound. Stepping into the humid air was the first shock, like running into a wall; it knocked me back as I felt short of breath. I took a couple more breaths, and then after what seemed like an eternity going through customs, we met my father's extended family for the first time. It was awkward but strangely beautiful; through the traditional bows and painfully shy smiles, I could definitely sense the burgeoning delight that only comes from a happy family reunion. My father's eyes were bright, and my mother laughed easily and told jokes. My cousins chattered excitedly with us and their parents. I just tried to take it all in. The rest of the time was a whirlwind of staying with both my father and my mother's siblings and their families, in the city of Seoul, outside of Pusan, the seaport, and in the little village out in the country where my father's parents had spent almost their entire lives. Initially when we drove up to my paternal grandparents' village, my heart sank because it seemed so primitive; I was a little frightened even. It ended up being the place I loved the most, and where I felt a profound sense of belonging and home. We traveled out to the rice fields. A neighbor caught a little bird for us to have as a friend during our stay, and cows would often walk through the front yard to visit with us. My favorite memory was the walk with my grandmother to the open-air market that seemed to be a few miles away. She tightly clutched my hand in hers and held an empty container with the other hand. Soon the container would be overflowing with food. She carried it on top of her head as easily as though it were an extension of her. This image is etched into my mind as a reminder of the contentment in the journey being a part of me, too, through her.

During times of feeling tossed and turned by storms of confusion caused by the world on this side of the ocean, I forgot some of those moments, especially the feeling of being rooted in a family and story that was so tangible. The next chance I had to go back was in 2004, this time during the summer after I had graduated from seminary. I went as a chaplain to a group of late high school and college-aged Korean American students sponsored by the Presbyterian Church (USA) and the National Korean Presbyterian Council Men's group. I saw it as a wonderful opportunity that fell into my lap. What better way to transition back into the "real world" after completing my seminary education than with a trip back to the motherland? My objective, according to the brochure, was to help these young souls engage in a spiritual pilgrimage. I facilitated discussions about how visiting the large Korean Presbyterian churches, perusing the historical museums and war memorials, and visiting the Presbyterian Seminary were pertinent to our faith. What did it add to our faith lives? How did it shape our faith perspectives? Where are we in these stories? I realized afterward that these questions were for me, too, questions that I had been living since that first journey across the ocean. The discussions were rich and lovely and awakened so many possibilities in me.

But the most important realization that trip solidified for me was the same conclusion I had come to after graduation from seminary:

I feel most at home in the questions. I originally thought when I stepped into my first theology class that I would find the solutions to everything about God, faith, and the church, right then and there, even in the books I carried in my backpack. I ended up leaving after three years with questions spilling out of my already-full bag. Eventually I realized that I felt most at home in the questions because they compel me to journey. But I do so with assurance and hope, whether the journey leads me physically across oceans or spiritually across whole worlds, because I know that no matter what obstacles or barriers, I have the strength and light of my family ahead of me, behind me, and next to me.

2

Fidelity, Prosperity, Longevity

The Asian American Woman

It is the questions we ask that move us from stage to stage of our growing . . . however simple the questions may seem.

—SISTER JOAN CHITTISTER

"The crane, and the origami crane developed in Japan several hundred years ago, has long been a symbol of longevity. In Asian mythology, it is said that cranes live for 1000 years. Cranes choose only one mate and never separate."[1] I have heard stories about a crane dance that used to be presented in one of the more famous temples as a way to tell the story of the crane's long life and good luck. As my mother and I would fold tiny pieces of paper to make these delicate creatures, I would dream of making thousands of them to give someday to someone I loved as a symbol of faithfulness. But I could not imagine feeling that way about someone. I would often linger over the thought of how something so small and fragile could last or symbolize anything eternal and timeless. It was strange to me. Now I think of my mother and how small and fragile she sometimes looked in my eyes and of how amazing it was that she held everything together in her life and her family with such strength and patience.

Only in recent years have I begun realizing that this resilient spirit, as often associated with the crane, was passed on to me from my mother. Perhaps I knew it but was ashamed or too proud to admit it; perhaps I even thought that I had somehow cultivated it myself. I saw her life experience as so different from mine and from the way I would want to be as a grown up, especially in the ways she experienced various levels of limitation, whether external or internal. I did not want to associate myself with an inadequacy that seemed rooted in being a Korean female. At the same time, I struggled with what it meant to be a girl, and eventually a young woman, feeling pulled by so many different stories that sought to imprint on me various versions of how to be a woman. My life felt like the paper that was in our hands, with forced folds and creases. Some felt natural, and some didn't seem to make any sense, but all of it was making me into some sort of creation. Most of the time I experienced a pull to and fro in a strange dance that was difficult to follow, because I just did not feel the music.

Sexism: Beyond Suzie Wong and Madame Butterfly

Sexism was a strange word to me when I was growing up. Since I resided in more traditional contexts, it was impressed upon me that this was almost a "dirty" word, a word associated with only the crazy, liberal fanatics and the "femi-nazis." When I started to feel the effects of injustices that seemed to happen over and over, and only to females, and how they clashed with an ideal I felt within me, I needed to name it. There was no label for it, except for the word that was avoided like the plague. But the feeling needed to be given voice.

Standards

When I was growing up, my parents had a number of expectations for me. Besides being successful academically, they desired for me to be adept at the basic domestic skills of cooking and cleaning. Unfortunately, I was always too much of a tomboy, too wild and too scatterbrained to have the attention span necessary for cooking a meal. At the same time, I became more aware of the subtle difference between my family's expectations of me and the standards set by the surrounding culture. My parents expected me to possess the characteristics of a "good Korean girl"—that is, someone who is quiet, demure, and obedient. My memories are peppered with their voices constantly pleading and admonishing, "You are too wild, don't be wild, you need to calm down." The dominant culture around me would sometimes echo these sentiments for women in general, but I saw that the image of Asian American women specifically included some level of exoticism and mysterious appeal. At the same time, I was becoming confused by feminist ideals of independence, liberation, and power. They seemed irreconcilable with any of these other depictions of Asian American women, listed by Jessica Hagedorn as follows:

> Pearl of the Orient. Whore. Geisha. Concubine. Whore. Hostess. Bar Girl. Mama-san. Whore. China Doll. Tokyo Rose. Whore. Butterfly. Whore. Miss Saigon. Whore. Dragon Lady. Lotus Blossom. Gook. Whore. Yellow Peril. Whore. Bangkok Bombshell. Whore. Hospitality Girl. Whore. Comfort Woman. Whore. Savage. Whore. Sultry. Whore. Faceless. Whore. Porcelain. Whore. Demure. Whore. Virgin. Whore. Mute. Whore. Model Minority. Whore. Victim. Whore. Woman Warrior. Whore. Mail-Order Bride. Whore. Mother. Wife. Lover. Daughter. Sister.[2]

Some of these labels may be familiar as they illustrate images of Asian women that are prevalent in movies, literature, and art. Interspersed throughout the list is the word *whore*, perhaps the image that is the most pervasive–a woman who is physically, mentally, emotionally, and sexually passive, someone who is simply a toy or plaything. Though not as overt in contemporary society, these stereotypes and expectations continue to be present in the social consciousness of Americans and the dominant majority culture.

In various social images–particularly in the media, through magazines, music, and other facets of popular culture–we begin to have a glimmering of the wide breadth of perceptions concerning gender that shape the identities of Asian American women. The common thread throughout these images is a one-dimensional human being stripped of emotion and humanity and, at times, a creature that is simply an instrument for the use and pleasure of those who seek to dominate her. While the perpetual foreigner syndrome and model minority myth are applicable to Asian American women, these categories are colored slightly differently when the gender issue is added to them. Primarily, Asian American women are seen as sexually available, exotic, and expendable; moreover, they experience objectification as conquerable territory. In addition, they are perceived with a mixture of fascination, fear, and contempt.[3] According to Kim, some examples of images of women in earlier literature by Asian American male writers reflect these sexist images: mothers who suffocate their sons, vapid girls who are unable to appreciate the complexity and sensitivity of their Asian boyfriends, and arrogant assimilationists who operate in complicity with white racists, scorning the young Asian man's search for self-respect and recognition.[4]

Many writers, even Asian male writers, have propagated an essentialist distinction between Asian American men and women. The origin of these stereotypes for Asian American women is not only in the East/West dichotomy, in which they are viewed as the Other. In addition, Asian American women are viewed as the Other in another relationship–that is, in the male/female dichotomy, which operates as another experiential paradigm. Thus some Asian male writers have concluded that manliness means "'aggressiveness, creativity, individuality, just being taken seriously,'" while femininity means "'lacking daring, originality, aggressiveness, assertiveness, vitality.'"[5] It is no wonder that this sentiment is familiar to Asian American women:

> We have been taught to play the role, to take care of our men. We are objects of desire or derision. We exist to provide sex, color, and texture in what is essentially a "white man's world." We have learned as Asian females to settle for less–to accept the fact that we are only decorative, invisible, or one-dimensional.[6]

I distinctly remember the conversations my mother and I had some time after I had gotten into seminary and begun classes. I was almost on a rampage, really feeling the deep conviction that all women needed to be free from the oppressive system that forced them into silence and subservience. I thought I needed to liberate my own mother first. The conversation became heated, and I could not fathom why she did not see the way she was allowing herself to be limited by these cultural forces. What was keeping her from being more, doing more, and pursuing more than the tasks around the kitchen, both in our home and in the church? She eventually got angry with me, frustrated and annoyed with my ironically oppressive "be free" speech, which was having the opposite effect on her. Then I saw it. I saw a little fear–totally understandable now that I felt it in her and in me–at the possibilities of what it would mean to live outside of the system that had become comfortable to her. It was familiar to her, and even though she might not live out her fullest potential, she would live intertwined with the rules that shaped her and kept her because in the long run, it was easier, it was safer, and it would require less work and effort. Sometimes I honestly can feel and understand it in my own bones, because trying to break out of those patterns is painful and lonely.

As a result of the experience of this type of sexism, Asian American women find themselves navigating through any number of combinations of these categories. It is a complicated system, and once you get in a spot or niche, you find it difficult to come out of it. I have seen this in my mother and experienced it myself. Asian American women must face the various complicated layers of race dynamics as an Asian American person. These dynamics include the images both of the perpetual foreigner and of the model minority. Yet, as the model minority, besides the expectation for having a high standard of intelligence and musical ability, Asian American women encounter the expectation for their unwavering subordination. Often these experiences are further complicated by the expectations of women as seen through the lens of their specific Asian culture, as experienced in relationship to the other women and men (like their immediate families) in the Asian communities–relationships that are normally rooted in patriarchal structures. Likewise, Asian American women are compelled to constantly take into consideration the surrounding dominant culture and the expectations of non-Asian men and women. The complicated structure of these relationships often acts as a further barrier to these women when it comes to identity development in the home, in the church, in the political arena, or in the workplace.

Silence

Whenever the Korean families from our church would come over, the men would immediately kick up their socked feet on the couches while the women would cheerfully take their places in the kitchen bustling like the proverbial busy little bees. Being young, inexperienced, and obviously awkward, I stayed on the fringes of the kitchen area, against a wall like some kind of strange house plant, secretly observing the ritualistic happenings around the sink, fridge, and stove like a scientist on the verge of discovering a new society. The exuberant chatter always intrigued me, but the volume and the intensity frightened me at the same time. I found myself relieved whenever the conversations dissolved into laughter, but I was always amazed at the way the female guests would move so easily about a kitchen that did not belong to them with such poise and grace, stirring a pot here, frying and grilling over there, spooning out perfect mounds of rice into little bowls. I could never spoon out the right amount–it was always too much or too little–and my mounds looked more like smashed ant hills. I would invariably hear, "*Mi-Yah, slow down, bik-yuh-bah, move over, neh-gah-heh, I do it.*" These dinners are one of the few memories

I have of the Korean women in my life not being silent, and really asserting themselves, especially in the Christian community, though technically from within a domestic space.

One of the most considerable expectations of Asian American women by the larger dominant culture, and often more so by their specific Asian communities, is the notion that they will be silent. They belong in the shadows of the dominant male culture, at home, chiefly in the kitchen or in the laundry room. One woman wrote about constantly facing overwhelming parental expectations for academic and material success and, it almost goes without saying, for expertise in the kitchen.[7] Thus it seems Asian American women are relegated to very limited spheres where speaking up or speaking out is not a necessity. Still they are expected to achieve a success that in most cases requires communication skills. The underlying expectation of Asian American women is the inability to communicate correctly and competently. In other words, Asian American women are just not skilled at articulation or expression; thus they should simply remain silent and unseen: "Don't draw attention to yourself."

Of course, I think of finding my own voice wrapped up in my call to ministry. It came about in an unexpected way. Moments of irony hit me hard. I think because I subconsciously hold up my worldview like a blanket wrapped around me, with these expectations and preconceived notions woven together tightly in my brain, when something outside of my usual assumptions happens to me, it knocks me out cold and stays with me for a while.

I grew up in a traditional Presbyterian home, culturally Korean on the inside and culturally attempting to be American (whatever that means) on the outside. An undeniable hierarchy ruled in the house, as well as at our church home. My father was the breadwinner, and my mother was the homemaker. At the church, only men were the elders, the leaders, the pastor, and any visiting preachers during the yearly weekend revivals. The women were always deacons, literally servants of compassion and hospitality for the church. Essentially, that meant they rotated bringing food, washing dishes, and cleaning the kitchen every Sunday after the fellowship lunch. They also headed up the church bazaar fundraisers. This was my world, and I never gave it any thought until my dad attended seminary while I was beginning my undergraduate studies.

At the same time, as I reflect back, I remember it wasn't so black and white. I brushed off the little moments of contradiction but kept them on the back burner. My mother, solely responsible for taking care of the home, also managed a few stores, businesses that my parents attempted to start up in various parts of the city during various parts of my childhood. Over and over again they would tell me their dreams for me were that I enter into some kind of successful, public profession (medicine, law, education), but they seldom mentioned marriage, family, and a home life. I went to a church service once where a woman preached, and I was simultaneously repelled and enthralled by it. Perhaps these moments caused the little rips and tears that would make the entire cover almost completely unravel at the seams that one fateful day.

When I started my undergraduate studies, I had planned on going premed (I know, so stereotypical of Asian Americans. Actually, a number of my Asian American friends are in medicine). Then I fell in love with the humanities courses I was taking in the religion, English, history, and philosophy departments. I was also involved in various ministries to high school and college students. I began to feel a tug toward the Church and ministry. But I would never have considered it in a million years until one particular conversation with my father in the middle of my freshmen year. He was attending Princeton Seminary at the time and enjoying the classes and community with numerous women who were studying to also become . . . *pastors*. "Pastors???" I interjected. "But the Bible says that women are supposed to submit to men . . . and church leaders are supposed to only be men. I can't imagine a woman being able to do it!!!" I argued with him over the phone, and we went back and forth.

And there's the irony.

My father, the symbol of Asian patriarchy, told me stories of how women had been leaders of the church for a long time. Many were elders in the Presbyterian Church, and some were also becoming pastors all around him. They had a voice. My father admired and respected them; in fact, he supported them. He reminded me that the first people to preach the gospel after Jesus' resurrection were women. He was taking a class on feminist/womanist theologies, the same class that would deeply impact me some years later during my own seminary coursework.

"And you can be a leader, too–an elder, a pastor, anything you believe God is calling you to be in your own life," he said to me.

These words turned everything upside down, in a frightening way, but they gave me a voice, or at least the possibility of having a voice in the context that was most dear to me, the Church. That moment was truly redemptive, one of the first few tastes of grace for me. As I think about it now, I cannot help but think of the words to a song that I had grown to love: *Redemption comes in strange places, small spaces calling out the best of who we are* . . . I look back and see that was certainly the case here. I was left with bits and pieces of yarn, string, remnants of that shroud of cultural pressures I had hung onto for so long, and I realized that these pieces were an invitation to create something new because I was given the ability, power, and freedom to do and be something more . . . *This is grace, an invitation to be beautiful* . . . *This is grace, an invitation* . . . So here I am on the other side, thankful for that one moment and all the *small inspirations* in this journey that have helped me become more of me and a more faithful me, encouraging me to respond to God's call courageously, and most of all, to share it . . . *And I want to add to the beauty* . . . *to tell a better story* . . . [8]

Still, self-effacing attitudes toward possessing a voice are all too familiar. A young Asian American girl wrote,

> Language is a barrier to me. I grew up silent, but burst-ing with the glimmering desire to describe everything I observed in the closest detail . . . Years passed, and my Eng-lish progressed, but I remained ever silent; . . . I knew that if I ever faltered, I would be reminded at recess, at the water fountain, and during day care.[9]

For some reason, Asian American women experience enormous pressure to verbalize according to certain standards or to be silent. They have internalized the illegitimization of their voices, and thus of their perspectives and experiences. Again, this internalized characteristic is rooted in the influence of the stereotypes of Asian American women as the perpetual foreigner and model minority, but moreover, as exotic, inferior, and one-dimensional. In essence, the stripping away of these women's voices is a removal of their individual personhood, humanity, and autonomy.

Sexuality

The subjugation of these women's voices is connected to expecta-tions concerning the Asian American woman's body image, beauty, and sexuality. Sometimes, these women are portrayed as the "rebel girls" who represent a taste of what is outside the normative like Jade Cobra Girls: sexy, defiant, fabulous images flaunting tight metallic dresses and spiky cockscomb hairdos streaked electric red and blue.[10] At other times, they may simply be portrayed as benign creatures, as in *The Joy Luck Club*, a movie about the stories of four Asian American daughters and their immigrant mothers. Asian American women confront expectations from the white culture and from their own specific Asian culture concerning their bodies and sexuality. As the perpetual foreigner, the Asian American woman may be seen not simply as unfamiliar but more as appealingly and invitingly exotic. Inherent in the image of the Asian American woman is the perceived provocation to access the mysterious in her, which is usually in terms of sexuality.

This furthers the necessity for the image of the Asian American woman to fit a specific body image in order to fit into the correct stereotype, as expressed by Phoebe Eng: "For Asian American women, our unique issues of our body image intersect directly with the complicated ways in which we view our sexuality."[11] Likewise, among the South Asian second generation what is most expected of them is maintaining the traditional culture and strong family ties. "South Asian daughters are expected to uphold the culture, to remain chaste and not bring in the pollution of outside people's cultures," said second-generation Sayantani DasGupta, a writer and physician.

> While heterosexual South Asian men are out pursuing and preserving the model minority myth, the women are told, "Leave your business shoes at the door, put your chappals on and do puja, the traditional prayers." This is the dominant theme for the second generation. Issues of dating, sexuality, and marriage are really code for controlling women's sexuality.[12]

Thus Asian American women are viewed as spaces to sexually occupy by either culture, whether for manipulation or containment.

What fueled my egalitarian views of empowering women of all cultures and generations first came out of Serene Jones's articulation and her use of the feminist theory of oppression. It is, of course, applicable to Asian American women. She refers to women's oppression as the dynamic forces, both personal and social, that diminish or deny the flourishing of women.[13] She goes on to describe it as a phenomenon that requires a materialist and cultural analysis as well as an examination of the relations between power and domination and how they constrain potential collectivities of women.[14] Iris Young describes the categories of this experience as the five faces of oppression: exploitation, marginalization, powerlessness, cultural imperialism, and violence.[15] While Asian American women may be able to identify with each type, Jones writes, "the value of these theories rests on their abilities to illuminate women's experience of oppression," and she encourages readers to use their own experiences of oppression to measure these theories. They are not meant to be exhaustive, nor are they meant to apply to every woman, but engaging these categories keeps feminist theories of oppression "on the move."[16]

The category of powerlessness is one of the tangible ways in which the Asian American woman can experience oppression. This face of oppression has to do with how decisions are made and power is distributed in a community. It is the inhibition of the development of one's capacities, lack of decision-making power in one's working life, and exposure to disrespectful treatment because of the status one occupies.[17] It concerns what is called "having a voice" and what one does with one's body. For example, Asian American women rarely find themselves in management positions or positions of authority. Thus others are usually telling Asian American women, whether in employment, academic, or even social situations, what to do, what to think, and how to act. Claire Chow shares her experience of becoming a licensed therapist and entering a profession where she faced clients and colleagues who doubted her ability because their initial impressions of her were overshadowed by her race (would she be able to relate to non-Asians?) and gender.[18] This sense of powerlessness makes women feel infantilized, patronized, made invisible, and not respected. They feel trivialized and silenced by the majority culture.[19] This powerlessness is rooted in the hierarchical structures that Asian American women encounter not only in their specific Asian cultures but in the larger dominant culture—for example, in the typical workplace, which perpetuates the structure that keeps the feminized worker (who is passive, obedient, less rational, and dependent, whether male or female) and the more "qualified" and powerful boss in specific roles. The powerlessness is maintained when these structures remain static and Asian American women find themselves trapped within them.

The other category that seems the most pertinent to the Asian American woman's experience is cultural imperialism. Cultural imperialism involves the dominant meanings of a society rendering the particular perspective of one's group invisible while at the same time stereotyping one's group and marking it out as the Other.[20] This has to do with the way groups develop and apply cultural standards for defining, interpreting, and regulating beliefs, actions, and attitudes.[21] This occurs when a more powerful group universalizes its standards and imposes them on less powerful persons. Cultural imperialism results in these dominant meanings causing the Other, the outsider, to experience the qualities of powerlessness, that is, invisibility and marginality. In this case, Asian American women experience cultural imperialism as their image is often based on certain stereotypes that denote their Otherness, specifically in terms of their sexual availability. This basically affects the Asian American woman's identity because the imposition of this standard construes her identity as supplemental to the dominant standard, whether masculine or "white." Part of this is reflected in a specific standard of beauty that is imposed on the Asian American woman: a slim, petite body; long, black, exotic hair; and sun-kissed, tanned, unblemished, creamy skin. A number of women share stories of their struggle with this imposed body image, including the experience of depression and eating disorders to compensate for the influence of this unrealistic expectation.[22] All these standards are connected to the root issue of the consequences of the cultural imperialism Asian American women face in the standards that regulate their voice, bodies, and sexuality and that ultimately limit their perspective and power.

Thus Asian American women experience racism, sexism, and cultural imperialism in unique ways. They share with Asian American men others' perceptions of them as perpetual foreigners and model minorities. Asian American women must also face issues of gender, which add another layer of meaning for them. Standards, as they manifest themselves concerning the Asian American woman's voice and body, overlap a great deal. The main issues revolve around these struggles, especially those of acquiring an identity free from the containment of those cultural impediments imposed on them by those in power. Of course, this discussion is by no means exhaustive. The issues are quite complex, but for me, and I hope for others, this will be a helpful and productive starting point.

*   *   *

My mom and I took a while to connect at a level beyond parent/ caretaker and child. I had often thought that I was, and even prided myself in being, more like my dad. He had power and agency. He made decisions. He was in leadership positions at the church. He had education. He engaged in conversations. He and I would often get into long, verbose arguments about everything. They would usually end with both of us exasperated, throwing up our hands and him exclaiming, "You need to seriously consider law! You like to talk too much!" Usually they included long dialogues about why my younger brother was allowed to do so much more than I was in terms of sports, going over to friends' houses, and in general being favored by our parents. (This kind of sexism can be typical in Asian families–favoring sons over daughters. I have fought against it my entire life, but I don't deny that I was obnoxious.) When I went away to seminary, it seemed my mother's worry and anxiety about how I would live out my call to ordained ministry as a woman and hopefully someday as a wife and mother were often barriers between us. She was uncertain how I would be able to do it all and maintain emotional, physical, and spiritual health. At the time, I thought she doubted my ability to do it, and it pained me, this feeling that I would fall short of her or anyone's expectations, that I would not fit the mold. But as I look back, and as we talk about family and raising children, I realize now her concerns were a lot simpler. She just wanted me to be happy.

When Andy and I were married, one thing changed for sure–the nature of my relationship with my mom. It seemed my relationship with my mother transformed almost overnight as we connected through conversations around simple topics like food and cooking, grocery shopping, cleaning, and taking care of our health. A tenderness developed that I had never felt before. I know something shifted in my perspective, and I think it had to do with my finally stepping into her world a little. I began to see a little better what her life must have been like, not really as an immigrant or as an Asian, but as an Asian American woman these last almost thirty years.

I began to see a new pattern in her life because I was slowly living out the pattern in my own life. It seemed I was finally in step with her and not at odds with her, as I had been in my earlier life. I loved it, but I was frightened by it. It was not an easy tension, trying to glean as much as possible from all her practical domestic lessons–ones that perpetuate the stereotypical gender roles–while at the same time maintaining an egalitarian lifestyle at home, since both my husband and I worked full time.

Nevertheless, in my mother, I began to appreciate and understand the kind of faithfulness she exhibited so naturally and regularly. Faithfulness is about that overarching commitment to another person, but it has a lot to do with the "little" things, too. No matter what kind of disagreement or fight they may have had earlier that day, she will always have three meals on the table for my dad. Even if we've had an argument on the phone, she will still call later and initiate a conversation. She adores my younger brother, and will always stick up for him, especially if I am giving him a hard time about anything. In the church, in her own quiet way, she is quick to serve, jump into the kitchen, and make sure everyone has enough on their plates. No matter what her role, her ability, and the expectations of her, she is faithful through and through to the moment.

Thankfully, a balanced view is second nature for Andy. He grew up in churches with women ministers on staff. His mother was a teacher for almost thirty years. He dated and married me. I have no doubt about Andy's and my commitment to each other. Still, for whatever reason—perhaps my rebellious, and as Andy often likes to describe it, "wild horse" nature—my new relationship with Andy took a longer time to settle in me. Marriage with Andy brought adjustments and transitions that still take so much work for me. I am naturally a selfish person, and marriage requires selflessness. Eventually I discovered that selflessness is a quality obligatory in all my relationships.

This type of faithfulness requires a level of sacrifice. One of the first heart-to-hearts my mom and I had was on a road trip she and I took together alone while I was in seminary. My parents were living in South Dakota at the time, and I had to go to my home presbytery for a meeting. It was about a six-hour drive from where they were in Sioux Falls, so we decided that we would do it together, so I would not have to make the trip by myself. My father could stay and go to his own meetings.

We started off. Soon we discovered we had been going the wrong way for a good hour, so we had to turn back around. This stressed me out. I cannot recall what triggered it, but we had an argument where we were full-out shouting at each other. I honestly do not even remember what we were yelling at each other. I had never responded to her in that way. For a moment, I heard her in my voice—that loud, harsh Korean woman screech. After we had calmed down and apologized to each other, we began to talk about what it was like for her in the early years of her marriage, and it all came spilling out. Stories about her original plan to come to the United States to become an art teacher and get her elementary education certification, her sisters convincing her to get married first, her excitement and fear of having children so quickly after their marriage . . . and how she had to put all her plans on hold when they first got here. They never got a chance to leave the ground, and though she may periodically have regrets, she has said she is thankful that she poured all she could into us so that we could live happily and healthily. After all, someone did have to stay with the kids, keep the house clean, and have the meals ready. Someone had to give it all up.

3

Fight, Struggle, and Survive

The Asian American Woman's Resistance

*Sometimes we speak out to try to change the world, and other times
we speak to try to keep the world from changing us.*

—Elie Weisel, author and Holocaust survivor

I have romantic visions of birds migrating for long distances
between the warm and cold seasons traveling over oceans or huge
land masses for days on end, somehow miraculously never stopping
unless for food or water. It is hard to imagine that they would run
into any obstacles or dangers during their journeys, because I figure
they would just fly above or away from them—the beauty of having
wings! Of course, that's completely wrong! Is there anything in this
world that does not experience struggle or conflict?

I have read that migrating birds being blown out to sea is just
one of the many dangers they encounter on their hazardous journey.
Exhausted, small land birds like warblers have landed on ships far
out on the ocean; many others must drown without finding a refuge.
Storms often blow both land and oceanic migrants far off course. If
they cannot find a resting place and food and get back on track, they
will not make it. Migration takes a tremendous amount of energy,
and smaller birds especially must "refuel" regularly to survive the
flight. When the birds are tired and hungry, they are more likely to
be caught by predators and other larger birds.

Adaptation: Compartmentalization or Assimilation

Survival is a tricky but interesting phenomenon. There is no simple way to categorize it. For instance, I grew up in various parts of suburbia, mostly on the north side of Colorado Springs in a neighborhood with houses, fences, and big SUVs. If we had to drive to the mall or the local grocery store to get anything, it was safe. It was familiar . . . and it was home. We could ride our bikes in the streets and kick a ball around on someone's front lawn. My favorite memories are of playing with my little brother and friends, simply running around in our backyard catching grasshoppers or digging holes in the dirt in the garden (much to our mother's chagrin) and taking our bikes up to the elementary school. I remember and feel as if there is something almost mind-numbing, like a sedative, in living this lifestyle. It is comfortable. And, it is easy to become self-absorbed and inwardly focused here. Survival is not a pressing need.

At the same time, I have been reflecting on the different modes of survival in this world and realizing that even in suburbia a survival mentality actually reigns. On the surface, it may seem to involve trying to get to all the sports practices, the dance rehearsals, and the band concerts. In reality, a deeper resistance is taking hold—families trying to stay connected to one another, people trying to stay afloat emotionally and physically, and in general, people trying to stay sane. In suburbia, problems continue to arise. People struggle with alcoholism and other addictions, with divorce, with loneliness, with avoidance of reality, with illness, with death and loss. All this is to say that no one is beyond the need for strategies of survival and that all of us in this world are trying to survive in one way or another—whether in Third World countries or in the townships of Pennsylvania or in the mountains of Colorado—animals, men, children, and women.

What is pertinent here is the reality that different situations and the people in them will choose varying survival techniques to keep afloat and maintain their lives. No one really has a way to exhaust all the possible survival strategies. One description isn't enough even with my own family where the personalities are so different. My mom and her sisters are all equally distinct in the way they adapt to stress and difficult moments, but no one can doubt that we are all affected by the same system of expectation and marginalization. The stress within this system we experience is a result of the expectations placed on us because we are Asian and female.

Survival Modes and Strategies in Faith Identity

Growing up in the church, specifically in a Korean American Presbyterian community, I found myself trying to keep two worlds separate from each other. I learned the art of compartmentalization. On the weekends, I was a Korean involved in church activities and actively engaged in my faith and in the community. I have early memories of going to church before dawn, sleeping on my mom's shoulder in the pew, and snoring through the sounds of this small group of devoted Korean immigrants, which included my parents, voices raised in earnest song and supplication to a God they believed would somehow be responsive to their limited existence. Though I did not realize it at the time, the feeling of solidarity rooted in culture and faith was palpable to my parents, so much so that it would rouse them every morning before sunrise to drive twenty minutes to this church six days a week. In the evenings at home, it was Korean food for dinner, Korean church topics, and Korean language.

During the weekdays, when at school or participating in other extracurricular activities, I lived in another world, one where I tried to understand what it would look like to be someone "normal," guzzling miniature boxes of chocolate milk, talking enthusiastically about various cartoons, and digesting as much information about American history and society as possible. This compartmentalization became more pronounced at a number of levels as I grew older and tried to juggle the various experiences–racial, cultural, spiritual, and psychological–that often seemed at odds with each other. As I continued to delineate more boundaries between these two worlds, I found myself increasingly at odds with myself. I started to lose what it meant to be myself as a Korean American Christian, a legitimate follower of Christ. Because my identity as a Christian was tied to my identity as a Korean American, I did not know how to act on my faith in daily engagement with the surrounding American culture. My faith identity felt the most central to me, but it became the site of the most confusion and uncertainty. Often I would find myself feeling ashamed of my Korean experience of faith, specifically the language or community. It just seemed like being a Korean American Christian was somehow qualitatively different from, even inferior to, being an unhyphenated American Christian.

So I learned the art of assimilation. I realized my inability to completely separate and maintain these two worlds, but at the same time, I saw I was not going to be totally accepted by the dominant culture because of my slanted brown eyes and dark hair, my essential diet of rice and *kimchee*, and the hybrid of Korean and English I spoke with my parents. I just was not like everyone else around me. Even though I spoke "perfect" English, was devoted to Johnny Depp, and loved pizza, hot dogs, and skateboards, I was seen as perpetually foreign and exotic, or as the silent, model minority–perceptions that were deceptively destructive. Even in Christian circles, though I professed the same faith as many of my peers, I always felt as if I were on the outside, always a bit of a mystery or enigma, not completely able to relate to them.

I suppressed this awareness and made huge efforts to persuade myself and others around me that I was the same as those who inhabited the dominant culture. For a while, I even went as far as to say that I was just "American" (in my brain this translated as "white" and Anglo), echoing the sentiments of my friends who claimed they saw me not as Korean but as simply the same as them. I grew up participating in high school fellowship groups like Young Life, and in college I continued in Young Life, joined Navigators, and attended Campus Crusade for Christ and the local Presbyterian Church college group. After much work convincing these mostly Anglo communities, and myself, that I was basically one of them by taking on their identity, their culture, and their language, I found I had lost something essential but not quite nameable. Though these communities did much to encourage and solidify my faith experience to a certain degree, it was at a cost: I forfeited an essential part of me to be received by what I hoped would fulfill me.

The harsh realities of the unfulfilled American dream for the Asian American require a paradigm that allows him or her to function at various levels. Throughout each day, much of life feels like a pendulum swing between expressing one's self and following convention. A number of women offer stories of growing up trying to maintain the expectations of both their parents' world and the world outside–in the hallways of the schools, in relation to the advertisements in malls, and in keeping with popular television shows.[1] One way of navigating through these different worlds while still fulfilling the expectations of both worlds is through compartmentalization. I define this as separating elements in one's life into specific compartments according to the appropriate cultural standard or expectation. Thus the Asian American is able to maintain in his or her mind the illusion of wholeness by separating out what are often conflicting expectations. Asian American women offer stories that fit into this phenomenon where they are drawn to two different worlds, whether it is through the external expectations of others based on images of race and gender, the pressure from Asian communities, or the desire to achieve material success in a "white world."[2]

An Asian American woman described this phenomenon to me as "keeping nice, neat little packages" that contain all the necessary elements of her identity in what she perceived as hard-earned order. The boxes could hold completely contradictory notions. One box stored the Asian characteristic of devoted obedience to parents, and another box had the American ideal of differentiation and individualism. With her separate boxes she was able to maintain her sanity by knowing which box to inhabit depending on the time, location, or circumstance. I pointed out that she probably expended much energy to mentally maintain these boxes, but she emphasized that it became second nature to her and that it was in fact a part of how she understood herself and interacted with others.

One of the main problems I see in compartmentalization is the illegitimization of the Asian culture. While compartmentalization allows for both cultures to exist, it is at the high price of subordinating the Asian culture to the white culture. Even if the means to achievement are often viewed as a product of the Asian drive and work ethic, the standards of success are still perpetuated by Anglo-American culture. To some extent I understand the need for this type of life response, holding up the tension between the desire to invest in both cultures and the desire to maintain a distinction between the two experiences. The surrounding dominant culture is undoubtedly powerful, and because it is necessary to engage in order to function successfully within it, many want to identify with it more.

Still, many Asian Americans find themselves influenced by their heritage or the particular Asian culture passed on to them specifically by their parents and immediate families. The families are the groups where one finds commonality and a sense of belonging, so Asian Americans may seek to uphold the Asian culture to honor their families and maintain communication with them. Sometimes, at another point, Asian Americans will find themselves identifying more so with the Asian culture. Kim writes, "The Asian American search for ways to articulate the emerging Asian American identity involved trying to identify with Asian cultures. But, the result, for the most part, has been confusion and disappointment."[3] To counter this confusion and disappointment, Asian Americans might compartmentalize not only the actual groups of people but also these expectations, and even these emotions. These external cultural forces cause them to vacillate between trying to establish identity in one group or the other, but the communities do not necessarily embrace them with open arms and solidify this sense of belonging. Neither world is accommodating in terms of identification or full acceptance.[4]

Yet another response often materializes as the phenomenon of assimilation. I define assimilation as being subsumed into a specific culture, normally the dominant culture, so that one finds ultimate identification there. This manifests itself as an alternative to compartmentalization because it maintains the illusory notion of a life without inner conflict or confrontation. This response allows the Asian American to feel he or she has chosen such a life, and though it feels like a simplifying measure, it feels absolute or final. This phenomenon is not so simple. Asian Americans who are assimilated into the dominant culture might be identified by their Asian counterparts as "white-washed," "twinkies," or "bananas," because they are viewed as "yellow on the outside, but white on the inside." The desire of assimilation is acceptance by the dominant culture, which is often a motivating factor for this choice, but acceptance needs to occur on a number of different levels.

First, the Asian American is required to accept certain tenets from the dominant culture. Kim writes, "One of the most powerful effects of white supremacism on Asian Americans, according to many Asian American writers, has been their acceptance of the view of themselves presented by their detractors."[5] Acceptance of this external view is normally based on the stereotype of the Asian American as being a "foreigner" or "minority," and certainly not "American." This means accepting certain Asian cultural elements as foreign, and thus necessarily rejectable. This acceptance is a necessary part of reception into Anglo-American culture, and thus a part of the Asian American's effort in assimilation. Once the individual subordinates himself or herself to these external views, assimilation becomes an easier choice. Asian Americans do experience some sense of personal acceptance in their adoption of these views and rejection of their heritage. For instance, Asian Americans are forced to accept Anglo-American standards of value and beauty even if this means rejecting the "Asian" look.[6]

What happens in reality is that Asian Americans become alienated from the dominant culture because they have simply perpetuated these external views of foreignness by accepting the view of themselves as foreign. In accepting these standards they have rejected themselves. They end up excluding others who do not look like or are not in this homogeneous community. Furthermore, they are ostracized from the Asian community because they are seen as people who have aligned themselves with another culture because they have denied the validity of Asian culture and values. Often, Asian Americans who have chosen assimilation are viewed with contempt because they appear to have "sold-out" their culture by propagating the dominant Anglo cultural standard.

Assimilation is often tempered by conflicting obligations and is not an easy route for many Asian Americans. Kim writes "Auto-biographical writing by second-generation Asian Americans such as Pardee Lowe, Jade Snow Wong, and Monica Sone are important documents of individual responses to the social contexts of all Asian Americans and of individual attempts to win acceptance and under-standing of certain segments of the group. It would be misleading to conclude, however, that the self-contempt and euphemization that generally characterizes them were in fact the most typical responses among Asians in the United States to social segregation and race discrimination."[7] Again, immediate family and the Asian commu-nity have played an influential role in the development of the Asian American identity. "Even among American-born Chinese, rejection of the Chinese American community, romanticization of their Chi-nese heritage, and the desire to 'disappear' by being fully assimilated into larger society have always been complemented by an attitude of rebellion against oppression and by expression of a need for pres-ervation of cultural integrity within the American context."[8] Hence Asian Americans are normally unable to purely experience the kind of assimilation that is often idealized in their minds. "By far the most common response among American-born Asians to the discrepancy between their aspirations and the realities that confront them intensi-fied identification with their own ethnic communities in the United States."[9]

Many Asian Americans have become aware of the deeper con-sequences of this assimilation. Kim writes further, "In recent years, Chinese and Japanese Americans have expressed intense resentment that they had been encouraged to emulate Anglo-Americans as their superiors or to objectify their racial heritages into exotic jokes for the benefit of Anglo-American ethnocentrism."[10] Even though the "option of 'assimilation' is in fact 'cultural genocide'"[11] and threatens to strip Asian Americans of their true past while preventing them at the same time from full and equal participation in the present, the deeper, more powerful desire is authentic recognition, a sense of belonging and connection with others, especially with those who are in power and set the standards. They will achieve this acceptance no matter the price. One Chinese American youth writes that he learned as an elementary school pupil that crying or becoming angry never won acceptance from the other children, but self-denigration would win them over.[12] Again, acceptance was won at the cost of personal dignity. Likewise, Asian Americans found acceptance from Anglos through an appeal to their interest in "exotic" Asian foods, customs, or artifacts, which would serve as nonthreatening, quaint objects of curiosity.[13] Thus elements of the Asian culture become another form of objectification that is easily manipulated so as to be marketable to the approval of the dominant culture. The question remains whether or not what is sacrificed for the sake of this assimilation is worth the illusory acknowledgment of the dominant culture.

These two responses to the general social contexts are attempts to navigate between two different worlds. Whatever the response, the cost is great and the separate demands are difficult to reconcile within the person. The attempt to maintain one's identity psychologically, emotionally, and spiritually in these ways is bound to take its toll on any human being. With no easy solution in sight, and sometimes not even a way to articulate the struggle, the transforming and liberating power of "naming" and acknowledging it is hopefully a beginning step, particularly in the Christian-faith context.

Asian American Feminism:
Warrior Lessons of Rage and Resistance

Before I went to college, the older congregants of my home church warned against taking too many "liberal" courses, particularly those of the Women's Studies department. They were afraid I would somehow be contaminated by flaming leftist notions about women's liberation because then I would refuse to do my duty in the kitchen and I would forget my place in the home or society. Anyway, this was silly because I was terribly inept at a number of the domestic skills, so both the kitchen and the expected female role were obsolete. But I remember avoiding these classes and viewing the department with a sort of desperate fascination. I sensed that these classes held a key that would unlock important doors to my own identity and relationships.

For Asian American feminists, what becomes necessary at the very least for survival and progress in these social contexts is the ability to voice the particular injustice of the cultural oppression and imperialism over Asian American women. Although the endeavors of feminist theory are often found to be in opposition to some of the deeply entrenched patriarchal elements of most Asian communities in the Unites States, more and more Asian American women, particularly those of the second generation or those educated in the United States, are open to exploring the possibly transformative power of feminist thought.

One Asian American woman, Pandora Leong, writes,

> I embraced feminism because it fought the attitude that women were born to please men. Asian women also fight a racial characterization that further entrenches these archaic assumptions about sex . . . As an Asian woman today, I find myself in the same struggle.[14]

Feminism is associated with Anglo, upper-class, educated women, so Asian American women seem to want to adopt a feminism particular to their own experience as evinced in the radical writings and performances of contemporary Asian American women. Leong writes:

> However, my experience suggests that within the subculture of Asian women, I am also fighting a cultural consciousness that favors a duty to society over the spirit of independence. Individualism may have been a Western male value, but at least it was a Western value. White feminists only had to democratize it; as an Asian feminist, I must introduce it. Asian society places a premium on social order and the advancement of the community.[15]

Thus an Asian American feminism must counter two levels of patriarchy by giving voice to individual experience, which is crucial to this development. In one sphere, Asian American feminists must fight to legitimate this struggle, but in another, they must simply fight for the right to have a voice. A "white feminism" is simply not enough to speak to this experience.

Many Asian American women are a part of creating a new type of feminism, one that is consistent with the pursuit of critiquing the individual and collective thought processes and institutions that prevent the flourishing of women.[16] Creating our own definitions can take a lifetime. Leong became a feminist because of how others would view her. She became an activist because she wanted to change how she was treated as a result of those gazes: "Feminists come in every flavor; we are not just vanilla anymore, if we ever were . . . I began describing myself as a feminist because it gave voice to my anger at the treatment of women in society."[17] Leong's feminist views are rooted in the tangible experience of the sociopolitical world through her activism. Though it is distinctly her views and experience–that is, an Asian American perspective–she feels it is relevant and gives voice to the injustices toward all women.

> When I invoked feminism, my political positions were at the fore rather than obscured within the boxes in which people thought my body belonged. Feminism tempered the power of society to label me, or at least interjected my own terms into the debate.[18]

Feminism provided her the space in which she would be able to engage issues that were important to her as a unique human being, and specifically as an Asian American woman.

Vickie Nam's anthology of stories by young Asian American women has a section titled "Dolly Rage," in which women express their frustrations toward their constant association with the stereotypical fragile porcelain doll. They experience anger at the power of these stereotypes as evinced in the model minority student, the china doll, and the subservient massage parlor girl that gloss over the unique painful realities of our marginalization.[19] What is remarkable is the wide diversity of voices. In *Making Waves*, the editors write, "It would be inaccurate to talk about a homogenous Asian American community when discussing class, education, national origin, economic status, or the potential for economic mobility."[20] Accordingly, a second effort of the development in Asian American feminism is to broaden the space to accommodate the wide array of women and their unique perspectives and experiences. It provides a space for the formation of community necessary for the development of Asian American feminism. Elaine Kim writes, "The links Asian American women cannot establish with their men they seek with one another."[21] Again, this is seen in new writings that reflect these new efforts in which women are seeking to be identified with one another rather than finding their identities in their association with men. Motivated by the sense that there exist few adequate portrayals of Asian American women in American literature, Asian American women writers have been attempting to depict the uniqueness and diversity of that experience as an integral part of the American and Asian American tradition,[22] as shown especially in these lines from a performance in 1979 at an art museum:

Woman Warrior

We are unbinding our feet
We are women who write
We are women who work
We are women who love
Our presence in this world[23]

These works are unveiling the specificities of not only the Asian American experience but also the Asian American woman's experience. Likewise, Kim describes Maxine Hong Kingston's *The Woman Warrior,* a story about a Chinese American woman's attempt to come to terms with the paradoxes that shape and often enrich her life so as to find a distinctly Chinese American voice to serve as a weapon for her life. The little girl narrating the story sees double almost all the time. "She has two vantage points, and the images are blurred. Continually confronted with dualities, contradictions, and paradoxes, she struggles to discern 'what is real' from what is illusory by asking questions, trying to name the unnamed, and 'speaking the unspeakable.'"[24] The narrator fights against the haunting possibility of the "antiself, an alter ego, another Chinese American girl who represents the fragility and softness of the victim as opposed to the survivor . . . the narrator imagines herself stomping on the other girl's imagined bound feet with iron shoes, forcing her to speak."[25] In this projection, through her voice and iron shoes she is resisting the power of an oppressive silence.

Contemporary Asian American writers are experimenting with new language, new combinations of forms and genres that they say best express their particular perspectves and experiences...Certain images and characters do recur in contemporary Asian American literature: Chinese American writing is filled with images of trains and journeys, images that express the Chinese American heritage of railroad building and of searching for a place in American society. In Japanese American literature, images of the desert recur, usually when the internment experience is depicted. Women who rebel against the strictures of racism and sexism are frequent, as are the grim and resilient old men whose silent strength is expressed in their lean and spare dialogue.[26]

Thus the social history and this radical new form of expression of Asian American peoples, particularly women, contribute to the creation of a specific Asian American feminism. It provides substance in which new images can be appropriated to symbolize in visceral ways the struggle Asian American women experience. Here, the emphasis is on encouraging the creation of these particular stories and allowing that endeavor to shape this new type of feminism. It is in the development of these stories and a new feminism that Asian American women will be able to find pride in themselves.

> It is okay to be somewhere in between–to be a so-called Asian American. We grow up being taught that all men are created equal. We are told not to worry because that statement implicitly includes us. We begin to wonder if Asians or women deserve more than they have received in the form of a few meager pages and minor footnotes in American history. We fail to take pride in our predecessors' contributions. We feel neglected in this melting-pot nation. We almost melt away. We then try to be "Asian" instead. We fail. We remember that some great white man once said that all men are created equal. We want to be men but cannot. We feel condemned as the non-Asian, non-American race and the nonimportant gender. We are confused, until we learn that there is a term that describes who we are–*Asian American women.* We like it. We find comfort in each other. We find pride. We find the term *Asian American women* more in the American history we are making.[27]

The constant creation of new Asian American literature expresses the passionate emotions of a feminist movement toward a space for freedom and renewal. "The anguished battle cry of many racial minorities against racism was a rejection of the notion of assimilation into what they viewed as the spiritual bankruptcy, cultural sterility, imperialism, materialism, and racial self-denial of the Anglo-American ideal."[28] "The rage of contemporary Asian American poets against racism and oppression emerges not only as a rejection of old stereotypes but also as a celebration of a new, self-determined identity, of new heroes and heroines whose first task is to speak the unspeakable and to reverse attempts to destroy Asian

American culture and identity, both by fighting injustice now recognized and admitted and by reaching out to one another in love and communion."[29] "The anger expressed in the new Asian American literature is not the anger of alienation. It is a fierce urge towards affirmation, unity, and community."[30] Asian Americans are realizing the common bonds shared by all Asian American groups.

Rashmi Luthra explores

> the methodologies of cultural resistance being invented by them, and the characteristics of the third spaces being created by them. As filmmakers, photographers, authors, activists, the women work in, through and toward a "differential form of consciousness" as elaborated by Chela Sandoval (2000).[31]

Part of the resistance involves more creative cultural forms invented by women to express a new way of being and engaging the world. She writes further,

> They are located at the interstices, the border, of different social orders, and this location enables the creators to offer third ways, ways of seeing that pierce through debilitating binaries. Both the form and content of their work exhibits a metis or *mestizaje* mode of perceiving and acting (Anzaldua, 1987; Lionnet, 1995), a mode of survival but also a means to liberation.[32]

The image of the intersections, the borders, and generally those spaces on the periphery provide an alternative and equally coherent perspective that dismantles long entrenched perceptions. There is undoubtedly a liberating quality to this kind of resistance. Luthra wraps up her abstract this way: "As Maria Lugones (1996) reminds us, 'If something or someone is neither/nor, but kind of both, not quite either . . . it threatens by its very ambiguity the orderliness of the system, the schematized reality.'"[33] The embrace of this essential occupation of both spaces, of being "both/and," is a venue for imaginative disruption of the system, and it potentially has far-reaching effects not only for Asian American women but for anyone who does not fit so neatly in the system.

Ultimately, Asian American feminism calls women to be active agents, specifically, warriors and not victims.[34] Although the imagery of the woman warrior is not without its flaws, it is an attempt to powerfully eradicate an image that keeps women in these oppressive cultural bindings. It supports Asian American women's efforts to speak out, share stories, and identify with one another. Honestly articulating the stories of Asian American women, whether through art, film, or other media, means pointing out injustices and the power of sin and evil. It compels Asian American women to embrace the humanizing effects of liberation and empowerment; thus this expression is the tool to wield against those who would make these women into passive, silent victims.

In a seminary class, I felt myself awakening to the fight that was beginning to surface within me. It was almost a snowball effect–the more I read and heard, the more I felt the urge to join in the conversation. But I needed an outlet, something different from screaming or crawling into a hole; this came pouring out of my pen after reading Claire S. Chow's *Leaving Deep Waters*:

paper margins

before beginning the lesson on America's story
the teacher called attention to the class
and held up a piece of yellow construction paper
next to the soft underside of her arm
and said, "See, she's not really yellow."

according to the teacher, the white teacher
says this model girl is not really yellow
just similar to yellow they say

this model I suppose for all minorities
so the other minorities end up hating her
she's not a model for the majority
since she sits somewhere in the middle
the very middle of the class
her last name is Lee or Kim
she is always in the middle somewhere
surrounded by people

and yet, inside she feels like no one is familiar
everyone else is foreign
but she knows she is really on the margins
these same notebook paper margins
on which she doodles with a
bright crayola absentmindedly
daydreaming not about paper cranes or ghost tigers

but about Johnny Depp, bicycles with pink streamers
and the Smurfs and the Brady Bunch

when the teacher is reading from
some book about the history of the people around her
something about pilgrims, slavery, wars, the Great
    Depression
it is supposed to be her history, too
but no one looks at her and thinks that
this yellow girl belongs in the same story
this story of America

this not-really-yellow girl is not really anything
and it is worse because not only is she yellow
she is a girl, so that both the yellow and white
and other crayola-colored people tell her
how to be a girl

a girl is this and that
and sometimes it sounds the same
for the yellow girl and the white girl
the brown girl, the black girl
sitting next to her in class but mainly

in this story she hears a girl
is not better than a boy
like when she was born some wished
she was not a girl but a boy
but since you are here anyway, okay

these are the places for the girl:
be in the kitchen, in the garden, at the piano or violin
    and
in front of the washer and dryer, you girl are
a baby-machine, too
did I mention in the kitchen?

not really barefoot because
your feet are in bindings
not just your feet but the world inside you
but then, wait forget the kitchen
until you are married, here in America
you, yellow girl, go to an Ivy League

do math and business
become a doctor or lawyer or engineer

and prove yourself our little
yellow girl, prove to us that you are a model
human being
that you belong in this story of America

This writing was a release, and even more so when I shared it during a presentation at the end of the semester for that same class. It resulted in much more writing, reflecting, and pursuit of dialogue surrounding these issues. There is something incredibly liberating and redeeming in allowing oneself to be completely genuine in front of others. It made my ears and heart more sensitive to the stories of resistance all around me, whether they came out of the mouths of my Asian American brothers and sisters or from my African American counterparts. I hungered for more, and longed to share and pass on more stories.

*   *   *

During a Pacific, Asian, and North American Asian Women in Theology and Ministry (PANAAWTM) conference in 2007, one of the speakers shared stories of "The Rainbow Center," which is located in Flushing, New York. The center originally came about as a response by Korean American Christian women who wanted to help those women who were impacted by marriages to US military personnel while living in Korea. Often they come back to the United States and face unspeakable emotional and physical distress, and even abuse. One woman was actually displaced when she returned to the United States with her husband because he abandoned her as soon as they set foot back in New York. For some reason, she was legally caught between two governments and ended up not having a legitimate citizenship in either country. She could not go back to Korea, and she had no services or help available to her here. So the Rainbow Center was created to offer bilingual support services to women of Korean and other Asian descent in bicultural family crises. Founded in 1993, the organization offers these services to enhance the women's sense of dignity and self-respect and to help end their oppression from sexism, racism, and classism. The Rainbow Center's primary role is to provide a temporary shelter and community for women and children who seek support and professional help. Specific services include a crisis hotline, temporary shelter, legal advocacy and translation, peer support, bilingual group and individual counseling, transportation, job counseling and training, housing facilitation and settlement, volunteer training, an open lunch program, feast and fellowship, reunification of families, and physical and mental health maintenance.

I am heartened by these stories. At a certain level I feel as though a window has opened up so that I can see–looking back to my own life–those moments of resistance initiated by the women around me. I constantly witnessed moments where the women around me were resisting the structures that contained them in tangible ways. Our little Presbyterian church, like many Korean churches, had a Women's Association, a group for women to participate in fellowship and mission within the community. As expected, they headed up anything that had to do with food and fellowship at the church, which meant preparing huge buffet-style meals on the Sundays that were before the special holidays, like Thanksgiving, Christmas, Easter, and Korean Independence Day. These women were equally adept at preparing turkey and *kimchee*, hams and *dduk-mahn-doo* (a beef soup with rice cakes), regular BBQ food and *bul-go-gi* (BBQ beef). The abundance made every occasion incredibly festive. Moms were always piling food on our paper plates even if we had already gone up once or even twice. I see now how their exuberant hospitality was an expression of resistance to me.

I remember one Sunday standing near the doorway to the kitchen as the women were cleaning up and dividing up the food after one lunch. One of the women insisted an older woman who lived alone take some home in a wrapped-up plate. The older woman seemed reluctant to receive the food, like she was ashamed to be taking a handout of some sort; but the woman, who was in a close circle with my mom and reminded me of one of her sisters, kept on pushing the plate covered in tinfoil on her. The older woman finally gave in, and I did catch a little embarrassment but gratitude, too. I do not recollect our church doing much in the way of food pantries or soup kitchens, and probably not a lot of Korean churches were doing that sort of outreach. I do remember these kinds of moments, usually initiated by the women, when someone who was on the periphery of our community was cared for in such a small, but lovely way. I did not recognize the feeling at the time, but I felt happy and inspired by it. A small act of kindness goes a long way, and when witnessed unexpectedly, it is equally moving. It made me see the way compassion and grace are forms of resistance, too, for when hospitality happens even in the midst of oppression and limitation, some barrier is overcome in that moment.

4

A New Flock

Currents from Asian and Asian American Feminist Theology

If I were really asked to define myself, I wouldn't start with race; I wouldn't start with blackness; I wouldn't start with gender; I wouldn't start with feminism. I would start with stripping down to what fundamentally informs my life, which is that I'm a seeker on the path. I think of feminism, and I think of anti-racist struggles as part of it. But where I stand spiritually is, steadfastly, on a path about love.

—BELL HOOKS

Besides the intense light of a sunset or the downpour of stormy rains, flying birds are basically the most hazardous phenomenon to me as a driver on the highway. Certain spots remain empty of any human distraction but are frequented by enormous flocks of birds–perhaps because of the wind and the high perches on top of city signs or in huge corn fields. I'm not part of an Audubon society or birding club, so I can't tell the species, but usually the birds are small and black. At least a few hundred birds at a time fly, hover, swoop, or rest in one place. They always draw my eyes. I rubberneck as if there were some terrible accident on the side of the road. Not unlike in Hitchcock fascination, I am morbidly intrigued by the sight of so many birds congregating in one place and by the way they seem to move together so fluidly, changing directions without appearing to fly into each other,

49

much like a school of fish. Some birds seem to fly easily and confidently, creating the necessary "maneuver waves"—subtle moves that radiate outward to guide the rest of the flock. And then I always notice a few stragglers, those newbies that seem like they're trying out their wings and working to keep up with the rest of the fliers.

They all look so natural and comfortable, at home whether they are roosting on top of a street light or tree or flying in a seemingly random circle to alight on another precarious ledge as the cars fly by underneath them.

I have felt glimpses of those waves in other ways when it comes to life and faith, and they always resonate with me. The recent theological work of Asian and Asian American women scholars has moved me, as I seek to fly into their air streams. Some of these currents articulate something in me that was there all along, and some of the themes expose perspectives and a reality that I did not even know existed in me. In every case though, I believe that the work is not only relevant to my life situation, or to my mother's or future daughter's lives, but also necessary for the life of the whole Church as we seek to maneuver faithfully through this world together. The divine drafts that have most lifted me up are familiar theological tenets: courageous naming, creative forming, cogent reorienting, clarion liberating, and crucial communing.

Courageous Naming: Revelations about God and Self

Revelation is commonly understood as an important theological starting point. But it had little meaning for me growing up, except for the book of Revelation, which I viewed with fearful awe as if it were a horror film. I'd "sneak" reading it. My parents sometimes forced me to attend a Korean revival service, though I didn't understand a single thing that was said or sung during the two-hour ordeal, so to occupy my mind, I'd turn to Revelation and try to decipher the cryptic messages. I thought that something in it would reveal the secret of the end times at the very least, if not the secrets of the universe. Perhaps what drew me to the book was the feeling that there was something superstitious about it. That intrigued me, especially since my parents often shunned such fantastical notions, while paradoxically holding onto them, as they seeped into our conversations anyway through admonitions about not sleeping with my right arm over my eyes because it's bad luck, the meaning of dreams, and how certain herbs or vitamins had miraculous powers. In retrospect, I did get a taste of revelation, as I received many revelations about my parents and what was important to them, even if it was a little crazy.

When I was getting ready to attend seminary, my father gave me a bright blue paperback, Shirley Guthrie's *Christian Doctrine*, saying that reading it would be "a nice way to dip into theology." Guthrie begins almost at the beginning with a section on "general revelation," which he prefaces with these ever-familiar existential questions: Why am I here? Where did I come from? Where am I going? What is the meaning of my life?[1] How we seek out and respond to these questions–that is, the very process of pursuing any semblance of the answers–expresses our religious sensibilities and what we believe about God and how God reveals God's self in the world. In the next section he speaks of "specific revelation" and writes, "The content of revelation is a Person."[2] Much of the chapter is centered on the person of Jesus Christ. The story of our faith is laden with very messy, complex moments throughout history–as my Sunday school teacher would say, "from Bible times" on–but it is undeniably irresistible because it is a story about a God longing to be in relationship with all of humanity. God, unbound by any of our language, is always in free communication with us, inviting us to join God in revealing God's self to the world.

God's revelation inspires all the many names for God, as spoken by kings and prophets, by disciples and followers throughout the Bible. It never ceases to intrigue me that God would have so many facets of personality and character but also so many names. Sometimes God gives us a name for God's self, like "I am," or more often, God responds to names like Shepherd or Deliverer. Both the process of naming and names themselves are incredibly sacred, rooted in acknowledgment and recognition and anchored in community. This is shown by various ceremonies, including the Jewish ceremony when newborns receive their names and baptismal rites in the church when the whole community "names" the infant or adult as "God's beloved."

Naming becomes problematic when it is imposed on another as an oppressive tool or becomes inadequate. Nami Kim challenges traditional perspectives on naming and identity. Her work invites me to examine even the most fundamental parts of this endeavor–namely, the labels. Kim emphasizes how important naming is for one's "personhood, rather than simply being inscribed upon by larger social or cultural forces." Her engagement of "the categorical and representational term 'Asian'" looks at how "it has been used by Christian theologians to describe a theology that aspires to be relevant and liberative to people and their lives in an Asian context."[3] A complex history lies behind the label that is often hyphenated with the familiar label "American." She purports that these terms

> in their current categorical and representational usages in theological discourse are inadequate for a pertinent and liberative feminist theology in the face of increasing forces of globalization that compel us to rethink national borders, citizenship, identity, and community.[4]

Thus the challenge is to find "ways in which feminist theological discourse can use the term 'Asian' without reinscribing the dominant racist, nationalist, and colonialist constructions of 'Asian' identity."[5]

"One of the strategic applications of the term 'Asian' is in its political use by Asian North Americans within the context of the struggle against racist oppression and the dominant usage of *Asian* as a racial, ethnic category."[6] The identity associated with the word *Asian* has social and political connotations. "Acknowledging the danger of using the term *Asian*, Asian [North Americans] have attempted to conceptualize *Asian* not as an already-constituted racial ethnic entity but as a political denominator that binds a group of people together based on the common history of oppression and struggle in the United States as well as struggle against American imperialism in Asia." It behooves those who employ this label to scrutinize this "unified subject of resistance" in terms of the implications of one name for a group that is incredibly diverse.[7]

> Identifying oneself as an Asian feminist theologian means that one is willing to engage in a strategic use of the term *Asian* while simultaneously engaging theology from a feminist perspective. Asian feminist theology then can be claimed and articulated by those who want to participate in an "imagined community" of struggle, not because she or he is seen as Asian because of her or his country of origin or through racial ethnic affiliation, but because she or he is willing to engage in a critical theological discourse that unceasingly challenges the dominant racist, nationalist, and colonial discourse and that simultaneously can provide a theological vision for a better and just world.[8]

The point of the discourse is not to stalemate the issues and silence those involved in the conversation, but to make all of us aware of what naming and labeling can do to people in terms of causes, relationships, and communities, and how it will always have the potential to exclude or alienate others. As Kim has already admonished, the "imagined community" is one that will involve all people who understand the purpose of being a part of a larger vision of the world. This will happen when we truly understand that though God's revelation to the world in Jesus Christ was a word, a label, it was something that signified grace and love, and when we take on the name "Christian" and identify ourselves with Christ, we are called to reveal God's love to others in radical ways.

Creative Forming: Creation and Partnership

Genesis holds the story of creation for Jews and Christians alike. This drama is beautifully methodical and clearly intentional. At the same time, it is often a site of controversy, particularly between science and faith, though even this conversation is experiencing a shift as some seek to find common ground. But the "Christian doctrine of creation does not begin with an analysis of creation itself and try to deduce what the Creator is like."[9] and Creation in itself is not the main point! Creation points to what is central. The Reformed Christian belief does not begin with creation, but rather with the Creator as the doctrine tells us: God is good, God is the Creator therefore, God's creation is good. Our being a part of God's creation, specifically created in the image of God, is significant, especially when it comes to the wonderful realization that we are then also cocreators with God, a tenet I often heard in my seminary classes. This partnership is applicable in many contexts, including the stewardship of our lives and resources, maintaining relationships in community, and literally creating–forming stories, dramas, and perspectives.

This creative forming, and cocreating, occurs at many levels, but it is poignant when it comes to reading the familiar stories of the Bible. I am particularly struck by Gale Yee's reading of the Book of Ruth. She writes,

> Ruth has captured the attention of many scholars interested in feminist and multicultural interpretations of the text. The book conjoins issues of gender, sexuality, race/ethnicity, immigration, nationality, assimilation, and class

in tantalizing ways that allow different folk to read their own stories in into the multivalent narratives of Ruth and Naomi.[10]

The basic story goes as follows: During the time of the Judges when there was a famine, an Israelite family from Bethlehem–Elimelech, his wife Naomi, and their sons Mahlon and Chilion–immigrate to the nearby country of Moab. Elimelech dies, and the sons marry two Moabite women: Mahlon marries Ruth, and Chilion marries Orpah. The two sons of Naomi then die. Naomi decides to return to Bethlehem. She tells her daughters-in-law to return to their own mothers and remarry. Orpah reluctantly leaves; however, Ruth says,

> Entreat me not to leave you, Or to turn back from follow-
> ing you; For wherever you go, I will go; And wherever you
> lodge, I will lodge; Your people shall be my people, And
> your God, my God. Where you die, I will die, And there
> will I be buried. The LORD do so to me, and more also, If
> anything but death parts you and me." (Ruth 1:16–17 *NKJV*)

The two women return to Bethlehem. It is the time of the barley harvest. To support her mother-in-law and herself, Ruth goes to the fields to glean. The field she goes to belongs to a man named Boaz, who is kind to her because he has heard of her loyalty to her mother-in-law. Ruth tells her mother-in-law of Boaz's kindness and continues to glean in his field through the remainder of the harvest season.

Boaz is a close relative of Naomi's husband's family. He is there-fore obliged by the levirate law to marry Mahlon's widow, Ruth, to carry on his family line. Naomi sends Ruth to the threshing floor at night and tells her to "uncover the feet" of the sleeping Boaz. Ruth does so, Boaz awakes, and Ruth reminds him that he is "the one with the right to redeem." Boaz states he is willing to "redeem" Ruth via marriage, but informs Ruth that there is another male relative who has the first right of redemption.

The next morning, Boaz discusses the issue with the other male relative before the town elders. The other male relative is unwilling to jeopardize the inheritance of his own estate by marrying Ruth and so relinquishes his right of redemption, thus allowing Boaz to marry Ruth.

Boaz and Ruth get married and have a son named Obed (who by levirate customs is also considered a son or heir to Mahlon, and thus Naomi's grandson). The genealogy that concludes the story points out that Obed is the descendant of Perez, the son of Judah, and the grandfather of David.

According to Yee,

> the book of Ruth utilizes two words to describe foreigners: *ger* and *nokriyah*. A *ger* is a foreigner who has immigrated into and taken up residence in a society in which she or he has neither familial nor tribal associations . . . the text implies Ruth is a *ger*.[11]

Yet what is interesting is the shift in identity Ruth experiences in her interaction with Boaz. For some reason, she calls herself a *nokriyah*, another word for foreigner, but one that "is generally negative highlighting the person's otherness and separateness from the dominant culture . . . [This] is particularly underscored by the fact that Ruth was a Moabite, one of Israel's traditional hated enemies."[12] Though the "impartial" narrator hints at Ruth being a *ger*, Ruth describes and labels herself as otherwise. Interestingly enough, the negative connotations of Ruth's foreignness are not completely erased in the book.[13]

Yee connects one aspect of Asian American experience, the model minority myth, to the story of Ruth. Ruth evinces the characteristics of the model minority, by highlighting the fact that

> the deeper the enmity between Moab and Israel, the greater the valor in Ruth's resolve to embrace the latter and its God. Her rejection of Moab and its negative links with Israel transforms her into the Jewish convert par excellence.[14]

Indeed, Ruth is not only the model convert but also an exemplar for the Jewish people. Yee quotes LaCocque, who writes,

> Ruth's heroism is to become more of a Judean than those who are Judean by birth! Retrospectively one can say that her fidelity toward the people and their God provides a lesson to those who should have been her teachers.[15]

Yee observes further:

> The construction of Ruth as the model émigré is similar to the model-minority stereotype of Asian Americans. Ruth is held up for propagandistic purposes, either to expunge any contamination of Moabite descent for David or to critique Ezra's and Nehemiah's policies against intermarriage. She

thus reveals what a virtuous foreigner can teach the nation. As model minorities, Asian Americans supposedly exemplify traditional values, such as respect for elders, industry and hard work, and family loyalty. Similarly, Ruth incarnates the quality of *hesed* in her overwhelming devotion to her mother-in-law; in her willingness to support her by diligently gleaning in a strange man's field . . . and in her conversion to another God. As Ruth the Moabite teaches Judeans the meaning of *hesed*, Asian Americans educate others on how to be "good" minorities who know their place in a white society . . . Ruth's disappearance in chapter 4 after the birth of her son leads one to question whether Ruth has been successfully assimilated as a foreigner into Judean society or ultimately abandoned once she preserves the male lineage.[16]

We hear some incredibly familiar overtones here concerning the Asian American experience of silence and invisibility and of general acceptance by the dominant cultures at great expense. Yee also looks at the flip side of the model minority stereotype, which is the perpetual foreigner syndrome: "Just as Asian Americans are consistently perceived as being more Asian than American by the dominant white society, so is Ruth continually called Ruth the Moabite, rather than Israelite, even after her immigration."[17] "Issues of class, especially as they intersect with ethnicity and gender in Ruth"[18] are part of an analysis by Roland Boer that Yee calls perceptive. "The economic gulf between Boaz, as owner of the land, and Ruth as foreign gleaner of the land's leftovers is wide."[19]

The character of Ruth in this biblical narrative contains numerous dimensions and wonderful tensions. She is not simply a passive damsel-in-distress, who in fairy-tale fashion meets her knight-in-shining-armor only to be swept away to a new life. Yee concludes, "On the one hand, the book of Ruth is a (fairy) tale about a devoted widow who rejects her homeland and her idols to accompany her mother-in-law to a new country. In this scenario Ruth becomes a model émigré (*ger*) who teaches the Chosen People the true meaning of God's covenantal *hesed*."[20] What an eye-opener: to imagine that the word most associated with God in terms of love, dedication, and faithfulness could be represented by a foreign woman! Still, that position is not without its complications and costs. "Ruth is also the perpetual foreigner–a *nokriyah*–whose consistent label of *Moabite* implies that she, like the Asian American in the United States, is not fully assimilated in the text's consciousness of what it means to be Israelite . . . Ruth's story becomes an indictment against those of us who live in the first world and exploit all those who come to the first world."[21] But Yee's biblical reading is an offer to all of us to see in new ways and to partner with others in formulating and creating new narratives and significantly important interpretations that involve all of humanity.

Cogent Reorienting: Incarnation and Bodily Experience

Central to Christian doctrine is the person of Jesus Christ, God's ultimate revelation to the world and the fullest expression of humanity. In John's gospel, we read, "And the Word became flesh and lived among us" (John 1:14). Guthrie writes, "In this real flesh-and-blood man, Jesus of Nazareth, God was uniquely present in the world."[22] God walked around on Earth a little more than two thousand years ago, and his name was Jesus. Growing up, trying to understand the incarnation of God in Jesus Christ, God-with-Us, fully human and fully divine, was like trying to hold onto a slippery fish. The math just didn't add up–100 percent and 100 percent? Whenever we had youth group, our youth pastor would lead us to pray to Jesus, and when we were in our separate worship services led by the sweet and very traditional, Anglo American wife of the former pastor, we'd often pray to God. Somehow they felt different. They had different characteristics from each other, as if they were siblings or cousins. I saw a family resemblance in them, but they played different sports or, like twins, were similar but pursued different hobbies.

Sometimes, when I would sit in church with my parents I'd hear the scattered chanting of the older ladies of the church. During the people's prayers in response to the minister, the ladies would chant *Ye-Su*, the Korean word for Jesus. Their chants sounded like pleas, but the emotion and the strain in their voices, unfamiliar to me, somehow made him seem more tangible, like he was in the room. As I grew older, it became increasingly impressed upon me that I should pursue a relationship with Jesus, just like any relationship with family members or friends. I finally got it, I think, in high school. I got something, and it was unexplainable and still didn't make a whole lot of sense, but it was undeniable. I felt his presence when I prayed and read my Bible in the mornings. It was warm, like an embrace, and left an ache in my heart. In those moments, I had no doubt that God was real and that Jesus was with me.

While those sensations do not come now as often or as intensely, one of the things that impacts me the most about the incarnation is

the reassurance that when Jesus was on Earth, he was very much
a human being, he had a family and friends, he suffered thirst and
hunger, and much more. He also simply had a story.

Rita Nakashima Brock poignantly shares bits of her story using
the familiar metaphors of food and body imagery:

> My identity resembles my mother's eclectic meals, a fusion
> of ingredients annealed by the fires of growing up on three
> continents as a Japanese, mixed-race woman and a liberal
> Protestant educated in the second half of the century in
> U.S. schools. This cross-cultural process has resulted in
> a consciousness I call "interstitial integrity." Integration
> brings many diverse parts together, the way a collection
> of ingredients finally makes a dish. Integrity is how we
> know ourselves and make choices that sustain our values
> in relationship with others. It is a complex, evolving pro-
> cess over time, captured in moments of self-awareness
> and self-acceptance–brief interludes of consciousness that
> appear within the tossing turbulence of many people and
> places. "Interstitial" comes from *interstitium* and is used in
> biology to describe tissue situated in vital organs. The tis-
> sue is not organ tissue, but, rather, it connects the organs to
> one another. It lives inside things, distinct but inseparable
> from what would otherwise be disconnected . . . It is how I
> mix a life together from myriads of ingredients.[23]

Her body and life is the site of many processes and has resulted
in a compelling phrase, "interstitial integrity," that describes the
complex pieces of her history and how they have resulted in an
organic mix of various factors, influences, decisions, and relationships. She writes further about her own agency in coming to terms
with and accepting herself and in constructing her life as a mixed-
race, Asian North American woman:

> The United States prefers its citizens to be pure racial types
> and monolingual people who can be categorized easily
> as friend or foe, elect or damned, patriot or terrorist. This
> emphasis on purity is deeply embedded in the founding
> myths of the society. It continues to structure relation-
> ships in the larger culture racially, religiously, and sexually.
> In understanding that I have an American identity and

citizenship, I have sought to take responsibility for the ambi-
guities of this identity.[24]

Her embrace of the various intersections in her life has led her to
confront the problematic ideal of "pure" races and groups of people
and to speak to the reality of the resulting consequences that come
from upholding something that is not genuine. In seeing the ambi-
guities in her own identity, she is able to accept the same in others.
These worlds are a necessary part of her humanity. She writes,

> I would have to learn to live in the interstices of several
> worlds, to live with several worlds inside me, not simply one
> or even two, while struggling to make a life neither totally
> within nor totally outside these worlds.[25]

Like Jesus, who operated and lived within various layers of
identity while exemplifying the possibility of a new kind of humanity, Brock emphasizes that navigating these assorted worlds and
expectations is also a part of human nature. Specifically, for Asian
Americans:

> This system of layers—of identities claimed and denied, of old
> conflicts sublimated and transplanted, and of hybrid forms
> integrated interstitially—characterizes the development of
> an American identity from Asians and their descendants.
> It is the story of race and immigration on North American
> soil . . . Interstitial integrity more accurately describes how
> human beings construct a self in any culture. We draw life
> from every relationship in our lives. We are imprinted with
> the voices that give us language, the emotional inflections
> and words by which we identify feelings, the body rhythms
> we enact, the ways we examine the world and interact with
> it, and the knowledge that we come to make our own . . . We
> are constituted by these complex relationships to the world
> as we internalize them.[26]

This is the other piece to Jesus' humanity: the reality that our relationships are not simply external to our lives, but that they inhabit us
internally in the ways they shape us, give us identity and an ethic for
making decisions, and shape our emotional response to the reality
around us. To be made aware of this requires an acknowledgement
of Jesus' incarnation as manifested as "interstitial integrity," and our
own. But interstitial integrity helps us to be attuned to the fullness

of life, to appreciate its many pleasures, and to participate in its ever-changing rhythms and patterns, rather than to be starved by unrealized hopes or a thin nostalgic past.[27]

Of course, interstitial integrity is a work in progress and needs constant attention and dialogue, particularly with oneself:

> My self is a constant conversation . . . I am as much the traces of Japanese grammar, which shaped my first fluency in language, and the cultural sensibilities of my first caregivers as I am my education in US military schools and liberal higher education.[28]

No doubt some painful pieces have to be held up as well. Some worlds are not easy or simple, and some cause a great deal of agony. Perhaps they are even locked away, but we can be in this world in various ways. More opportunities avail themselves to us when we see their presence within us. We can certainly find comfort and reassurance that we are not alone in this struggle, and that there is even a divine element in this human experience, as exemplified by Jesus, both fully human and divine.

Clarion Liberating: Counternarratives and Redemption

As a young person, I attended youth group retreats, at which I had experiences that were similar to the revival meetings the adults had once a year at the church. There was intense preaching, plenty of singing, and a lot of crying. Of course, in addition the youth had crazy games and skits, which I imagine our parents would have enjoyed as well, if they had not been trying so hard to keep up appearances. It's interesting to think we had those occasions in common with them, particularly the service on the last night of youth group retreat that included something like an altar call, sprinkled with a lot of prayer, with nearly everyone in the room. It was both strangely therapeutic and cleansing, and also freeing. For the adults and youth, these revivals focused our identity as Christians being rooted in God. In other words, we are made complete and whole, we are accepted, we are *justified*, we are made "right" with God through God's salvific initiative.

Guthrie talks about justification in a simple, convicting way. I can almost hear my old Young Life leader explain it in this way, too: "You cannot justify yourself. That was the first point. The doctrine of justification is first of all a call to give up. Surrender. Stop trying to be something you are not."[29] You can give up attempts to be holy/

sufficient/clean/accepted/sinless, because they are unnecessary. Only God can do this work, and God does it. These words are also incredibly freeing to think–despite what my parents, the world, the church, and even the tenets of faith expect of me, I don't need to bother trying to do it all, at least not for the sake of winning God's love, because God already did everything that was necessary for me. God's grace is a gift (Rom. 3:24). God's free grace–God's justification–is truly a simple concept, and yet for some reason, it has become so complicated in my life, and I know I'm not the only one who feels this way.

The truth of God's unconditional love is one that often gets swallowed up by material and cultural expectations. But Anne Dondapati Allen offers a compelling description of acceptance and justification from the context of Indian Christian theology in terms of the identity of women and the issue of sexuality. She gives a thorough background to the religious sensibilities of the people and its effect on the image of women. From a culture that gave the world the Kamasutra, the erotic architecture of the Ajanta and Ellora caves, and the seductive undulations of the Bharatanatyam and Kuchipudi dances, the term "de-eroticized Indian woman" seems a contradiction.[30] For centuries the Indian woman epitomized sexuality and sex. Allen writes, though, that

> the unconquered body of the chaste Hindu woman was the ground on which the redemptive story would be constructed. Out of the ashes of a people who were conquered and a culture that was violated would rise a nation that was wounded but not obliterated, sullied and yet impenetrable to the onslaught of an alien civilization, bruised but resilient–endowed with the image of Mother India. By acknowledging the fallenness of the nation, the nationalists achieved two significant goals: (1) they glorified the insurmountable, indomitable spirit of the nation, Mother India, in spite of the degeneration of the culture; and thereby, they solidified the perception of a cohesive, continuous, and glorious past; and (2) they issued a challenge to men and women to restore Mother India to its past glory.[31]

The people of India reappropriated the image and body of the woman and recast it as a unifying source for all Indians, that is, one that would inspire the people to a resurrection of their culture and people. Allen observes,

A more notable outcome was the unquestioning acceptance . . . If the Indian Hindu woman was constructed
as the salvific figure for burgeoning nationalism, and her
chaste body was the source for bringing forth a new India,
the task of prescribing approved codes of conduct would be
legitimate.[32]

For the sake of unity and the creation of a new, glorious India, it
was necessary to change the image of the Indian Hindu woman; "in
other words, women would become the sacred sacrificial object to
compensate for the inadequacy of the Indian male."[33] The Indian
woman would be subjected to physical and moral oppression so that
India would be birthed anew.

The consequences of such a limited perspective were far-reaching
for the women. Perhaps it would be akin to the tension between the
Virgin Mary and Mary Magdalene–a chaste, sacred, feminine image
versus a sexual and impure image of a woman. The significance here
is that the Indian Hindu woman found herself caught in between
these two unrealistic ideals. Once again the issue manifested itself in
terms of sexuality,

Indian cultural contexts acknowledge female sexuality and
desire, but they are described and valued to fit the agenda of
patriarchal structures . . . Sexual desire in women, although
found in religious beliefs, proverbs, folklore, and the subversive ways women claim their desire, is, nonetheless
viewed as an abject condition. It is characterized as inferior,
irreversible, and destructive.[34]

These views impact Indian women deeply, touching on issues of
their personhood, agency, and basic dignity. Furthermore, these

views allow the society to regulate, discipline, and nor-
malize all life stages of women to curb the condition. The
hierarchical and negative construction of female sexual
desire thus validates families, society and religion as systems of control . . . Outside motherhood [sexual intimacy]
is an amoral, obscene act.[35]

Thus women only found acceptance within these parameters set
by religious systems, and they were limited in experiencing a fullness of life. Yet, Allen writes, there were ways in which these women

nevertheless resisted the system and sought to embrace their worth at all levels.

> Subversion is a process by which disenfranchised groups surmount systemic oppression through subtlety by appropriating resources from within their cultures and faith traditions. Women subvert the constrictions of nationalist gender norms both by creating counternarratives and by using gender norms to appear conformist while becoming agents of power outside women's traditional confinement to home and motherhood. A.K. Ramanujan suggests that tales centered around and told by women provide a venue for expressing beliefs and customs contrary to those found in Hindu classics, allowing women to rid themselves of the societal shackles, if only in imagination. This countersystem is crucial to the survival of women within an otherwise physically restrictive, emotionally stifling, and spiritually repressive world.[36]

Though these counternarratives did not directly seek to overturn the identity restrictions of the women, they created cracks in the system from within the system. The countersystem was a powerful mode of resistance for these women, imaginative rather than physical, but still pragmatic and tangible. Allen describes the way this countersystem was passed on and transmitted through the community from woman to woman:

> Oral traditions, particularly folk songs, provide another example of subversion . . . For instance "Rajasthani folk culture, transmitted in women's songs and stories, supplies many images of females that are simultaneously seductive and fertile, erotic and domestic, and positive . . . This lore gives an impression of women as sexually playful and exuberant, taking pleasure in their own bodies and celebrating their bodies' capacities both for erotic engagement and for painful but fruitful birth giving." [Raheja and Gold] These lighthearted songs seem to undermine the existing values systems . . . Women's songs are remarkable in their ability to move between the realities of their social circumstances and their created fantasy worlds without much tension . . . The abjection of sexual desire within social gender hierarchies is subverted as the women's fantasies take flight within artistic

expression . . . Countersystems exist as a powerful media
for communicating the unresolved conflicts giving voice
to emotions, desires, and fantasies that subvert the social
order without posing a tangible threat . . . Some resource-
ful women have subverted the teachings of their religious
communities and have used their traditions to give voice to
their agency.[37]

Countersystems are subversively redemptive tools that effect
liberation for these women. The beauty in these countersystems is
that liberation manifested itself in the ordinary and mundane humming and chanting and in the songs sung during everyday work.
The result is the ability for these women to occupy the dichotomous
realities and move fluidly and naturally between them. That space
between offers a refuge for women to create a new reality. More
importantly, these modes of resistance impact those stubbornly
entrenched hierarchies by leveling them out. In Indian Christian
theology, this equity–in economic terms as well as social and political–is a pertinent issue as Christianity was often associated with
the high caste and measures of one's economic station and upward
mobility.

Propriety, constraint, and chastity were established as a
measure of respectability for women . . . Indian Christian
theology that arose in the nineteenth century in response to
neo-Hinduism was mainly the work of high-caste converts
to Christianity. In the hands of the Christian elite, theology
advanced the interests of their caste communities. Hence it
was guilty of maintaining oppressive gender norms as well
as perpetuating caste structure. By excluding the voices of
the oppressed and marginalized majority, Indian Christian
theology became an instrument of "co-option" rather than
"human liberation."[38]

Christianity maintained the status quo, particularly for women.
Those who saw the problematic characteristics of replacing one religious system with another sought to challenge Christian theology
for more redemptive structures. Allen writes, "The key is to find
liberative resources within one's traditions that understand the full
humanity of all people."[39]

In this case, resources are available to Christian women in the
non-Christian cultural expressions, even if it may not be encouraged
by those in authority or by those who uphold tradition. The point

is that the countersystem, the subversion of the status quo systems is available.

> This is particularly true for Christian women in India, who are in dire need of a message that is transformative and liberative. To be human embodiments of the Christ, we must all love others as gifts of joy and pleasure . . . In a redeemed state, adult love is lived out in mutuality and in the company of equals . . . For Indian Christians our struggle must be to understand how this liberating truth may be both a counternarrative drawn from India's cultural traditions and a new, liberating truth drawn from our faith.[40]

Allen's conclusion is that the truth of God's love needs to be lived out in all people as a total and holistic acceptance–a justification that is not rooted in the oppressive structures of Christianity or Indian culture. But a full out rejection of both is not the answer. Rather, it is in the interplay between the two traditions, which provides possibilities for new experiences of redemption. The challenge is to create a space for the life-giving words of grace found in both Christianity and in Indian culture, and to allow that grace to shape all lives.

Crucial Communing: Compassion and Church

It is difficult to imagine what it would have been like for me and my family to live in the United States had we not had our church family. I could sense my parents' loneliness from time to time. Though my mother had one sister and family who lived in the same small town that we lived in, anytime we went out to the grocery store or to a choir concert, I could see how displaced my parents felt among the people, and sometimes I could even feel an ache in my own body, too. Thankfully, though, we did belong to a local Korean church. There is no doubt in my mind that the community was vastly important for my parents' faith, as well as my own development. My father experienced his call to ministry while there, and my brother and I received a foundation for our faith that we would not have been able to find had we not gone to church at all. The community was not just about what we learned from the Bible and faith, or even about the feeling of family and belonging. Something bigger was definitely happening every time we gathered together.

Again, Guthrie provides some practical descriptions, saying that the church is a community of people who *know* they are sinners, a community of *dissatisfied sinners*, and a community where all are gathered in the name of Jesus Christ.[41] In other words, it is a place that exemplifies a unique kind of community, where everything seems a little upside down and different from the world outside. We have a particular governing structure that is manifested in various ways in different churches. In each case, Jesus is viewed as the head, as we are the body of Christ (1 Cor. 12:27). We have a purpose and mission that has to do with the care of the immediate community within the church as well as a responsibility to the people around us. We experience and enact rituals within the walls of the church that have to do with Jesus' last supper and baptism as found in the gospels. Finally, we believe that we are a part of something that is much greater than any of the single churches, and we celebrate it. Of course, there's much more, but these are some of the familiar essentials of being the Church.

Still in many ways the Church, specifically the people or the leaders, has "failed" in its purpose and mission in more than one way. At the end of the anthology, Boyung Lee writes about her own experience with community in terms of her educational process and the significant role her mother played not only in teaching her to cook but also in helping her learn to teach and to be a part of something bigger than herself:

> Expressing my frustration [at the traditional Korean cookbooks], I asked my mother how someone like me could ever learn to cook. My mother told me to (1) start with a dish that I had eaten many times before; (2) try to remember the taste; (3) try to create the taste by using ingredients suggested by cookbooks. "Then as I re-create the dish from [my] memory . . . I will create something of my own." Later . . . my mother added one more lesson for cooking that I consider the most significant part of creating a good dish: she said that good food is created by the cook's *sonmat*, which literally means the taste of one's hands. As most Korean dishes are supposed to be made by hands, mixing all the ingredients in an appropriate way during an appropriate time, a cook's hands decide the flavor of food. This is the reason that *sonmat* is the key for good food. My mother also said, "Even though you use the best materials to make good food, if your hands do not have right condition, the food will not turn out good. No matter what is going on in your life and in the world, don't let the world define who you are and who

you should be. When your mind and heart are in peace, your body will be in a calm and peaceful condition."[42]

This perspective shaped Lee's understanding of life and relationships–she must know first for herself without anyone else defining her. She writes further that "the pedagogy of *sonmat* reflects some of the core features of pedagogy as practiced by many Asian and Asian North American women; it is holistic, communal, ontological, and political."[43] Lee describes a community that lives out this pedagogy: "Many Asian North American women who teach in academic contexts also practice this holistic pedagogy. For example, in 1999 several of the faculty advisors of the Pacific, Asian, and North American Asian Women in Theology and Ministry (PANAAWTM), a grassroots movement of Asian and Pacific North American women in theological education and ministry, developed a communal project that provides materials and strategies for teaching Asian and Asian North American women's theologies in North America."[44] The community is a crucial part of the larger Church in the way it encourages men and women to live out their fullest potential and capabilities.

Most relevantly, the pedagogy of *sonmat* of Asian and Asian North American women is also communal in both its purpose and its process. Lee writes,

> As I said above, while I was remembering the taste of the food, the entire community related to the food came to my mind and heart. In other words, even though I was cooking by myself in my kitchen, I was in communion with many people to whom I was indebted, for whom I am and to whom I am accountable. For example, whenever I make a certain Korean pork dish or whenever I see big pots, I ask myself whether my current theological work is contributing to the lessening of the suffering of the marginalized of our society. While I was a graduate student in Korea, I worked with poor Korean women living in huts illegally built on government land in Seoul. On every Sunday between morning and evening services, these women took me to their homes so that I could rest, and they fed me with the most delicious food imaginable. Often the table was laden with a big pot of pork and a bowl of rice, which meant that we all ate from the same pot and rice bowl. To me that was the most meaningful experience of communion and theology.[45]

Lee describes in beautiful terms the impact that community, especially in the least expected places, has had on her and can have on anyone, when one's hands are open to the possibility. The presence of the Church is not contained by four walls, just as a person's worth cannot be contained by cultural expectations or limitations: "The involvement and presence of community is one of the most integral parts of the pedagogical formation of women of Asian heritages . . . Asian and Asian North American women have developed communal personhood."[46] Although one of the first lessons she received from her mother was to not let others define her, she emphasizes that the most important aspect of the Church is the reality that we are eventually shaped by the people around us. God shapes people through their relationships, and this happens in good and, unfortunately, bad ways. The community of Asian American women shapes others like them, but it also ends up having an effect on the Church at large. This emphasis on community is evident in much of Asian linguistics:

> Unlike individualism, which values each person's individuality and independence, the value of the individual in communal Asian societies depends on how well a person adopts communal norms and functions to promote social harmony. Attachments, relatedness, connectedness, unity, and dependency among people are much more important than are independence and individuality. For example in Korean linguistics, the I-ness words such as "I," "my," and "mine" are rarely used. Koreans prefer the word *uri*, meaning we. Almost everything is called "our (something)," instead of "my (something)."[47]

Likewise, Japanese linguistics also exhibits communal selfhood: The English word "self" is usually translated by the Japanese word *jibun*, and vice versa. However, unlike the English word, *jibun* connotes "one's share of the shared life space"–that is, oneself is an inseparable part of ourselves.[48] There is a sense of radical communing, which tends to be passed on through the churches, inherent in Asian cultures. Still, Asian cultures are by no means perfect, and many Asian and Asian North American women seek a communal personhood that respects their being and experiences as women.[49] It is helpful that both men and women are engaged in dialogue about ways the Church can be faithful to its members who have traditionally been seen as inferior or lesser. The manifestation of the Church requires a collective endeavor, with everyone's equal participation, because to remember and recreate the taste of the food and to create one's own recipes is a rich, collective pursuit.[50] It is a way the Church is living out its purpose and participating in something greater than itself. It is a way the Church offers a place for courageous naming and understanding revelation, creative forming and partnering in creation, cogent reorienting and seeing incarnation, clarion liberating and living out redemption, and crucial communing, and sharing in transformation.

The work of these theologians, these writers and artists, these architects has and will continue to make enormous waves within the Church, and offer a way to be faithful, compassionate, and hopeful in new and fresh ways.

Confident Unfolding: Syncretism, Vulnerability, and Imagination as Expressions of the Work of the Holy Spirit

The concept of the Trinity has always seemed a compelling way to talk about God. Even though I could not completely articulate it, I am sure I was subconsciously drawn to the implicit expression of community in the Divine interrelationships. But the Holy Spirit always eluded me. I grew up calling him/her the "Holy Ghost," an expression of my campfire fear and fascination with this nebulous part of God. It always seemed as if the Holy Ghost were God's spy lurking in corners and darks closets. But lately I have found myself feeling more "charismatic," even going so far as to labeling myself as a "Presby-costal" because I feel not only in my own spirit, but also my flesh and blood, a connection to the religious faith of the people we worshiped and worked with in the Dominican Republic for almost six summers. The Dominicans we lived with for ten days at a time were part of a Pentecostal denomination–raucous music, dancing, spontaneous and lengthy prayers in worship drenched in the Holy Spirit–and all of it woke something up in me. In so many ways they opened me up to the Spirit, and informed my recent inclination toward a strong pneumatology.

But I did not find many resources that spoke to a theology of the Holy Spirit. In some ways it felt like an oxymoron. To try to talk about something almost abstract did fit in a little with the task of theology, and yet the emphasis on the lived experience of the Holy Spirit made that a challenge. Still, it has always felt pressing and necessary. According to George Hendry, "in his old age, Barth told of a recurrent dream he had of a theology which would be centered on the Holy Spirit rather than on Christ, but which he, like Moses, was permitted to see only from afar."[51] This suggests that perhaps even Barth, who was in the eyes of many severely entrenched in a christocentric theology, recognized the need for a robust pneumatology. Some others suggest that he in fact incorporated one. Hendry reviews *The Spirit as Lord: A Pneumatology of Karl Barth*, in which author Philip Rosato "disputes the assumption of the dream and undertakes to show that Barth, despite his apparent preoccupation with Christology, was also deeply concerned with the doctrine of the Holy Spirit, and he might as well be described as a pneumatic as well as a christocentric theologian."[52]

In the face of increasing globalization where numerous cultures and religions are accessible, it makes sense to rely intentionally on the work of the third person of the Trinity–the Spirit–to be present in these conversations. More than that, as for many contemporary theologians, it behooves us to integrate the work of the Spirit into our theological constructions. Feminist and liberation theologians clearly are leading the way in this endeavor, and we can reap the benefit of their explorations.

While some Christians may not feel comfortable talking about the Holy Spirit, many people in general talk easily about spirituality. A popular sentiment today is "I'm spiritual but not religious." Although some associated with religious institutions may find this a watered-down comment about one's lack of religious commitment, others seem open to what it means to be "spiritual but not religious" for this generation. At the very least, spirituality certainly seems a viable starting point for talking about religious *experience* and even how the Spirit plays a role in it. Professor of ecumenical studies Chung Hyun Kyung begins this way and gives a compelling description of women's spirituality in her first book, *Struggle to be the Sun Again*, in the specific context of Asian women. She asks the following:

> What is emerging Asian women's spirituality? Out of their daily struggle for full humanity, Asian women are giving birth to "a spirituality that is particularly women's and specifically Asian." When Asian women gathered together at Singapore in 1987 to articulate an emerging Asian women's theology they described it as: Faith experience based on convictions and beliefs which motivate our thought processes and behavior patterns in our relationships to God and neighbor. Spirituality is the integral wholeness of a person

syncretizing his/her faith through their daily life experience. Asian women's spirituality is the awakening of the Asian women's soul to her concrete historical reality–poverty, oppression and suffering. It is a response and commitment of a soul infused by the spirit, to the challenge for human dignity and freedom, and new life of love.[53]

An emphasis on spirituality and, specifically, the Spirit, calls for a descriptive theology rather one that is prescriptive or instructive. And while emphasis is on the Spirit, and spirituality, it relies heavily on the embodied and lived experience of the people, especially in the context of community. It requires connection between a person's inner life and the people and circumstances around her–the stronger the connection the more urgent the resistance toward injustices and inequities within the larger system. Spirituality does not have to do simply with quiet or passive meditation in a dark room, though it often can begin here. Rather, it calls for brave and courageous engagement of life.

It naturally entails employing a *syncretistic* method –an expression of relying on the Spirit to reveal God outside of our own contexts and limited assumptions.

Syncretism: The Holy Spirit as Revelation

Chung goes on to describe this syncretism: They assert that their new spirituality is "integral, outgoing, community-oriented, active, holistic, and all embracing." To be syncretistic originates from concrete life experiences, and in this case of Asian women.[54] She speaks of this spirituality in three rhythms: impasse, choice for life, and reaching Out. The notion of impasse has to do with the paralysis that comes from an "experience of economic political cultural and psychological oppression" and it is "suffering pain, poverty, oppression, and marginalization."[55] It is feeling stuck and a sense of hopelessness.[56] But the choice for life is "a way out of impasse – the intentional choice of life. Accepting responsibility for and control over our lives."[57] Although I am hesitant to employ an imperative to those in oppressed circumstances to accept responsibility for a system that barely allows for even mere survival in many cases, I tentatively agree with and would like to explore the potential sense of empowerment that happens in rejecting a victim mentality. Yet whether the perspective is that the oppression is so large and multi-layered and therefore, out of the victim's control, or that those who are oppressed and who are the oppressor, or even bystander, are all complicit in this broken system, this calls for a more nuanced engagement and specifically a reliance on the Spirit's movement. Chung offers an example of an Asian woman who did confront the unjust system that perpetuated these circumstances, and what she discovered about herself:

> Asian women's honest admission of shared responsibility in sin, but with hope and faith in the grace of God, which brings wonders and new creation" is the foundation of Asian women's emerging spirituality "that motivates their action and reflection." To take full responsibility for oneself and to discover and claim one's own identity means to grow into full adulthood. For Mary Dunn, a Burmese woman, to be a fully adult woman today means being a woman who can define who she is and prove what she can do because she has found an identity of her own.[58]

Mary Dunn did not discover this in isolation as an ascetic in a cave. This confirms Chung's emphasis on the most important piece: reaching out and building a community. It is not only abstract connection, but an awareness of the myriad of spaces in which this connection can occur between women. The experience of God, faith, and the Spirit is not limited to classrooms or sanctuaries, but rather, as Chung writes: "Women's spirituality is a living experience – found 'in kitchens, laundries, fields and factories,' and it is 'the divine living on grassroot levels.'"[59] It is in the ordinary, everyday, and mundane where the Holy Spirit can manifest this interconnectedness. It is in these places of nitty-gritty life, where all economics and luxuries are stripped away, and the fields are leveled, where people encounter each other in authentic ways, that is, in shared sweat and tears. This is not to say that those of privilege are not able to connect, but the material and consumerist goods of the world seem to be a barrier to authenticity, and therefore, true community. Chung talks further of this communal spirituality, and emphasizes that it is not an inert or individual experience:

> Since women live their spirituality in their everyday lives they can feel for others and opt for the needy ones. They call it "compassionate spirituality." It comes from the experiences of women giving birth, and caring, and nurturing their children and family. Women give of themselves to

others in order to give life and to provide for others so that all may live.[60]

I appreciate the perspective that the Spirit calls men and women out toward compassion; in other words, a spirituality that is actually physical, tangible, and relevant in the surrounding culture.

Engaging culture is a significant component in crafting a pneumatological theology. Likewise, Grace Ji-Sun Kim integrates culture, specifically Korean culture, in her incorporation of faith language in *The Grace of Sophia*. She offers a helpful point by discussing the meaning of *inculturation*:

> It is the necessity of the historical intersection of cultures and determination to blend them with an integrity that respects both faith and cultures. Inculturation thus has to do with the interaction of what may be referred to as "faith" on the one hand and culture on the other–the ongoing dialogue between faith and culture.[61]

This ongoing dialogue–"the process of inculturation is one of integration, in the sense of an integration of the Christian faith and life into a given culture and also an integration of a new expression of the Christian experience in the Church,"[62]–is rooted in a posture toward the movement of the Holy Spirit, who seeks to connect and integrate, and make whole. To integrate and make oneself literally a person of integrity, a whole person, means openness and engagement of the fluid and ever-changing nature of culture. It results in an intentional incorporation of other cultures with the attitude that they will help us understand our own stories even amidst conflict and differences. Kim gives the example here, in the relevancy of the experience of the immigration of Korean North American women

> who are at times torn between two cultures as they try to embrace both and live by them both. One key to resolving such a tension between two cultures is to maintain a bicultural existence, through selecting appropriate elements of both cultural worlds to make the best adaptation according to the demands of social circumstances.[63]

But the process of integration is not smooth or without pain and sacrifice. Often the work of assimilation or appropriation can be the result of oppression and coercion–a tension with subversive efforts of resistance. To name and understand the struggle of these circumstances often experienced in the process of difficult inculturation, Kim begins with the Korean concept of *han,* which is

> a mode of responding to the tragic situation of the oppressed. In terms of its etymology, *han* is a psychological term that denotes repressed feelings of suffering, through the oppression of others or through natural calamities or illness. Sometimes translated as "just indignation," *han* is deeps spiritual pain that rises out of the unjust experience of the people . . . It is a dominant feeling of defeat, resignation and nothingness.[64]

Han, both deeply physical and spiritual is actually connected to the Spirit. At first glance, though it sounds fairly depressing and debilitating to life, there is an emphasis on confronting hardship and embracing vulnerability. How is this going to be helpful to people who are entrenched in oppressive structures under the thumbs of the privileged? Are not vulnerability and *weakness* the opposite of resisting structures and gaining power? Kim answers, "on the other hand, *han* is a feeling with a tenacity of will for life which comes to weaker beings."[65] There is more to *han* than just stoic suffering and pain, and a fragility. *Han* has a kernel of resistance that once nurtured and cultivated becomes much more.

Vulnerability: The Holy Spirit as Redemption

Han may seem like too culturally specific a phenomenon. To make this particular concept theologically relevant, Kim, like Chung, explains the necessity for syncretism, which in essence is another expression of openness to the Spirit: "Blending concepts from beyond Christianity in order to clarify and illuminate the gospel for this time and place, and for these people."[66] Syncretism is helpful here in that it offers a way to absorb other cultural expressions in theologically faithful ways and opens the dialogue up to the Spirit. But it involves an initial pursuit of the Spirit's presence in order to do this respectfully and honestly. And in the case of *han,* though a particular cultural experience, through the syncretic work of the Spirit it can become accessible and universal.

Han has another side to it that makes it complete. Wonhee Anne Joh in *The Heart of the Cross: A Post-Colonial Christology* joins the dialogue by approaching *han* through the Korean concept of *jeong.* While Korean theologians have articulated a liberation theology through an analysis of *han,* Joh also shows how *han* might be understood to non-Koreans through Julia Kristeva's notion of abjection (an in-between stage normally associated with marginalized peoples–literally between "object" and "subject"), in relationship to *jeong.*[67] She cites Jae Hoon Lee's description of *han* in universal terms as a "form of suffering, a broad and deep image that speaks to all human beings about the mysterious source of both suffering and creativity."[68] But j*eong* is not a dualistic opposite of *han,* rather "*han* is inevitably interwoven with the presence of *jeong.*"[69] It seems that an understanding of *jeong* solidifies, but thickens in some ways, redeems, and completes the experience of *han,* and finds parallels then to Kristeva's notion of abjection by providing a both/and kind of reality. I find compelling the emphasis on *jeong* rather than *han* as the inspiration for the Son's voluntary suffering on the cross because it is *jeong* that makes space for identifying with another's suffering, as well as providing an avenue to connect to the reality that Christ, the Abjected One, possessor of both *han* and *jeong,* is the one who is able to appropriate and overcome *han.* Joh writes further, "Jesus' agency on the cross results not only from his confrontative actions but also from his embodied *jeong.* By living the way of *jeong,* Jesus risked the wrath signified by the cross."[70] *Jeong,* as the source of *han,* deepens the reality and existence of *jeong* as exemplified in Jesus:

> The suffering of Jesus on the cross, then, signifies the *jeong* he embodied in his solidarity with the abject while, at the same time, the cross defies the powers that repress *jeong.*[71] My Christological claim is that the cross is not a benign story of the Father and the death of His beloved Son, but might it not be the event of a full presence of the repressed/abject? The cross would then represent not an end to life but rather a resurrection, a return of the abject: those who have been repressed, expelled, persecuted, executed, oppressed– all those who have been *han*-ridden.[72]

This is a powerful way to approach a theology of the cross. Joh suggests "it is fruitful for a theology of the cross to highlight *jeong* because the cross embodies and continues to function as an embodiment of abjection and love, both *han* and *jeong.*[73] Once again, the work of the Spirit, namely, a syncretistic view, allows for a richer understanding of the cross. Joh writes more, "*Jeong* has power to unravel *han* through heart and connectedness in the midst of differences...This unraveling requires an entry into the Third Space of hybridity, and Christ on the cross becomes that entry into the Third Space.[74] This connectedness happens in unexpected ways, which is another expression of the mysterious work of the Spirit, and hybridity is often a possible result of that work. The syncretistic work of opening oneself to a seemingly impossible connectedness produces new creations, and thereby richer experiences of the Divine.

Similarly, in *The Holy Spirit, Chi, and the Other,* Kim describes these new creations in terms of hybridity, which "becomes a form of resistance as it eliminates the dualistic and hierarchical constructions of cultures and illustrates that cultures grow and are dependent on constantly borrowing from each other and affecting one another.... Hybridity becomes an important tool for liberation."[75] In scripture, this is expressed in pneumatological terms as well: "Now the Lord is the Spirit, and where the Spirit of the Lord is, there is freedom," (2 Cor. 3:17). I would go further to say that hybridity is not only a tool for liberation, but also an expression of liberation.

The way hybridity operates is by shifting "the conceptualization of identity because identity is no longer a stable reference point... It creates a new paradigm in which liminality, instability, impurity, movement, and fluidity inform the formation of identities."[76] The nebulous nature of this paradigm is also an expression of the Spirit, and while a lack of structure produces unknown vulnerabilities and may seem terrifying to many, it is a doorway to a new way of being as inspired by the Divine through God's Spirit. The space in which hybridity occurs is in the Third Space Joh mentions earlier. It is in those peripheral and nontraditional places. One example of this Third Space is the diaspora.

Imagination: The Holy Spirit as Resource

Kwok Pui-Lan in *Postcolonial Imagination and Feminist Theology* describes "diasporic discourse," which has "become a fluid and challenging site to raise questions about the construction of the center and the periphery, the negotiation of multiple loyalties and identities, the relationship between the 'home' and the 'world,' the political and theoretical implications of border crossing, and the identity of the dislocated diasporized female subject."[77] Diaspora communities around the world are disruptive to the local culture by virtue of introduction to different cultural elements. They are bubbling with potential for many syncretistic expressions, hybrid possibilities, and expressions of *jeong*. In even more tangible terms, they are compelling sites in which lines and boundaries are blurred in potentially creative ways, and allow for the Spirit to move and work to change the larger communities. Kwok cites James Clifford's description of the situation of those living in diaspora:

> Diaspora communities, constituted by displacement, are sustained in hybrid historical conjunctures. With varying degrees of urgency they negotiate and resist the social realities of poverty, violence, policing, racism, and political and economic inequality. They articulate alternate public spheres, interpretive communities where critical alternatives (both traditional and emergent) can be expressed."[78]

These alternative realities–perspectives, lifestyles, and methods–are also conduits for the Holy Spirit, which in turn, continuously opens the way for more possibilities, and therefore, a richer, multivaried reality. Kwok writes about "diasporic imagination," which works to

> decenter and decompose the ubiquitous logic and "common sense" that says that the cultural form and norm of Christianity is defined by the West. It resists a predetermined and prescribed universalism and a colonial mode of thinking by insisting on re-territorization of the West and by tracing how the so-called center and periphery of Christianity have always been doubly inscribed and mutually constituted . . . It recognizes the diversity of diasporas and honors the different histories and memories.[79]

Rather than creating divisions between people, if approached with a spirit of compassion and openness, and anchoring in one's shared humanity with all people, it provides a way to connect in intense ways. She writes further that "a diasporic consciousness finds similarities and differences in both familiar territories and unexpected corners,"[80] and in the same way *jeong* can awaken a sense of interconnectedness, and the possibility of profound help from fellow human beings, "one catches glimpses of oneself in a fleeting moment or in a fragment in someone else's story."[81]

Kwok says, "André Aciman, a Jewish writer originally from Alexandria who writes about exile, diaspora, and dispossession and who calls himself a 'literary pilgrim,' may be right when he says:

We write about our life, not to see it as it was, but to see as we wish others might see it, so we may borrow their gaze and begin to see our life through their eyes, not ours. Only then would we begin to understand our life story, or to tolerate it and ultimately, perhaps to find it beautiful."[82]

It is the Holy Spirit, working through the disruptive nature of the confrontation between the center and periphery of these communities, who helps us discover a better understanding of all our life stories. The new creation is not something born *ex nihilo* but with the pieces of our lives connecting in beautiful and surprising ways. It is a work that requires sensitivity to the Holy Spirit as we encounter it in each others' cultural traditions and stories, in each others' *han and jeong,* and in these manifestation of communities that blur the lines at so many levels. To experience the Holy Spirit fully, and therefore the Trinity, and each member of the Godhead, we must take syncretistic risk, embrace a *han* vulnerability, and employ a *jeong* imagination. When we do, we will discover the Divine unfold and reveal itself in incredible ways through the human beings around us.

The work of all these theologians and more, writers and artists, cultural architects have and will continue to make enormous waves within and without the Church. It is a way for the Church to offer a place for courageous naming and understanding revelation, creative forming and partnering in creation, cogent reorienting and seeing incarnation, clarion liberating and living out redemption, and crucial communing and sharing in transformation. It is, ultimately, a space for the Spirit to unfold our lives and communities anew.

5

Freedom Songs of Long Life

Let us consider how to provoke one another to love and good deeds, not neglecting to meet together, as is the habit of some, but encouraging one another.

—HEBREWS 10:24-25

As long as I can remember, I have loved Disney movies. As a child, I was enthralled with the idea of princesses, witches and villains, rescue missions, and all the glorious musical numbers. I especially loved the scenes with the main female protagonist in the woods, birds singing and chirping around her, maybe even alighting on her shoulder. The day was sunny, and the princess/heroine usually sang a song. It was a charming picture—to be so one with one's self and nature that even the birds felt comfortable enough to roost in your hair. Unfortunately that will never happen to me because I have always hated the sound of a lot of birds, particularly in the morning. I am an incredibly light sleeper, and not a morning person in the least, so the sound of all the varied chirping, squawking, and screeching rouses me from my shallow slumber, leaving me in quite the foul, dark mood. I have no romantic or poetic thoughts of birds chirping cheerfully around me as I break out into song while getting ready for work or school, not in the least. I will never be a Disney princess. I am comforted by the thought that now that I know there were some deeply misogynist and sexist tendencies, as well as racist overtones, in Disney movies, I would not want to be in one anyway. I can have my musical numbers in another way.

Growing up, thankfully, music was always a part of my life. It may not be a surprise to find out that my mother signed me up for piano lessons at the ripe age of four. For more than a decade, I would find myself sitting at the piano for at least two hours a day, with her next to me making sure I practiced for the full time. Don't get me wrong–despite the tediousness of the work day in and day out and the slight pressure I felt with my mother constantly sitting with me, I loved having music in my life. I would pick up the violin and then the cello for a couple of years during elementary school (though I eventually quit playing cello, as I found it difficult to walk to school each day dragging the huge instrument behind me). I sang in choirs at school and church, picked up the guitar in college, tried out for a capella groups, and just could not imagine a moment without being able to express myself through music. Early on I had sensed that there was something universally connective in music. It was its own language, and I saw that anyone could speak it because it was clearly rooted in something cosmic and eternal as well as deeply human.

Music was a way to connect to others, particularly to my mother. When I would play the piano, she would sometimes come over while in the middle of cooking dinner or doing some household chore. Usually she would listen to whatever I was working on at the moment, but periodically she would choose certain hymns for me to help her practice for church choir or simply to sing because they were her favorites. In one of those rare moments she would break out into song, I relished hearing her voice–like a window opening up bringing in fresh air. I could always hear an earnestness, a struggle, and resistance in her effortless and pure vibrato. There was a fight in her song, and it was inspiring to me, too. It made me want to break out and sing and sometimes to dance; I felt a glimmering of inexpressible contentment. Perhaps this is why Anne Dondapati Allen's description of the use of folk songs by Indian women to subvert the oppressive system of their society is also a compelling template for me as I seek to articulate the effects of collision and fragmentation. Embracing song is subversive and healing at the same time.

Living in the Collision and Embracing the Fragmentation

The words *collision* and *fragmentation* do not necessarily connote the most comforting feelings or thoughts. I am reminded of a car accident I was in once, my first and worst one. I was a sophomore in college. I had borrowed a roommate's car to take my brother and a couple of friends to the airport. I had never been there before. We got turned around, and I was in a panic. Their departure time was close, and I feared they would miss their plane. I did not see a red light in an effort to figure out a place to turn around and collided with another car coming through the intersection at that moment. It was a horrific feeling. My brother slammed his knee against the dashboard, and it immediately swelled up like a balloon. The girl sitting behind him somehow broke her glasses and got a cut on her eye. We all went to the emergency room, including the woman driving the other car. As I waited for my friend to get stitches, I bawled uncontrollably. It was incredibly surreal and terrible at the same time. I remember wanting to get as far away as possible from that point in time. I could not get sounds of the cars crunching together and the picture of the shattered glass on the ground out of my head for a long time.

Thankfully, while some are much worse, not all collisions are so violent and traumatic. In this case, I use collision as a metaphor to mean the ongoing encounter of stereotypes, expectations, standards, and conflicting realities that lead to fragmentation. In moving toward an Asian American feminist theology, I emphasize the necessity for theological work to be rooted in the possibility of dynamic play in the midst of fragmentation, and the resulting conversation among Scripture, tradition, and experience. I also find useful a theology of the body because it stresses embodiment and the lived-out experience of faith. I believe a dialogue between these salient experiences of Asian American women and other theological perspectives will be helpful in showing how this conversation can point us to a fresh theology and provide space to live into and out of God's whole redemption. The metaphor of collision resonates deeply in me as expressive of the experience for Asian American women in its connection to the fragmentation that occurs in daily life.

These days I continue to learn the art of fragmentation. This is both a positive and a negative process: a continuous recognition of the numerous sources of my identity, deconstruction of these influences, and then, most important, a work of intentional reconstruction. While it is an interpretive work in recognition of the complicated layers of meaning in relationships and identity development, there remains a creative component to the process. It calls for radical and courageous thought, words, voice, and song. For my own process, all of this is done in a theological framework alongside Scripture and traditional and historical Christian influences, in conversation with other oppressed or silenced groups, through other disciplines, and in the context of the specific social history of Asian Americans in this country. As I reflect on my faith journey, I realize a number of painful pieces that make up who I am. Some pieces I have chosen for myself, but other pieces have been forced on me, whether according to assumptions and stereotypes, or in relation to categories about race, culture, gender, or generation. I am learning how to feel this fragmentation by embracing the disjointedness as my own unique experience while recognizing the necessity for engagement and inquiry. I am slowly realizing how I have navigated and continue to operate and live through this fragmented existence. The evangelical Christianity I grew up in remains legitimate in my mind, an undeniably important piece of my history. Much of my faith language was born out of this evangelical community. This process of reflection and conversation is the preliminary work for a lifelong project in which I seek a new Word, a new song that articulates the promise of God's whole healing and redemption in me as an individual and in society as a whole.

As an ordained Minister of the Word and Sacrament, I am particularly struck by the power of words, that is, symbols and metaphors to convey meaning. So I am compelled by the possibilities of meaning in the images of collision and fragmentation. I am hopeful that this might resonate with the experience of Asian American women because as we develop our identities and communities in a fluctuating culture, we constantly face the phenomenon of this collision of images, ideologies, expectations, and beliefs concerning race and gender. Often, this may lead to fragmentation, which may incite different adaptive responses, like compartmentalization or assimilation. Zia writes about the discomfort of this experience of fragmentation. For instance, this fragmentation is seen in the response of the Asian American community to the death of Vincent Chin, a Chinese American who fell victim to a hate-race crime during the labor shortage plaguing automobile factories, which was viewed as the result of overseas competition in Japan. Although some of the local Asian American organizations worked for and demanded a more just sentence met by the courts' judgment of the perpetrator's crime, most national Asian American organizations were uncertain how to respond because they questioned exactly where they fit in America. They had never been included in broad discussions on race, nor had they interjected themselves into such discussions. This was a moment of collision. Zia writes,

> Organizing over race might make us seem like troublemakers, as African Americans were often perceived, but we

lacked the numerical strength and political power of blacks; if we stepped out of the shadows to make waves, wouldn't we risk becoming targets again?[1]

Thus Asian Americans' view of themselves and their social reality disintegrated in light of the injustice toward Vincent Chin's family and community.

Zia goes on to write in reference to the Red Apple Boycott, which I mentioned in chapter 1, that what was disturbing and more damaging to the Asian American identity, was "the relative ease with which Asian Americans could move back into the shadows, even with Korean Americans on center stage as the target of black discontent. The paralysis shifted Asian Americans back into a place of uncertainty over where we belonged in the landscape of a white-black society, afraid of stepping on the moving fault lines, looking to others for safety rather than taking our own principled stand. How could we build and maintain relations with African Americans and other people of color while safeguarding the equal rights of Asian Americans?"[2] In this collision of events, clashing agendas, and mixed communication, the fragmentation Asian Americans experience is facing this uncertainty and instability, as well as the elements within their experience that seem irreconcilable. This fragmentation is seen in Asian American literature; for example, the fragmented Japanese American community in a novel called *No-No Boy* crumbles during the course of story. The main character, Ichiro, is himself characterized as incomplete and fragmented.[3] This is only one example that reveals the way fragmentation, although not always named as such, is a familiar concept to Asian Americans.

Similar to compartmentalization and assimilation, fragmentation has alienating tendencies. There is no sense of belonging or of home in this phenomenon. Phoebe Eng writes,

> Comfortable enough in America, Chinatown, and even Honk Kong or Taiwan, we seem to belong everywhere. Because of this, we might also belong nowhere. "Home," it seems, ends up being a mixed-up notion that must be redefined if it is to have meaning for many of us.[4]

Dina Gan, editor in chief of several magazines, writes,

> "Asian America" is a frame of mind, a spiritual place that is located neither in Asia nor America, but hovering somewhere above, between and around the hearts and souls of

the people who belong to it. Especially for those of us who were born here—we feel alienated in America and estranged in the countries our parents came from—Asian America is the closest thing to a place to call home.[5]

This Asian America is still in the stages of development in the minds and hearts of the Asian Americans who are making enormous sacrifices to create it. Jenny Kim writes,

> It's impossible to even attempt to quantify the Korean versus the American in me; it's not as easy as doing an autopsy to find *kimchee* next to a Big Mac in the gastric lining and declaring the corpse Korean-American. At times it is existentially dizzying to try to separate and count how many times I ran around East and West, cultural reality and fiction. I've begun to see Korean and American cultures as two fluid worlds that sometimes mesh, sometimes conflict, but always form the identity *I* claim.[6]

Thus these destabilizing tendencies, the disequilibrium experienced in this fragmentation has the most potential to bring awareness to the problematic social existence of Asian American women, which I believe is the route to a more engaged interaction and transformation.

Embodied Process: An Emphasis on Praxis

Delving into this theology, I am guided by a number of trustworthy resources. Mark Taylor's emphasis on highlighting praxis in any theological work is significant. In the introduction to *Remembering Esperanza*, he writes,

> To say that Christian theology emerges from praxis, then, is to point to a complex mélange of thinking and doing. In this mélange, action has primacy, but is not antithought. The components of theory make a contribution to action. To accent praxis as I do here is also to highlight the socially and politically conditioned character of theology . . . Praxis is also not just individual or personal acting and doing, though, again, those are included. Praxis is primarily all this as a communal or intersubjective process laden with social and political freight.[7]

The emphasis on praxis results in the incorporation of the social context, history, and literature of Asian American woman's

experience. Such impetus particularly highlights some of the prod-
ucts of the power dynamics in the United States–namely, the
experience of racism and sexism and the different forms of adaptation to these power structures. I agree with Taylor that it is necessary
to develop sensitivity to the "communal and intersubjective processes" rather than to impose certain abstract criterion. Otherwise,
this work would fall into the same category of oppression as that
of cultural imperialism, neocolonialism, and commoditization. Taking into consideration the social and political elements of the Asian
American woman's experience has a rehumanizing effect that coun-
ters the dehumanizing effect of stereotypes and images inherent in
these structures of oppression.

Moreover, throughout this project, I have intentionally interjected autobiographical elements along with real stories of Asian
Americans as an example of this praxis. This supplementation is
more than a peripheral element. It is essential! Peter Phan writes
about a new theology and a new way of doing theology:

> Asian theologians insist that theology is only a second act
> critically reflecting on the first act which is commitment to
> and solidarity with those who are victims of poverty and
> oppression. Theology is not "God-talk" based on some
> canonical texts in search of practical application. Rather, it
> originates from Christian praxis . . . moves to critical reflec-
> tion, returns to praxis, and the spiraling movement of praxis
> . . . in ever new contexts.[8]

Theology is a double method of social analysis and introspec-
tion. Autobiography, generally stories and narratives, are a necessary
element of this praxis. Likewise, Taylor writes, "It is better to focus
on autobiographical elements less as a linear sequence of events and
more as a recurring set of emphases or themes that come to light
through reflection on the shape and nature of remembering."[9] Thus
the biographical elements of theology are totally legitimate and even
natural in the formation of an Asian American feminist theology.
"To reassess the forces that are already established as the only viable
references for constructing realities for everyone, un- and under-rep-
resented people have to learn to take their own autobiographies and
the stories of their own communities seriously. For no social being
is an isolated island; and no autobiography is completely divorced
from other biographies. Indeed, human identities are grounded in

and through relationships with others."[10] These interactions create the drama of the most extraordinary stories.

Embodied Proclamation: A Theology of the Body

I move beyond Taylor and Phan by also being guided by a basic *theology of the body*. For collision and fragmentation to resonate as metaphors, theology must be rooted in the physical and flesh-and-blood—in the mess and chaos of humanity. This theology of embodiment is grounded in the reality of God in Christ Jesus. It finds its roots in a doctrine of the incarnation of Christ that highlights the importance of apprehending Jesus Christ in a particular human, social context. This, then, becomes the basis for validating our own social histories and situations. We are able to view our own lives as the center and subject of stories rather than in relation or association to what is considered normative. The emphasis is placed on human experience in the body more than on abstract ideas of the mind as the starting point for understanding God, so body experiences are positively viewed as occasions of revelation.[11]

A theology of the body connects the incarnation of Christ to the flesh-and-blood reality inherent in all of humanity. What this means is Christ's incarnation affirms everyone's humanity since Christ also shares this same humanity. So Christ's story matters not only to those in the center, or those in majority culture, but to those on the periphery. Though he is at the center of Christian faith, he himself lived a life on the margins. Everyone can therefore find that their own stories are necessary. Thus it becomes imperative that an Asian American feminist theology emphasize on calling the Asian American woman's situation radically into question, as she discovers what it means to live out this justification as a legitimate human being. Specifically, it is vital to this theological formation that she identify with and in Christ—the one who shares humanity with all—and that she realize that as an Asian American woman her identification with Christ is as valid as that of every other person. Christ, and not the dominant culture's views on her as a foreign, exotic, or sexually conquerable person, becomes the sole source of her identity, and she lives out her story through the encouragement of Christ's shared humanity.

This is relevant to Asian American feminist theology because it legitimizes bodily experiences and the resulting stories of Asian American women as valid spaces for encountering God, which is necessary for this theological work. Asian American women's lives become a legitimate starting point for these narratives. Moreover, a theology of the body is about bodies in relationship to one another, hence the need to emphasize community. These stories create and shape the community of Asian American women. Thus the community is an essential place for the creation of an autobiographical narrative and theology particular to Asian American women. David Ng writes, "Autobiographical theology or theological autobiography, my biography is not a solo, isolated life story. It is communal and of necessity includes the lives of other persons and of my own life-in-community."[12] Stories and autobiography require bodies–bodies that move, speak, sing, and also struggle, fail, and rise up again and again . . . together.

Journeys at the Intersection

Collision and fragmentation are incomplete in my mind without some engagement of that space between impact and splintering. Just as within community, overlap and junctures are necessary for formation, other spaces–a third way, a place of cross sections–also inform this journey in conjunction with the beginning impulse to engage what is practical and physical. These intersecting points do not inhibit the creativity necessary for identity and community development, though in some ways they may complicate it; but still, they sustain and enrich it, in the same way harmonies supplement melodies by generating beautiful layers and depth.

Embodied Resistance: Feminist Theories

Body theology has roots in feminist theories as well, so it may be helpful to cover some of the basics of feminist theory. Feminist theory is often divided into two different schools of thought: the essentialists and the constructivists. Essentialism relies on a language of "universals" to communicate that some "things" possess certain "natural" qualities. Some feminists embrace an essentialism that values the uniqueness of women's bodies and think it is necessary to celebrate these essential qualities of women. Critics often respond that assigning a specific nature to women is inevitably oppressive and perpetuates a gendered, hierarchical, dualistic, and thus limited perspective on the world.[13] For instance, a heavy essentialist view on women's roles is fairly pervasive in Asian cultures.

On the other hand, feminist constructivism focuses on the social, cultural, and linguistic sources of our views of women and women's nature. Constructivists use the term to point out that supposed eternal truths of women's nature are historically and culturally variant, so consequently, gender is "formed" rather than "given."[14] Critics of this theory express concern over the political effects of de-centering women, the removal of the "central anchors, called 'essentials,'" and the resulting "shifting complexity of forces and histories that constitute our ever changing identities."[15] As with most theories, these two always raise the possibility of some kind of backlash from the other extreme. In constructivist thought, the backlash potentially leads to a cultural determinism. In some ways, this could be more oppressive than a determinism based on essentialism.

Jones's "strategic essentialism" seems most in harmony with an articulation of a feminist theology. Strategic essentialism is described as a position between essentialism and constructivism that "applauds constructivist critiques of gender but feels nervous about giving up universals altogether."[16] It takes "a path between willingness to stake a claim and openness to constant revision and challenge, between belief in universal truth and recognition that we are radically constructed and constrained in our ability to know that truth objectively."[17] The invitation to maintain a tension, a both/and, feels much more authentic to human experience, particularly for women. In theological terms, Jones calls this an "eschatological essentialism": a theological vision of an already/not-yet future and a vision of God's will for a redeemed humanity where all persons live in right relation to God and one another. This is an intersection, a third way, and a space where both realities are acknowledged and lived out.

"Strategic essentialism" does recognize the need for some normative criteria, like notions of freedom, injustice, and redemption,[18] as well as the dynamic aspects of a constructivist analysis that reexamines these notions in new seasons and contexts. The constructivist aspect of this eschatological essentialism encourages "localized thick descriptions,"[19] "additive approaches,"[20] and an emphasis on embracing challenge, question, and dialogue as inherent in this process. Jones suggests that a language of "landscape" provides a way to view doctrines as constructions in an imagistic and conceptual terrain in which people of faith locate themselves.[21] For people who journey and are aware of their physicality, this language is compelling. Thus, to do this work faithfully, an Asian American feminist theology must engage classical theological perspectives while maintaining an awareness of how doctrines mediate gender and race relations that structure the multiple levels of oppression.[22] Then, set in this framework, feminist theology becomes a "remapping." It is not, however, a reconstruction of the terrain. Rather, feminist theology offers new marks for traveling through the terrain in new ways.[23]

Jones's framework is a space that opens up the possibilities of a coherent and creative Asian American feminist theology. Again, I am working with the fundamental metaphors of collision and fragmentation as images that potentially symbolize one aspect of the experience of the Asian American woman. A feminist theological perspective can use this inimitable experience of fragmentation, which often results in marginalization, Otherness, and the more troublesome components of her experience. A feminist theological perspective does not condone the oppression of Asian American women, but it does emphasize recognizing the existence of such oppression and the need to confront it. Although fragmentation may be viewed as a negative phenomenon, I see it as a potentially positive occurrence. What is required in this potentially positive occurrence is allowing for a theology of the body. Such a theology includes recognition of the embodiment of our experience, especially our process and voice, and advocating an openness to emotions, in particular anger and rage. Validating these bodily emotions allows for the Asian American woman to validate the social and spiritual reality of the specific injustices she experiences in relationship with others. Then channeling this energy and engaging this fragmentation leads to a new way of confronting these oppressive structures. This phenomenon forces the individual to question the causes of this fragmentation. In examining the sources of this fragmentation, she potentially becomes more aware of another redemption that does not rely on the acceptance of the oppressive dominant culture. She can give voice to the sources of this fragmentation, and furthermore, it can empower her to work for change at the deepest levels of society.

Embodied Revolution: Liberation Theology

Much like an orchestra or choral group, other voices add a bountifulness that helps make the music of theology more meaningful. I cannot help but be moved and influenced by other voices within liberation theology, particularly those of Aloysius Pieris, Gustavo Gutierrez, and James Cone. While their social contexts are vastly different from the Asian American woman's context, they provide some articulations about universal, human tendencies that are potentially applicable and add more dimensions to my own understanding of the need for liberation for all people. I found myself drawn the most to Pieris for his discussion on Asian culture and poverty, but the resonant themes that arise throughout all the writings include economics, ecumenism, ecclesialism, and emancipation.

Pieris offers a pertinent perspective that engages economics and poverty, one that is often overlooked in the United States because of the assumption that all Asian Americans are successful, experience no racism, and are able to cast off the cultural burdens of their homelands. It is rooted in the model minority myth, as mentioned earlier. But the stories, superstitions, and religious sensibilities of our ancestors seep in whether or not we are paying attention. Pieris offers more than an "Asian sense in theology,"[24] systematically providing a thorough analysis of the relationship between poverty and liberation (in sociological, ecclesial, and spiritual terms) and between religion and liberation within the context of Asian cultures and the phenomenon of enculturation and indigenization, and finally moving toward a theology of liberation in Asia. He writes, "A valid theology of liberation in Asia is born first as a formula of life, reflecting an ecclesial praxis of liberation continually internalized by being symbolically reenacted in the liturgy, before it is shaped gradually into a confessional formula."[25] There is a need for an Asian theology to engage a language that embraces cultural translation resulting in a liberative expression.

Through the process of enculturation and indigenization Western Christian theology has tended to oppress Asian communities, whether through compounding a cultural gap that had an unavoidable economic gap[26] or through theological vandalism and cultural commoditization/commercialism.[27] Across the broad spectrum of these supposedly well-intentioned methods of evangelization, Western Christianity has left little room for the indispensable process of "translation" both culturally and contextually. Thus the "mission crisis [became and is] an authority crisis."[28] The backlash of colonialism inherent in Western Christianity has created this mission crisis, which in turn affects not just the authority but the language–that is, the vehicle and means by which Christianity is heard by Asian culture. So, Pieris writes,

> Asians are called upon to resurrect a new credible symbol of God's saving presence among our peoples, an authoritative word from a source of revelation universally recognized as such in Asia. In short, we are summoned to fashion the contours of a *new missionary community* truly qualified to

announce God's kingdom and mediate the liberative revolution inaugurated by Jesus through his life and death . . . what is asked of us is nothing short of an *ecclesiological revolution.*[29]

According to Pieris, the cultural translation offered by Western Christianity, and even by Latin American liberation theologians, does not suffice to bring about the necessary contextual revolution in Asia. What is lacking is a liberative expression rooted in dialogue with the pervasive religions in Asia. This is applicable not only for those who reside in Asian diasporas around the world but also for those in the context of the United States, who continue to experience the effects of colonialist and imperialist endeavors, which are often masked by the dominant group's evangelical Christianity.

This liberative expression must find its roots first in acknowledging Jesus' grounding of spirituality in poverty: "for both Jesus and his followers, spirituality is not merely a struggle to be poor but equally a struggle *for* the poor."[30] Pieris continues: "Poverty is not merely a material rejection of wealth." It is struggling against "a subtle force operating within me, an acquisitive instinct."[31] Thus the liberative expression finds itself in the modern-day appearance of the poor masses in Asia–that is, in the lives of those who have few material goods but are rich in culture. Pieris affirms that this theology must be rooted in their language:

> Learn first the folk language. Assist at the rites and rituals of the Asian people; hear their songs, vibrate with their rhythms; keep step with their dance; taste their poems; grasp their myths; reach them through their legends. You will find that the language they speak puts them in touch with the basic truths that every religion grapples with, but each in a different way . . . in short, the struggle for full humanness.[32]

He writes further that "theology is not mere God-talk,"[33] but it most definitely must be rooted in the life, struggle, and call for liberation in Asian communities. This language is more than "liturgy,"[34] the appropriated and enforced worship/spiritual language of Western Christianity, and certainly more than "ideology,"[35] a social and political language focused on a programmatic worldview.[36] It is language that needs to legitimately include the soteriological elements of Asian religious experience; acknowledge Western, colonialist, capitalist, technocratic evangelization; and engage Asian religion and poverty. Rather than being a seeming deterrent to the gospel, or to the Christian struggle for liberation, this dynamic interplay opens the door for a richer dialogue and theological expression for the Asian Church and the Asian American Church in which women have power and responsibility.

Though theology is not solely linguistics, it is language in that it is fluid, constantly shifting and adjusting to be relevant, fresh, and helpful in making a seemingly cavernous reality more accessible. Theology is a "sign of," "symbolic of," "points to," and is never complete or accurate in and of itself, and yet, it connects. Theology has the power to bring mountains to destruction, transform the course of history, to call life out of death. Pieris' work affirms that this language is needed in every context, *economically* and *ecumenically.*

Likewise Gustavo Gutierrez posits that theology must respond to the question "Does God love us?" and—even more difficult—"How to say to the poor, that God loves them?"[37] Thus theology must be "a reading of the word of God from within the situation that the believer is living." Gutierrez claims that language, a cultural institution, must be used faithfully in relation to God and man's reality.[38] He seeks to engage theology—not only liberation theology but all theology—also in terms of *language*: "Thus we seek and make a language about God (that is, a theology) together with a people living the faith in the midst of a situation of injustice and exploitation which is a denial of God."[39] Language certainly has the potential to oppress, but it has equal potential to bring to light, break down walls, and transform beyond our imagination—and certainly beyond the physical reality.

Most notably, Gutierrez sets forth the need for a new *ecclesialism,* and again, a language of commitment and community: "[Theology] is an ecclesial function."[40] "To do theology is to write a love letter to the God in whom I believe, to the people to whom I belong, and to the Church of which I am a part."[41] This language expresses the commitment we make to God. But first it expresses the covenant God has made with us. God promises to be a God with us as Emmanuel, and in Karl Barth's words, a "God for us." Moreover, our language must not only exhibit community, but it also must have roots in the community of the Church. That must especially include being a "church of the poor," as Gutierrez reiterates numerous times. "The answer to that reality of death is to proclaim life: to proclaim the kingdom of life as an expression of God's love for every person."[42] The Church is called to engage at all levels in life to proclaim God's love. But to speak of liberation does not mean, as some people think, adopting an enthusiastic and facile optimism. On the contrary, the language of liberation can only come from an experience of oppression and death, without which liberation itself has no meaning.[43]

We are called to share in the suffering, oppression, and death of Christ and Christ's people, for when we do this faithfully we are responding to God's call to be the Church. In the space of the fellowship of the believers, the practice and manifestation of language can be redemptive.

Similarly, James Cone offers another perspective that is rooted in the salient experiences of the African American narrative. Specifically, the component of liminality in theology is especially key in Cone's work–that is, those moments of intersection where the realities of human life are brought to its outer edges and limits, and Something breaks through to challenge what is normative, and that Something is conveyed in language to the masses. For Cone, this was foundational for his "points of departure." This foundation expressed itself as a serious Liberation Theology, with the intention of literal liberation:

> The task of black theology, then, is to analyze the nature of the gospel of Jesus Christ in the light of oppressed blacks so they will see the gospel as inseparable from their humiliated condition, and as bestowing on them the necessary power to break the chains of oppression.[44]

In using collision and fragmentation, particularly in intersection, for the case of Asian American women, I am trying through language and narrative to get at something similar to this rupture, a moment that challenges what is normative.

In chapter 6, "Jesus Christ in Black Theology," Cone addresses the role of the historical Jesus, examining the previously established discussion on Jesus based on the question "Who is Jesus Christ?" as posed by Albert Schweitzer.[45] In light of black theology, Cone writes that "the historical kernel is the manifestation of Jesus as the Oppressed One whose earthly existence was bound up with the oppressed of the land."[46] Cone also addresses the character of the New Testament Jesus, pointing out that the stories highlighted are his birth, baptism, temptation, death, and resurrection, all of which have strong elements of oppression. The dimension of liberation is embedded in the names of Jesus.[47] Finally, he proposes a literal Black Christ: "The black Christ is he who threatens the structure of evil as seen in white society, rebelling against it, thereby becoming the embodiment of what the black community knows that it must become," writes Cone.[48] It expresses the concreteness of Jesus' presence today.[49] To sum up, Jesus represents in his very body a connection to the oppressed and to *all* those in need of liberation. The power of these words is indescribable.

Cone takes a further step by not merely situating himself within these moments of intersection. He constructs black theology by emphasizing these points of departure as those moments wherein communities must undertake the work of theology by a courageous willingness to depart from what is normative, especially that which includes dialogue and participation in the liberation of the oppressed. This is pervasive throughout his work. For instance, in his discussion of "The Kingdom of God and the Black Christ," he expresses God's kingdom as salvation, and repentance arises as a response to God's liberation.[50] Thus liberation is a key component in black theology in that it is crucial in the experience of salvation. Cone, in essence, seeks to "resurrect" the notion of salvation by emphasizing that "to be saved meant that one's enemies have been conquered and the saviour is the one who has the power to gain victory." "This is not to deny that salvation is a future reality, but it is also hope that focuses on the present" and "has to do with earthly reality."[51] Salvation is lived out in the here and now as *emancipation*, an embodied liberation. The source of this freedom, which is available to all, is in the One who conquers all, that is, Jesus Christ.

These theologians and others are driving the work that is necessary for all of humanity, as Gutierrez offered once, for both oppressed and oppressor as paraphrased here: Liberation for some actually means liberation for all. Feminist and liberation theologians provide us with powerful and transformative words that parallel each other with themes of language and liberation. What they all show is that the song requires equal and effective voices from those in the center and the margins. For it to truly be indicative of God's kingdom we must seek to be radically inclusive so all the voices make the song rich and resonant.

6

Food for the Journey

A Third Space and Threshold Theology

*Liberation theology seeks to be a way of speaking about God.
It is an attempt to make the word of life present in a world of
oppression, of injustice, of death.*

—Gustavo Gutierrez

Apparently, birds in preparation for migration become hyperphagic. That means they eat more food, which is stored as fat for their long journey. Fat is normally 3% to 5% of the bird's mass. Some migrants almost double their body weights by storing fat before migration. The ruby-throated hummingbird weighs only 4.8 grams and can use stored fat to fuel a non-stop, 24-hour flight across a 600-mile stretch of open water from the U.S. Gulf coast to the Yucatan Peninsula of Mexico.[1]

This would probably have been the ideal way to travel on road trips with my family because my father hated to stop for even a moment, fearful of the time lost with every pause to go to the bathroom or to deal with other emergencies. After a while he relaxed and became a little more laid back. These days, though, when Andy and I go on road trips, losing time is the least of our concerns. We both tend to need to take breaks. One of the things I look forward to most is packing the food, but I also love stopping for food. Usually, I will stock up on bottled water, sugar snap peas, bananas, Pringles, and sourdough pretzel nibblers. If we stop off at a gas station or rest stop, my drink of choice is an orange Fanta and maybe Cheese Nips. On a flight, I crave either a ginger ale or tomato juice, and lately, Bloody Mary mix. Food and journeys go hand in hand; they are a necessary part of the travels, as my dad would always remind us–"Eat carbs; they're good for your brain."

When I think of food, my mind invariably turns to the kitchen, a space that inspires both anxiety and comfort for me. It can represent so many troubling stereotypes and expectations for women; but according to feminist and *mujerista* theology, it is a potential third space, brimming with redemptive possibilities. At the very least, it is a place for creative dialogue about women's work. It is important to note the various injustices that occur both at home and in the workplace for women. For many women work is an experience in a dual space, both at home and at a place external to the home. Feminist theologians have drawn on feminist theory to analyze the sexual division of labor, the separation of the spheres of home and work, and occupational segregation of "men's jobs" and "women's jobs" as dynamics contributing to discrimination against and devaluation of women and their work.[2] Feminist theory deconstructs the assumed naturalness of gendered divisions of labor. Womanist, *mujerista*, and some feminist theologies also point to the role of race, class, age, and sexual preference in constructing unjust divisions of labor.

The issues concerning work are engaged by feminist theologies, though these theologies differ somewhat on goals and strategies for redressing discrimination against women's work. Some want women's maternal, domestic roles valued more highly than they currently are in the public sphere and advocate child or family allowances as one way of doing this.[3] Others want equality between women and men at work and at home. They advocate equal educational and employment opportunity, and possibly affirmative action, to overcome the occupational segregation of women into traditional women's jobs such as clerical work. Pay equity or comparable worth is advocated by some to redress the lower wages paid to women in such jobs.

Others advocate radical social transformation that replaces hierarchical relations of domination with more egalitarian social relations as necessary to good work for both women and men.

Many feminists contend that women's sole responsibility for domestic work is a significant factor in women's oppression. Maria Pilar Aquino's argument that Latinas' "double oppressions reside in their double workload" is applicable to other doubly or triply oppressed women. This double workload is understood to be some kind of wage work, "in generally more disadvantaged conditions than men's," as well as the sole responsibility for domestic work in their own homes.[4] As I noted in reference to Gerbara's piece, women's work in the home is another potential avenue for oppression. The relegation of women to a limited space seems to limit their ability to influence change, especially in the ways women are caught in these vicious cycles of oppression rooted in economic, political, and social forces.

Faithful Journey: A Third Space

Despite the potential of the home space as the symbol of domesticity to become a space of oppression, it is beginning to be perceived in a new light as a revolutionary space. Marguerite Renner reviewed Glenna Matthews' book on domesticity as a cultural phenomenon during the nineteenth and twentieth centuries. In the book, Matthews argues that nineteenth-century domesticity represented a high point in prestige for women and in respect for women's work in the home. Renner describes Matthews' views as follows:

> She even terms the mid-nineteenth century the "golden age of domesticity" and describes women's roles in antebellum years as an "epic role in which the home provided a touchstone of values for reforming the entire society." Changing material conditions, including technological development, and the availability of servants, she argues, combined with the values and attitudes of republican motherhood to allow women the opportunity to expand their emotional, social, religious, and political roles in the home.[5]

The home was a central space that potentially offered women a chance to expand their influence into the public sphere. The women had power over their families and through their husbands who were able to act in larger society. With an increasingly dynamic community life, due to these "changing material conditions and technological development," women were able to creatively manipulate the impact of their roles. Thus Renner writes further:

Domesticity elevated women to a position of respect and prominence that earlier generations had not known . . . That stature in the home generated a new self-image and sense of importance for women, which they were able to use to move beyond their homes into the public arena. This part of Matthews' argument depends on recent revisionist scholarship . . . Her argument daringly moves beyond much of the scholarship to argue that domesticity became central to American culture. Males played a role first in "helping to create and perpetuate" domesticity, she argues. Beyond that they were instrumental in making it part of mainstream culture. As she states, "What has been insufficiently recognized . . . is the extent to which men, too, entered into the ideology of domesticity, helping to create and perpetuate it. In so doing they took the home beyond the boundaries of 'women's sphere' and into the national arena."[6]

Though males may have had a role in creating and perpetuating these roles, it is more significant that the boundaries of the women's sphere eventually appeared to spread out to impact other spheres of life. At the same time, the lines between the roles of men and women became less definable, which allowed for women to navigate between these various spheres. Thus, while men's roles remained fairly rigid, women's flexibility and capacity to maneuver through a diversity of spaces also increased their potential impact at multiple levels creating the road toward some kind of pseudoequilibrium. This understanding of domesticity is challenging and provides a lens for feminist theologians to reengage the various spaces in which women might be able to effect tangible change.

The domestic space is a place that is engaged in various works of art and literature. It is a place of warmth and comfort, and it can be subversively used to further the cause of women both at home and actually in the workplace. No doubt it is a place with roots and anchors, where stories of origin are offered in vivid pictures. It is a place that shapes identities and makes space for the creation of stories, and it is a place to garner energy and power. The work of love that characterizes raising a family can also potentially be stretched beyond the home to connect members of the community of a town, a city, a nation, and a world. But it requires imagination, and a little bit of faith and grace, for this kind of expansion to be possible. It needs to be seen as a threshold, a place of creation and birth.

Faith-Filled Journey: Threshold Theology

Threshold connotes being on the brink or verge of something, of inception, a dawn, and a beginning; in terms borrowed from physics, it has great potential energy. It also suggests the quality of being on the border, the fringes, and the margins. The image of the threshold is therefore a potentially appropriate ingredient for a theology that speaks to and from the context of Asian American women.

On marginality, one Asian American theologian writes, "To a person or community in need of recovering a sense of subjectivity due mainly to historical erasure, invisibility, and constant misrepresentation, self-reflections and autobiographies are viable means of reclaiming wholeness."[7] These self-reflections can occur when the Asian American woman recognizes the sources and effects of her fragmentation. In doing so, she is better on the road to true healing and wholeness in facing the collisions that produce this fragmentation in her. In addition, she is able to embrace her own humanity and thus the humanity of others, including those who oppress her. One Japanese American theologian verbalizes the pain of being interned in the United States. But despite the harsh reality that marginality meant being a nonentity or a nonperson, he became aware of the connection between marginalization and Christ's Incarnation during his search for identity. Moreover, he became better able to identify with the oppressed, the marginalized, and the dehumanized, and at the same time to see himself as a person, made in God's image and likeness and loved by the Creator. He writes powerfully, "Marginality has led me to discover my humanity."[8] Recognizing and boldly claiming this marginality highlights these injustices for the Asian American woman; she is able to acknowledge the margins because she sees the oppressive structures as instruments of manipulation, exploitation, and destruction. At the same time, in a noncomplicit way, she can positively embrace them, and in turn, subvert this oppressive system by redefining the margins. For example, this analysis can lead her to realize the way Asian American women's bodies are being ravished by the dominant culture as a space for the construction of racial and gender stereotypes and certain notions of sexuality and redefine not only these definitions but also the space. On the other hand, Young Lee Hertig offers a new perspective on marginality, explaining what is lacking for her in solely relying on the feminist perspective. She writes that the word *yinist* popped into her head one day and filled the void.[9] She doesn't seem to intend it as a comprehensive term, but she offers it as an open door to women who identify themselves specifically as Asian or Asian American. She explains,

> It is taken from the word *yin,* the female energy in Taoism. This female energy is comprehensive because it encompasses gender, ecology, nature, health, and God. The *yin* is holistic, dynamic, synthesizing, and complementary with *yang,* the male energy. *Yinist* feminism, therefore diffuses false sets of dichotomy deriving from the dualistic paradigm: male against female, human being against nature, God apart from human being, this world apart from the other world.[10]

Hertig observes further through this lens that Jesus, throughout the gospels, models balance. He pays attention to marginalized people, thus giving them voices. The yin-yang dynamic is meant to dismantle the dualistic perspectives that dominate Western thought and to provide an interpretation of God and faith, and reinterpreting the center-margin dialectic. Hertig points out that

> the Bible is full of opposites in harmony. A Benedictine sister Joan Chittister articulates the harmonious dynamics of *yin* and *yang* through the spirituality of embrace: "Scripture is full of the coming together of opposites–Joseph and his brothers, Moses' mother and Pharaoh's daughter, Jesus and the Samaritan woman, the young woman Mary and the old woman Elizabeth." Yinist feminism seeks co-existence without male or female domination . . . It accepts dialectic tension between harmony and conflict.[11]

It seems holding up this tension could lead to an alternative space as well, but what it is difficult for me here is trying to embrace an Eastern spiritual perspective that is culturally unfamiliar to me as an Asian *American.* Still, I do see the prospect of fruitful dialogue, especially concerning the social relationships between those in the center and those on the margins.

Even as we continue to confront the deconstructive aspects of fragmentation, my hope is that it leads to a reconstructive work. I see reconstruction already, for instance, in the way contemporary Asian American writers are immersed in this imaginative work of challenging old myths and stereotypes by defining Asian American humanity as part of the composite identity of the American people, which is itself still being shaped and defined.[12] Likewise, Asian

American theology can participate in this creative work by engaging these issues theologically in the language of justification, redemption, and wholeness. Thus a feminist theology can begin to address how the Asian American woman can reclaim her body by being aware of these social constructions and, rather than being a passive blank template, she can speak out, write, and express on her own initiative. In doing so, she creates her own identity. One woman poignantly writes,

> My mom used to tell me life is just a blank book when you are born. Then you write all your strokes in it—calligraphy, drawing, spitting, whatever you want to do. It all depends on how you want to turn the pages.[13]

Embracing this fragmentation opens up the Asian American woman to realize the implications of adaptation—namely, the deceptive wholeness achieved by compartmentalization or assimilation. The very fact that an Asian American woman daily faces the inevitability of adaptation to the surrounding culture signifies the need for a theological response. Whether it means subordinating one's own space to include the dominant cultural views or accommodating space for the sake of maintaining dominant cultural views and thereby losing one's own space to the effects of cultural imperialism, the perceived need for this false adaptation results in an inability to fully experience her own humanity. Through this type of adaptation, the Asian American woman allows those in power to define her belonging, acceptance, and justification. An Asian American feminist theology encourages choice rather than coercion or manipulation. This freedom begins in the threshold of fragmentation where the Asian American woman is invited to engage the disequilibrium. She experiences a glimmering of it in the very throes of collision. This is where she can hold up different pieces of reflection because she can affirm different standards. Elaine Kim calls these pieces of reflection "multiple mirrors and many images," which are new directions as seen in Asian American literature. It is an indication of Asian Americans' need to reimagine their experiences and create new ones through multiple mirrors and lenses.[14] Mark Taylor writes, "Remembering is reconstituting and restoring to connection what is often fragmented."[15] This process of remembering will allow the Asian American woman to relocate her body, which is divided up into the stereotypical pieces imposed on her by the dominant culture, into an intentional process toward wholeness.

Since this is a theological work, it is natural to engage Christian doctrines. Jones writes about the way Christian doctrines act as both imaginative lenses and loose but nonetheless definitive dramatic scripts for persons of faith.[16] The language of an "already/ not-yet" experience resonates with the patterns of the Asian American woman's experience. As mentioned earlier, Jones appropriates this language in her notion of eschatological essentialism. This language comes specifically from Karl Barth's theology–a productive conversation partner, I think, in this formation of an Asian American feminist theology. Although there are some problematic expressions in Barth's theology about the roles of men and women–specifically in his language of women's subordination–there are some connections to be made between feminist theology and his political theology, which teaches that Christian community must manifest solidarity with the oppressed. While it is not a perfect fit, I think Barth's passionate articulation of basic Christian tenets has great potential in the dialogue about Asian American woman's experience, so I believe it is important to look at his work.

Specifically, Barth's construction of humanity's *justification* in Christ has promising opportunities for intersection with Asian American experience. Trevor Hart neatly summarizes Karl Barth's explanation thus: "For Barth justification is never something which involves the Christian in any cooperation or active involvement ('graced' or otherwise). It is, in this sense, wholly objective, standing over against us as a finished work."[17] This recognizes the reality of sin and the inability of the sinner to cooperate or merit, so justification is necessary; yet, while it is a finished work, humanity has yet to realize it in its fullest completion.

This echoes the Asian American woman's experience, in terms of her life as a work in progress and the way in which feminist theology provides lenses through which she can actively participate in–can, in fact be a creator of–this work. Yet, when fragmentation opens her eyes to see the corruption in the power structures, she recognizes the work is not yet complete. Thus Barth includes the notions of *simul iustus et peccator*, that is, the individual is simultaneously justified and a sinner.[18] So the Asian American Christian woman is completely both justified and sinner, as well as participator and creator of the work of her life in the same instant.

The presence of both justification and sin is a reflection of the individual as well as the sociopolitical structures of American society. The individual receives justification, but her fraudulent, oppressive surroundings remind her that sin remains present in the world; she experiences the sin within her and without her. Hart describes the concurrent reality that we are on a pilgrimage from an ever new past through an ever new present to an ever new future: "As man's past as a sinner is still his present, so his future as a righteous man is already his present."[19] The main potential correlation between Hart's description and the Asian American woman's experience is the language of journey and pilgrimage. She experiences this process not simply as progress or personal improvement, because these terms tend to rely on some arbitrary standards usually set by the dominant culture. Rather, process means the creation of a story, a narrative, a drama, a history; it is the journey from one mile-marker to the next and the drama that arises from this movement. The language of journey communicates that its process is not necessarily linear, but also not static, yet it is most certainly dynamic. Barth's Christology is ever present, reminding us that rather than turning to empirical or metaphysical explanation, we must turn to the concrete history of Jesus of Nazareth.[20] It is here that the eschatological future of God has broken decisively into history; it is here that our experience of ourselves and our situation is called radically into question as we are called upon to discover ourselves "in him" and in his situation.[21]

What is powerful and liberative for the Asian American woman is the reality that Christ is the standard, Christ levels the playing field, Christ destroys all barriers, and in justification she experiences that Christ is truly the source of her very being and calls her to respond and create in faith. Her body, her life, and her activity are marvelous, exciting expressions of Christ and Christ's work in her. Thus it is in Christ that we are to understand this justification, ourselves as *simul iustus et peccator*, considered in ourselves we are sinful and guilty people, but considered in Christ we are new creatures of God, faithful covenant partners. Jesus' history is our history, His death is our death, and in His resurrection and exaltation we share.[22] The Asian American woman is a new creation with a new history, and she shares in the life, death, resurrection, and exaltation of Jesus Christ according to God's word. Thus she can embrace this existence as God's real creation by embracing her history in light of Jesus' history and life.

There is a narrative quality to the dual focus of this justification—that is, it is accomplished in the actual events of the history of Jesus Christ, and because the Asian American woman of faith is justified in Him, His story is her story. Thus it is not some ontological or forensic status quo but an alien history, a "story," that we discover to be our own in the journey and that projects us into the urgent crisis of eschatological transition–living out the Kingdom of God in midst of the world, living by faith in that reality, which lies beyond our experience but stands as our reality nonetheless.[23] The term *alien* can then be appropriated by the Asian American woman's context in a new way. Initially, the term reawakens the experience of foreignness, but in this context, rather than being a negative reality, it becomes a positive phenomenon. Her "alien history" is authentic, and this specific "alien history" connotes faith. When she discovers this alien history to be her own story she is acknowledging in faith this justification and her own legitimacy.

According to Hart, who continues his discussion on Barth, "In him our justification is complete justification yet, we are *in via* in the sense of living out of this completed justification."[24] The Asian American Christian woman's life is this journey, this living out of a complete justification, but her life is ever on the way. This is where Barth explains that faith in its character of acknowledgment is a human activity in which something virtual is actualized; faith is that action in which we joyfully embrace something that is already real and already has our name firmly stamped upon it.[25] The Asian American woman is called into this human activity in which she embraces in joy what she has been given and what she can claim in her life, this unique experience of justification. This does not, however, render her passive, emotionless, or bodiless; rather, she lives out this human activity of faith in the fullest embodiment, activity, and passion.

The image of fragmentation and collision are symbols that can potentially transform the Asian American woman's fullest comprehension of justification. It demonstrates the Asian American woman's experience of constantly being "betwixt and between":

> To be betwixt and between is to be neither here nor there, to be neither this thing nor that. Spatially, it is to dwell at the periphery or at the boundaries. Politically, it means not residing at the centers of power of the two intersecting worlds but occupying the precarious and narrow margins where the two dominant groups meet and clash, and denied the opportunity to wield power in matters of public interest. Socially, to be betwixt and between is to be part of a minority, a member of a marginal(ized) group. Culturally, it

means not being fully integrated into and accepted by either cultural system. Psychologically and spiritually, the person does not possess a well-defined and secure self-identity and is often marked with excessive impressionableness, rootlessness, and an inordinate desire for belonging.[26]

This "neither here nor there" nebulous feeling can be a space for the expression of this justification. Jones writes that indeterminacy is not always viewed as a problem; sometimes it is seen as a promise of new things to come.[27] I view it as a space that is unbounded, an invitation to creation and expression, full of latent possibility. Moreover, it does not necessarily have to be lived out in solitude. The amorphous space Asian American women occupy can actually be a basis for community. The space calls us to reside in it. Thus, in past years, Asian American writers expressed an intense desire to live here in this space with the fullness of voice and perspective. In reading works by these authors it seems the general tone is a yearning to participate fully in the main currents of American life and culture. Today's writers are still concerned with defining their identity and roots in American society.

But another theme that underscores the contemporary body of Asian American literature is a need for solidarity and community, which affirms this justification in Christ: Asian American writers are attempting to build bridges that span generations, nationalities, and genders, connecting Asian Americans to each other and to other minority groups.[28] Rather than trying to find their identity in the dominant culture, or in the men within this culture, or even in the men of the specific Asian communities, Asian American women can establish their identities through associations with other Asian American women. Then this nebulous space that is called home will not seem so vast and empty but filled with the stunning expressions of these women, who are Christ's own. The stories and songs of these women will go out and heal not just Asian American women but women in countries where there is still violence toward their daughters, women who are forced into silence and seen merely as containers for children, and the women and men everywhere who are daily persecuted for their sexual orientation. What seems particular to just Asian American women will hopefully translate in meaningful ways to all who face oppression.

*   *   *

For as long as I can remember I have avoided the race and gender dynamic. I was taught to not "rock the boat," to be quiet, to prove myself through material success, to appropriate the language of the dominant Christian culture, and to superficially get along with everyone, male or female, white or black or brown. But I am realizing that these dynamics form a problematic trend that impacts everything from toys and films to employment, church growth, and international relations. Although this revelation is somewhat new, it remains ever provocative: Nothing is simply black and white. While I cannot help but be affected by this system of viewing and expressing race and gender, I, and many others like myself, do not fit easily into this system. Perhaps no one does. I am somewhere on the fringes and margins, somewhere in between here and there. I occupy a space that is nebulous and vague. I am in a space where there has been and continues to be a collision of worlds, perspectives, and languages. This collision tempts me to compartmentalize and assimilate, to essentially run away, to hide and cower, but through new lenses I am compelled to learn how to appropriate the broken fragments in my understanding of who I am in God and God's call to me. I am learning to rearticulate what it means to live out of my identity in Christ and to realize I am a unique expression of Christ's love, and through these seasons of faith and identity I am rediscovering God, God's salvation, and God's unique redemption of humanity.

Though located first in Christ's justification, our work on ourselves is necessary work, and it affects all. Zia puts it this way:

> Our demographics and achievements, trials and tribulations, tell a compelling story of a people who come together from markedly different backgrounds, without a common language or culture . . . We have forged a sense of shared experience and common future as Americans–Asian and Pacific Islander Americans . . . As we transform ourselves so we are transforming America.[29]

These are words full of promise, expressing the power of this journey together in the crossroads of life, in the experience of justification as an Asian American "already/not-yet" phenomenon, and in the midst of the images of collision and fragmentation. As Asian

American women, if we dare to respond, if we dare to claim this fragmentation, we may find ourselves in an amazing adventure as we navigate through this unbounded wilderness. But the hope is that when we immerse ourselves in this fragmentation with courage, we will also encounter the unexpected, the surprise, the joy of our restored sight, and then we will see what was hidden from us: the sight of glorious mountain peaks and lush and habitable green valleys and the freedom of endless blue skies. With voice and body and joined hands, as we move from threshold to threshold with confidence and courageous honesty, we will truly live out a hopeful and hope-filled anticipation that proclaims a fresh journey of wholeness and redemption not only to ourselves or to the Church but to the entire world.

The third space is a place of burgeoning possibilities, a place that is open to anyone. My hope is that Asian American women will be hosts to each other and offer it to all who need a place of refuge, to eat and be refreshed for the journey and continue on in God's work of love and compassion.

Epilogue

A Thousand Cranes

Everlasting Wishes

I never did end up ever making a thousand cranes for anyone. I have already found and been found by the love of my life, my husband Andy, but a thousand cranes would have been too few to express the depth of love and commitment I have toward him and the millions of wishes of long life, love, and fulfillment I hope for him.

But I do have a thousand hopes for the future, especially for all my mothers, my sisters, and all our daughters someday.

I wish for all my mothers a peace and contentment that surpasses all understanding.

I wish for all my mothers a space to create, write, and transform the world.

I wish for my mothers to share their wisdom with courage.

I wish for my sisters a fulfillment that comes from knowing and loving oneself.

I wish for my sisters hope in the midst of mind-numbing status quo and subtle but debilitating oppression.

I wish for my sisters vocations that allow them to live to their fullest potential.

I wish for the image that is reflected back at my daughters to be one that is pleasing and more than acceptable, no matter what the hair color or shape of the eyes.

I wish my daughters many opportunities to love openly and freely.

I wish that the world my daughters and their daughters will live in will be one that celebrates their beauty and intelligence.

I wish for strength for all women around the world who are furthering the cause of those who suffer injustice.

I wish for the world to be turned radically upside down so that those in power who are catalysts of terror and torture would be brought low.

I wish for God's kingdom to be brought to bear in every country and community, a kingdom of peace and radical grace.

There isn't enough space for all the wishes, but I dream that this endeavor will be a part of the greater struggle, one of the many songs that speak out for the sake of those who experience silence and oppression and one that furthers the work that has already been initiated by many more.

Notes

Foreword

[1] Grace Ji-Sun Kim, "Asian American Feminist Theology" in *Liberation Theologies in the United States: An Introduction,* ed. by Stacey M. Floyd-Thomas & Anthony B. Pinn (New York: New York University Press, 2010), 131.

[2] Harry H.L. Kitano & Roger Daniels, *Asian Americans: Emerging Minorities,* 2nd ed. (New Jersey: Prentice-Hall, 1988), 113.

[3] Ibid., 113, 116, 118.

Chapter 1: Flight and Migration

[1] Shirley Hune, "Rethinking Race," in *Contemporary Asian America: A Multidisciplinary Reader,* ed. Min Zhou and James V. Gatewood (New York: New York University Press, 2000), 668.

[2] Frank H. Wu, *Yellow: Race in America beyond Black and White* (New York: Perseus, 2002), 20.

[3] Helen Zia, *Asian American Dreams* (New York: Farrar, Straus and Giroux, 2000), 92.

[4] Wu, *Yellow,* 79.

[5] Ibid., 87.

[6] Elaine H. Kim, *Asian American Literature* (Philadelphia: Temple University Press, 1982), 4.

[7] Ibid., 5.

[8] Edward Said, *Orientalism* (New York: Vintage, 1978), 3.

[9] Seth Arjun, "Silk Routes," in *Edward Said and the Production of Knowledge* (University of Maryland), accessed April 20, 2007, http://www.silkroutes.net/Ref/OrientalismWikiArticle.htm.

[10] Wu, *Yellow,* 8.

[11] Ibid., 144.

[12] Ibid., 145.

[13] Ibid., 146.

[14] Wu, *Yellow,* 40.

[15] Lucie Cheng and Philip Yang, "The Model Minority Deconstructed," in Zhou and Gatewood, *Contemporary Asian America,* 464.

[16] Zia, *Asian American Dreams,* 47.

[17] Ronald Takaki, *Strangers from a Different Shore* (Boston: Little, Brown and Company, 1998), 475.

[18] Wu, *Yellow,* 44.

[19] Takaki, *Strangers,* 476.

[20] Zia, *Asian American Dreams,* 47.

[21] Takaki, *Strangers,* 477.

[22] Cheng and Yang, "Model Minority," 473.

[23] Zia, *Asian American Dreams,* 46.

[24] Takaki, *Strangers,* 485.

[25] Wu, *Yellow*, 39.

[26] Ibid., 50.

[27] Ibid., 49.

Chapter 2: Fidelity, Prosperity, Longevity

[1] Michael G. LaFosse, Richard D. Alexander, and Greg Mudarri, *Japanese Paper Crafting* (Berkeley, Calif.: Periplus Editions, 2007), 52.

[2] Jessica Hagedorn, "Asian Women in Film: No Joy, No Luck," in *Asian Americans: Experiences and Perspectives,* ed. Timothy Fong and Larry Shinagawa (Upper Saddle River, N.J.: Prentice Hall, 2000), 264.

[3] Ibid., 265.

[4] Elaine H. Kim, *Asian American Literature* (Philadelphia: Temple University Press, 1982), 196.

[5] Ibid., 198, quoting Frank Chin, "Confessions of the Chinatown Cowboy," *Bulletin of Concerned Asian Scholars,* fall 1972: 67.

[6] Hagedorn, "Asian Women," 269.

[7] Claire S. Chow, *Leaving Deep Waters* (New York: Penguin Books, 1998), 39.

[8] Lyrics by Sara Groves, *Add to the Beauty*, Columbia Records/Sony.

[9] Vickie Nam, *Yell-Oh Girls* (New York: HarperCollins, 2001), 184.

[10] Hagedorn, "Asian Women," 265.

[11] Pheobe Eng, *Warrior Lessons* (New York: Pocket Books, 1999), 131.

[12] Helen Zia, *Asian American Dreams* (New York: Farrar, Straus and Giroux, 2000), 213.

[13] Serene Jones, *Feminist Theory and Christian Theology* (Minneapolis: Fortress Press, 2000), 72.

[14] Ibid., 72–73.

[15] Ibid., 78.

[16] Ibid., 79.

[17] Ibid., 86.

[18] Chow, *Leaving Deep Waters*, 152.

[19] Jones, *Feminist Theory*, 86.

[20] Ibid., 87.

[21] Ibid., 88.

[22] Nam, *Yell-Oh Girls*, 146.

Chapter 3: Fight, Struggle, and Survive

[1] Claire S. Chow, *Leaving Deep Waters* (New York: Penguin Books, 1998), 2.

[2] Ibid., 187.

[3] Elaine H. Kim, *Asian American Literature* (Philadelphia: Temple University Press, 1982), 242.

[4] Chow, *Leaving Deep Waters*, 22.

[5] Kim, *Asian American Literature*, 226.

[6] Ibid., 229.

[7] Ibid., 89.

[8] Ibid.

[9] Ibid.

[10] Ibid., 228.

[11] Ibid.

[12] Ibid., 229.

13 Ibid., 230.

14 Pandora Leong, "Living Outside the Box," in *Colonize This!*, ed. Daisy Hernandez and Bushra Rehman (New York: Seal Press, 2002), 351.

15 Ibid., 352.

16 Serene Jones, *Feminist Theory and Christian Theology* (Minneapolis: Fortress Press, 2000), 4.

17 Leong, "Living Outside the Box," 353.

18 Ibid., 354.

19 Vickie Nam, *Yell-Oh Girls* (New York: HarperCollins, 2001), 115.

20 Asian Women United of California, ed., *Making Waves* (Boston: Beacon Press, 1989), 16.

21 Kim, *Asian American Literature*, 253.

22 Ibid.

23 The Unbound Feet 1979 Performance at the San Francisco Art Museum.

24 Kim, *Asian American Literature*, 199.

25 Ibid., 205.

26 Ibid., 220.

27 Nam, *Yell-Oh Girls*, 34.

28 Kim, *Asian American Literature*, 224.

29 Ibid., 248.

30 Ibid.

31 Rashmi Luthra, *Cracking the Mirror: South Asian Women Creating Resistive Third Spaces*, http://www.allacademic.com//meta/p_mla_apa_research_citation/0/1/5/1/3/pages15139/p15139-1.php.

32 Ibid.

33 Ibid.

34 Kim, *Asian American Literature*, 253.

Chapter 4: A New Flock

1 Shirley Guthrie, *Christian Doctrine* (Louisville: Westminster/John Knox Press, 1994), 53.

2 Ibid., 54.

3 Nami Kim, "The 'Indigestable'Asian: The Unifying Term 'Asian' in Theological Discourse," in *Off the Menu: Asian and Asian North American Women's Religion and Theology*, ed. Rita Nakashima Brock et al. (Louisville: Westminster John Knox Press, 2007), 23.

4 Ibid., 24.

5 Ibid., 26.

6 Ibid., 37.

7 Ibid.

8 Ibid., 38–39.

9 Guthrie, *Christian Doctrine*, 147.

10 Gale Yee, "She Stood in Tears amid Alien Corn: Ruth, the Perpetual Foreigner and Model Minority," in Brock et al., *Off the Menu*, 47

11 Ibid., 53.

12 Ibid.

13 Ibid., 54.

14 Ibid.

15 Ibid., 55.

[16] Ibid.

[17] Ibid., 56.

[18] Ibid.

[19] Ibid., referring to Roland Boer, *Marxist Criticism of the Bible* (London: T & T Clark International, 2003).

[20] Ibid., 60.

[21] Ibid.

[22] Guthrie, *Christian Doctrine*, 243.

[23] Brock, *Off the Menu*, 126.

[24] Ibid., 127.

[25] Ibid., 135.

[26] Ibid., 136.

[27] Ibid., 139.

[28] Ibid., 136.

[29] Guthrie, *Christian Doctrine*, 318.

[30] Anne Dondapati Allen, "No Garlic, Please, We Are Indian: Reconstructing the De-eroticized Indian Woman," in Brock et al., *Off the Menu*, 183.

[31] Ibid., 186.

[32] Ibid.

[33] Ibid., 187.

[34] Ibid.

[35] Ibid.

[36] Ibid., 188.

[37] Ibid., 189, citing Gloria Goodwin Raheja and Ann Grodzins Gold, *Listen to the Heron's Words: Reimagining Gender and Kinship in North India* (Berkeley: University of California Press, 1994), 44.

[38] Ibid., 191.

[39] Ibid., 192.

[40] Ibid., 193.

[41] Guthrie, *Christian Doctrine*, 357.

[42] Boyung Lee, "Recreating Our Mothers' Dishes: Asian and Asian North American Women's Pedagogy," in Brock et al., *Off the Menu*, 293–94.

[43] Ibid., 294.

[44] Ibid.

[45] Ibid., 297.

[46] Ibid., 298.

[47] Ibid.

[48] Ibid., 299.

[49] Ibid.

[50] Ibid., 300.

[51] Rosato, Philip, "Book Review: *The Spirit as Lord: The Pneumatology of Karl Barth*," http://theologytoday.ptsem.edu/oct1986/v43-3-bookreview1.htm, accessed May 2, 2012.

[52] Ibid.

[53] Chung Hyung Kyung, *Struggle to be the Sun Again: Introducing Asian Women's Theology*, (Maryknoll, N.Y.: Orbis, 1990), 85–86.

[54] Ibid., 86.

[55] Ibid., 86.

[56] Ibid., 87.

[57] Ibid., 88.

[58] Ibid.

[59] Ibid., 89, citing Mary Dunn, "Emerging Asian Women Spirituality," Consultation on Asian Women's Theology–1987, p. 1.

[60] Ibid., 89.

[61] Grace Ji-Sun Kim, *The Grace of Sophia* (Cleveland: Pilgrim Press, 2002), 28.

[62] Ibid., 29.

[63] Ibid., 79–80.

[64] Ibid., 56–57.

[65] Ibid., 57.

[66] Ibid., 82.

[67] Wonhee Anne Joh, *The Heart of the Cross: A Postcolonial Christology* (Louisville: Westminster John Knox Press, 2006), 19.

[68] Ibid., 20, citing Jae Hoon Lee, *The Exploration of the Inner Wounds-Han* (Atlanta: Scholars Press, 1994).

[69] Ibid., 22.

[70] Ibid., 100.

[71] Ibid., 101.

[72] Ibid., 114.

[73] Ibid., 83.

[74] Ibid., 115.

[75] Grace Ji-Sun Kim, *Holy Spirit, Chi, and the Other* (New York: Palgrave MacMillan, 2011), 96.

[76] Ibid.

[77] Kwok Pui-Lan, *Postcolonial Imagination and Feminist Theology* (Louisville: Westminster John Knox Press, 2005), 45.

[78] Ibid., 46, citing James Clifford, *Routes: Travel and Translation in the Late Twentieth Century* (Boston: Harvard Univ. Press, 1997), 261.

[79] Ibid., 48–49.

[80] Ibid., 50.

[81] Ibid.

[82] Ibid., 51. Aciman quote is from André Aciman, "A Literary Pilgrim Progresses to the Past," in *Writers on Writing: Collected Essays from "The New York Times,"* (New York: Henry Holt, 2001), 6–7.

Chapter 5: Freedom Songs of Long Life

[1] Helen Zia, *Asian American Dreams* (New York: Farrar, Straus and Giroux, 2000), 70–71.

[2] Ibid., 108.

[3] Elaine H. Kim, *Asian American Literature* (Philadelphia: Temple University Press, 1982), 150.

[4] Phoebe Eng, *Warrior Lessons* (New York: Pocket Books, 1999), 2.

[5] Vicki Nam, *Yell-Oh Girls* (New York: HarperCollins, 2001), 30.

[6] Ibid., 185.

[7] Mark Taylor, *Remembering Esperanza* (Maryknoll, N.Y.: Orbis Books, 1990), 19.

[8] Peter C. Phan and Jung Young Lee, eds., *Journeys at the Margin* (Collegeville, Minn.: Liturgical Press, 1999), xiv.

[9] Taylor, *Remembering Esperanza*, 5.

[10] Jung Ha Kim, "But Who Do You Say That I Am?" in Phan and Lee, *Journeys at the Margin*, 111.

[11] Lisa Isherwood and Elizabeth Stuart, *Introducing Body Theology* (Sheffield, England: Sheffield Academic Press, 1998), 11.

[12] David Ng, "A Path of Concentric Circles," in Phan and Lee, *Journeys at the Margin*, 83.

[13] Serene Jones, *Feminist Theory and Christian Theology* (Minneapolis: Fortress Press, 2000), 29.

[14] Ibid., 32.

[15] Ibid., 37.

[16] Ibid., 44.

[17] Ibid., 54.

[18] Ibid., 9.

[19] Ibid., 39.

[20] Ibid., 37.

[21] Ibid., 17.

[22] Ibid.

[23] Ibid., 19.

[24] Aloysius Pieris, *An Asian Theology of Liberation* (Maryknoll, N.Y.: Orbis Books, 1988), 81.

[25] Ibid., 112.

[26] Ibid., 40.

[27] Ibid., 42.

[28] Ibid., 35.

[29] Ibid., 35.

[30] Ibid., 15.

[31] Ibid., 16.

[32] Ibid., 70.

[33] Ibid., 85.

[34] Ibid., 23.

[35] Ibid., 24.

[36] Ibid., 25.

[37] Gustavo Gutierrez, *The Density of the Present* (Maryknoll, N.Y.: Orbis Books, 1999), 179.

[38] Ibid., 13.

[39] Ibid., 174.

[40] Ibid., 173.

[41] Ibid., 207.

[42] Ibid., 98.

[43] Ibid., 99.

[44] James Cone, *A Black Theology of Liberation* (Maryknoll, N.Y.: Orbis Books, 1986), 5.

[45] Ibid., 111.

[46] Ibid., 113.

[47] Ibid., 122.

[48] Ibid., 121.

[49] Ibid., 123.
[50] Ibid., 125.
[51] Ibid., 128.

Chapter 6: Food for the Journey

[1] Kerry Scanlan, Vicki Piaskowski, Michelle Jacobi, and Steve Mahler, "Bird Migration," http://www.zoosociety.org/Conservation/BWB-ASF/Library/BirdMigrationFacts.php.

[2] Pamela K. Brubaker, "Work," in *Dictionary of Feminist Theologies*, ed. Letty M. Russell and J. Shannon Clarkson (Louisville: Westminster John Knox Press, 1996), 320.

[3] Ibid.

[4] Ibid.

[5] Marguerite Renner, review of *"Just a Housewife": The Rise and Fall of Domesticity in America*, by Glenna Matthews, *History of Education Quarterly* 29, no. 2 (Summer 1989), http://links.jstor.org/sici?sici=0018-2680%28198922%2929%3A2%3C339%3A%22AHTRA%3E2.0.CO%3B2-2.

[6] Ibid., 341.

[7] Jung Ha Kim, "But Who Do You Say That I Am?," in *Journeys at the Margin*, ed. Peter C. Phan and Jung Young Lee (Collegeville, Minn.: Liturgical Press, 1999), 111.

[8] Paul Nagano, "A Japanese American Pilgrimage," in Phan and Lee, *Journeys at the Margin*, 66.

[9] Young Lee Hertig, "The Asian American Alternative to Feminism," in *Asian American Christianity Reader*, ed. Viji Nakka-Cammauf and Timothy Tseng (Castro Valley, Calif.: The Institute for the Study of Asian American Christianity, 2009), 306.

[10] Ibid.

[11] Ibid., 310.

[12] Elaine H. Kim, *Asian American Literature* (Philadelphia: Temple University Press, 1982), 279.

[13] Vickie Nam, *Yell-Oh Girls* (New York: HarperCollins, 2001), 76.

[14] Kim, *Asian American Literature*, 159.

[15] Mark Taylor, *Remembering Esperanza* (Maryknoll, N.Y.: Orbis Books, 1990), 5.

[16] Serene Jones, *Feminist Theory and Christian Theology* (Minneapolis: Fortress Press, 2000), 17.

[17] Trevor Hart, *Regarding Karl Barth: Essays toward a Reading of His Theology* (London: Paternoster Press, 1999), 50.

[18] Ibid., 55.

[19] Ibid.

[20] Ibid., 58.

[21] Ibid.

[22] Ibid., 60.

[23] Ibid., 62.

[24] Ibid., 63.

[25] Ibid., 67.

[26] Peter C. Phan, "Betwixt and Between: Doing Theology with Imagination" in Phan and Lee, *Journeys at the Margin*, 113.

[27] Jones, *Feminist Theory*, 9.

[28] Kim, *Asian American Literature*, 278.

[29] Helen Zia, *Asian American Dreams* (New York: Farrar, Straus and Giroux, 2000), 310.

Bibliography

Aciman, André. "A Literary Pilgrim Progresses to the Past." *Writers on Writing: Collected Essays from "The New York Times."* New York: Henry Holt, 2001.

Arjun, Seth. "Silk Routes." *Edward Said and the Production of Knowledge.* University of Maryland. http://www.silkroutes.net/Ref/OrientalismWikiArticle.htm.

Asian Women United of California, ed. *Making Waves: An Anthology of Writings by and about Asian American Women.* Boston: Beacon Press, 1989.

Brock, Rita Nakashima, Jung Ha Kim, Kwok Pui-Lan, and Seung Ai Yang, eds. *Off the Menu: Asian and Asian North American Women's Religion and Theology.* Louisville: Westminster John Knox Press, 2007.

Chow, Claire S. *Leaving Deep Waters.* New York: Penguin Books, 1998.

Chung Hyung Kyung. *Struggle to be the Sun Again: Introducing Asian Women's Theology.* Maryknoll, N.Y.: Orbis Books, 1990.

Clifford, James. *Routes: Travel and Translation in the Late Twentieth Century.* Boston: Harvard Univ. Press, 1997.

Cone, James. *A Black Theology of Liberation.* Maryknoll, N.Y.: Orbis Books, 1986.

Eng, Pheobe. *Warrior Lessons.* New York: Pocket Books, 1999.

Fong, Timothy, and Larry Shinagawa, eds. *Asian Americans: Experiences and Perspectives.* Upper Saddle River, N.J.: Prentice Hall, 2000.

Guthrie, Shirley. *Christian Doctrine.* Louisville: Westminster/John Knox Press, 1994.

Gutierrez, Gustavo. *The Density of the Present.* Maryknoll, N.Y.: Orbis Books, 1999.

Hart, Trevor. *Regarding Karl Barth: Essays toward a Reading of His Theology.* London: Paternoster Press, 1999.

Hernandez, Daisy, and Bushra Rehman, eds. *Colonize This!* New York: Seal Press, 2002.

Isherwood, Lisa, and Elizabeth Stuart. *Introducing Body Theology.* Sheffield, England: Sheffield Academic Press, 1998.

Joh, Wonhee Anne. *Heart of the Cross: A Postcolonial Christology.* Louisville: Westminster John Knox Press, 2006.

Jones, Serene. *Feminist Theory and Christian Theology.* Minneapolis: Fortress Press, 2000.

Kim, Elaine H., and Laura Hyun Yi Kang, eds. *Echoes upon Echoes.* New York: The Asian American Writer's Workshop, 2002.

Kim, Elaine H. *Asian American Literature.* Philadelphia: Temple University Press, 1982.

Kim, Grace Ji-Sun, *The Grace of Sophia.* Cleveland: Pilgrim Press, 2002.

——, *The Holy Spirit, Chi, and the Other.* New York: Palgrave MacMillan, 2011.

Kwok Pui-Lan, *Postcolonial Imagination and Feminist Theology.* Louisville: Westminster John Knox Press, 2005.

Lee, Jae Hoon, *The Exploration of the Inner Wounds-Han.* Atlanta: Scholars Press, 1994.

Luthra, Rashmi. "Cracking the Mirror: South Asian Women Creating Resistive Third Spaces." http://www.allacademic.com//meta/p_mla_apa_research_citation/0/1/5/1/3/pages15139/p15139-1.php.

Nakka-Cammauf, Viji, and Timothy Tseng, eds. *Asian American Christianity Reader.* Castro Valley, Calif.: The Institute for the Study of Asian American Christianity, 2009.

Nam, Vickie. *Yell-Oh Girls.* New York: HarperCollins, 2001.

Phan, Peter C., and Jung Young Lee, eds. *Journeys at the Margin.* Collegeville, Minn.: Liturgical Press, 1999.

Pieris, Aloysius. *An Asian Theology of Liberation.* Maryknoll, N.Y.: Orbis Books, 1988.

Renner, Marguerite. Review of *"Just a Housewife": The Rise and Fall of Domesticity in America,* by Glenna Matthews. *History of Education Quarterly* 29, no. 2 (Summer 1989). http://links.jstor.org/sici?sici=0018-2680%28198922%2929%3A2%3C339%3A%22AHTRA%3E2.0.CO%3B2-2.

Russell, Letty M., and J. Shannon Clarkson, eds. *Dictionary of Feminist Theologies.* Louisville: Westminster John Knox Press, 1996.

Said, Edward. *Orientalism.* New York: Vintage, 1978.

Scanlan, Kerry, Vicki Piaskowski, Michelle Jacobi, and Steve Mahler. "Bird Migration." http://www.zoosociety.org/Conservation/BWB-ASF/Library/BirdMigrationFacts.php.

Takaki, Ronald. *Strangers from a Different Shore.* Boston: Little, Brown and Company, 1998.

Taylor, Mark. *Remembering Esperanza.* Maryknoll, N.Y.: Orbis Books, 1990.

Wu, Frank H. *Yellow: Race in America beyond Black and White.* New York: Perseus, 2002.

Zia, Helen. *Asian American Dreams.* New York: Farrar, Straus and Giroux, 2000.

Zhou, Min, and James V. Gatewood, eds. *Contemporary Asian America: A Multidisciplinary Reader.* New York: New York University Press, 2000.

CPSIA information can be obtained
at www.ICGtesting.com
Printed in the USA
JSHW031924210920
8001JS00005BA/12